Frank Preston Stearns

The Life of Prince Otto von Bismarck

Frank Preston Stearns

The Life of Prince Otto von Bismarck

ISBN/EAN: 9783337383831

Printed in Europe, USA, Canada, Australia, Japan

Cover: Foto ©Raphael Reischuk / pixelio.de

More available books at **www.hansebooks.com**

THE LIFE

OF

Prince Otto von Bismarck

BY

FRANK PRESTON STEARNS

AUTHOR OF "SKETCHES FROM CONCORD AND APPLEDORE," "LIFE OF TINTORETTO,"
"MODERN ENGLISH PROSE WRITERS," ETC.

PHILADELPHIA AND LONDON

J. B. LIPPINCOTT COMPANY

1899

TO

PROFESSOR EDWARD T. REICHERT

OF THE

UNIVERSITY OF PENNSYLVANIA

THE GAME OF LIFE

The life of man is like a game of chess,
  The which he plays according to his art ;
Winning or losing, he does nothing less
  Than to obey the dictates of his heart.
Himself against himself, he ever sets
  His pawns, knights, castles in a brave array ;
His soul the stake he on the issue bets,—
  Too high a prize to risk in thoughtless play.
Honor and conscience do the white men guide
  Desire and his self-love the red direct
An angel and a demon on each side
  O'erlook the game,—for its result elect.

If thou wouldst win and not thy fortune rue,
Subdue thyself, yet to thyself be true.

PREFACE

BISMARCK'S memoirs, although his advanced age is sometimes perceptible in them, contain a mine of wisdom for the practical statesman; and yet they are not in the true sense an autobiography, for they are not a record of the man's own life. Likewise there are valuable incidents in Dr. Busch's voluminous sketches of the German chancellor; but Dr. Busch's acquaintance with his employer only began in 1870, and he makes no attempt to explain Bismarck's policy or how he accomplished his mighty work. Mr. Lowe's larger English life of Bismarck is a dignified study of the subject, but it was published many years before his death, and is written too much from the English Tory and monarchical stand-point to please American readers. Von Sybel's history of the foundation of the new German empire contains the only adequate statement of Bismarck's statecraft between 1862 and 1870; but the period comprising the last twenty-five years of his life was hardly less important than that which immediately preceded it. What Americans now require is a clear statement of the character of the man, the principal events of his life, and an explanation of his policy as related to the historical events of his time. This is what I have undertaken to give in the present volume.

In order to do Bismarck justice, however, we should divest ourselves for the time of our national antipathy to royalty. The name of king is hateful to Americans, as it was to the ancient Romans, and with good reason; but in order to do justice to Bismarck and recognize him as he was, we must endeavor to place ourselves in the position of a man who was born and brought up with the idea that loyalty to his sovereign was an ethical principle, and who, even after he had somewhat outgrown this belief, found it useful as a basis—perhaps the only basis he could find—on which to raise the political superstructure of his own life's work, the elevation of Germany to its proper position in the family of nations, and its liberation from those evils from which it had suffered for centuries, owing to its interminable subdivisions and its liability to foreign intrigues.

I think it will be admitted that so grand and difficult an undertaking, and one accomplished in so short a space of time, could in all probability have only been carried through in the manner that it was ; and this probability is largely increased by the fact that during the succeeding twenty years of Bismarck's administration he is credited with not having made a single important political blunder. If he had joined the revolutionists in 1848 and rendered himself conspicuous as an opponent of royalty, it is impossible to imagine how he could have accomplished it.

The notion that Bismarck was a sort of political Mephistopheles, which originated long since with a sensational writer for the *Edinburgh Review*, becomes dissipated in the light of historical investigation like mist before the sun. His worst enemies have never been able to prove a single discreditable act against him in his public or his private life. His remark that Dr. Busch would write the secret history of his time must have been ironical, for no secret history of Bismarck's diplomacy has come to light. He was sometimes violent and domineering, but never for personal ends. He appears always in the light of a disinterested statesman, whose whole thought and activity are concentrated on what he considers the welfare of his country.

F. P. S.

CONTENTS

CONTENTS

THE LIFE

OF

𝕻rince 𝕺tto 𝖛on 𝕭ismarck

CHAPTER I

THE BISMARCKS

POMERANIA lies between Brandenburg, the Baltic, and Prussia proper. It is rather a dreary waste, with little to recommend it either to the common traveller or the student of history. The soil is sandy, and, like the adjacent Holstein, better suited to grazing than agriculture. Long reaches of pasture-land are dotted with small hamlets and peasants' cottages, and broken up by occasional patches of woods and more extensive game-preserves. Its chief advantage consists in a healthy and bracing climate, which, with an habitually cloudy sky, makes toil pleasant to the laborer, and has built up a race of men as strong and vigorous as those of the Scotch border-land, a tract which it closely resembles. It was originally a portion of the old Vandalic territory, and is still inhabited largely by their descendants, who have a dialect of their own, and until the reforms of Von Stein were mostly in the condition of serfs. Through the centre of Pomerania flows the Oder, which near Stettin is joined by the Biese, a smallish river on whose bank are situated the town and castle of Bismarck.

It would be natural to suppose that the name Bismarck had been derived from the river Biese, but this does not appear to have been the case. It should be a warning to the fine-spun arguments of archæologists to learn that the earliest spelling of the name on record—early in the thirteenth century—was Bischofsmark, or mark of the bishop, nearly all Germany being divided at that time into marks or marches, and the Bishop of Havelberg being in authority over the district where the castle of Bismarck stands. It is a very old castle, belonging to the great days of the German empire, perhaps as early as the tenth century, and must have been inhabited by the Bismarck family long before the earliest record of them. We do not even know what their surname was, which, like that of the Hohenzollerns, was exchanged or fell into disuse after residing at the castle. The name of the Hohenstaufens (Weiblingen) has been preserved to us by Ghibelline tradition, though the family became extinct with Conradin.

In those early times of political integration men improved their fortunes chiefly by valor on the battle-field and discretion in the hour of victory, qualities for which the Bismarck family would seem to have been always distinguished. To judge by their descendants, they were powerful and athletic men, such as would carve their way to fortune with the edge of the sword, and maintain it against all comers. There are some historical evidences of this, especially of a Nicholas von Bismarck, whose father left the family castle about the time when Dante was chief magistrate in Florence, and removed to the city of Stendal, where he and his son became important in civil affairs. Nicholas especially dominated for a time over Stendal and the adjacent districts, but was finally driven out of Stendal to seek his better fortune in the service of the Margrave of Brandenburg. This resulted in the Bismarcks' removal from Pomerania; and Nicholas, for his valuable assistance in peace and war, received from the Margrave the estate and castle of Bergstall, one of the largest baronial fiefs in the Altmark, as the Prussians continue to call it. We do not, however, hear of other notable Bismarcks from this time forward, though the family continued to hold its position, and was represented in all the great German wars down to the time of the French Revolution. They were tyrannically treated by the Elector John George of Hohenzollern, who dispossessed them of the valuable property of Bergstall, and removed them to a much inferior piece of property during the latter part of the sixteenth century.

In spite of this unjust affront, they continued to serve the Hohenzollern family with true mediæval loyalty. We find a Colonel von Bismarck in the army of Duke Bernard of Weimar, at the defeat of Nordlingen; after which he returned to Brandenburg to fight under the Great Elector, and came through the whole period of the Thirty Years' War without injury, so far as we know. Between 1570 and 1650, however, three branches of the Bismarck family had perished,—a witness to the terrible ordeal of that period,—though in what way we are not informed, and only the present Schön-hausen line survived to represent the family. Crevese and Schönhausen are the two estates which the Elector John George had, with a bonus of two thousand thalers, presumed to consider an equivalent for the Bergstall property. It is stated that he also made a present of an hundred florins apiece to each of the ladies, to console them for their change of residence![1] Frederick William I., in like manner, attempted to console the relatives of Lieutenant Katte for the execution which depended entirely on his own will.

Prince Bismarck's third grandfather married a lady of the Katte family early in the eighteenth century, and the Prince's great-grandfather was a contemporary of Frederick the Great and much in favor with him, but, unfortunately, was killed in 1742 at the battle of Czaslau, where Frederick defeated the Austrians with inconsiderable loss. He was a colonel of hussars, and we may judge him to have been the ablest of the Bismarck family in recent times until the present Prince. The most distinguished connection of the family, though the Bismarcks of our time are not descended from him, was Lieutenant-General Ziethen, the great hussar commander of the Seven Years' War, whose daring exploits and hair-breadth escapes have become a household legendary store among the

---

Prussians. The Germans consider him to have been fully
the equal of Murat, and there is an attractive statue of him
by Schadow in Dessau Place at Berlin,—a rather slender
man, in a dreamy, nonchalant attitude, as if life were a matter
of indifference to him. So it probably is to the bravest kind
of men.

We cannot discover anything in the Bismarck genealogy
which would lead us to expect the appearance of a first-class
genius in the family. Prince Bismarck's own father, Carl
Wilhelm Ferdinand von Bismarck, born in 1771, was a man
of rather imposing personal appearance, with refined features
and a forehead that reminds one of Goethe, but left no record
which distinguishes him in any way. As Kaunitz said, Nature
has to rest before producing a great statesman. Carl Wilhelm served in the king's body-guard for a time, but we do
not hear of him as taking an active part in the defence of his
country against the French. His one distinction is that he
chose a most excellent wife. Three months before the battle
of Jena he was married to Louisa Wilhelmina Menken, not
of a noble family, but, what was much better, the daughter
of Privy Councillor Menken, and in all respects a superior
woman. Councillor Menken was a man of ability, of liberal
tendencies, and much trusted by Frederick the Great in his
last years. It is from this direction, evidently, that Prince
Bismarck derived his diplomatic talent, and, perhaps, his intellectual ability. Carl von Bismarck saved his young wife from
the anxiety of his presence at the battle of Jena, and lived
thenceforth a rather retired and very domestic life, chiefly given
to the oversight of his estates, of which he had two in Pomerania, besides his head-quarters at Schönhausen,—and to the
shooting of ground game. His children were many, and
their birthdays extended over the space of twenty years.
Otto was the fourth in order, but his eldest brother died in
infancy, so that he became his father's second son, a position
among noble German families which commonly requires of a
young man either to earn his living as a soldier, or to make
some unusual exertion if he wishes to secure a place for
himself in the great world.

LIFE OF BISMARCK

Great events are the stars which preside over the birth of remarkable men. There is every reason why they should have this stimulating effect, and sufficient instances are known to bear witness to it. Webster, the defender of the constitution, was born while the Constitution of the United States was under discussion, and most of the great men of the nineteenth century came into existence during the wars of Napoleon. Bismarck was the last and most important of these. He first saw the light on the first of April, 1815, when all Europe was in an uproar. Napoleon had been welcomed back to France, and received in Paris with enthusiasm; the Vienna Congress had dissolved itself in haste, and armies everywhere were in motion. The effect of this on some women might have been slight enough; but the Frau Louisa Wilhelmina von Bismarck was a person to recognize its significance, and it may have had a determining influence on the future of her second son. As events have proved, a more unfavorable circumstance for the fortunes of the Bonaparte family could not have happened than the advent of Otto Edward Leopold von Bismarck. The Frau von Bismarck could not be blamed if she felt a hostility towards the French; for in 1806 she had only been saved from the insults of Napoleon's soldiers by a stout oaken door at Schönhausen, which still bears the marks of their violence. If Otto von Bismarck bore any ill will towards the French as a nation, this is sufficient to account for it.

He was not, however, brought up at Schönhausen, for his parents removed the following year to the estate of Kniephof, in the vicinity of Naugard, Pomerania, and not very distant from the old castle of Bismarck, where the family had acquired its knightly character seven or eight centuries before. There was no place for Count Carl Wilhelm in the rejoicings and congratulations after the return of the Prussian army from Paris, and his high-spirited wife must have felt this keenly. They lived in retirement for the next seven years or more, during which time Otto grew to be a strong, vigorous boy in the bracing air of Pomerania, with a liking for domestic animals, woods, and country life which never left him. The Pomeranians are the tallest men and accounted the bravest soldiers in the German army, and Bismarck, both in mind and physique, was a typical example of them.

He inherited his father's figure and his mother's mental endowment, as well as the vigorous and clear-sighted intelligence of the old Privy Councillor Menken. His mother was a master of the game of chess, as well as a fine linguist and a reader of the best literature. She possessed sufficient insight into character to discover that her son Otto was well suited for the profession of a diplomat, and destined him at an early age for his future career. It is probable that there was more of the Menken than of the Bismarck in him.

It would be well if we could know more of Otto's childhood, and the manner in which his mother brought him up, but we never shall unless he has left some record of it himself. The Prussians believe in severe discipline, and it is this which gives the slight stiffness to their manners, and the Frau Louisa Wilhelmina was no exception. When Otto was exactly six years old she placed him in charge of Dr. Plamann, who kept the strictest school in the city of Berlin. He afterwards confessed that this was the severest portion of his life. His elder brother, fortunately, was with him, also a bright and vigorous boy, and was no doubt much of a help to him, but there were no entertainments, such as make school-life pleasant to English and American boys. They could not go out to walk except in charge of an instructor, like the pupils in a convent; and to a child so full of life and energy as young Otto this was very oppressive. He suffered from homesickness, a mental malady which some children never become acquainted with. Though not fond of his studies,-he made excellent progress, was liked by his companions, and at the age of eleven years and six months he entered the Friedrich Wilhelm Gymnasium to prepare for the university.

German *gymnasia* are secondary schools of instruction, and something more than that. The name would seem to be badly selected, unless it refers to the unclothed condition of the youthful mind at that time of life. The graduate of a gymnasium is supposed, however, to be thoroughly versed in Greek, Latin, mathematics, and such modern languages as his parents may designate for him, and altogether as well equipped as a junior in our best colleges. He then goes to the university and commences the study of his profession, taking parallel courses in history, philosophy, art, and literature. In this manner time is saved, and the youth is not thrown upon his own resources at too tender an age, before he knows properly how to care for himself.

Otto troubled himself about his Latin and Greek only as much as was necessary to pass the examinations. All through life he cared little for such things as were not of practical use to him. In the modern languages he made better progress, and was always an assiduous reader of history, the true foundation of good statesmanship. Besides the regular curriculum, his ambitious mother inflicted on her sons French and English tutors during the summer vacation, so that there was practically no cessation to their studies. No expense was spared for their education, and they were as carefully guarded against evil influences as the sons of wealthy Athenians in the time of Plato.

The Frau von Bismarck was much given to theological reading, and felt the influence of the great wave of religious liberality which swept over Europe and America between 1820 and 1840. She was a warm friend and devoted admirer of Dr. Schleiermacher, of Berlin, who was not more remarkable for his profound scholarship than for the eloquence of his discourse. No German theologian of the century has exercised so extended and long-continued influence in America as Schleiermacher, and the prudent liberality of his views has largely contributed to the moulding of such minds as Channing, Beecher, and Phillips Brooks. At his mother's desire, Otto was confirmed in the church of the Trinity at Berlin, at Easter in the year 1830, an event whose importance the distinguished clergyman did not live to recognize, but which may have had a decided influence on the future of his young neophyte. The path in religion pointed out by Schleier-

macher and his mother was the one which Bismarck followed
throughout life, as his frequent conversations on religious
topics bear witness. With creeds and theological tenets he
did not concern himself much, but his faith in an all-wise
ruler of the universe remained unshaken through all the
physical and metaphysical scepticisms of the nineteenth century. It is true that after his diplomatic service began Bismarck did not often attend church, but there were always
religious books on his table, and he carried them on his campaigns to France and Bohemia. One of Napoleon's most
sensible remarks was, that, as a rule, it was best for every
man to adhere to the religion in which he was brought up,
and Bismarck exemplified this.

Obstinate and unruly school-boys often make able men,
but are always narrow-minded. It is because they cannot see
both sides of a subject that they act as they do. Young Bismarck's conduct at school was such that he rarely required
correction, and never severe punishment. We like this better
than that more perfect behavior which results from too strict
a consideration for form,—the behavior of the martinet. Dr.
Bonnell, who was one of Otto's instructors for whom he
acquired an enduring affection, and in whose family he re-
sided from his sixteenth to his eighteenth year, has said of
him that he was a thoroughly amiable and unaffected boy,
showing a decided preference for domestic life, not given to
roaming about at night. His only fault was that he was
rather domineering and exacting with servants, as sons of
the nobility too often are. He made few friends at school,
but those few he retained through life. This may have been
because he did not often find in others those substantial
qualities on which lasting friendship is based. At Kniephof
he learned to ride and shoot, as a matter of course. He was
always a daring horseman and an expert swimmer, besides
being a good fencer and dancer. He was not, however, so
fond of these amusements as to neglect more serious business
for them. Gymnastics he never cared for. He grew up tall,
but a rather slender figure, and it was not until middle life
that he broadened out as we now see him in his pictures. He

was much attached to a great Danish dog which his father purchased for him at this time, and which became his constant attendant for many years.

GÖTTINGEN

Having graduated from the Berlin gymnasium with honor, Bismarck wished to go to Heidelberg, where there is always a large corps of Prussian students; but his mother, who had long since obtained control of all the family affairs, preferred Göttingen for him. It is sufficient evidence of her strong will that she could thus prevail over the wishes of her strong-willed son. It is said that she objected to Heidelberg for fear Otto might contract the habit of beer-drinking there, for which she had an especial dislike;[1] but she could assign a better reason than that, since Göttingen is in Hanover, where the purest German is spoken, and this for a diplomat was also of importance.

Otto went accordingly to Göttingen in May, 1832, and remained till November, 1833, studying law, and whatever else he had time or fancy for. He went alone, and, what seems strange, was wholly unacquainted with his fellow-students. Inexperienced and left to his own devices, for the first time in life, with an exceptionally active mind and full of Pomeranian energy, he plunged from one mishap or blunder into another. His record at the university was a turbulent one, not unlike that which Schiller describes in his account of Wallenstein. He had already fought his first student's duel, a very boyish affair, in Berlin; and one morning, being laughed at in the streets of Göttingen for his rather eccentric attire, Otto in his confusion or disgust knew of no better alternative than to challenge the whole party. This, however, had consequences that could not have been foreseen. The second of the Hanoverians, who called on young Bismarck to arrange a meeting, found so little ill will and so much good humor in him, that he was strongly attracted towards him, and offered to bring about a reconciliation, which was accordingly done. The Hanoverian

---

[1] Hesekiel's Biography, p. 98.

soon afterwards became Bismarck's chum, and, being older and more experienced, persuaded him to leave the Brunswick corps, to which Otto then belonged, and to join his own, since there was no regular Prussian corps at the university. Thus early did Bismarck evince his indifference to party attachments.

The Brunswickers, however, were highly offended, and their leading man challenged him to fight with the schläger, from which Bismarck escaped with a few blows, and his opponent with a cut in his face. Of course, the Brunswickers were not going to let him off on such terms as this, and Otto was challenged successively by all their ablest swordsmen. It was a miniature of his after-experience as a statesman with the great powers of Europe. Bismarck is credited with having fought twenty duels with the schläger during the first year, and in every instance but one he had the advantage over his antagonist. In his encounter with a student named Biederwig, whom he afterwards greeted on the floor of the Reichstag, the latter's sword-blade broke as Bismarck was parrying his attack, and gave him a slight cut on the cheek. A convention of experts, however, decided that such an accident did not constitute a victory for Biederwig, though the gentleman himself always held a different opinion. In this way Bismarck became the champion of the Hanoverians, and, though only eighteen, he became the admired and most dreaded fencer of the university. It is the fair explanation of his duelling experience, which otherwise might be difficult to account for. Though of an aggressive nature, he was not quarrelsome, but rather conciliatory.

It is a peculiar custom, this schläger duelling of German students, and seems to take the place with them of those athletic games which the Saxon race so much delight in. It was only at a later period that English foot-ball was introduced at Heidelberg. Though their encounters rarely result in a more serious injury than a permanent scar on the face, these scars are so common that they would almost seem to be the mark of an educated German. From the earliest times the Germans have been given to such rude tests of personal courage, and there is no doubt a certain advantage in them. Schläger-fighting trains the nerves and hand for the more serious emergencies of life, and is as useful to the surgeon or lawyer as it is to the soldier; but the idea of sending one's sons to college to be marked in this manner is not very pleasant, and perhaps it would be quite as well if German students found some other method of proving their manliness.

The pistol duel, with which Bismarck was connected in January, 1833, was in no wise to his discredit. An Englishman, named Knight, had fallen out with a young German baron, and they had arranged for a deadly encounter. At the last moment the baron's second disappointed him, and Bismarck was asked to fill his place. This he did from that sentiment of loyalty to his countrymen which is the best virtue in early life; and he showed on this occasion that masterful trait in his nature arising from a clear perception of the case before him, and readiness to act according to his thought. The principals were too nervous to hit each other at the first fire, and Bismarck, who had purposely lengthened the distance between them, proposed a cessation of hostilities, which all parties were glad enough to agree to. Such affairs of honor, however, were contrary to the laws of the university, and the participants in it were severely punished; the rector allotting Bismarck for his connection in it eleven days of solitary confinement, though public opinion spoke loudly in his favor. At another time he was accorded four days' confinement for having associated with an illegal organization, but what this was we are not informed.

Among the friends that he made at Göttingen were Dr. Windhorst, afterwards his most active opponent in the Reichstag, and John Lothrop Motley, the historian of the Dutch Republic. There were other Americans there at the time with whom he became friendly, and assisted in the celebration of the Fourth of July with pleasant international courtesy. He has himself recorded his acquaintance with Motley in a letter to Oliver Wendell Holmes, dictated in March, 1878, as follows:

LIFE OF BISMARCK

"I met Motley at Göttingen in 1832; I am not sure if at the beginning of Easter Term or Michaelmas Term. He kept company with German students, though more addicted to study than we members of the fighting clubs. Although not having yet mastered the German language, he exercised a marked attraction by a conversation sparkling with wit, humor, and originality. In the autumn of 1833, having both of us migrated from Göttingen to Berlin for the prosecution of our studies, we became fellow-lodgers in the house No. 161 Friedrich Strasse. There we lived in the closest intimacy, sharing our meals and out-door exercise. Motley by that time had arrived at talking German fluently; he occupied himself not only in translating Goethe's poem 'Faust,' but tried his hand even in composing German verses. Enthusiastic admirer of Shakespeare, Byron, Goethe, he used to spice his conversation abundantly with quotations from these his favorite authors. A pertinacious arguer, so much so that sometimes he watched my awakening in order to continue a discussion on some topic of science, poetry, or practical life, cut short by the chimes of the small hours, he never lost his mild and amiable temper. Our faithful companion was Count Alexander Keyserling, a native of Courland, who has since achieved distinction as a botanist." [1]

This is an invaluable letter, for it throws light on the deeper thought and feeling of Bismarck during his academic years. Motley would not have found pleasure in discussing Shakespeare and Goethe with him, if Bismarck had not also been a man of ideas. They were evidently kindred spirits.

Bismarck escaped his second incarceration by suddenly changing from the University of Göttingen to the one at Berlin, where he continued his study of law with Sarigny, the Ulpian of Germany. Sarigny's lectures on the Roman law, however, did not interest him. He cared little for the ancients or their methods, and lived wholly in the present time. Although seemingly neglectful of his college duties, he nevertheless accomplished a good deal of work, and in the spring of 1835 passed the rigid Prussian examination for admission to the bar,—an exceptional age, and a severe mental ordeal.

---

[1] Holmes's Life of Motley, p. 18.

He seems to have disliked lectures, and preferred studying alone, with the occasional help of a tutor.

BARRISTER AND SOLDIER

Through the influence of his family Bismarck was immediately appointed an examiner in one of the intermediary courts of Berlin, where he found active employment during the year 1835–36 in taking the testimony of witnesses. According to the practice of the civil law the evidence in court is not elicited by the counsel on either side, but by state examiners, and after they have finished, the counsellors are also permitted to make inquiries. This has the advantage over the common law of preventing witnesses from being brow-beaten and otherwise imposed on by unscrupulous lawyers who often entertain the jury at the witnesses' expense; but in exceptional cases it has the disadvantage of allowing the government too great an influence over judicial proceedings. Bismarck distinguished himself in this new avocation by his pertinent and searching questions, and the slight impatience of his manner was ameliorated by an evident personal interest in the witness. He here became acquainted with human nature as it appears in the substrata of society, which is sometimes hidden altogether from those who are fortunately born, and learned to know men and women as they really are at heart more clearly than he could have done in any other way. He was particularly impressed, as he afterwards related to Dr. Busch, by a woman who was required to sign a certain document, but absolutely refused to do so, although he, and the judge as well, tried all their powers of persuasion upon her.

In the same year he was introduced at court, where his commanding figure and the strong stamp of his face attracted the attention of royalty itself. His future patron, William I., was then commander of an army corps, and it was thought that if he only had a chance to distinguish himself he would make a celebrated general. These two men, afterwards so indispensable to each other, met and parted without the least anticipation of their future relations. Prince William was

devoted to the army, and Bismarck to the law; but his experience at court was excellent discipline for him, after the neg-
ligent ease and freedom of German student life. Old Dr.
Johnson said in regard to his interview with George III., "It
does you good to talk with your king: one cannot become
angry with the king."

In 1836 Bismarck exchanged his Berlin office for the position of referendary at Aix-la-Chapelle, a government position
which afforded him small pay, and work of even a smaller
description; but it was considered important that he should
become acquainted with the government system of bureaucracy and the details of its administration. It is likely that
Frau von Bismarck had a hand in this, though she was now
in failing health and lived in retirement for the most part at
Schönhausen, for Aix was the resort of French, English, and
Hollanders, with whom Otto might be expected to improve
his knowledge of those languages. So, at least, it turned
out, for we find him making English and French acquaintances there; reading *Hamlet* and *Richard III.,*—the last, perhaps, from a curiosity to learn what Shakespeare would make
of such a hideous character. The close neighborhood of the
Rhineland, which, with its old castles, romantic scenery,
wines, and dreamy atmosphere, seem like an enchanted region
to the inhabitants of prosaic Prussia, was an allurement that
attracted Bismarck strongly. "How much time," he said
afterwards, "I wasted in my youth, strolling, drinking, dan-
cing, and flirting on the Rhine!" Unhappily he was obliged
to pay for this youthful Elysium by an equal period of sad-
ness and melancholy afterwards. It was a midsummer
night's dream, in which folly and delusion were mingled with
delight. It was from Aix that he made his first journey to
England, and was cautioned, after landing in London on Sunday morning, for whistling in the streets. The solemnity of
the English Sabbath did not impress Bismarck favorably, but
he noticed the great advantage which the country had derived by its exemption from the ravages of war.

Hesekiel suggests that Bismarck did not leave Aix of his
own free will, but whatever happened there could not have

been very serious, for he still remained in the government's service. The following year (1838) we find him at Potsdam engaged as a referendary, and at the same time doing service as a private in the Jäger (riflemen) battalion of the Royal Guard, which had formerly been Blücher's guard also in the French campaigns. To see the Jäger battalion drill at Potsdam is a spectacle like the Strasburg clock. In 1839, however, Bismarck removed again to Greifswald, where there was an agricultural academy, for the purpose of learning better how to manage the paternal estates, which he foresaw would soon require his personal attention. Here also he united the duties of a soldier with those of the civilian, thus completing his two years of service to the Prussian state. In this way he finished the circuit of his accomplishments, and might step forth now into the great world a complete and well-rounded man, illustrating the words of the poet,—

> "Who takes his hand from the ploughing,
> The kingdom is not for him."

The great world, however, was still far enough off from Otto von Bismarck. His happy student life, the splendor of the Berlin court, and the festivities of the Rhineland were a dream of the past never to return. At Potsdam he again met his brother Bernhard, who had served four years in the dragoons and now also accepted office as a referendary; and it was about this time that the two brothers discovered that the family exchequer was wellnigh empty. Their chess-playing mother had not proved a wise manager of the Bismarck estates. It may have been good policy to spend liberally on her children during their years of education, but she was also given to agricultural experiments and expensive improvements which did not bring the return she expected. A visit to the Pomeranian properties of Kniephof and Jarchelin satisfied Bernhard and Otto that the time had come for them to interfere. They accordingly went to their father and laid the case plainly before him. They persuaded him that the only way to relieve the financial embarrassment of the family was to make over the Pomeranian estates to his sons

LIFE OF BISMARCK

for good and all. This was acceded to, and Külz, which was
quite equal to the two other properties, fell to Bernhard's
share, while Otto received Kniephof and Jarchelin. Frau
von Bismarck died in 1839, leaving her children well equipped
for the race of life, but still near the foot of the ladder. Her
husband followed her six years later, having lived to witness
the revival of prosperity in the hands of his energetic sons.

Bernhard von Bismarck was a man of ability, and would
have given the family a national distinction if he had not been
overshadowed by his more brilliant brother. He did well at
Külz, and later in life became a member of the King's Privy
Council. Otto now began work in earnest, and applied the
knowledge he had learned at the agricultural college to till
the soil of Pomerania in a practical manner. He was present
in many places and feared in all. His expression as applied
to ineffectual work, " *Noch lange nicht genug*," [1] has become a
proverb in Germany. Gradually the condition of his two
properties began to improve. Better crops were raised; order
and economy enforced; small obligations liquidated. The
condition of the tenants was also looked after. When Otto
found that they were working on Sunday in order to make
up for extra hours in his service, he ordered that they should
till their own ground before they attended to his affairs, and
he found himself the gainer by this arrangement in the good-
will with which they afterwards worked for him. It was not,
however, the life that Bismarck was intended for by destiny.
The harness of his daily routine galled him as it might a
Pegasus. The management of a farm requires as much
thinking as the management of a railroad, but of a very different kind. His mental activity had to find an outlet in
some other direction. "If you plant an acorn in a flower-
pot," says Goethe, "either the oak will die or the flower-pot
will break." Neither were his prospects for the future encour-
aging. He had left the government service, not in disgrace
certainly, but without such official commendation as might
encourage him to think of it again. Would he always have

---

[1] " By no means sufficient."

26

LIFE OF BISMARCK

to continue in his present mode of life? Hesekiel says of his
Kniephof days:

" When Bismarck, at the age of twenty-three, in the most pressing circumstances, without credit or capital, undertook the conduct
of the wasted estates, he evinced prudence and activity, and, as
long as bitter want pressed upon him, he found solace in agricultural activity; but when, by his means, the estates began to rise in
value, and everything went on smoothly, and he was able to rely
upon able subordinates, the administration gave him less satisfaction, and he felt the circle in which he moved too contracted for
him. In his youthful fancy he had formed a certain ideal of a
country Junker; hence he had no carriage, performed all his journeys on horseback, and astonished the neighborhood by riding
twenty to thirty miles to evening assemblies in Polzin. Despite
of his wild life and actions, he felt a continually increasing sense
of loneliness, and the same Bismarck, who gave himself to jolly
carousals among the officers of the neighboring garrisons, sank,
when alone, into the bitterest and most desolate state of reflection.
He suffered from that disgust of life common to the boldest officers
at certain times, and which has been called 'first lieutenant's melancholy.' The less real pleasure he had in his wild career, the
madder it became; and he earned himself a fearful reputation
among the elder ladies and gentlemen, who predicted the moral
and pecuniary ruin of ' Mad Bismarck.' " [1]

This was Bismarck's Wertherian period, which developed
itself according to the peculiarity of his nature. It has been
more than hinted that he also had his Charlotte, not the wife
of another man, but an unmarried woman, who did not appreciate him. He made one more visit to the Rhineland, and one
only. The gay *Fräulein*, who admired him as a government
official, with prospects of promotion, was not well pleased at
the idea of burying herself in the country. Bismarck returned to Kniephof with his spirits at a very low ebb, not
realizing that he had made a fortunate escape, and that he
was yet to find a much better helpmate. To a nature so
ardent and intense such an experience brings a strong reaction,—a disgust of life, an indifference to self, and a contempt

[1] Life of Bismarck, p. 109.

27

for human nature. To the rejected admirer the world for a time seems upside-down, the sunshine a mockery, and happiness an illusion. Bismarck went to Paris, went to London, and thought of more distant journeys. He revelled with the officers of the neighboring garrison; pistol-shots were heard in the night at Kniephof; nobody could predict what Bismarck would do next.

A man so full of energy, and with the wine of youth in his veins, has to let off steam in some manner or he will explode. We do not hear that Bismarck ever injured a human person, —except in his schläger-duelling,—and the tales about him were probably very much exaggerated after he became distinguished. The faults of great men are ever looked at through a magnifying-glass. Certain it is that Otto von Bismarck came out of this moral fermentation perfectly sound in mind and body, whereas a few years of genuine dissipation will commonly abbreviate a man's life before he is fifty.

In the midst of it all he astonished the prophesiers of his future ruin by an act of heroism which has become historic. Going with his groom and others one morning to a neighboring horse-pond, the banks of which were somewhat precipitous, the groom's horse stumbled and suddenly pitched its rider into deep water. Either the man could not swim or he lost his presence of mind, and was in evident danger of being drowned. Bismarck, alone among those present, went to his rescue. Tearing off his sword and coat, he plunged in, and, though at one time they both disappeared, and Bismarck was in great peril from the convulsive struggles of the groom, he finally succeeded in bringing him to land. The on-lookers do not appear to have offered their assistance, though by forming a chain in the water it would seem as if they might have done so effectively.

Bismarck, having learned the duties of a private soldier, applied for and obtained in 1842 the commission of a lieutenant in the Landwehr battalion stationed near Kniephof, and in 1843 he exchanged this position for a command in the Uhlans at Graiffenberg in Pomerania. His military duties were not so exacting but that he was able to continue the oversight of his estates. A Prussian nobleman considers a practical knowledge of military affairs as an essential part of his education, and in the evening of his life Bismarck expressed his regret in a letter to the emperor that he had not made military science his profession instead of diplomacy. We are unable to trace, however, any decided inclination during his early years for the career of a soldier; though we cannot but think, with his rare presence of mind, decisiveness in action, and mental ingenuity, he would have become one of the famous captains of the century. Inclination shapes our lives quite as much as mental endowments, and in this field he would have encountered a rival of a genius quite equal to his own, while among diplomats he was *facile princeps*. It is doubtful if the perpetual restraint of army life could have long been endured by a nature so impulsive, irrepressible, and full of original designs. As it happened at Kniephof, Bismarck was repeatedly summoned before his commanding officer, either for breach of discipline or neglect of duty, and this would have seriously interfered with his chances of promotion. With his powerful physique and immense vitality he was also endowed with a nervous system more sensitive than that of the average woman, and though his head was one of the coolest, this might have proved a disadvantage to him on the field of battle.

Thus he continued farming, drilling, hunting, drinking, and reading for a number of years,—not a model life by any means, but an exceptional one, which somehow suited Otto von Bismarck, and proved more fruitful than many a model life has been; though we could not advise our young friends to imitate it. In 1844 his sister Malwine became betrothed to Oscar von Arnim, who had been his friend at the Friedrich Wilhelm Gymnasium and had remained so ever since. This was a great satisfaction to him, and his letter of congratulation to her has a playful affectionateness which suggests the coming of brighter days. His father died in 1845, leaving his estates equally divided between Bernhard and Otto,— an unusual practice, rendered still more so by his willing the ancestral residence of Schönhausen to his younger son. It may be surmised from this that he realized Otto's exceptional ability, and looked to him as the one who would give distinction to the name of Bismarck.

Some time in 1847 Otto von Bismarck became acquainted with the young lady who was to be his future wife. She belonged to the Prussian family of the Puttkamers, time-honored in the service of the state, and her given names were Johanna Frederica Charlotta Dorothea Elinore.[1] She was not beautiful, but what is much better, a pleasant, sensible person. From the first she seems to have appreciated him, which is also important in such cases. This is evident from the fact that Herr Ernst von Puttkamer did not understand Bismarck at all, and at first disapproved of the match. The wild life of the country squire may not have been so much of an objection as his unconventional behavior; but the man who was to conquer kingdoms was not to be defeated by a Puttkamer. Only a woman who is true to her heart can see into the future. Fräulein Johanna knew her man and stood by him with creditable firmness. It was a love-match on both sides,—not a common occurrence where large properties are at stake,—and the parents were finally persuaded to give way. Bismarck was married to her on July 28, 1847. Their wedding journey included a visit to Switzerland and Northern Italy, and at Venice they accidentally met and were entertained by the King of Prussia, Frederick William IV. Ernst von Puttkamer and his wife never had occasion to regret the marriage of their daughter.

---

[1] These long personal appellations have a charm for the German nobility which others know not of.

CHAPTER II

GREAT political convulsions produce men of equal magnitude. Napoleon was the fearful offspring of the first French revolution; Bismarck the colossal child of "forty-eight." Metternich foresaw and predicted the revolution of 1848, but hoped to defer it to a later time by a repression of all the tendencies which he thought might lead towards it; but by this policy he only helped to precipitate it.

While the first French revolution was confined to France and was a great success, the revolution of 1848, extending from Warsaw to Lisbon, proved a failure. In only one country at least did the seed which was sown by it come to be harvested, and that country was Prussia. Everywhere else the reaction that followed upon it produced a condition of affairs less favorable to the development of liberal institutions than the conditions that preceded it. Yet the heroes who died for it under the walls of Rome, in the plains of Lombardy, and in the valley of the Danube did not fall wholly in vain.

The revolution possessed a different character in different countries. In France, where it originated, there was less occasion for it than anywhere else. The government of Louis Philippe was mild and liberal. The position of the king differed only from that of a president in the title and hereditary right. It was Thiers's history of the first empire and the lack of an aggressive foreign policy which upset the Orleans dynasty. The revolution was inaugurated by the socialists and taken advantage of by the Bonapartists. France is now substantially republican, but in 1848 republicanism was confined to Paris, Lyons, and Marseilles. The election of Louis Napoleon as president was an ominous event, which plainly foreshadowed the second empire.

In Italy there had been for centuries sufficient cause for revolution, and looked at broadly it was a hopeful sign that it should have succeeded, even for a single year. The temporal power of the pope was looked upon as a perpetual evil by Macchiavelli; and if he thought so it certainly must have been. Yet we must give Pius IX. the credit of having been the first to inaugurate reforms, and the frivolous assassination of his *nuncio* was a commencement of bad augury for the revolution. Sardinia and Tuscany were well governed, and the people of those states expressed little desire for a change of form; Naples was badly governed; and the Austrian portion of Italy, after its quasi-independence under Napoleon, was continually fermenting under a rule which felt no interest in its welfare beyond the collection of taxes.

In Austria proper the complaint arose from a bureaucracy of such long standing that the government machine had come wholly into the possession of a limited number of families, who provided for their relatives in comfortable offices of which the outside public could obtain no share. The professional and commercial classes suffered from a burden of feudatory privileges like those of France in the eighteenth century, though not to the same extent. The Hungarians, who had proved the shield of Austria in the Napoleonic wars, had been deliberately oppressed by Metternich, from a cowardly anticipation of what they might demand in return for this. They were governed almost entirely by Austrian officials, obliged to use the German language for all public business and forms of legal procedure, and could only obtain redress for their supposed grievances through the bureaucracy of Vienna, a dubious and wearisome method of procedure. What the people of Hungary wanted was to manage their own affairs; but the revolution there commenced with a wanton act of cruelty also, which prejudiced the thinking world against it.

The people of Prussia and the smaller German states wished for constitutional government and a fulfilment of the broken promises of 1813. Besides this, the desire for national unity, and the political theory which looked for a republican government as the most direct means of effecting this, stood ready to take advantage of any situation which might seem favorable for the attainment of its wishes. Everywhere in 1848 there were three distinct revolutionary elements,—constitutional government, republicanism, and socialism. In France, however, Bonapartism was substituted for the first of these, and in all countries except Hungary the socialistic element preponderated over the republican. In Germany there was little true republicanism, for the reason that the class of people who form the solid material of republican institutions—those who see their objects at shooting distance—perceived plainly that for the present a republic was impracticable there. They accepted the socialists as allies for the time being, but they did not aim beyond a constitutional monarchy.

It was socialism that handicapped the revolution in France, Italy, and Austria, and prevented its success. The struggle of 1848 had neither the grandeur nor the disinterestedness which gave a terrible momentum to the revolution of 1789. It was largely a warfare of class against class; and, though this was justified to a certain extent, it was what evidently interfered, like a frost, to prevent its proper fruition. Otto von Bismarck would seem to have perceived this at the outset, and to have taken in the political situation at a glance.

There is ample evidence of his always having been interested in political affairs,—that he was a public-spirited man. His discussions with Motley may have been largely on this subject. The one was a democratic monarchist, and the other an aristocratic republican. For that matter, there are plenty of people in America who are less accessible than the German and English nobility. French and Italian noblemen are different, and much, of course, depends on the individual. Bismarck's military associates at Kniephof considered him much of a liberal. We find him, in 1846, soliciting Oscar von Arnim for his company to attend a meeting of the Society for the Improvement of the Working Classes at Potsdam. As early as 1843 Bismarck was a candidate for nomination as a delegate to the Provincial Diet of Pomerania which met at

Stettin, but he does not appear to have desired this. Two years later he was elected, although Prussian politics at that time were more underground than on the surface of events.

In 1846 he began to take hold in earnest. There was a rumor in the air that a great crisis was at hand. Everybody felt it, and, as usual at such times, there was a requisition for serious and determined men. The king had summoned a national assembly to meet in the White Chamber at Berlin in February, 1847, and Bismarck was active among the electors of his district, and made no secret of his desire to represent them. He would go, however, as a conservative candidate, pledged to support the throne above all; and as for other matters, he would do what he considered for the best interest of the nation, without special regard to party lines. Bismarck rode much about the country on his horse Caleb, in the autumn and winter of 1846, explaining his views on politics to all who were willing to listen. The electors were satisfied with his views, but did not select him for their delegate. He was chosen, however, as a substitute, when something happened to prevent the regular delegate from attending at the White Chamber. What a chance this was!

There is no enemy equal to an imprudent and over-zealous friend. Bismarck's first German biographer, by introducing his own political opinions where he should have contented himself with an explanation of those of his hero, has produced an impression of ultra conservatism on Bismarck's part, which has continued to the present time. He has suffered more in this manner than from all the hostile attacks of French and Austrian journalists. In his remarks on the revolution of 1848, Hesekiel shows himself a narrow and intolerant partisan of absolute monarchy, who, like Metternich, can see nothing in the demands of the Prussian people for a constitutional government, but the spirit of insubordination and the lust of power. It is to be feared that he has done very slight justice to Bismarck's position in 1847, which was at first like that of a mediator between contending factions, repressing the extravagance of the revolutionary party, but ready to accept such propositions or changes in the existing political status as might be prudent, practical, and conservative. He was comparatively a young man among those about him in the Diet, but he appears already as the most clear-headed and resolute figure in the Prussian state.

Otto von Bismarck was always superior to party. He recognized political parties exactly for what they are worth, and his unvarying success has been due to this cause in a greater degree than to any other. He stood on the high ground of national patriotism, which is above all parties, and this has prevented his running into those extravagances by which political parties are shipwrecked. A political party may be patriotic, but it is always selfish, and, except on those rare occasions when a whole nation rises to its feet, it always represents the interests of a class. Bismarck was from 1867 till 1878 the leader of the German National Liberals, which under his guidance remodelled Central Europe. His impartial attitude towards general politics cannot be better explained than by the following extract from a letter which he wrote in 1861 : " Nor do I see, moreover, *why we should recoil so prudishly from the idea of popular representation, whether in the Diet or in any customs, or associative parliament.* Surely we cannot combat an institution as revolutionary which is legally established in every German state, and which we Conservatives even would not wish to see abolished, even in Prussia. In national matters we have hitherto regarded every moderate concession as valuable. A thoroughly conservative national representation might be created and yet receive the gratitude of the Liberals." The true statesman is he who not only can see both sides of a question, but can weigh both sides in the balance, and decide where to apply his force when the time for action arrives.

We hear of Bismarck as having belonged originally to the *Junker Partei* in Prussia, but no explanation accompanies this statement which might help us to a conception as to how the *Junker Partei* is constituted, and what it desires to accomplish. As a matter of fact there is no such political party, but the younger sons of noblemen form a class by themselves, usually proud and indigent, whose only prospects in life are to be found through service in the army or civil positions under the government. That they should be the most conservative of conservatives is, therefore, to be expected. Bismarck was not a true Junker, though he was frequently called so in 1847, for his sufficient patrimony placed him above the necessity of seeking office as a means of livelihood. We all begin life, however, from the family stand-point, and it was inevitable that Bismarck should begin it as a conservative. Another young German of those days, a man of rare ability, was destined to take the opposite side, to be imprisoned, and as an exile in America to become one of the foremost statesmen of the western hemisphere. If Bismarck had been born in the same position as Carl Schurz he might have taken a similar course, though, perhaps, not have gone quite so far; and if Schurz had been a Junker, he also might have supported the government. Late in life they met together at Schönhausen and discussed old times with mutual respect and admiration. It was fortunate for Bismarck and for Germany that he took this course in 1848, for otherwise he could never have gained the confidence of the king, which was essential to his future success.

THE DAYS OF MARCH

Violent revolutions are bad, and to be avoided if possible. The loss of life and waste of property which they cause are not so much to be regretted as the disturbing effect which they have on public affairs, the unsettled state of public feeling which they produce, and the reaction which is sure to follow them. Sometimes, however, they are not to be avoided. The slow, gradual transformation of society which has been going on in Germany for the last hundred years is much more effectual, accomplishes its work with much less friction, and is more likely to be enduring than those spasmodic efforts at reform which meanwhile have taken place in France.

To understand the position of Frederick William IV. and his advisers during the days of March it should be considered that they were not only obliged to resist a pressure from

within the capital, but a more distant and equally real pressure
from without. Max Müller speaks in sincere praise of Frederick William IV., whom he knew personally, but he was a
man of too retiring a nature, too much given to literature and
philosophy, to make a very effective king. He might have
been more distinguished as a professor or in the pulpit. A
timid deference to Metternich and the Tsar had become habitual with him, yet he struggled somehow through the storm
of 1848, and though he appeared at one time as the forcible
repressor of the revolution, and afterwards as the leader of it,
we need not, therefore, consider him inconsistent. The story
of his being seen by Bismarck reading Shakespeare in the
forest, with a stag watching him from behind, is one of the
prettiest in all the annals of royalty.

Bismarck soon found himself in a small minority in this
assembly. The revolution of forty-eight was not inspired by
the noble impulse for rational reform and philosophic government with which the revolution of 1789 began. Before 1789
socialism had not been thought of. It was a development of
the revolution,—as Madame de Staël said, an invasion of the
barbarians,—owing to the general prostration of governmental
power. In 1848 it was a deliberate and well-developed theory,
and asserted itself, not in the spasmodic manner of the Reign
of Terror, but with a persistent energy which made it much
more dangerous. There can be no doubt of what a majority
of the Prussian people wanted, and that was a parliamentary
government like that of England, but the socialistic element
was also strong.[1] The meetings of the Diet were occupied
with long-winded harangues full of patriotic sentiments, but
without much practical consideration of the application of
means to ends. Bismarck soon discovered that the assembly
was composed of such diverse and chaotic elements that no
ultimate good could come from it, and that the only prudent
course was to support the government without reservation.

---

[1] During the March revolution of 1848 a mob collected in front of the royal
palace in Berlin, shouting the French war-cry, "Liberty, equality, and fraternity," to which the king sent the reply, "Infantry, cavalry, and artillery."

Nothing alarmed him so much as the tendency to socialism, for he knew, as every clear-sighted person must, that socialism could only end in anarchy and the utter ruin of civilization. The personal attacks on the royal family angered him, for though the ceremonial of court life was distasteful to him, and he had not as yet made acquaintance with Frederick William, he knew the royal family to be worthy people, and he resented these reflections upon their character as a man of spirit always will in such cases. The worst of democracy and popular elections is the advantage it gives to calumny as a political weapon, which is very effective among the illiterate, and always has less weight in proportion to a man's intelligence.

Bismarck, though inexperienced in parliamentary debate, soon became the leader of defence. He was too rapid a thinker to be a very good speaker, and he never cultivated the graces of oratory, but his cool-headed and determined manner was not without its effect. He replied to the bursts of patriotic eloquence by a well-considered statement of the legal aspects of the question, which could not but have weight with those in the Diet of his own profession. The platform he stood on was rather a shaky one, but he made the most of it. It was no other than the divine right of kings, a platform which at that time might be considered on its last legs, and which now exists no longer. The divine right of kings seems absurd enough in America, but during the Middle Ages it formed a solid basis of political right, and answered much the same purpose that a national constitution does at present. It was, in fact, an unwritten covenant between a sovereign and his subjects, and was as much an obligation upon the former to do what was right, as it was for the latter to fulfil whatever their sovereign considered it best to do. This, of course, left a large margin to the personal interest or caprice of the prince; but its influence on such men as Saint Louis and Barbarossa cannot be questioned; and without it there would have been nothing but temporary expediency and the right of the strongest. It was essentially a Germanic principle, and was more efficacious in Germany than in other countries. It was on account of the disregard of it in England that the Magna Charta was extorted from King John; and in Italy, where it never obtained a foothold, the numerous crimes of small potentates may readily be accounted for by the insecurity of their position. It is not to be supposed that this moral covenant was strictly observed in Germany, but German mediæval history has a much more humane and benevolent tone than that of England or France, and political executions were rare in it.

Although the Prussian people in 1848 were mainly in the right, and Bismarck and the king mainly in the wrong, the position which Bismarck assumed had a sound legal basis. The divine right of kings was a right *de facto*, and would continue to be until either the king had retreated from that position or had been driven from it by a permanent revolution. The constitutional agreement between the English Parliament and William of Orange was brought forward in debate, and Bismarck replied, "The English people were then in a different position from that of the Prussian people at present; a century of revolution and civil war had invested it with the right to dispose of a crown, and bind up with it conditions accepted by William of Orange." This was a valid argument; for as a new proprietary right can only be acquired by adverse possession for a prescribed length of time, so the loss of a similar right can only happen by a similar dispossession. The change in public opinion could no more effect it than public opinion in America could change the Constitution of the United States by a single election.

The German people were inexperienced in parliamentary government, and their first attempts at it were awkward and ineffective, as might have been expected. The Diet at Berlin, after speechifying, discussing, and amending for about three months, wound up its proceedings with a series of demands and resolutions, some of which were needful and to the point, but others so impracticable that it is not to be wondered that Frederick William and his cabinet decided to reject them altogether. The work of the Diet was not good enough to pass muster, and was returned to be done over again, like an ill-constructed piece of furniture. The Prussian people would not believe this, and it caused great irritation, destined to result the following year in the only revolt that has ever taken place against the Prussian government.

After his return from his wedding journey,—and no pleasanter excursion can be imagined,[1]—Bismarck settled down to matrimonial life at Schönhausen, where he could watch the events at Berlin from a closer stand-point than at Kniephof. There his eldest child, Mary Elizabeth Johanna, was born in August, 1848. He added the name of Schönhausen to the family appellation of Bismarck, though it has not become customary to use it except on official documents. That his early married life was happy and contented we learn from the letters to his wife when absent from her on public business, of which there was plenty in store for him. Marriage and an active profession was all that Bismarck needed to balance his natural forces. After this we hear nothing more of his mad frolics and other eccentric behavior, though he always continued to be unconventional outside of court circles. Count Herbert was born at Berlin in December of 1849, and William Otto Albert at Frankfort in 1852. These were his only children. Frau Johanna von Bismarck became distinguished as an exemplary housekeeper and a skilful manager of her husband's estates during his long periods of absence. The hams she cured were supposed to be the best in Germany, though the name of Bismarck perhaps served as a spice to their flavor.

Bismarck's utterances during the days of March, 1848, are no more to be seriously considered now than the profane exclamations of a shipmaster when his vessel has gone ashore in a fog. He remained mostly at Potsdam, in order to learn what events were taking place, and to serve the government if called on; but no call came for him. It continues to be a disputed point to this day how the collision between the troops and the insurgents took place in Berlin. The order to clear the streets was attributed to Prince William, afterwards Emperor Wil-

---

[1] Switzerland and Northern Italy.

liam, who went to England in exile for some months in consequence, but this has been denied by a competent authority.[1] The case was similar to the Boston massacre in 1774. It was necessary that a collision should occur, in order to disinfect the movement of its socialistic element and give the constitutional party untrammelled freedom of action. The troops remained masters of the streets, but not of the city, and, worn out with fatigue, were finally obliged to retire. The king dismissed his ministers and approved the organization of a citizen guard, chosen from the better and more reliable class, to preserve order in Berlin. It was an affecting spectacle, when the corpses of those who had been killed in the barricades were brought to the court-yard of the Schloss, and the king and queen surveyed them and bowed their heads before them. Three days later the victims of the revolution were buried in a common grave in the Friedrichshain, accompanied by a funeral procession of twenty thousand people, to which Frederick William paid his respects, decorated with the black, red, and gold of the revolutionists. Historians may call this weakness, vacillation, or whatever they please; but it was the best policy he could have adopted, for it showed the people that, after all, they and the government were one.[2] A constitutional convention was appointed to meet on May 22.

The behavior of this convention, to which Bismarck declined an election, was such as to justify the government in more rigorous measures. Knives were drawn on the more moderate and conservative delegates, in order to compel them to vote for the most extravagant resolutions. A large party urged a declaration of war against Austria, in order to assist their democratic brethren in Vienna, and the wrangling was so fierce, over questions like the annulling of patents of nobility, that no progress could be made.[3] No enduring govern-

---

[1] Professor William Müller, of Tübingen.

[2] It is only fair to state that Bismarck could never see this, and never became reconciled to the revolution. In his memoirs he attributes the conduct of Frederick William IV. to mental and physical frailty. If so, it was a fortunate frailty for Prussia.

[3] The presiding officer of this convention was one *Herr Unruhe*, or Mr. Unrest, a name singularly appropriate to the occasion.

ment has yet been founded in such a manner, and it was not long before the saner portion of the convention became convinced of this. The storming of the city arsenal by a disorderly mob created supporters of the monarchy by the ten thousand. The liberal ministry resigned, and was replaced by a more conservative one. The convention was prorogued to meet again in November at Brandenburg, and General Wrangel, a popular veteran of the War of Liberation, was summoned to Berlin with a strong force to preserve order, for which the citizen police had been found ineffectual. Meanwhile Bismarck was busy in his own way,—on the street, in the gallery of the convention, in the palace, watching events and writing his opinion of them for the newspapers, especially the *Kreuz Zeitung*, like a common reporter. As his letters were unsigned, they can only now be guessed at from the vigor and decisiveness of their style, but it is fair to presume that they exercised a decided influence on the public mind. The adjourned convention met on November 27, but, as a majority of the members absented themselves, no business could be transacted. A few days later a sufficient number of socialists and republicans appeared to constitute a quorum; but after entering a protest against the transferrence from Berlin, where they could be supported by the mob, they disappeared again, and the convention adjourned *sine die*. As the popular assembly had failed to bring forth the constitution, Frederick William now proposed one drawn up by his own ministers.

The revolution was successful and went just far enough, a creditable fact for all parties concerned. Nothing more was heard of the French war-cry,—liberty, equality, and fraternity. Frederick William granted the Prussian people a much more liberal constitution than the Magna Charta which was extorted from King John. Its fundamental principles, however, were the same: the right to levy taxes and to enlist soldiers was vested in an assembly called the Landtag, elected by the people; but the king retained an absolute veto on all changes of the laws or of the constitution. An upper chamber of notables, similar to the House of Lords, was to reconsider the action of the Landtag in certain cases, pass judgment on constitutional changes, and legislate on all matters appertaining to the nobility. This, certainly, was not a very liberal constitution, for it provided no means for controlling the executive action; but the difference between an absolute veto and a two-thirds majority is not so very great; for where public opinion is nearly unanimous it will generally accomplish its object, even in an old-fashioned monarchy. If the Prussian army had fraternized with the insurgents in 1848 as the French army did in 1792, the Hohenzollern dynasty would have come to an end, at least for a term of years.

Much more important than the Prussian fiasco was the national convention which assembled at Frankfort, to consider measures for the establishment of German unity. In this assembly were gathered the most notable men in Germany, outside of the royal families, and some of them more distinguished than any monarchs of their time. Simson, the jurist, afterwards president of the North German Reichstag, was one of its prominent members. There were poets, philosophers, lawyers, and historians. A more dignified assemblage could not be imagined, and yet all its labors came to naught, as Bismarck predicted, because they were not supported by any material force. It was a convention on paper, and carried no more authority with it than an unsigned writ of *habeas corpus*.

They were too high-minded for the people, and too far removed from practical affairs for the princes. It was an ominous mistake that they should have selected for president Henry Gagern, frequently called Jupiter Gagern from his imposing figure, grandiose features, and thundering voice; the most popular orator in Germany, but whose speeches were not of such material as would convince an audience like the Roman Senate. Bismarck, in his slashing way, called Gagern "the watering-pot of phrases."

The Frankfort Convention spent over a year on its work, and elaborated a constitution much after the pattern of the unwritten constitution by which England is now governed.

It was to have an all-powerful national assembly, a chamber of princes for the sake of appearances, and an emperor at the head who would possess as little authority as Queen Victoria. Frederick William IV. was offered the honor of this precarious position, and a deputation of members, including Gagern and Simson, went to Berlin to confer with His Majesty. All Germany was breathless with interest while the King of Prussia and his ministers consulted on its acceptation; and great was the disappointment when the offer of the convention was rejected. Frederick William, however, could do nothing less; for its acceptance would have placed him in antagonism not only to the smaller princes of Germany, but to the Emperor of Austria, and would inevitibly have involved him in an unequal conflict, where he would have had to depend on his own resources, without any assistance from the wise men of the Frankfort Convention. In fact, it was much to be feared that at the first sound of the bugle they would disappear like foxes in their holes. A marked majority of the new Prussian assembly passed a resolution recommending the king to accept the imperial crown, but he declared that it would only make him the servant of the revolution. Bismarck, who had been chosen a member of the first Prussian Landtag, made a speech on the occasion, in which he objected to the imperial title on legal grounds. The Frankfort Convention, he said, proposes that the king should surrender the crown which he had inherited from his ancestors, and receive in place of it one which bore the stamp of popular sovereignty, and which he would hold merely in fief from the people of Germany, who might afterwards revoke the gift whenever they thought fit. The Frankfort crown seemed to him too much like a tinsel affair, and he could not advise the acceptance of so dubious a present.

The revolution in Germany did not find such able leaders as Mirabeau and Danton. Simson and Gagern were talkers and thinkers, not men of action, and the German people are slow to turn aside from their daily mill-round. Yet the fine oratory at Frankfort was not without its influence on the time. It served like a breeze to waft the destiny of the German people on its appointed course. A fresh impulse had been given to the aspiration for national unity, and Bismarck may have noticed that the proposition brought before the convention which caused the most animated discussion was whether the Austrian empire should be included as a whole in United Germany, or only the two German provinces of it. The Austrian delegates declared that either their empire must be accepted in its completeness or excluded altogether. Here was a problem for any future statesman who hoped to accomplish national unity to reflect on.

Bismarck relates an amusing interview which he had with Jupiter Gagern on behalf of Frederick William IV. in order to effect some kind of a bargain or compromise with the party or group of which Gagern was the leader. General Manteuffel, who was then in the ministry, brought the two together and then left them to fight it out. Bismarck says, "As soon as Manteuffel was gone, I commenced to talk on politics, and explained my whole position in a very sober and business-like way. You should have heard Gagern. He put on his Jupiter face, lifted his eyebrows, bristled up his hair, rolled his eyes about, fixed them on the ceiling till they all but cracked the plaster, and talked at me with his big phrases as if I had been a public meeting. Of course, that got nothing out of me. I answered him quite coolly, and we remained as far apart as ever." When Bismarck told this story[1] he could not remember whether it was in 1850 or 1851, so that it is impossible to place it exactly in the events of that time; but it contradicts those biographers who assert Bismarck's ultra conservatism during the revolutionary period, for in that case the king would not have employed him as a mediator with the opposition. The anecdote also discloses Gagern's lack of practical sense in dealing with men.

In the winter of 1849–50 Bismarck went to live in Berlin, and occupied the first story on Dorotheen Strasse, No. 37, and there his son Herbert was born in December, and the boy was christened in February by a Lutheran pastor in the

---

[1] November 18, 1870. Cf. Busch.

orthodox Prussian manner. Bismarck's letter to his sister, Frau von Arnim, and others this year are more filled with domestic affairs than the politics which seemed to absorb him. His political work was disinterested enough in one sense, for he received no remuneration for it, and the income from his estates only enabled him to live in a very modest way with two establishments, one at Schönhausen and the other at Berlin. His parliamentary duties were but a small portion of his daily business, and his chief entertainment was an evening hour in a beer-saloon, where a number of Conservatives were in the habit of congregating.

It was at another establishment of the kind that Bismarck committed the only act of violence for which he is held responsible. A saucy Radical, or Socialist, came into the beer-garden evidently for the purpose of bucking the tiger. He soon commenced to talk politics, and indulged in some very offensive expressions in regard to the royal family. Thereupon Bismarck informed him that if he did not leave the room he would break a beer-glass over his head, and as the man continued obdurate he kept his word. The Radical was not seriously injured, and appears to have received small sympathy from the by-standers, but it is barely possible that such a blow might prove fatal.

There is no phase of this many-sided revolution so difficult to understand as the Convention of Erfurt. The imperial offer of the Frankfort delegates had in no wise been solicited by the King of Prussia, and yet the act was considered by foreign courts, especially Austria, as a dangerous precedent for which he was directly responsible. Prince Schwarzenberg, who had succeeded to Metternich's policy, and was himself an inferior kind of Metternich, informed the smaller German governments that the exclusion of Austria from German affairs was a subject not to be considered, and that the Frankfort Diet must be restored under Austrian supremacy. This was a diplomatic attack on Prussia, and Frederick William attempted to offset it by establishing a league of German princes in which Prussia would become the military and diplomatic leader. The kings of Saxony and Hanover supported this plan, but Bavaria held aloof from it. A convention of delegates was convened at Erfurt to consider the subject. Bismarck was present, and his keener intelligence foresaw that the result of the movement would be to place Prussia, though really at the head of the confederation, in a position subordinate to the votes of princes, like the Elector of Cassel and the Grand Duke of Baden. It was now that he showed himself the true statesman. Though a conservative delegate, he was expected to support the project, but he turned against it and expressed his opposition plainly and boldly. The leadership of Prussia in such a confederation would not be a real leadership, but one so fettered as to make the direction of its affairs intolerable. His first principle was that the independence and integrity of the Prussian monarchy must be maintained. If such a confederation of princes could be established it would possess no enduring vitality. German nationality must be achieved in some other manner.

In fact the Erfurt Convention and the Frankfort Convention would seem to have been supplements of each other, the one representing the wishes of the people, and the other constituted under popular influence by a number of isolated governments. Each was a fraction by itself, and only by the union of the two could German nationality be accomplished. The adoption of either plan would have placed the Prussian government at the mercy of an uncertain influence, and could only have resulted in Prussia breaking through the legislative net-work by a sudden revolution to its former position. Bismarck was rejoiced when the intervention of Austria overturned the Erfurt Constitution. Prince Schwarzenberg proclaimed the restoration of the Frankfort Diet, and invited all the German powers to send delegates to a meeting there on the 1st of September. Frederick William IV. and Count Brandenburg refused to do this, and issued a circular protesting against the re-establishment of the Diet. The Emperor of Austria accordingly threatened the withdrawal of diplomatic relations, and was supported in this by the King of Bavaria. For a short time German affairs assumed a war-like appearance, but the questions at stake were too ephemeral to carry either government to such an extreme. Both sides appealed to the Tsar Nicholas, who decided in favor of the old Frankfort Diet, but without granting any special favor therein to Austria. Thus the revolution in Germany suddenly came to an end. The Erfurt Convention had at least served like a bogus railroad to prevent an Austrian hegemony, and Bismarck gained in prestige what he may have lost in favor with the Prussian Ministry.

The polity of the Roman Republic, the best government of ancient times, was worked out through a protracted struggle between patricians and plebeians. So the present constitutional government of Prussia, and of all Germany, resulted from the obstinate struggle between the king and the people in 1848. It will be observed that of all the European revolutions at that time this was the only one which was not carried too far, and was the only one which bore good fruit. The Parisians, who expelled Louis Philippe with so much ease, were soon obliged to accept a military government in his place. The Athenian democracy, which Mazzini and Garibaldi established in Rome, was suppressed by a French army, and Pius IX. returned to establish a Roman despotism for twenty years longer. The King of Sardinia's support of the revolt in Lombardy cost him his crown, and the Hungarian revolution was suppressed with a severity which left that unfortunate country little to hope for in the future. Prussia, however, had made a distinct step in advance; and yet it was a step on a dangerous path. As the Berlin papers said, she "was on the constitutional," and so much the better for her good health and internal condition; but she was surrounded by jealous rivals, who viewed this change in her form of government with slightly disguised hostility, and were eager to find a pretext for interference in Prussian affairs so as to produce a counter-revolution, and a return to the previous political condition.

CHAPTER III

FORTUNATE are the people who are strong and numerous enough to establish national unity. Without this there can be no lasting independence, and without independence no superior national development. The world is becoming crowded; nations press against one another, and their population increases so that it everywhere is straining to find an outlet. Those that are not strong enough to maintain themselves in this continual struggle become absorbed by others, and disappear as independent communities. At the same time the spirit of nationality has never been so daring and self-assertive, so that every small branch of the Aryan family is ambitious to attain it. These are the centrifugal and centripetal forces of Europe.

The numerous French invasions of Germany from the time of Louis XIV. to that of Napoleon I. had sufficiently developed the need of a closer consolidation of the German states and national interests. Austria, lying most remote from France, was the only German community sufficiently powerful to offer a substantial resistance to the ambition of French rulers; and the interest of the Austrian government in provinces situated on the Rhine was wholly a philanthropic one, an element which cannot safely be counted for much in international affairs. Though the aggrandizement of France was always something of a menace to the Austrian empire, this would not become serious so long as the French confined themselves to the left bank of the Rhine.[1] Frederick the Great formed a league with the Protestant German states for their better protection against both France and Austria, but

---

[1] It is only fair to say in justice to the French that, as the Rhine was the ancient boundary of Gaul, they have always felt that they had an immemorial right to it, though such a right could not be considered legal or international.

this was broken up by the first French revolution. So Alexander Hamilton made use of the history and condition of Germany as one of his strongest arguments in favor of our national government. He says in the *Federalist*, No. 19: "The history of Germany is a history of foreign intrusions and foreign intrigues; of requisitions of men and money disregarded or partially abortive, or attended with slaughter and desolation, involving the innocent with the guilty; of general imbecility, confusion, and misery." Again, in No. 22, he says: "German empire is in continual trammels from the multiplicity of the duties which the several princes and states exact upon the merchandises passing through their territories, by means of which the fine streams and navigable rivers with which Germany is so happily watered are rendered useless." This condition continued, with some amelioration, during the nineteenth century, until it was brought to a close by Bismarck's new German empire in 1871. So long as the Holy Alliance endured there was no danger to Germany from foreign invasion, but the Diet established at Frankfort for the regulation of customs duties and the settlements of differences between German states could accomplish little, for the simple reason that it possessed no material means with which to enforce its decisions. The conflicting interests of so many small commonwealths were not easily reconciled, and the proceedings of the Diet were characterized by interminable discussions and a "masterly inactivity." This much may be said, however, in favor of Metternich, that he honestly desired to maintain peace in Europe, and that his policy towards other governments was always conciliatory. So long as he guided the power of Austria the King of Prussia could depend on friendly consideration, but after 1848 there was a change in the attitude of Austria which was felt both by the representatives in the Diet and by the Prussian ambassador at Vienna. The causes of this were twofold.

In the first place, Austria had emerged from the revolution with victorious banners. Hungary and Lombardy had been placed under military government, and the concessions wrung from the emperor by the Vienna mob were easily cancelled by his abdication and the inauguration of his son, Francis Joseph, who was too young to resist the tide of reaction even if he desired to. The adoption of a constitution in Prussia was looked upon in Vienna and St. Petersburg as a confession of weakness, and at the same time produced a feeling of estrangement like that which results from a change of political parties. The sudden rise of Louis Napoleon was considered an ephemeral event, and henceforth Austria and Russia were to determine the destinies of Europe.

Near the close of his life Talleyrand pointed out that there was a strong tendency to a closer political organization in Germany, which either Austria or Prussia would be likely to take advantage of, and which might prove detrimental to the interests of France. Hegel, a South German, born in Stuttgart, but who in middle life was called to the University of Berlin, preached the doctrine of national unity boldly and vigorously from 1820 to 1830. He found many proselytes and successors among philosophers and historians, and the professorial class exercise an influence on public opinion in Germany like that of the newspapers in England and America. Such instruction could not fail to have its effect on a people intellectually vibrating with the music of Beethoven and the poetry of Goethe and Schiller. One of the peculiar phenomena of the revolution was a national assembly of three hundred and twenty delegates, chosen by popular suffrage independently of the governments of the German states, which met at Frankfort with deliberate intention of replacing the old German Diet and inaugurating a new German empire. The high-minded and patriotic men who composed this organization evidently did not take into account that their deliberations could have no actual value without the support of a military force, and when they finally offered the imperial crown to Frederick William of Prussia, disregarding the Austrian government, which at the time had its hands full with the Hungarian rebellion, the honor was unhesitatingly rejected. Only men experienced in public affairs know how dangerous it would have been for the King of Prussia to have accepted a title which would not only have brought him into direct conflict with the Emperor of Austria, but with most of the smaller German princes. The king and his ministers perceived plainly enough that such a result could only be reached through a European convulsion. The event, however, had a significance which cast a long shadow into the future. It was the handwriting on the wall, which served to warn the duodecimo monarchs of Germany, as well as the Emperor of Austria, of a danger to their absolutism which they might some day be obliged to encounter, and the method they adopted to strangle this baby Hercules was an instance of that short-sighted political narrowness which often brings to pass the very result which it desires to prevent. Nothing could be further from the unambitious mind of Frederick William IV. than to assert a superiority over the kings of Saxony, Bavaria, and Hanover, but this did not prevent him from becoming none the less an object of suspicion to them.

The Frankfort Diet resumed its sessions on May 30, 1851. General von Rochow was the Prussian delegate, and Bismarck accompanied him in the position of secretary,—much the same as a secretary of legation. In the course of the first year, however, von Rochow resigned, weary, perhaps, of the dulness and monotony of the Diet, and recommended Bismarck for his successor. The king readily acted on this suggestion, for it had come to be rumored in Berlin that there was no better man for any kind of business. The position, which in the hands of another might have been little more than an empty form, was soon infused by Bismarck with all the character of his sturdy nature and penetrating intelligence.

Bismarck seems to have found from the first a hostile attitude in the Diet towards Prussia, and it is more remarkable that this was quite undisguised. The mythical story that he asked the Austrian delegate for a light for his cigar at a meeting of the Diet has been reduced by Bismarck's own statement (and that of his biographer) to a private interview, in which the Austrian delegate received him smoking, and offered him neither cigar nor chair. Bismarck took a cigar out of his own pocket, asked the other for a light, and made himself comfortable. After that, however, the conference could come to nothing; the slight almost amounted to a direct insult, and the campaign of 1866 may be said to have originated at that moment.. Subsequently Bismarck was so roughly treated by the Austrian delegate, that he challenged him to fight. This policy was steadily maintained by the Austrian court for the following sixteen years.

The leaders of this new movement of the Austrian cabinet were Prince Schwarzenberg and Count Buol Schauenstein. A more shallow, empirical policy than theirs could not easily be imagined, and in the result it brought Austria to the verge of ruin. Among other motives, they would seem to have been actuated by personal ambition and a vainglorious spirit. It was not difficult for them to find allies among the German states. Saxony had been deprived of half its territory by Prussia, in return for the French alliance of 1813. Hanover and Nassau were under English influences, and England had been the ally of Austria for more than two centuries. Bavaria was Catholic, and was inclined towards Austria on the score of religion. By means of a majority vote these states hoped to discipline Prussia, and control the Diet wholly in their own interest.

It is a shrewd statement that, no matter how autocratic a monarch may be in theory, he is practically surrounded by barriers which it requires a strong man to overleap.[1] The youthful Francis Joseph could hardly have been expected to overleap the barriers with which this court party surrounded him, and as he grew older he evidently lacked either the ability or the will to do so. The first important consequence of this policy was the Italian campaign of 1858. Count Cavour was not a statesman to be blind to what was going on around him, and the isolated position which the Austrian cabinet thus made for itself served as a tempting bait to the ambition of Napoleon III. Austria might control the Diet at Frankfort, and regulate the customs duties in a way unfavorable to Prussian industry, but Lombardy was lost in con-

---

[1] E. J. Lowell, in The Eve of the French Revolution.

sequence. The French emperor would not have dared to attack a united Germany, for he could not have done so with any prospect of success.

Bismarck's attitude at the Diet was firm and dignified, but appears to have been conciliatory. At least his letters have this tone, and he could not otherwise have served the gentle-spirited Frederick William, who shrank from anything like a collision. Nevertheless, there was always the same compact majority against everything that Prussia wanted, as Bismarck said himself during the campaign of 1870.[1] He went on a special embassy to Vienna in 1852, and had a personal con-ference with Schwarzenberg and Francis Joseph himself, but he was met there with the same overbearing spirit as at Frank-fort. They thought they were masters of the situation, and intended to make the most of it. He wrote to his wife from Vienna:

"In business, however, there prevails great nonchalance; either people don't want to arrange with us, or they think we look upon it as more important than appears to them. I fear that the oppor-tunity of coming to an understanding is gone, which will prove a bad result for us; for it was thought that a very great step towards reconciliation was taken in sending me, and they will not soon send another here as desirous of coming to an understanding, and who at the time can deal so freely."

The same sentiments were expressed in a report from Count Bernsdorf, the Prussian ambassador, to the king, from Vienna, on the 11th of February, 1851:

"According to Schwarzenberg's plan, no notice is to be taken of any objection from the minor states. Prussia is to assist in this,— that is, to drop her allies, and with her own hand help form a Direc-tory in which she would always be in the minority, and which

---

[1] The Saxon-Austrian premier, Von Beust, says in his Memoirs (i. 313), "I do not deny if my appointment had been made previous to 1866, I could have been more useful, especially in regard to German affairs. I am sure that I would have succeeded in preserving *Austria's dominant position*, and in averting dis-asters like those of 1866." This innocent confession from one of Bismarck's chief opponents is the best vindication of Bismarck's policy.

would be of great advantage to her bitterest enemies. Russia is expected to support Austria. The two powers, which a short time ago were ready to fight Prussia on account of violation of the treaties of 1815, now urge a reckless abolition of those treaties. If the question concerned the transferrence of the executive into the hands of the two great powers alone, this would be a progressive step for the attainment of which it would be worth while making considerable sacrifice. But rather than establish a many-handed Directory, in which Austria would not share the power with Prussia, but with the lesser states, it would be decidedly better for Prussia to return to the old Confederate Diet." [1]

The despatches of a foreign ambassador are intended to convey the exact truth, for otherwise they would be of no value to his government. In Bismarck's circular note to the German courts of January 24, 1863, he said:

"Before 1848 it had been unheard of that questions of any magnitude should have been introduced in the confederation without the concurrence of the two great powers previously being secured. Even in cases where the opposition had come from the less powerful states, as in the matter of the South Germany fortresses, it had been preferred to allow objects of such importance and urgency to remain unfulfilled for years rather than seek to overcome opposition by means of a *majority*. At the present day, however, the *opposition of Prussia*, not only to a proposal in itself, but in reference to its *unconstitutionality*, is treated as *an incident undeserving of notice*, by which no one is to be restrained from pursuing a deliberately chosen course to any extent whatever."

This is a memorable document. Nothing could be clearer or more explicit as a description of the political situation. Voting seems like peaceful and harmless business; but when it takes place on certain definite lines, and continues so year after year, the minority will always resort to arms if they can do so with the probability of success. The condition of affairs was the more galling to Prussian patriotism because the Austrians had never been found a match for the Prussians on the field of battle; and though the Austrian empire

---

[1] Von Sybel's German Empire, ii. 101.

held a much greater population than Prussia, the German portion of Austria was not much larger than Bavaria. Bismarck attempted a reconstruction of the Diet, by which delegates would be chosen *pro rata* instead of according to the system then in vogue. This would have placed Prussia in a more advantageous position, and the absurdity of so large a kingdom being offset by the vote of Saxony or Baden must have been apparent to every one. Bismarck probably did not expect his plan to succeed. Too much stress cannot be laid on the point that previous to 1848 no proposition was introduced into the Diet by either of the great powers without a previous consultation with the other. In this way their conflicting interests were harmonized before the smaller German states could have a chance to pass judgment upon them.

How dangerous was the path that constitutional Prussia was likely to tread we may judge from the outcome of the Hessian revolution of September, 1850. The house of Cassell had been a pestilent disgrace to Germany for nearly a hundred years. The Elector of Hesse, who sold the lives of his subjects to the British government during our War of Independence, is reported to have had over a hundred illegitimate children.[1] Napoleon abolished the state entirely, but after his downfall the electoral family was restored to its rights and properties by the Congress of Vienna. When the reaction came, in 1849, the reigning Elector of Cassell formed an ultra-conservative ministry, with a Count Hassenpflug at the head of it, a man formerly prosecuted for forgery, and universally mistrusted by the Hessians. He immediately proceeded to such arbitrary actions that the people arose in wrath against him and expelled him from the state. King Frederick William, not liking such an unprincipled neighbor, and, perhaps, also actuated by a sense of right and justice, supported the Hessian people, and expressed a wish to have the Elector form such a ministry as would be acceptable to his subjects. Schwarzenberg, however, insisted that the Elector should be supported, right or wrong, and that Hassenpflug should be

---

[1] See E. J. Lowell's account of him in The Hessians in America.

restored to power. Prussian and Austrian troops were mobilized, and for a few weeks war seemed imminent. The result could hardly have been unfavorable to Prussia, but Frederick William's courage could not be brought to the sticking point. In a moment of weakness he accepted the mediation of the Tsar Nicholas, and a conference was held at Warsaw. Contrary to the whole course of Russian diplomacy, Nicholas, instead of conciliating the Prussian government by a compromise, threw his whole power into the Austrian scales. Hassenpflug was recalled; the unfortunate Hessians were saddled with Austrian troops after the Metternich method, and obliged to endure such humiliation that many of them emigrated to Prussia. Schwarzenberg had played with loaded dice; there was evidently a bargain between Nicholas and himself; and it seems incredible now that an Austrian chancellor should have deliberately consented to the aggrandizement of Russia at the mouth of the Danube. Nicholas already had the invasion of Turkey in his plans, and the Cassell affair was one of the steps which led ultimately to his own humiliation.

The liberation of Schleswig and Holstein had been fairly accomplished by their own troops and the Tenth Prussian Army Corps, but the intervention of Russia and Great Britain brought it to an untimely end. Great Britain might have some reason to fear the aggrandizement of Prussia in this instance, but the interest of the Tsar could not possibly coincide with this, and his course would seem to have been instigated by hostility to constitutional government. Schleswig and Holstein had never been placed on an equal footing with the other provinces of Denmark, but rather governed after the manner of conquered territory. They seem now to have been subjected to a more shameful treatment than the Hessians. The historian, Wilhelm Müller, says: "No land in all Europe was abused and trodden under foot with such cynical brutality as Schleswig, and every German with a spark of honor in him, while cursing a diplomacy which in the nineteenth century still treated the people like cattle, and execrating a system of government which could dispose in that wholesale way of so many German souls, blushed for shame and rage when he heard the name of Schleswig-Holstein."

"Individuals," says Froude, "have suffered by millions in this world, but the community which permits the injustice to be perpetrated is finally obliged to atone for it to the last drop of blood that has been shed." So it is with nations. The brutal oppression of the Hessians and of the people of Schleswig-Holstein met with a more speedy atonement than has often happened in such instances, and resulted in a European convulsion which extended from Paris to Constantinople.

Such were the subjects which Bismarck had to reflect on during the monotonous sittings of the Diet at Frankfort. What conclusions he formed on them can only be judged by his subsequent course. His position required him to keep a close watch on his tongue and pen; but his letters at this time breathe a spirit of calm confidence which show that his faith in the future of Germany, and especially of Prussia, had the character almost of a religious belief. The greatest actors in the world's history have always been strong believers, and Bismarck's assertion during the campaign of 1870 has been recorded by Dr. Busch, that but for his faith in God and immortality he could not have remained at his post a single day; but he added, "I live in an age of unbelievers." His post of duty had not yet become a dangerous one, nor had the cares of his position begun to worry him, and we find in his letters from Frankfort plenty of calm, healthful enjoyment, especially enjoyment of nature. His ardent love of nature is much in Bismarck's favor. As Emerson says, the sighing of the pine-tree has a meaning which only the pure can understand. Bismarck always preferred a ramble in the woods to an evening at the opera. He was fond of solitary excursions, as many a great man has been before him. He went alone to Rüdesheim on the Rhine, to spend the night and swim in the great river. As the evening was warm (August, 1851), he went in bathing by moonlight, and floated down the river to the Rat Tower, "where," he says, "that wicked old bishop came to his end."[1]   He luxuriated in the sea-bathing at Ostend, and was always very fond of water, either fresh or salt.   He made visits to old Metternich at Johannisberg Castle, and listened to his old stories about Napoleon and Alexander I. Metternich's stories were not much to be trusted, and Bismarck appears to have come to that conclusion, for he did not afterwards speak of Metternich with any great respect,— a remarkable diplomat, but not a constructive statesman. Metternich, on the other hand, would seem to have recognized Bismarck's genius, and to have delighted in his society.

Bismarck's letters to his wife from Frankfort, and also from Hungary, are the finest literature of their kind; not sentimental, but warm-hearted, considerate, and clear-sighted, and written in language, whether you call it German or English, not easily excelled.   He had only been married three years, and more than half the time had been separated from her by the necessities of his political life.   His descriptions of natural scenery remind one of Byron.   They properly belong to this period, and we meet with little of them in his later writings, which are too business-like and diplomatic to be particularly entertaining.

The loneliness of his situation at Frankfort and indifference of the people about him lead him to reflect on his past life, and in a letter to his wife, July 3, 1851, he says:

"I cannot understand how a man who considers his own nature and yet knows nothing of God, and will know nothing, can endure his existence, from mere contempt and wearisomeness.   I know not how I could formally support it; were I to live as then, without God, without you, without my children, I should not indeed know whether I had not better abandon life like a dirty shirt; and yet most of my acquaintances are in that state, and live on!   If I ask of an individual what object he has in living on, in laboring and growing angry, in intriguing and spying, I obtain no answer.   Do not conclude from this tirade that my mood is dark;

---

[1] The Rat Tower could never have been the habitation of a bishop or any person but an anchorite.   It appears to have been an old Roman tower, converted, perhaps, into a granary.

on the contrary, I feel like a person who looks of a fine September morning on the yellowing foliage; I am healthy and cheerful, but I feel some melancholy, some longing for home, a desire for forests, ocean, wilderness, for you and my children, mingled with the impressions of sunset and of Beethoven."

Bismarck sits in his study, penning long epistles to his wife, with his great Danish dog looking solemnly at him across the table. He repents of the idleness and frivolity of his youth; he finds little satisfaction in his diplomatic honors, true trait of a veracious nature; he longs for the society of his wife and children; to see the sunset from his own home, and for a little of Beethoven's music. Such was the man of "blood and iron," of whom an English magazine hack, with these letters before him, wrote in the *Edinburgh Review* in 1869, after affirming that Bismarck's political ideas were not in accordance with the nineteenth century, and that his career, though brilliant, would undoubtedly be a brief one:

"He knows how to flatter his interlocutors by assuming an air of genuine admiration for their talents; they leave him charmed by his condescension, *whilst he laughs at the fools who took his fine words for solid cash. His contempt of men is profound;* he dislikes independence, though he probably respects it. There is not a single man of character left in the ministry or the more important places of the civil service."[1]

Truly this writer's soul must have been as arid as the desert of Gobi. We wonder if he could appreciate Beethoven, and preferred the society of his own household to wandering about at night. It is safe to presume that this judgment on Bismarck came into his head after he had taken up his pen, and it is a fair example of the mendacious criticism to which great men are exposed in our time. Surely it is these literary gadflies, and not the Napoleons and Bismarcks, who are the tyrants of the nineteenth century. Bismarck's chief sin consisted, of course, in his being a Prussian. If he had been an

---

[1] We trust the reader will weigh this last sentence as he would a dubious piece of money. How does the reviewer know so much?

Austrian premier, and the battle of Sadowa had been an Austrian victory, he might have been glorified to an equality with Palmerston and Disraeli. The remarkable part of it is that editors should publish such contributions and readers believe them. Those who enjoyed personal interviews with Bismarck did not find him to be either a flatterer or a cynic.

Legislative assemblies are often dreary enough, especially to a man of active temperament and executive ability. Bismarck analyzes the customary proceedings of the Frankfort Diet in a caustic and amusing manner. He writes to Frau von Bismarck:

" I am making enormous progress in the art of saying nothing in a great many words. I write reports of many sheets, which read as tersely and roundly as leading articles; and if Manteuffel can say what there is in them, after he has read them, he can do more than I can. Each of us pretends to believe of his neighbor that he is full of thoughts and plans, if he would only tell; and at the same time we none of us know an atom more of what is going to happen to Germany than of next year's snow. Nobody, not even the most malicious sceptic of a democrat, believes what quackery and self-importance there is in this diplomatizing."

In a similar strain Bismarck spoke of the Frankfort Diet twenty years later. He was no political pedant, to be charmed with a show of empty formalities. We find, all throughout his life, that nothing had an interest for him except what was real and veritable, such things as might bring some good to Prussia, to himself, or to some other person. Can anything be more irksome to such a man than learning the art of saying nothing in a great many words? Yet Bismarck went through this Frankfort discipline diligently and effectively, as a soldier marches day after day under a hot sun on a dusty road. To do whatever he undertook with Prussian thoroughness and precision, that, evidently, was his motto.

His letters from Hungary are intensely interesting, for they afford such a clear and graphic account of that half-European, half-Oriental land, with whose fortunes so many Americans

have sympathized. He went there not long after the revolution had been crushed out, and found a melancholy condition
of affairs, Tartar-like bands of robbers patrolling the country,
so that it was dangerous to venture far from the cities without
a military escort. Many of these may have been Kossuth's
disbanded soldiers, and no wonder; but not a word escapes
Bismarck in regard to politics, for, as he says, his letters will
certainly be opened before they reach their destination. He
likes the Hungarians, however, and admires their country.
"If you could be here for a moment," he says, "and could
see the silvery stream of the Danube, the dark mountains on
a pale red ground, and the lights twinkling up from Pesth,
Vienna would sink in your estimation as compared with it.
You see I am also an enthusiast for nature." It would seem
as if he might also have been a landscape painter.

This was in the summer of 1852, and one year later German
politics and the quiet proceedings of the Diet were cast into
shadow by the threatened invasion of Turkey by Russia, and
the rumor of an alliance between France and England, a
novelty in international politics unheard of since the Crusade
of Richard Cœur de Lion. The impression current in
America at that time that the object of the Tsar was to
obtain an appanage for the Grand Duke Constantine was an
erroneous one, arising from insufficient knowledge of Oriental
affairs. Wars between Russians and Turks have much the
same character as the Crusades.[1] The Sclavonic inhabitants
of Bulgaria and Servia have always been most grievously
oppressed by the Turks, and the Russian people have felt
this as the Germans did the oppression of Schleswig and
Holstein. The Greeks also belong to their church, and are
united to them at least by the bonds of religious sympathy.
Moreover, a great nation whose commerce is restricted to one
sea-port on the Baltic and another on the Black Sea cannot
be blamed for desiring better advantages in this respect.
Samuel Johnson, one of our finest Oriental scholars, satisfied

---

[1] The general in Tolstoï's "Invaders" says to a lady, "Remember, I have
taken an oath to fight the infidels."

himself that the Crimean War was a popular war in Russia, and that Nicholas was not more responsible for the Crimean War than the Russian people were. On the other hand, if the Russian government should once obtain possession of Turkey in Europe, it would not be long before it obtained possession of Turkey in Asia, and thus create an empire of semi-civilized nations which would endanger the existence of all higher forms of civilization, in Europe at least. This is one of the possibilities of the future, and may assist in bringing forward that second decline and fall which Neibuhr and other historians have predicted for the modern world.

What an historical problem is this! How difficult to decide the right and wrong, not to say the expediency, of it. Certain it is that both parties to such a conflict will be sure to consider themselves in the right, and feel justified in opposing each other to a bloody issue. Nicholas believed that the time had come when Austria should reward him for his support in Hungary, in the Hessian troubles, and in the Schleswig-Holstein question. The Turkish problem concerned Prussia least of all the great powers, and though her king sent a lukewarm note of protestation, his opposition to the movement went no further. Nicholas, however, might have hesitated but for the character of the English ministry at that time,— the ministry of Lord Aberdeen, who was strongly opposed to foreign interference. Here we come upon an exceptional peculiarity of the English constitution, which causes its weakness in dealing with foreign affairs, and in the present instance served Nicholas in the way of a trap. The President of the United States may change or modify his policy, but he and his cabinet cannot be turned out of office within twenty-four hours. The King of Prussia may change his ministry, but his well-known character remains the same, as well as his pledges to other governments, and both can be counted on to a certain extent. It is not so in England, and that is the reason why a British alliance is worth so little to other nations. In the present instance Lord Palmerston rose in Parliament, and by a speech of two hours' duration overturned the Aberdeen ministry. The aspect of events was wholly changed for Nicholas.

Louis Napoleon's English alliance has been considered a master-stroke of policy, and it certainly does credit to his judgment. His motives, however, in this affair still remain unknown to us. It has been supposed that he wished to give prestige to the second empire by brilliant military achievements; and if so, he succeeded better than might have been anticipated. In the Crimean War the French army carried away all the honors. They turned the Russian position at the battle of the Alma, rescued the English army when it was surprised by the Russians in a fog, and captured the Malakoff Tower while the English were repulsed from the Redan. Whether Napoleon III. took broad, statesmanlike views of the situation it is difficult to say. Bismarck asserts that Napoleon III. was not the person to conceive great designs,—ignorant of many things, especially of geography, and a man likely to be plucked at an attorney's examination.

In reading Louis Napoleon's " Life of Julius Cæsar," it is easy to perceive what was running in his mind: Napoleon Bonaparte was the modern Julius, and in this he was not far wrong; and Napoleon III. was to be the modern Augustus. To a certain extent he succeeded in this. He remodelled Paris, and made it not only the most elegant city in the world, but the most thoroughly constructed.[1] He divided with Louis of Bavaria the most judicious patronage of art since the sixteenth century, and his internal administration was so excellent as to cast a doubt on Bismarck's criticism of him. France was never in a more flourishing material condition than during his reign.

It is evident, however, that Napoleon III. did not possess " the piercing judgment of Augustus," as Tacitus calls it. His foreign policy succeeded well for the first ten years, but after that proved a miserable failure. It is easy to see now that his Mexican adventure was ill-judged and badly carried

---

[1] The portion of Paris between the Seine and the church of La Madeleine may be expected to last two thousand years.

out,—an imprudent attempt to graft monarchical institutions on the American tree,—but there were many who perceived this at the time. It seems as if a man with true political foresight could not have made such a blunder. Then his small political trafficking in 1866 was, if anything, still worse. It has been supposed that Napoleon III. was guided during the first half of his reign by his half-brother, the Duc de Morny; but of the Duc de Morny we know too little to form a decisive opinion.[1] On the other hand, it is certain that he had the advantage of Cavour's advice. Minister Bancroft said to General Grant in Berlin, " The three great statesmen of our time have been Bismarck, Cavour, and Gortchakoff;" to which Grant added " Hamilton Fish." Whatever place may finally be assigned to Gortchakoff and Fish, Cavour certainly stands next to Bismarck. He was to Italy precisely what Bismarck has been to Germany, and, considering the means at his disposal, the results he accomplished were quite as remarkable. Both were actuated by the same motives, and based their action on the same political principles. That Napoleon III. was drawn into the Italian war by Cavour's influence is well known, though this was not, as has been represented in various popular magazines, contrary to Napoleon's interest; but Cavour was frequently in Paris before that, and it is certain that a corps of Sardinian officers accompanied the French army to the Crimea ; but, unfortunately for Louis Napoleon, Cavour and De Morny both died before the Mexican expedition.

During the Crimean War, Francis Joseph was in the rather comical position of a man who suffers from a pain which he is endeavoring to conceal. Schwarzenberg had made his bargain with the Russian government, and the Austrian emperor did not like to keep it. He was indebted for his throne to the Tsar Nicholas, but he did not like to pay for this by the Russian possession of Bulgaria. The Austrian people, who felt anything but gratitude towards Nicholas, as well as Aus-

---

[1] Bismarck's story of De Morny's French carriages and their sale at the embassy in St. Petersburg will be remembered. Bismarck said " he was unprincipled, but a very good fellow."

trian mercantile interests, pressed powerfully for intervention. The Hungarians especially were in a great ferment. Still, Francis Joseph was reluctant to break his pledge, and the course he adopted was characteristic of the man.

There was a period during the Crimean War when the allied armies suffered greatly from sickness, and the capture of Sebastopol appeared to be almost hopeless. If the army of relief which Nicholas despatched to the beleaguered city had not been buried alive in a snow-storm, the result might have been different. It was then that Francis Joseph and Count Schauenstein believed their opportunity had come. They intrigued in the German Diet to obtain an united German movement against Russia. Simultaneously French and English envoys appeared to urge the intervention of Germany, and particularly of Prussia, in the interest of *peace*. Whether a generous slice of Poland was offered as a bait to Prussia in this transaction we do not know, but it is probable enough. It was now that Bismarck won his first diplomatic triumph. He perceived the snare, and opposed the movement for intervention with all the energy of his nature. He was assisted in this by those central German states on which Francis Joseph had previously counted; for their princes knew well enough that they had nothing to gain and much to lose in the event of a Russian war. Bismarck here established a principle which he ever afterwards followed consistently,—that Prussia should not fish in troubled waters, or interfere with the affairs of other nations so long as it could possibly be avoided. This was precisely the opposite of Louis Napoleon's policy.

Francis Joseph, now baffled and thoroughly alarmed, concluded a defensive alliance with the Sultan, which proved of no value to either party, and only served to exasperate Nicholas against him. Bismarck no doubt noticed this in his observing way, and remembered it for a future occasion. The storming of the Malakoff Tower, which has never been excelled as a military feat, placed an end to the war, and the humiliated Tsar died of chagrin. His successor, Alexander II., the best of all the house of Romanoff, and not inaptly called by the Germans the Lincoln of Russia, naturally resorted to the traditional policy of an alliance with Prussia. Austria was now isolated in Europe, and Count Cavour was just the man to take advantage of the fact.

Bismarck's political activity, however, was not limited to the desultory proceedings of the Frankfort Diet. From 1851 to 1855 he was in such constant request at Berlin that, he says, in one year he travelled not less than ten thousand miles on German railways. Frederick William IV. wished continually to consult with him and use him for numerous small diplomatic negotiations, for which Bismarck had already proved his dexterity. In one instance the House of Peers had set itself obstinately against the policy of the Russian cabinet; and Bismarck, not being directly connected with the king's council, was required to bring them to terms if he could possibly do so. He accomplished this so effectively that, although the leaders of the different cliques in the House remained firm, when the vote came up they found themselves deserted by their followers, who all went over to the government side. As a rule, however, Bismarck found that his advice was either unfavorably received or not acted upon afterwards, so that he soon came to wonder why he was so often consulted, until he perceived at length that this habit of asking the opinion of a variety of counsellors was a chronic infirmity of Frederick William, who could not understand the political situation, and was too indecisive even to allow his ministers to come to a conclusion for him. When pressed by Manteuffel to adopt a definite line of policy, he would appeal to Bismarck, Count Pourtales, or some other to sustain him in his opposition to it, and thus maintained a continuous ebb and flow of diplomatic intrigue at the court, which was exceedingly harassing to all concerned. He treated his ministers, said Bismarck, as if he were a schoolmaster listening to recitations.

Of course, under such conditions the ship of state could only drift with whatever tide was setting most strongly. Manteuffel may not have understood the situation clearly, but if he had done so he could hardly have succeeded in the hands of such a master; and one consequence of it was that by using Bismarck as a foil against him the king produced a suspicious feeling between them which does not appear to have ever wholly abated. Bismarck, in his retrospect of these court cabals, seems rather severe in his judgment on both Frederick William IV. and Manteuffel; for it should always be remembered that the king's health was precarious, and that he was gradually nearing the mental malady which ended his life. Manteuffel, also, was a faithful public servant, and if he did not succeed in penetrating the mists that rose up around Germany after the revolution of 1848, this proved, in the end, quite as well for Prussia and Bismarck himself. No wonder if Bismarck was impatient and vexed, after going repeatedly to Sans Souci to unfold his great designs before the king, only to find that the whole project had gone to water two days afterwards. Count Gerlach, who was Bismarck's most faithful friend during this period, speaks of Manteuffel at one time as unprincipled and untrustworthy, and not long after (in a fit of penitence) admits that only Manteuffel could hold the position of minister-president for more than four weeks at a time, and writes to Bismarck, " Because of my genuine love and esteem for Manteuffel, I should not like to assist in bringing about his fall." This of itself is sufficient to indicate the situation of affairs previous to the regency of William I., or, as he was then denominated, the Prince of Prussia. Bismarck's correspondence with Count Gerlach is as plain, straightforward, and disinterested as that with his wife. There is not a trace of personal ambition or personal animosity through the whole of it, but impatience enough at the manner in which Prussian affairs were being conducted, and plenty of exasperation against those who could not perceive what was plain enough to his own mind. Once, when he asked for leave of absence to visit his sick wife, Frederick William complained that Bismarck cared more for his own family than he did for the destiny of Prussia. Bismarck was a royalist by profession, but no king-worshipper, and he has exposed the peculiarities and foibles of Napoleon III., Christian of Denmark, the King of Hanover, and even of William I. with a telling plainness of speech.

LIFE OF BISMARCK

On October 23, 1857, Frederick William IV. resigned the affairs of state to his more vigorous brother William, who acted thenceforward as regent of the monarchy. This, however, did not immediately improve the political situation, at least according to Bismarck's notion of it. The regent surrounded himself with excellent counsellors, but they were divided in their judgment, and perhaps for the time being it was best that they should be. The princess, afterwards Empress Augusta, imagined that she understood politics, and, being a person of energy and a brilliant talker,—very persistent withal in carrying her point,—she caused her husband and his ministers from first to last a great deal of annoyance. Bismarck believed that she had articles written for the daily press to represent her views, which she afterwards placed on the regent's breakfast-table as an evidence of public opinion. She had certain prejudices which were ineradicable. She liked the English and Austrians, but despised Louis Napoleon as a *parvenu*, and disliked the Russians because they lacked elegant manners. As sometimes happens with her sex, she easily persuaded herself that her personal inclinations were identical with the interests of the Prussian state. As Bismarck had already become identified as a determined opponent of Austria, and believed in conciliating the Russian government as an offset to Austrian intrigue, he quickly fell under her displeasure, and remained an object of aversion to her during the rest of her life. In after-years, when Bismarck had entirely won her husband's confidence, William I. sometimes consulted with him in regard to his troubles with his wife, whom he more than once denominated as *feuerkopf*,—fire-brain.[1]

William I. does not appear to have trusted Bismarck in the beginning to the same extent that his brother did. Frederick William recognized the entire loyalty of Bismarck's nature,

---

[1] Bismarck says that during the revolution of 1848 he was approached by a gentleman of the prince's household with a proposition that Frederick William should resign, that the Prince of Prussia should be set aside, and that the princess should become regent for her son, then eighteen years old. This must have originated with Augusta herself.

and the frequency of their consultations shows that he had confidence in his judgment, although he could never resolve to adopt the policy which Bismarck advocated. The expression attributed to him of a "red-hot reactionary" may have resulted from one of Bismarck's uncomplimentary bursts of frankness; or Count Vitzthum may possibly have invented it. William I. proceeded more cautiously, and when he had once gained access to the secret springs of Bismarck's nature he trusted him implicitly; nor was he ever disappointed in his man. Bismarck had expected that the regent would give him a portfolio in the ministry, and Bismarck's friends supported him for this; but William, with rare good judgment, decided to send him to St. Petersburg, although Bismarck himself would have preferred to have remained at Frankfort. William said, however, that he considered the Russian mission as the most important post which he had to bestow, and added, "You do not belong to yourself alone; your existence is bound up with Prussian history, and you should do as I request you, even if it is contrary to your inclination."[1] The appointment was a fortunate one, for Bismarck learned in Russia how strongly both official and public feeling had turned against Austria there since the Crimean War, and this served him as a future base of diplomatic action, which he improved by a thorough knowledge of Russian court life and the more important personages concerned therein.

Before leaving Frankfort, Bismarck met with an adventure which must have astonished him not a little, and may have had a certain share in determining the future policy of Prussia. Immediately after the announcement of his transfer to St. Petersburg he received a letter from a Jew banker named Levinstein, informing him of a lucrative speculation which he might find for his interest to consider. Bismarck paid no attention to the note, and a few days later Levinstein called on him with a card from Count Buol-Schauenstein, and requested a private interview. He then proceeded to explain the nature of the lucrative speculation, which proved to be

---

[1] Bismarck's Memoirs.

nothing less than an offer from the Austrian government to
represent the interests of Francis Joseph at the Russian
capital for a salary of thirty thousand thalers a year. This
was, of course, intended for a bribe, and Bismarck attempted
to get a statement of it from Levinstein in writing; but the
Jew was too sharp for him, and equally pertinacious in endeavoring to effect a bargain; so that Bismarck was finally
obliged to lead him to the staircase and threaten to pitch him
down headlong before he could get rid of his remarkable
tempter. The exposure of this unblushing attempt would
have created great scandal, and have excited strong indignation in Prussia against the Austrian government; but Bismarck prudently kept it to himself, only informing the regent
of it on his way through Berlin. It may have proved a good
card for Bismarck with his next sovereign.

ST. PETERSBURG AND PARIS.

The tendency of recent writers is to underestimate the importance and ability of William I., and to represent him as
the inevitable shadow of royalty which accompanied Bismarck
in all his undertakings. General Hazen, in his report on the
Franco-German war, speaks of the Crown Prince Frederick
as if he were a man of more intellect and ability than his
father. He may have been a more accomplished scholar, and
he was certainly an admirable soldier; but the diary which
he has left, and his behavior in the Battenburg affair, make
it only too evident that he lacked good political judgment.
This was precisely what his father possessed,—good judgment in regard to men and practical affairs. It is not so important that the chief magistrate of a nation should be a man
of genius as that he should be a man of character, able to
recognize character and genius in others. To penetrate
character itself requires intelligence of the highest order.

It should be remembered that during the first five years of
William's sovereignty Bismarck was absent from Berlin, and,
though in frequent communication with the king, the latter
could hardly be supposed to have enjoyed the benefit of his
counsel. It was during this time that William reorganized

the Prussian army, and with the assistance of Von Moltke perfected that military machine which is universally admitted to
be without its equal. As a tactician, Von Moltke has never
been surpassed, even by Napoleon; and whether William I.,
thorough soldier as he was, would have succeeded as a military leader we have no means of judging. But who was it
that discovered Von Moltke? Men of rare executive ability
are not apt to be popular, and the quiet, reticent hero of
Sadowa would not have been likely to attract the attention
of a superficial potentate like Francis Joseph. Here, as in
Bismarck's case, we recognize an innate similarity between
the men which brought them together. There was no blind-
ing vanity in William I., but rather a grand simplicity of
nature which fitted him admirably for the part he had to play
in this triumvirate. It was not only Von Moltke, but throughout the army and in all branches of the Prussian government
he filled the highest offices with the best qualified men. At
the battle of Sadowa he exposed himself so fearlessly as to
excite Bismarck's alarm for the safety of his sovereign,
though, as he afterwards remarked, " I had rather see him so
than over-prudent." At Gravelotte, the most stoutly con-
tested of the French battles, he assumed the chief command,
although the movements on that occasion would seem to have
been directed by a council of war held upon the field. His
occasional differences with Bismarck are sufficient to indicate
that William I. had a mind of his own.

Among the hereditary rulers of the nineteenth century,
Dom Pedro, of Brazil, was certainly the ablest and noblest,
and next to him stand William I. and Alexander II. If manliness, modesty, and good judgment deserve success, William
of Prussia may be said to have deserved it, but he was also
one of the most fortunate men of whom there is any record.
Endowed with a magnificent constitution, he came to the
throne at the age of sixty, and yet lived to take an active par-
ticipation in the greatest events of his country's history. His
temperance was such that he preserved his mental and physical
vigor much beyond the average age of man. He was fortunate in the long life of his estimable wife, fortunate in his

children. He never met with a reverse, and until the last year of his life was never acquainted with grief. There are incidents in history which seem like special providences, and no one knew so well as Bismarck how invaluable that life was to him and to Germany. Without its continuance he might not have been able to place the capstone on his edifice. If he had been obliged to deal with a visionary like Frederick III., or with the present incumbent, all his work might have gone to naught.

The peculiar strength of the German and Russian foreign policy resides in the fact that their cabinet ministers study foreign affairs in the different capitals of Europe, and do not derive their knowledge of them at second hand. The British government, on the contrary, has a regular corps of foreign diplomats, who are transferred from one court to another, and rarely return to England until they retire from active service. An English premier rarely travels abroad, except on a pleasure excursion to Italy or Switzerland, and most of them have known little about the character and condition of foreign peoples. If Beaconsfield and Gladstone had comprehended Oriental politics, the former would not have sent Sir Louis Cavagnari with his escort of seventy Englishmen to be murdered at Cabul, and the latter would not have attempted to pacify the Arabs of the Soudan by moral influence and the help of Chinese Gordon. Such instances may be placed beside the Mexican speculation of Napoleon III. Bismarck remarked in regard to the Afghanistan muddle that treaties with semi-civilized nations were a waste of parchment.

William I. inherited Bismarck from his brother as a precious legacy, which he was determined to make the most of. The latter had already made one or two visits to Paris, where he found Napoleon III. in quite a friendly mood towards Prussia, as was natural enough, since he was preparing for war against Austria. Early in January, 1859, he was designated as envoy to St. Petersburg, and set out for that frozen capital in midwinter, prudently leaving his family behind him. His journey is memorable, because it seems to have originated the ill health which, combined with his excessive work, made Bismarck's life henceforth a penitential pilgrimage. The account of his journey is enough to terrify the stoutest traveller. The railway was not yet finished, and travelling by stage through the deep snow for several nights in succession, he could obtain no sleep. He wrote to his wife: "I was outside all night, and we changed from one to twelve degrees Réaumur. The snow was so deep that we literally remained sticking in it with from six to eight horses. In one instance we were an hour in going twenty paces. It was impossible to sleep on account of the cold." When he reached the steam-cars he fell asleep at once, and remained unconscious for twenty hours.

This could not but have evil consequences in a new and exceptional situation. Bismarck was ill all through his first season at St. Petersburg; suffered severely from rheumatism, and still worse from his doctors, who treated him to large doses of iodine, without the least regard to its effect upon his nervous system. This was the first beginning of that harassing insomnia which caused him so much misery during the Franco-German war, and from which he never altogether recovered. It was the first physical infirmity from which he ever suffered. With one of the strongest physiques and a constitution like seasoned oak, he was endowed by nature with nerves as sensitive as those of a Correggio or a Mendelssohn. Such a combination is exceptional. People with sensitive nerves have commonly sensitive, if not irritable, minds. Bismarck became irritable from insomnia and the wear and tear of business; but originally he was as cool-headed and imperturbable as President Lincoln. During the stormy debates of 1847 few of his opponents equalled him in *sang froid* and good humor. In considering his life from this time forward, Bismarck's nervous condition should always be taken into account. As Wasson wrote in his admirable letters from Germany in 1873, he is a man for whom one has to make allowances. Even at Frankfort he was sometimes made dizzy by speaking in the Diet, so as to be obliged to go out into the open air; and it is a known physiological fact that when a man feels his nerves giving way within him he cannot control himself as he otherwise would do.

LIFE OF BISMARCK

The impression has been current, and even circulated by Bismarck's English biographer, that his life in St. Petersburg was rather a riotous one; that he drank slivovitch, and revelled into the morning hours; and this notion has been added to by a rather external letter from the historian Motley concerning the entertainments in Bismarck's home at Schönhausen. Motley had much of Macaulay's habit of heightening his statements by a catalogue of nouns, and it is remarkable that he should have visited Bismarck without having anything more interesting to say of him. Otherwise we have not been able to discover any better justification of this libel than Bismarck's own statement, that it was at St. Petersburg where his constitution first began to fail him. On the contrary, there is good reason to believe that he lived a quiet, sober, and methodical life there. During the first nine months he suffered greatly from ill health, and was finally obliged to return to Pomerania for rest and relaxation.

He studied Russian and mastered it,—no slight accomplishment,—so that for several years he was the only person in the foreign office at Berlin who could speak and write the language. The troubles of thirty thousand resident Prussians, some of whom were always getting into difficulty, in a country where only barbaric power prevails, gave Bismarck business enough to attend to. Besides this, he maintained a large political correspondence with various Prussian statesmen. Court parties and court ceremonies were equally laborious to him. He was obliged to work from eight to fourteen hours a day. He was glad of an opportunity to spend a quiet afternoon on the palace veranda at Peterhof with the empress dowager, a genial, motherly person, who was knitting some kind of light worsted work, and with whom he felt very much at home. He visited Moscow, and considered it the handsomest city in Europe, but, with customary prudence, made no reflections on Napoleon's expedition. During his second winter he wrote to his sister: "We have to attend a great many balls and *fêtes;* but they only begin at eleven o'clock, and we always leave at midnight."

He was on a vacation at Rheinfeld when he wrote the letter

of condolence to his brother-in-law, Oscar von Arnim, on the death of a boy fifteen years old, which has endeared Bismarck to the hearts of German women as much as his great exploits have exalted him in the minds of German men. That such a letter should have been published for the purpose of giving him popularity is out of the question; and we cannot regard its publication as unfortunate, though the subject is rather a delicate one. It is, in truth, a confession of faith as genuine as it was spontaneous. He wishes he could go instanter to his sister and her husband, but concludes that his strength would not be equal to the journey. Then he says:

"How do all the little cares and troubles which beset our daily lives vanish beside the iron advent of real misfortune! And I feel the recollections of all complaints and desires by which I have forgotten how many blessings God gives us, and how much danger surrounds us without touching us, as so many reproofs. We should not depend on this world, and come to regard it as our home. Another twenty or thirty years, under the most favorable circumstances, and we shall both have passed from the sorrows of this world; our children will have arrived at our present position, and will find with astonishment that the life so freshly begun is going down hill. Were it all over with us so, it would not be worth while dressing and undressing."

Bismarck rarely talked philosophy, and it is doubtful if he even attended Hegel's lectures at the university in Berlin. He certainly was not a disciple of Herbert Spencer or of any modern form of materialism, but believed that man has a soul in him, for whose well-being he is responsible. *Mind* to him did not mean "a collocation of cerebral processes," but an immortal spirit. So John Brown said in his Virginia prison, "Governor Wise, it is only for a few moments we remain on this earth, and there is a whole eternity beyond." Thus have heroic natures believed and prophesied in all times and countries.

We do not hear of Bismarck as fond of hunting in his youth, though he may have done more or less of it during his bachelor Kniephof days. In middle life he took to it for the benefit of his health, and as a relief from the weight of responsibility which pressed more and more heavily upon him. He was an expert shot with a rifle,—an evidence of the keenness of his perceptions,—and could take the heads off of ducks floating on the water. In Russia he soon became distinguished as a hunter of bears, a mighty Nimrod. It was like the schläger fighting at Göttingen in his youth. Nothing requires more nerve than shooting a bear on foot, and there are few of our Western huntsmen who dare to attempt it. Unless the brute is mortally wounded at the first or second fire you are lost. Bismarck is credited with having killed three bears in rapid succession. "Once," he says, "I was in great danger from a bear which I could not see distinctly, because he was covered with snow. I wounded him and he fell. I reloaded as quietly as possible, and shot him dead as he rose to his feet." Bears seem to be plentiful in Russia, and it is to be feared that they are a heavier incubus on the farmers than hares and foxes are in England.

Smoothing down the Russian bear is the special business of a Prussian ambassador at St. Petersburg. Bismarck did not find this difficult, for the current was now running in his favor instead of against him, as at Frankfort and Vienna. Alexander was more than wise enough to profit by the mistakes of Nicholas, and his mother's influence, also, was on the side of William I. Bismarck was just the man to promote a cordial understanding and feeling of security between the two governments, for to whomsoever he dealt with he always gave the impression of a veracious nature. He once said, "I have never learned to lie, even as a diplomat." This may be doubted, though he may have thought so at that time; but those who placed their entire confidence in him have never had reason to regret it. A Boston lawyer once inquired of a New York banker whether William Vanderbilt could be depended on to tell the truth in regard to his railroads, and the reply was, "How can he tell it?" Bismarck was often placed in such situations. Surrounded by enemies, conspirators, and imprudent friends, how could he tell the truth? His principle appears to have been to deal with others according to the measure in which they dealt with him. To those who trusted him he was frank and friendly, but woe unto those who tried to overreach him. He deceived Louis Napoleon; but was not Louis Napoleon attempting to deceive *him?* That is the only safe rule in politics or trade. The photographs of Bismarck, taken between 1865 and 1870, have all the appearance of a substantial, straightforward man, while the portraits of Metternich wear an expression of Mephistophelean cunning, and those of Louis Napoleon have the ingenious, suspicious expression of a man who lives by his wits. Bismarck's cranium was one of the largest, and his deep-set eyes looked out from under their frowning brows as if they were saying, " Tell me the truth now, or look out for yourself." The top of his head was almost a perfect dome, a fine subject for phrenology.

The pay-day was now at hand, when the Austrian government was to receive the first instalment of the reward for its Schwarzenberg-Schauenstein policy. Almost on the day when Bismarck set out for St. Petersburg, the King of Sardinia's daughter was married to Prince Napoleon Bonaparte; the press of Turin began to talk of the wrongs of an outraged Italy; and the Sardinian army was evidently being placed on a war footing. In reply to the request of Francis Joseph for an explanation, Cavour proposed a European conference to consider the condition of Italy. The Tsar Alexander showed his colors by supporting this proposal; but there was nothing the Austrian cabinet dreaded so much as an exposure of their methods of fleecing the Italian provinces. War was consequently declared against Sardinia; but in this way Cavour obtained the appearance at least of a defensive attitude.

Political intrigue usually goes hand in hand with official corruption, and in the campaign of 1859 we find an internal condition of affairs in the Austrian government that might well be compared to its foreign policy. In several divisions of the army whole companies were found on the pay-roll which had no actual existence; enormous frauds were unearthed in the commissary department, and much of the

soldiers' equipment was discovered to be of the sort denominated as shoddy in the first years of our Civil War. The Austrian emperor was in a rage, but so extensive were the pecu-
lations that he found himself unable to punish the offenders.
No wonder that such an army was repeatedly beaten, and the
success of the French and Sardinians was evidently more
owing to the weakness of their opponents than to the military
skill of their commanders. In fact, it soon became apparent
that the army of Napoleon III. had not improved in efficiency
since the Crimean War. The ill-fed and badly commanded
Austrian troops three times repulsed an attack on the hill of
Solferino, which was finally captured by a quick scramble of
the Zouaves.

There was no reason why William of Prussia should give
Austria assistance, and the wonder is that he and his ministers did not take advantage of the situation to improve the
position of Prussia in Germany. Bismarck would probably
have done this.

If William I. and his cabinet could have foreseen the immense advantage to Prussia from a liberated Italy, they might
have pursued a different course, but their intention evidently
was to prevent either party in the war from obtaining too
great an advantage. After the defeat of the Austrians at Solferino five Prussian army corps were mobilized and placed on
the French frontier, so that, if they had been directed, their
commander might have reached Paris before Napoleon. The
movement was injudicious, and caused Bismarck great anxiety.
It might have resulted in the evacuation of Lombardy and
the loss of all the Sardinians had gained. Fortunately, however, Francis Joseph undertook the management of the affair
himself, and was easily outwitted by Cavour and Napoleon.
The peace of Villafranca was hastily concluded, in order to
prevent Prussia from acquiring too great importance in
European affairs. The only advantage which Napoleon III.
gained from the loss of twenty thousand lives was a narrow
strip of territory on the Mediterranean, including the valuable city of Nice. Napoleon prudently declined Kossuth's
offer of an uprising of the Hungarians, as that would certainly

have brought Russia into the field of action, with a general European convulsion.

On July 2, 1859, Bismarck wrote to his wife:

"Our politics are sliding more and more into the Austrian groove, and if we fire one shot on the Rhine the Italo-Austrian war is over, and in its place we shall have to see a Prusso-French war, in which Austria, after we have taken the load from her shoulders, will assist, or assist so far as her own interests are concerned. That we should play a victorious part is scarcely to be conceded. Be it as God wills! It is here below always a question of time, nations and men, folly and wisdom, war and peace; they come like waves and so depart, while the ocean remains."[1]

William I. had no intention of provoking a war; but if Bismarck had been minister-president at this time it is possible that the whole Austrian-Prussian problem might have been solved with less friction and loss of life than afterwards happened. Prince Hohenzollern, who had succeeded Manteuffel, was more of a dilettante than a practical statesman.

An overdose of iodine was not the only medical blunder which Bismarck suffered from in St. Petersburg. In June, 1859, he contracted a slight rheumatism, and this settled in his left knee, which he had injured two years before by a fall while hunting in Sweden. As he intended to return to Berlin for the summer months, and wished to start in good condition, he imprudently consulted a German doctor named Waltz, who had been recommended to him by the Grand Duchess of Baden. This physician prescribed a plaster, which he assured the Prussian envoy would cause no inconvenience, but would fall off of its own accord in a few days. The plaster contained cantharides, which will commonly raise a blister in less than half an hour; and Bismarck, having gone to sleep with it upon his knee, awoke towards morning in most intolerable pain. On attempting to detach the plaster a portion of the flesh came off with it, and it was some years before his leg recovered wholly from the effects of this maltreatment. The doctor blamed the apothecary; and on Bismarck's sending for the prescription the apothecary declared he had returned it to the doctor. Bismarck afterwards discovered that Waltz was the son of a confectioner at Heidelberg, and was known as an idle student, although he possessed the faculty of making himself agreeable to ladies of rank. Bismarck returned to Berlin by way of the Baltic, and, meeting a distinguished surgeon named Pirogow on the steamer, consulted him in regard to his trouble, but was astonished enough when Pirogow advised him to have his leg amputated above the knee. The medical profession seemed to be in a conspiracy against him, and some of his friends were of opinion that Dr. Waltz's poisoning was not without an object; but Bismarck himself thought differently. Arrived at Berlin, he was soon sufficiently improved by honest medical treatment to walk and ride again, although with some discomfort.

In October Bismarck accompanied the crown prince to Warsaw for an interview with the Tsar Alexander; after which he went to St. Petersburg again, but was obliged to return to Berlin in the following March (1860) for sound medical treatment, and sat there as a delegate in the House of Peers.

The political situation in Berlin did not please him any better than during the last years of Frederick William IV. The ministry was divided, and the king indecisive. Prince Hohenzollern was the nominal president, and continued to be until 1862, but he had long since been outvoted, and Count von Schleinitz, an adroit courtier, who sided with the queen, wielded the greatest influence. Bismarck was invited to a cabinet meeting and asked for his opinion, which he gave only to find himself opposed at every point by Schleinitz, who had evidently prepared himself for the purpose beforehand. Bismarck was confident that the Prussian government would receive strong support from the Tsar if it only asserted itself in a spirit of manliness and independence. So long as Prussia followed in the Austrian channel, Alexander and Gortchakoff would distrust her. The queen and Schleinitz believed, on the contrary, that the greatest danger to the state was to be feared from a Franco-Russian alliance, and that it was important to maintain friendly relations with Austria, even at the cost of national self-respect, in order that Prussia should not become isolated. Von Roon, the Minister of War, and the one solid character in the cabinet, sided with Bismarck, but for the time being the queen and Schleinitz carried all before them.

What Gerlach had been to Bismarck in his Frankfort days, Von Roon was to be henceforward, a friend implicitly trusted. He was also to Prussia what Carnot was to the first French revolution, the ablest military organizer of his time. In the autumn of 1860 Bismarck returned to St. Petersburg again, and Roon helped him as a friend at court, who, believing in Bismarck's future destiny, served him more faithfully than he could have served himself. Many of his letters are dismal enough. The Landtag was ruled by the party of Progress, whose aim was to revolutionize Prussia after the English pattern, and obtain a ministry and a premier from their own ranks, without considering the difference between England and Prussia, and that the British Parliament, though nominally a popular body, is in reality controlled by noblemen and wealthy land-owners. The attitude of the ministry was disheartening to patriotic Prussians, and discouraging to the German national sentiment; so that the position of the government was growing continually weaker and more embarrassed. The violence of party feeling may be imagined from the fact that Edwin Manteuffel, Roon's chief supporter in the ministry, became involved in a duel with Twesten, a leader of the Progressists, and was placed under arrest for it. Von Roon wrote to Bismarck, July 24, 1861, " May God help us in future! I can do little more than remain an honest man, work in my own department, and do what is sensible. The greatest misfortune, however, in all this worry is the weariness and languor of our king. He is more than ever under the orders of the queen and her accomplices." The marriage of the Crown Prince to the Princess Victoria of England had brought in a lively young recruit to the queen's forces, who was not long in making her influence felt. It was rumored

at this time among the Hungarian exiles in America that the
Crown Prince of Prussia had taken a wife whose will was
stronger than his own. She was, in fact, almost the counterpart of her mother-in-law, and Prussia seemed to be verging
on petticoat government.

King William, however, was too much of a soldier to permit this order of affairs to continue indefinitely. His queen
was a more brilliant talker, and, as Bismarck says, an abler
critic, but William possessed what is so often deficient in
gifted natures, and that is plain, practical sense; and the inborn
manliness of his nature was of itself sufficient to provoke a
change in course of time. The coronation took place at
Königsberg, in old Prussia, on October 28, 1861, and Bismarck, being in attendance, found reason to suspect from the
queen's conversation that a radical divergence of opinion on
state affairs already existed between the royal pair. On his
return to Berlin, in the spring of 1862, he found that the
queen's faction was no longer in the ascendant, but the king
was still irresolute, and the confusion in his cabinet greater
than ever. It was one of the phenomena of political exhaus-
tion.

Prince Adolph of Hohenlohe had succeeded Prince Hohenzollern as president of the ministry in March, but he
found himself unequal to the position, and frankly informed
Bismarck that he would be glad to have him take it off his
hands. Bismarck himself was dispirited and badly out of
health; although he had been summoned by the king, little
attention was paid to him on his arrival. Fearing the evil
opinions which might result from apparent idleness, he begged
Count Bernstorff, the Minister of Foreign Affairs, either to procure him an office or to accept his resignation; and as a consequence of this determination he was immediately appointed
ambassador to France. On the 1st of June he was received
at the Tuileries.

The sudden transfer of the incorruptible Bismarck from
St. Petersburg to Paris created the liveliest excitement at the
Austrian court. Francis Joseph could not fail to be con-
scious that his policy during the Crimean War was considered

base ingratitude by the son of Nicholas, and visions of a Franco-Russian alliance, in which Prussia would serve as the mediator, and perhaps as a broker of whole provinces, floated before the mind of Count Buol. Prince Richard Metternich, then ambassador at Paris, was immediately notified to make the most friendly advances to Louis Napoleon, and to offer him any form of alliance which would be compatible with the integrity of the Austrian empire. Napoleon, who could not understand the exact relation which existed between Bismarck and Count Buol, was evidently puzzled at this, and concluded that the readiest means of enlightenment would be to inform Bismarck and see what kind of a counter-move he would make to this proposition. So, on June 26, Bismarck was invited to Fontainebleau, where he and the emperor took a long walk together, and the latter began by discussing the advantages of an alliance between Prussia and France, to which Bismarck prudently replied that an alliance between two great nations must have a definite object, and could not be based on mutual friendliness, or even on the expectation of indefinite mutual interests. Napoleon then informed him of the Austrian proposals, evidently in the hope that Bismarck would suggest an alternative which would be more favorable to French interests. He was well aware that there was no way in which Francis Joseph could assist him to territorial annexations, except through a war with Prussia ; and with the Mexican expedition on his hands, he was in no condition to undertake that. If, however, he could assist Prussia to a stronger position in German affairs and obtain the duchy of Luxemburg for his trouble, much might be gained at very small cost. As Luxemburg belonged to the King of Holland by inheritance, Bismarck may have thought the same, but he declined to commit himself, and returned to Paris, leaving Napoleon III. as wise as he was before.

Later in June Bismarck went to London, perhaps to allay suspicions of a Russo-Prussian alliance, and after that on a long expedition to the Pyrenees to recruit his health, which in the sequel was greatly improved by it. Late in August Von Roon wrote to him that the condition of uncertainty in Berlin still continued; that the ministry was practically without a head, and that Bernstorff, who had been acting in that capacity, could not decide whether to remain or to take the English mission; that he believed the outcome, however, would be Bismarck's appointment as minister-president. He added, "Concessions and compromises are not to be thought of; least of all is the king disposed towards them." Bismarck replied that he was ready to enter the ministry, or would be content to remain at Paris; but that he wished above all to know definitely what the king intended for him; that he had long been separated from his family, and that his household goods were scattered in various places. In his whole correspondence with Roon there is not a trace of personal ambition, and this may be taken as one reason why he succeeded where others failed. Only six days later he received the following telegram from Berlin:

"Periculum in mora. Dépêchez-vous.[1]
"L'oncle de Maurice,
"HENNING."

"Henning" was the middle name of Moritz Blanckenburg, a nephew of Von Roon, and this form of notification is significant of the secrecy that was required, in those perilous times, for communications apparently simple in themselves.

---

[1] Bismarck's Memoirs, i. 203.

CHAPTER IV

On Bismarck's arrival at Berlin he was immediately summoned by the crown prince for an audience on public affairs, and, supposing that this was done with the knowledge of the king, he immediately complied, although he considered it prudent not to commit himself on important points to a subordinate personage. It proved, however, an independent effort of the prince's to gain information, and came near shipwrecking Bismarck's preferment; for the king on hearing of it said, " You see, he is not to be trusted either," and it required all the earnestness of Roon's nature to convince him of the contrary. Whether this episode was due to youthful imprudence, or to the long-headed calculation of Queen Augusta, is a problem which no evidence can help us to solve.

Bismarck found the king in a most melancholy mood. He said, " I will not reign if I cannot do it so as to be answerable to God and to my conscience; and I cannot do that if I am to be dominated by the present majority in Parliament." This referred to the refusal of the Progressists to pass appropriations for the maintenance of the army, and their openly declared intention of reducing the king's authority to a level with that of the Queen of England. This, of course, was revolutionary, and could only be met by a counter-revolution. Bismarck perceived this at a glance, and in the course of a lengthy interview succeeded in persuading William I. that such a course was not only honorable but necessary for the interests of Prussia, and therefore justifiable. The draft of a letter of abdication, which the king had on the table before him, was destroyed in Bismarck's presence.

It is difficult for an American to sympathize with William I. in his struggle with the Prussian Landtag at this time; but this much is certain: if the king had given way before the majority in the Parliament, Bismarck could never have accomplished the great work of German unification. We see the course that history has taken, and we credit those actors in it who have been of service to mankind; but it is useless to consider how things might have been otherwise. Only those who were living and present at the critical moment may have been able to judge of this. The Prussian Landtag in 1862 cannot be fairly compared with the Assembly of the Third Estate in 1789. Prussia was suffering from no heavy grievances, and its representatives had no great wrongs to redress. The nation had always been well governed, according to the standard of the time; it had freedom of speech, popular education, and freedom of the press; its laboring classes already enjoyed the advantage of one agrarian revolution, and were the most prosperous in Europe. If their wages were not so high as in England, their expenses were considerably less. The administration of internal affairs is of great importance in every country, but in Prussia foreign affairs were and are even more important than internal affairs; for the very existence of the state depended on the conduct of them. This the Progressists could not and would not understand. They had no intention of creating a republic, but they wished to reform their government after the English pattern, in which, as Bismarck said, "the monarchy serves as a graceful cupola to the edifice of state rather than as its main sustaining column." Woe to the country in our time that undertakes to imitate English institutions!

The United States and Great Britain enjoy exceptional advantages from their geographical positions. American politicians are just beginning to find out that international politics is a science by itself, and one which heretofore they have had small occasion to study. During the Civil War our foreign relations were so admirably managed by Secretary Seward that they scarcely attracted public attention; but Seward spent nearly a year in Europe to make a special study of the subject, and was, moreover, a statesman of rare ability. So long as the British government maintains its supremacy at sea, its premiers can make blunders in foreign policy without endangering the independence of England. It is quite otherwise on the continent of Europe, where nations and races are packed together like sardines in a box. There a diplomatic mistake has to be atoned for sometimes by succeeding generations; and of all European states Prussia holds the most difficult position, being surrounded by all the others, with an extended frontier to defend, for which its population was formerly quite inadequate. The experience of Poland, Italy, and, in ancient times, of the kingdom of Antigonus, has shown that such nations are in danger of being divided up between neighboring states. It is, therefore, more important in Prussia than elsewhere that men should be at the helm of government who have had training and experience in foreign affairs; and this can only be obtained, like a sound knowledge of foreign languages, by residing a certain length of time in the capitals of other countries. Bismarck plainly told the leaders of the Progressists in the Landtag that they were not properly qualified to administer the affairs of government. "You wish," he said, "to remodel our constitution according to the English pattern; but we have not the class of people in Germany to draw upon for practical statesmen that they have in England, where they are often bred to it for generations." Alexander Hamilton in America, and, thirty years later, Hegel in Germany, pointed out that, although the corruption in English elections was much to be deplored, it had the advantage of maintaining in office a sufficient number of experienced statesmen. This is also true of the United States Senate, without any bribery; but the Prussian Landtag in 1862 was of a different complexion. The Landtag might be compared to the French Chamber of Deputies during the last years of the eighteenth century, when the French had obtained their liberty, but knew not how to make use of it. English parliamentary government is a growth of centuries, and cannot be imitated in a few years. It was a favorite saying of Bismarck that "Germany, once in the saddle, would learn to ride;" but it would first have to serve an apprenticeship. The object of the Progressists was not national, but particularist. Bismarck, intensely practical as he was, had always

the vision of a united Germany, powerful and respected by all
nations, floating before his eyes; and to this end his position
as president, his devotion to the king, and even his Prussian
patriotism only served as means. He was always more of
a German than a Prussian, and this the Progressists were not.
At the university Bismarck was republican, but he became a
monarchist because he saw clearly that it was the only practical course for him. If, instead, he had joined the Progressists, he might not have been so prominent and influential
as Twesten, Lasker, and other popular agitators.

The conflict was not more between the king and the Landtag than between the Landtag and the House of Peers. According to the constitution, the right of raising taxes and of
granting recruits for the army was vested in the Landtag, but
the House of Peers was obliged to concur with its estimates
before they could go to the king for approval. The Landtag
wished to reduce the term of service from four to two years,
and cut down the appropriations for the army accordingly.
This, in the face of Louis Napoleon's piratical policy and the
hostile attitude of the Austrian government, was altogether
too great a risk, and the House of Peers returned the bill to
the Landtag for reconsideration. The anger of the majority
in the popular assembly was so much the greater at this
action, because it was an exigency which they had never contemplated. After a stormy debate they absolutely refused to
change the estimates, and thus a deadlock took place between
the two legislative bodies, which left the government without
legal means of raising taxes for its continued existence. The
king offered as a compromise to reduce the army estimates
by four million thalers; but beyond that he declared he could
not go. The Landtag treated his message with scorn. Then
Bismarck declared in full Senate that he would govern without
appropriations, and levy such taxes as the exigencies of the
government required. Prussia was practically in a state of
revolution.

Such a condition of affairs had not been contemplated in
the constitution, and there were no provisions that could be
made to apply to it. Each side considered itself in the right,

and when Bismarck proceeded to make good his promise he was attacked with the most violent abuse by the Progressist newspapers, besides continually receiving letters with threats of assassination. He may have cared little for the invectives of his opponents, but he rightly concluded that inflammatory editorials were stirring up the minds of unbalanced men to desperate deeds. The Prussian constitution guaranteed free-dom of speech, but it had also provided that in times of great public excitement the ministry might exercise a censorship over the press.[1] Bismarck had this law enforced in a strin-gent manner. Public indignation could now find an outlet only in the Landtag, where the debate became continually more acrimonious.

At this juncture Bismarck's determination carried his policy through against the opposition of the public, the parliament, the royal family, and the majority of his colleagues. It was a single will pitted against the spirit of the age. William I. was never known to retract a policy to which he had once committed himself, but Bismarck could only depend on his active support so long as he was within reach. On September 30, 1862, the minister-president made a speech before the Committee on Appropriations which has become historical. He pointed out that the very configuration of Prussia, as it was then, necessitated a larger proportionate military force than that of other European nations. His expression was, "a suit of armor too large for the weak body;" that for its future se-curity the Prussian military organization would have to be ex-tended over all German-speaking people; and "that in order to secure this, they must place the greatest possible weight of blood and iron in the king's hands." This was the first inti-mation which Bismarck gave to the public of his future policy, and even his most devoted adherents were startled by it. "The suit of armor too large for the weak body," and the policy of "blood and iron," penetrated to every corner of Germany.

---

[1] Curiously enough, a similar censorship was exercised in the United States at this time.

The king was at Baden-Baden with his wife, and the effect of this speech on the royal pair may be judged from the fact that the king immediately telegraphed his return to Berlin, and requested Bismarck to meet him on the way. When Bismarck found him, quite alone, in an ordinary first-class *coupé*, the king seemed wholly unnerved, and commenced with the pertinent question, " Where is all this going to lead us ?" He then talked of revolutions, decapitations,—the fate of Louis XVI. and Charles I. Bismarck judged correctly that this mental condition was the result of the queen's influence, and knew how to counteract it. He appealed to the king's *esprit du corps* as a soldier. " What do you wear a sword for, your Majesty ? Are you afraid to die an honorable death ? Your Majesty is bound to fight : you cannot capitulate." Arguing in this strain, he soon dispelled the witchcraft meshes which had been woven about the old Hohenzollern ; and by the time the train reached Berlin, the king's mind was prepared not only to give his premier a confident support, but to show a bold front to the doubtful and more timid members of the ministry.

Bismarck's position was not without danger from the standpoint of legal procedure. The Landtag had already passed a resolution, by 274 to 45, that the ministers were responsible with their persons and fortunes for unconstitutional expenditure. This meant for Bismarck, in case of failure, imprisonment and confiscation. His friends even advised him to make over the estate at Kniephof to his brother, in order to prevent its alienation. To do this, however, would have been an evidence of weakness, and Bismarck knew the importance of preserving a confident tone to his own party and a bold front to his opponents. He played for the whole stake,—a Napoleonic game,—and the more daring opposition papers had already predicted that he would yet be seen picking oakum in felon's clothes.

The disaffection within the royal family reached the point of insubordination when on June 4, 1863, the crown prince, who had gone to Dantzic to hold a review of the regiments there, in reply to an address by the civil authorities, expressed

LIFE OF BISMARCK

his regret that the policy which his father had adopted was at variance with public opinion. Of the proceedings which had brought this about he knew nothing; he was absent, and had no part in the deliberations which had led to such a result. Sentiments like these, published in the Dantzic *Times* and copied in the London *Times*, were calculated to encourage a more determined opposition, if not open insurrection. On being requested by letter to make an explanation of his conduct to the king, the crown prince made the situation worse by tendering the resignation of his position in the army, asking his father's forgiveness, and at the same time persisting in his opposition to the ministry.

William I. was furious, and Bismarck was obliged to summon up all his diplomatic talent to prevent a violent rupture and such severe treatment of the crown prince as the king might afterwards repent of. " Let your Majesty decide nothing in anger," he said.[1] William I., therefore, accepted his son's apology, declined his resignation, and cautioned him to be more prudent in future. The return which Bismarck received for this magnanimous consideration was a letter from the crown prince, two weeks later, censuring the policy of the ministry in the strongest terms: he would entreat the king to permit him to take no further part in its proceedings. This was characteristic of the man, who, like his mother, had rather a brilliant mind, but lacked clearness in his ideas. He never had possessed a voice in the councils of state, but was requested to attend them for the sake of instruction in political affairs. An editorial in the London *Times*, which congratulated the Prussian people on having so important a champion,—a prince whose consort supported him in his liberal views,—gave to this miserable affair an international importance.

Strange to say, after the king's anger had once cooled down, he permitted his son to continue in this wayward course all through the summer; but this may have happened because at that season he enjoyed the protection of his

---

[1] This is Bismarck's statement, and it is all we shall ever know.

mother's tongue. In August the crown prince had an interview with Bismarck at Gastein, where "he spoke of his late behavior as one conscious of a native want of independence, and full of veneration for his father; modestly and gracefully tracing his error to its source in his imperfect political training." Yet early in September he wrote Bismarck a chilling letter in which he declared himself the determined foe of the ministry. Bismarck obtained another audience with him which narrowly escaped ending in an explosion of temper; and then the king took the matter seriously in hand. With Bismarck's assistance he made out a schedule of directions for his son's future guidance, by which he made him clearly to understand what his proper position was in the government, and the extent to which he might be permitted to criticise the ministry with due consideration for his royal father.[1] The crown prince appears to have accepted this as a guide for his future conduct, and to have caused the ministry little further annoyance.

How long this strange conflict would have continued between a visionary majority and a practical minority, and what would have been the final issue of it, would be fruitless to conjecture. Perhaps it was fortunate for Bismarck that external politics came to his assistance, and by developing his diplomatic skill and enlarging his reputation, won for him the confidence of the Prussian people in his management of affairs.

It was not long before his magnetic influence was felt in the foreign affairs of Prussia. He knew that all that was required to make the state respected abroad was a determined attitude and a well-disciplined army.[2] It was perhaps owing to his resolute position that the Hessians were encouraged to try conclusions again with their wicked old elector. It is not likely that Bismarck fomented the slight disturbances in Cassel during the winter of 1863,—he was much too busy at home,

---

[1] Bismarck's Memoirs, i. 358.

[2] In the light of subsequent events it is almost impossible to understand the suicidal attitude of the national assembly. Prussia evidently required an army equal in force to that of France or Austria.

—but at their first appearance he sent a notification to Kur-Hessen that the interests of Prussia required that he should change his ministry, and mend his ways in other respects. Bismarck, like Richelieu, always began with an attempt at conciliation. If that failed, his blow was sudden and crushing. Kur-Hessen looked for assistance from Austria, but Francis Joseph could no longer obtain the intervention of Russia, and after Solferino he felt no desire to survey another battle-field. Kur-Hessen was obliged to submit, and if Bismarck was now unpopular in Berlin, he was all the more popular among the Hessians. Nor could right-minded men all over Germany refuse him their respect for this summary act of justice. In England, on the contrary, as Kur-Hessen was related to the English royal family, the affair was represented as a high-handed piece of Prussian tyranny.

The Italian revolution had also produced its reflection in Poland. The insurrections in Russian Poland were hopeless from the beginning and easily suppressed. As Bismarck always maintained, the liberation of Poland could only be accomplished through a European convulsion. English editors poured out their ink in virtuous indignation against Bismarck as the coadjutor of Russian despotism,—the real grievance being a treaty with Alexander, which they rightly suspected might cover more ground than the French and English cabinets had information of. Bismarck knew that England was too much concerned with the American question to run the risk of a European complication, and paid no attention to the remonstrances of the British government. Speaking of the Polish insurrection of 1863, Von Beust says in his memoirs:[1]

" On the other hand, one must remember what Bismarck was at that time. The game, played with such brilliant success, of misleading the world by telling it sincerely in advance what he intended doing, was thus only in its first stage when both great and small states all looked on him as a restless spirit, possibly dangerous, but unlikely to remain long in power. By the general

---

[1] Vol. i. p. 221.

public, with the exception of the ultra-conservatives, he was not only underestimated, but also thoroughly disliked. That was the time when, as he said to me during one of our conversations at Salzburg, people spat on the ground when he passed. Bismarck's unpopularity, however, was the least of the evils he had to contend against. A wise man does not value popularity highly, and a brave man never fears its reverse.''

The course of the Austrian government from 1863 to 1866 can only be ascribed to an infatuation. The purblind Schauen-stein had been succeeded by an equally purblind Karolyi, who continued the anti-Prussian policy of his predecessors, despite the loss of Lombardy and the alienation of the Russian court. There is reason to believe that Pius IX. and his Jesuit counsellor, Antonelli, had a hand in this, as it is well known that they exerted an influence on the French empress and her party previous to the Franco-German war. Prussia was the only Protestant power on the continent, and could Prussia once be placed in the vocative some progress, at least, would have been gained by the Church of Rome towards the re-establishment of its former supremacy. The Jesuits expelled from Austria, France, and Spain during the middle of the eighteenth century found an asylum in the dominions of Frederick the Great, but after the wars of Napoleon they had returned to their former habitations, and were as active in intriguing as ever.

The anti-Prussian policy was fratricidal, and could only end by dividing the German house against itself. Even Machiavelli could have satisfied Francis Joseph on that point, but the Austrian emperor and Karolyi counted on the internal dissensions of Prussia, and felt confident of their majority in the Frankfort Diet. As Von Beust says, they considered Bismarck the creature of a day, who would soon come to the end of his rope, and be replaced by a more pliant and conciliatory minister. They vainly believed that the majority of the Diet carried with it an authority equal to its pretensions. The victories of Frederick the Great were supposed to have been due to his exceptional genius, and it was not likely that the Prussians would find another general to match him. The

Prussian army had not seen active service since 1815, while Austrian veterans had fought in Italy and Hungary. Foolish illusions, and not much to the credit of Francis Joseph, who counted as little on Prussian patriotism as he did on Von Moltke and the needle-gun.

Von Moltke had assured Bismarck that he could crush Austria at a moment's notice : all that he required was a full complement of men for his regiments. Bismarck, therefore, assumed a bold attitude. He informed Count Karolyi that the present behavior of Austria towards Prussia was unfriendly, and if continued could only result in a suspension of diplomatic relations. The count replied that the Austrian government could not relinquish its traditional influence on the German states ; and with this cool assertion of superiority the negotiation ended.[1]

This is Bismarck's own statement, and if correct, Karolyi's answer was evasive, and quite unlikely to promote a good understanding between the two governments. It is difficult to obtain the truth in regard to this international discussion, much of which was carried on by personal interviews, and is now unsupported by documentary evidence. We may suppose, however, that Professor Müller, of Tübingen, would be likely to give an unprejudiced account of it; for if any portion of Europe can be considered neutral ground in politics it is the duodecimo kingdom of Würtemberg. As South Germans the Würtembergers stand in a certain dread of Prussia, and their religion interferes with their being in complete sympathy with Austria, while their immunity from invasion prevents that hostility towards the French which is felt in Baden. Müller's account of the negotiations between Bismarck and Karolyi agrees substantially with that of Bismarck's biographer. We know, at least, what Bismarck's propositions were to the congress of princes which Francis Joseph summoned at Gastein in September, 1863, and they cannot be considered unreasonable, if any concessions were to be made at all to Prussia in the interest of peace and harmony. They

---

[1] Hesekiel's Biography, p. 341.

were substantially: the agreement of Prussia and Austria to be required for every war not undertaken in defence of German soil; the perfect equality of Prussia and Austria in the government for the arbitration of federal affairs, and a national representation to the Frankfort Diet of representatives chosen by the different states according to the ratio of their population, with more extensive powers than those of the present delegates. In the Diet as then constituted, Prussia, which contained one-third of the population of Germany, had no more electoral power than Cassel, which contained about a twentieth, and Bismarck's proposed modification would give the largest state in Germany more consideration, though never necessarily a majority. It would be certain to break up the existing cabal, and make the formation of a new one more difficult than formerly. It was met by Count Karolyi by a counter-proposition, which had the character of a blind alley, leading nowhere in particular, and evidently intended as a pretext for delay. The result of this was that King William declined to attend the congress of princes at Frankfort the following August, which accordingly dissolved without coming to any definite conclusions. The importance of Prussia in German affairs was at last becoming manifest.[1]

The quarrel in the Diet was mainly a question of tariff, but there was also an unlimited number of interstate regulations to be considered from session to session, and on both these subjects Prussia was always found in the minority. The vast portion of the Austrian empire is mainly agricultural, and,

---

[1] A characteristic instance in Austrian diplomacy was the embassy of Von Beust to Bismarck at Baden-Baden, in order to persuade William I. to put in an appearance at the congress. Bismarck received him cordially, but said, significantly, "You have come to drag us to destruction." Von Beust then suggested that if William I. would only come to Frankfort for a single day and plead indisposition, the congress would probably adjourn on the day following, but Bismarck was not to be caught in such a trap as that. "What you say," he replied, "is probable enough, but not certain." Dr. Busch was on hand to note down the conversation, portions of which Von Beust afterwards repudiated as pure inventions of the enemy. Without questioning the sincerity of either party it is enough to say that a diary written at the time is better testimony than the memoirs of after years.

though it was a disadvantage to the farmers, the government wished to maintain moderately high duties on imports on account of the revenue which it derived from them. The same was true of the smaller inland states, like Bavaria, Würtemberg, and Saxony. Prussia was the only large state which possessed an extensive commerce, and its people were inclined to free trade. In such cases there ought to be a compromise if possible. The German navy, which was of some advantage to Prussia, but little enough to Austria, caused a great deal of dissension during the first session of the Diet after the revolution had subsided, and the majority voted to dispose of it the following year. Such grievances do not seem of themselves sufficient to justify the resort to arms, but continued during a term of years the evil increases at compound interest until they form an intolerable burden.

Bismarck followed up his contemptuous treatment of the congress of princes by concluding with the French government a commercial treaty on behalf of Prussia, Mecklenburg, and a few smaller states, equally advantageous to both parties, but in direct violation of the authority of the Diet. This was practically nullification, and must inevitably have resulted in war between Austria and Prussia, or in the secession of the latter and the formation of a confederacy with the states that adhered to it. In his circular note of January, 1863, to the German states, Bismarck had said, " In order to bring about a better understanding I took the initiative and informed Count Karolyi that, according to my conviction, our relations with Austria *must unavoidably change for the better or the worse*. It is the sincere wish of the royal government that the former alternative should arise; but if we should not be met by the imperial cabinet with the necessary advances as we could desire, it will be *necessary for us to contemplate the other alternative and prepare for it accordingly.*" The relations of Prussia and Austria were now changing for the worse, but Count Karolyi found his diplomatic grave at the Frankfort congress of princes, which, without the King of Prussia, proved to be like a cart left without its horse. His successor, Count Rechberg, showed a more conciliatory disposition to-

wards the Prussian state, and it is possible, though not probable, that he might have succeeded in averting the impending
catastrophe, but for an event which unsettled the balance of
power in Germany and introduced a series of changes of the
grandest character.

CHAPTER V

THE time of retribution was now approaching for the brutality of the Danes in their German provinces. Lord John Russell is credited with having said that he never knew but two persons who understood the Schleswig-Holstein question, and he evidently did not understand it himself. These duchies had never been an integral portion of Denmark, but were inherited by a Danish king some time during the Middle Ages, after the manner of landed estates. Their inhabitants spoke a broad kind of German, and always felt a lively antagonism towards their seafaring neighbors. Now, according to English and Danish law, political rights could be inherited by females, but according to the German law they could not. We have seen that in 1848 the male line of Danish sovereigns became extinct, and according to German usage the two duchies would revert properly to the Duke of Augustenburg, but the Danes very naturally did not agree to this. The London conference, which settled the question at that time, confirmed the new King of Denmark's possession of Schleswig and Holstein, but on condition that they should not be incorporated in Denmark proper. The Duke of Augustenburg never acquiesced in this decision, nor would the German people have submitted to it, had it not been supported by Russia and Austria.

The new Danish king, Frederick VII., encouraged by the opposition of the English ministry to Bismarck, and emboldened by the continued dissensions of Germany, had an act of incorporation for Schleswig passed by his parliament in the autumn of 1863, and was on the point of signing it when he suddenly died; and this nullification of the London congress was completed by his successor, Christian IX., who soon discovered the difference between the professions of

Lord John Russell and the heart of the German people. The Schleswig-Holstein question suddenly became a popular movement, like the war of liberation in 1813. Max Müller has given us in one of his essays an interesting account of the campaign songs that were sung for the liberation of the two duchies.¹ Even the moribund Diet at Frankfort was carried off its feet in the general enthusiasm, and, without considering the protest of the Austrian delegate, passed resolutions denouncing the action of the Danish government as a violation of the treaty of London; and as this produced no improvement of the situation, on the 7th of December the Diet enacted a decree that the Kings of Saxony and Hanover should take possession of Holstein with a force of six thousand men each, and that the Austrian and Prussian governments should maintain a reserve on the border of the province in case the Saxon and Hanoverian army should not succeed in repulsing the Danes. A more ineffectual and absurd arrangement could not well be imagined.

"To be politically great," says Froude, "is to recognize a popular movement, and have the courage and address to lead it." What Bismarck's plans were before the Schleswig-Holstein question appeared on the stage will probably never be known. In the whirl of events which followed he may have forgotten them himself. We can perceive in retrospect that his one object was the elevation of Prussia from the depressed condition in which his country was suffering, and he made

---

¹ "GERMAN HONOR AND GERMAN EARTH.

"Spring, 1848.

"There came soldiers across the Elbe,—
Hurrah, hurrah, to the North!
They came as thick as wave on wave,
And like a field full of corn.

* * * * * * *

Good day, ye Holsten, on German soil!
Good day, ye Friesians, on the German sea,
To live and to die for German honor,—
Thus wanders and marches the host."

Müller's Chips, vol. iii. p. 134.

everything else bend to this purpose. Great statesmen, however, do not make definite plans, but suit themselves to circumstances as they arise. They allow themselves to be ruled neither by circumstances nor by such plans as they have already formed, but hold an even course like a sea-captain, who pays more regard to the safety of his vessel than to the time which he spends upon his voyage. The statements that have been made, that Bismarck predicted the course of events between 1862 and 1866, are not worthy of credit, especially as they come from his political opponents. Count Vizthum, who was minister of Saxony to England during this period, says that the leader of the opposition in Parliament informed him that Bismarck came to London in 1862 to explain his future policy as minister-president to her Majesty's government, with such a statement of it as it would be easy enough to write ten years later. Memoirs are always poor historical evidence; but how Count Vizthum could expect a fairly intelligent public to believe such a transparent absurdity as this it is not easy to comprehend. It presupposes not only that Bismarck was a sufficient fool to divulge his plans in advance to the friends of his adversaries, but that the British ministry should have been equally foolish in divulging them to their own adversaries. *Nicht möglich*, as the Germans say.[1]

To solve the Schleswig-Holstein problem was Bismarck's immediate task, and it was like walking Niagara on the tightrope,—one misstep, and he was gone forever. The people of Holstein held an enormous meeting, in which they offered themselves as subjects to the Duke of Augustenburg, whose title to the duchies was now under legal scrutiny. The question was, however, if the duke obtained possession, would he be able to support himself in the new state of Augustenburg against a Danish attack? If not, Prussia, as his nearest neighbor, would inevitably be called upon to support him; and what advantage would Prussia derive from the blood and

---

[1] In the same category may be placed Lord Ampthill's statement that Bismarck told him that he had "always managed to talk over, if not to convince, his royal master." Bismarck would never have made an English lord the repository of so undiplomatic a secret. The statement is malicious.

treasure expended for his benefit? Another problem was whether the Saxon and Hanoverian army could conquer the two duchies from Denmark, and if so, what benefit would Saxony and Hanover derive from their exertion? Nothing for nothing is the principle in politics as in law. Bismarck doubted the success of either scheme. If the work was not done effectually at this time, it would remain an open grievance and a stumbling-block for Prussia in the future. He was determined to have the affair settled once for all.

He negotiated with Rechberg, who appears to have been of the same opinion, though in fact there was only one course open to him. Bismarck told him that if Austria would unite with Prussia, well and good; otherwise Prussia would undertake the affair alone. It was a game of "heads I win, tails you lose;" and yet it could not be said that it was a game of Bismarck's invention. *The Diet* (which was established for Austria's benefit) *had drawn Austria into a net from which there was no escape, except by playing this game for Prussia's advantage.* In order to have a voice in the distribution of the conquered territory the Vienna cabinet decided to join Prussia in an invasion of the two duchies, though Rechberg must have perceived his own fate before him from that moment. A force of fifty thousand men was considered necessary for the purpose, and this in itself shows how inadequate were the provisions of the Diet. The Danish army numbered between thirty and forty thousand.

There was only one way in which such a campaign could end, with two great powers on one side and a small one on the other. The Danes screamed aloud to England for assistance, but high-toned denunciations of Bismarck in the London papers were the only succor they received. Nevertheless, the campaign was rather a difficult one. General Wrangel, who had fought against Napoleon in 1813, was commander of the allied forces, but the real leader of the Prussians was Prince Frederick Charles of Hohenzollern, one of the toughest fighters of the nineteenth century.[1] The national assembly re-

---

[1] It is to be regretted that his character as a man was not equal to his ability. He commanded in more than a dozen engagements, and always with success.

fused to grant the necessary funds even for this patriotic war, but Bismarck paid no attention to that. The allies entered Schleswig, the more northerly province, driving the Danes before them. Finally the Danish commander made a stand at the two fortresses of Düppel and Fridericia, but Frederick Charles stormed the former, though considered impregnable, and the latter was evacuated. The allies then advanced into Jutland, and occupied the mainland of Denmark without much opposition.

Napoleon III. may have concluded that so long as Prussia and Austria were united it was best for him to keep as quiet as possible, but the English ministry now interfered to prevent further bloodshed, and as the object of the war had been accomplished, there was no reason why this request should not be considered. Another London conference ensued, but came to no good. In fact, the Danes were their own worst enemies from first to last. It is surprising that Bismarck should have assented to the proposition that the two duchies should continue to be attached to the Danish crown, with permission to regulate their own internal affairs. Bismarck assented to it, but the Danish envoy would not. The Danes considered themselves inaccessible in their rock-bound islands, but Frederick Charles crossed Alsen Sound with his forces during the night of June 28 and succeeded in intrenching himself under the fire of the Danish batteries. During the course of the following day the Danes were defeated, their intrenchments stormed, and they were driven back to the further extremity of the island. The soldiers who performed these feats had never seen active service before, and it was evident that a Prussian was a Prussian still. Denmark was now reduced to Copenhagen and its adjacent islands. Christian IX. was compelled to sue for peace.

This war, looked at from a distance, had the appearance of a cowardly oppression of the weak by the strong, and so it was considered in America at that time, but on close inspection we find in it a true popular movement corresponding to the conquests of Naples and Sicily by Garibaldi. ' Professor Müller states that Bismarck frowned upon it from the first, and this is not unlikely, for when such a movement begins there is no predicting what course it will finally take. Bismarck's reticence, however, may have been like that of a man who sees an opportunity before him, on which he desires to wholly concentrate himself. It was predicted as soon as the war was finished that the victors would quarrel over the booty, and nobody was surprised when this came to pass. It is difficult to decide from the external facts of the negotiations which followed whether Bismarck wished to push Austria to the wall or not. He probably wished it, but might have hesitated if a common ground of agreement could have been discovered. It is doubtful if an arrangement satisfactory to the interests of both nations was possible.

Meanwhile the useless Saxon-Hanoverian army had marched into Holstein without opposition. Bismarck insisted that as the Danes had now been driven out there was no occasion for its remaining there, and requested the two kings to withdraw their respective forces. As they did not acquiesce in this immediately, the King of Prussia concentrated strong bodies of troops on the borders of Hanover and Saxony, a threat which in due course of time proved effectual. Bismarck's proposition that the two duchies should be governed by a mixed Austrian and Prussian commission, while one province was occupied by Prussian forces and the other by Austrian, would seem to have been fair, but did not prove acceptable to the Austrian cabinet. The objection probably was that the Austrian troops thus employed would be shut in by the Prussians, and in case of war between the two nations would prove an easy capture. The claims of the Duke of Augustenburg were next considered. Bismarck, perhaps to gain time, employed a number of lawyers to look up his title, from which it appeared that he was heir to only a portion of the duchies, while the Duke of Oldenburg was heir to another portion, and that the King of Prussia also had a small claim. This was fine business for the lawyers, interesting business, and must have paid them well, but it did not help the solution of the problem.

The people of Schleswig and Holstein, except the gentry

of Lauenburg, declared for the Augustenburger, and he was accordingly invited to Berlin. It is supposed, with good reason, that if he had been willing to make an arrangement by which his army would become an integral portion of the Prussian army (like that of Brunswick, and, we believe, also Mecklenburg) he might have obtained the princely inheritance, but he was under the influence of Austria and the Frankfort Diet, and would agree to nothing which gave Prussia a political foothold in either Holstein or Schleswig,— thus losing his opportunity forever.

Just before or after the battle of Sedan, Bismarck gave an off-hand account of his discussion with the Augustenburger, who was gallantly serving as an officer in the Bavarian army, on the Schleswig-Holstein proposals. " He might have done better for himself," Bismarck said, " if he had only been willing to make a few concessions. We wanted no more of him originally than the other princes conceded to us after the Bohemian campaign, but he was obdurate,—and I thanked goodness for it to myself,—and when I spoke of giving Prussia the right to Kiel harbor, he remarked that that was five square miles of water, a statement which, of course, I could not deny. He would make no military agreement with us, and so the negotiation came to an end without a result." It is likely enough that the Duke of Augustenburg was afraid to accept Bismarck's proposition lest it should involve him in difficulty with Austria, and he should become the centre of a conflict between two forces much beyond his power of control. If, however, he had taken his chances on the side of Prussia he might have done well for himself.

The subsequent course of the Schleswig and Holstein settlement was like that of a river twisting and winding to find its way out from a mountainous country. It is tedious to follow it, and requires so much patience that we cannot but admire the endurance and assiduity of the diplomats who were engaged in it and struggled through it. It must have been specially trying to Bismarck, with his sleepless nights and a hostile parliament to contend with at the same time. He had, at least, gained something for Prussia by taking the

question out of the Frankfort Diet and placing it before
Francis Joseph in such a form that he must either accept or
reject the Prussian proposals. Count Rechberg was replaced
by Count Mensdorff-Pouilly, whose peculiar talent appears to
have been that of procrastination. There could have been no
advantage to Prussia in dragging out the negotiations to such
a length, and the fact proves either that Bismarck was not
desirous of precipitating a war or that he found in Count
Mensdorff a wary and accomplished tactician.

After some cautious skirmishing on both sides, in February, 1865, Bismarck sent a despatch to Count Mensdorff,
in which, after taking notice of the fact that the Austrian government had repeatedly asserted that neither of the pretending
dukes (Augustenburg and Oldenburg) could support a claim
to the whole of the two duchies, he goes on to explain the
position of the Prussian government towards them as follows:

" Both internally and externally considered, the constitution of
the military system in that important country, which is our next-
door neighbor, cannot but be of the greatest interest for us. It is
an imperative duty to make the means of defence at the disposal of
Schleswig-Holstein, especially on the sea, as useful as possible for
Germany, and in commerce and trade Prussia and the duchies must
naturally be most closely related to each other. No one can blame
us if we regard these interests as of the first importance. We are only
fulfilling a duty to Prussia and to Germany when we insist, before
proceeding to any definitive decision, upon some guarantees for the
security of these interests, and when we declare our unwillingness
to be dependent upon the uncertain good-will of a future sovereign
and his estates." [1]

This communication may not have been unexpected, but it
produced uneasiness and ill-feeling at Vienna. It showed
only too plainly the inevitable drift of the Danish war, and
that Bismarck had no intention of letting slip an opportunity
which in its natural course would turn to the aggrandizement
of Prussia.

---

[1] Von Sybel, iv. 56.

" Prussia misjudges us," Mensdorff complained to Baron Werther. " You should not suppose that we envy you any aggrandizement; only in that case we must obtain an equal equivalent for ourselves. This is indispensable in the present state of public opinion here." He then declared that the emperor had no partiality for the Augustenburger, who had several times broken his word to them. He then made a lengthy statement to Bismarck, which was little more than a reiteration of previous statements, ending with the conclusion that there was danger of open rupture between the two nations unless Prussia adopted the Austrian programme. " Our imperative duty," said Mensdorff, " requires us to bring these negotiations to an end as speedily as possible." At the same time he proposed no adjustment of the question which could be satisfactory to the Prussian government. It is curious to see how both parties in this discussion make use of public opinion as a loop-hole of escape and as a last resort in argument. Public opinion in Austria would not permit the aggrandizement of Prussia without an equivalent to Francis Joseph. Public opinion in Prussia could not allow the surrender of Upper Silesia, which was the only equivalent which Austria could very well obtain;[1] for an equal division of the Elbe duchies between the two nations would be too favorable geographically for Prussia.

After a good deal more skirmishing, we find Mensdorff late in April proposing a united convention of the estates of Schleswig and Holstein, for the purpose of deciding their own political status. A discussion then ensued as to whether the delegates should be elected to the convention—which Bismarck approved on the ground of legality—according to the law of 1848, or the more liberal regulations of 1854; and Bismarck finally nullified the arrangement by advocating their election by universal suffrage. This was looked upon in Vienna as an amendment intended to defeat the motion,— and so it probably was. Nothing could be more hateful to

---

[1] One difficulty in the way of this was that the Silesians were Protestants and strongly objected to being placed under the Austrian government.

Francis Joseph than the suggestion of universal suffrage. The Duke of Augustenburg still continued to reside in Holstein, and the joint motion of Austria and Prussia in the Frankfort Diet to have him ejected had been voted down by the smaller German states. Bismarck considered his withdrawal from the country essential to a fair election, but Mensdorff deprecated the use of force, and would only agree to make an earnest protest to the duke for this purpose.

After peace with Denmark had been declared, the government of the Elbe duchies had been placed in charge of an Austrian and a Prussian general as commissioners, who administered affairs in a dictatorial manner. As it was not considered expedient that this should continue, a popular government was organized, having its focus in Holstein for both states, and administered by a board of six councillors, while the commissioners retained a right of supervision, and served as a court of final appeal. This form of government was satisfactory to the people of Schleswig and Holstein; but either the Austrian commissioner outwitted his Prussian colleague, or he was favored by public opinion, so that of the six councillors chosen five proved to be partisans of the Augustenburger. Thus the civil establishment of these two provinces was rapidly drifting into the Austrian channel, though the fortresses and military establishment were mainly under Prussian control.

On May 29 King William held a grand council at the Schloss in Berlin, to consider the Schleswig-Holstein question, at which all of his ministers, as well as the crown prince, were present. The king presided and introduced the subject by remarking that the problem was a German as well as a Prussian question, and would have to be considered from both points of view; that Prussia had made sacrifices in the late war which required compensation, and that Austria, with whom they had specially to deal, had never been left in doubt on that point. Bismarck followed, and called attention to the fact that previous to 1864 the relations between Denmark and Prussia had been sufficiently friendly, so that now the disadvantage of a hostile neighbor must be added to the loss of life and expenditure of money. Of the various plans proposed for the solution of the problem, only two seemed to him practicable.

The first was that the two duchies should be surrendered to the Duke of Oldenburg, on condition that they should pay a war indemnity of eighty million thalers and place their military organization under the command of a Prussian general. The second was that Prussia should make a formal demand for the annexation of the provinces. This would probably result in a war with Austria; but he believed that such a war was unavoidable so long as the Austrian government persisted in its systematic policy of repressing the interests of Prussia. He considered the European situation was favorable for Prussia in the event of such a conflict, and if it was to come at all it ought to come soon. Von Moltke gave his opinion that annexation was the only salutary solution for Prussia, and the crown prince supported the claim of the Augustenburger.

It must be admitted that the only fair way to solve this complicated problem would have been for William I. to have surrendered Upper Silesia to Austria, and in return to have annexed the Elbe duchies.

Unfortunately there was another question mixed up with this,—that of the hostile majority in the Frankfort Diet, which loaded it down like a phantom rider, and prevented a settlement. There was witchcraft in the broth. Even Bismarck's first proposition, which he had already advanced on February 22, was not unreasonable,—all circumstances considered,—though it afforded Prussia a decided increase of military power. The attitude of the crown prince was exceptional, and might be explained by his opposition to Bismarck, or by the influence of his English wife; but in itself it amounted to a second Olmütz, a surrender of every advantage which Prussia might have derived from a successful campaign.

Such a consultation at Berlin would not seem likely to lead to a peaceable conclusion, and this feeling was increased by the continued residence of the Augustenburger in Holstein, and certain public agitations there, intended to advance his interests and supposed to be instigated by him. Accordingly, about the middle of July, Bismarck sent an ultimatum to the Austrian government, in which he said:

"All negotiations concerning the future of the duchies are refused until authority is established there and all agitation done away with. When this is accomplished, Prussia will be ready to treat with Austria concerning the establishment of the Grand Duke of Oldenburg as sovereign. The candidacy of Augustenburg is entirely out of the question for us, so long as the hereditary prince persists in his attitude of usurpation."

This brought Francis Joseph to his senses for the time being, and a meeting of the two monarchs, with their respective ministers, was hastily arranged for the 8th of August at Gastein in Upper Austria; and there an agreement was concluded to the effect that Lauenburg should be ceded to Prussia for three million thalers, and that the rights of Austria and Prussia in the remaining duchies should continue undetermined, though the government of Holstein was to be undertaken by Austria, and that of Schleswig by Prussia.

It will be seen that nothing was positively decided by this arrangement except the disposition of Lauenburg. Count Belcredi, who had succeeded Mensdorff-Pouilly after the rotary fashion of the Austrian court, made another suggestion for Upper Silesia as a settlement of outstanding claims, but William and Bismarck would not listen to it. Bismarck had now the upper hand in the game, and played his cards accordingly. General Manteuffel, who stood next to the minister-president in the king's estimation, was appointed governor of Schleswig, and General Gablenz, an equally astute official, was nominated for Holstein by Francis Joseph. The evident intention of the two monarchs was to preserve the peace, if possible; but it was plain that the arrangement could not last, and the question everybody in Germany asked was, What will be the next scene in this political melodrama?

The stories that have been circulated in regard to an understanding at this period between Napoleon III. and Bismarck have no documentary foundation, and are improbable in them-

selves. *There was no necessity for such an understanding.*
The fact was that Bismarck was better informed in regard to
French affairs than Napoleon himself. Von Moltke's spies
had been everywhere through French territory, and had discovered that the *grande armée* was a chimera,—that Napoleon
was not possessed at this time of a hundred thousand efficient troops, although he supposed that he had nearly twice
as many. A portion of the French army was still in Mexico;
enlistments had been discontinued for the sake of economy,
and gross frauds had been practised similar to those in the
Austrian army previous to 1859. Bismarck knew that Napoleon was not in a position to take the offensive, and it was this
fact which made him so bold.

Unfortunately for the nephew of the great Napoleon, the
latter had written in his memoirs, " France is nothing without
Belgium and the Rhine," and this statement was to Louis
Napoleon like the words of a gospel. He had accomplished
much, but this still remained to fill the measure of his glory.
There has always been a sentimental opinion among the
French that they have a right to the boundaries of ancient
Gaul, but it is not the same description of right as that which
Frederick II. claimed to lower Silesia, which had been given
to his ancestors by the treaty of Westphalia and unjustly withheld from them by the Austrian emperors. It is impossible to
consider such claims when they go behind the Dark Ages,—
that long period of anarchy and confusion from which modern
Europe emerged. Napoleon III. had slight chance of accomplishing this final object so long as an alliance between Austria and Prussia was possible. What he might have done
safely enough, as Bismarck remarked afterwards,[1] "was to
have taken possession of Belgium. He had nothing to fear
except from England, and not much there." So long as the
liberal ministry were in power at Westminster the British
government would not have been likely to interfere with him,
nor could the British government have expelled the French
from Belgium without the co-operation of some continental

---

[1] Bismarck in the Franco-Prussian War.

power. The Belgians speak French, and it requires an experienced foreigner to distinguish a citizen of Brussels from a
Parisian. The province would have been five times as valuable to France as Rhenish Prussia, but Napoleon did not see
this opportunity. His eyes were fixed on the German quarrel, which he hoped to take advantage of to get possession
of Luxemburg and Cologne.

After the Gastein convention Bismarck was rewarded with
the title of count, which, at least, placed him on an equality
with most of his colleagues. To men of the grand sort such
honors are small compensation. It did not help to remove
the difficulties before him, and the following winter (1866)
was the toughest of his life. He felt the impending conflict,
and all Germans felt it, as we felt the same thing in America
during the last months of Buchanan's administration. The
Progressists in the National Assembly gave him more difficulty than ever,—men infatuated with an idea, and that an
impracticable one: intoxicated with it as they might have
been with brandy. They would pass no appropriations, and
Bismarck was in the same position as Julius Cæsar when he
borrowed of every banker in Rome in order to obtain the
consulship. It did not require a Bismarck to foresee that
such a course was ruin both to himself and to the king unless
he should meet with complete success. The royal family
perceived this, and opposed him as energetically as the National Assembly. The queen may have been influenced by
her near relationship to the Augustenburger, but this was not
likely to have affected the crown prince.

The king, however, remained firm, and Bismarck received
strong support from Von Moltke, the chief of staff, and Von
Roon, the scarcely less distinguished minister of war. These
were the men whom William I. trusted before all others, and
they knew those state secrets which were not divulged even
in the royal family, and which Bismarck counted on for success. His consultations with Moltke and Roon in the garden
adjoining his house in Berlin during the spring of 1866 decided some of the most important events of modern times.
The great marshal and the great chancellor never became

warm friends, and yet they acted together for the most part in such perfect concert that it might have been supposed that they had only one purpose and one mind.

Meanwhile the situation in Holstein and Schleswig was becoming gradually worse. The Holstein nobility seem to have disliked the Austrian government, and many of them signed a petition to William I. to have the province incorporated with Prussia. Bismarck may have instigated this, but they certainly would not have done it at his bidding. At the same time the Austrians encouraged demonstrations for the Augustenburger, and when the wife of his eldest son went on a journey through the province ovations were tendered to her at the railway stations, with expressions of the liveliest political sympathy.[1] This contagion spread over the border of Schleswig, but did not develop there to any considerable extent; a fact which indicates that it was encouraged by General Gablenz, the Austrian commander in Holstein, and repressed by General Manteuffel, who commanded in Schleswig. Both sides were intriguing, and the advantage was in favor of Austria, but this very fact gave Prussia a diplomatic advantage. The petition of a few nobles came to nothing, while the agitation in favor of the Augustenburger continued.

The Altona incident may be taken as an example of the whole affair. The leaders of the Augustenburg party arranged for a grand mass-meeting at Altona, in Holstein, for the 23d of January, 1866, at which noted speakers from Frankfort, Hesse, and Bavaria were to be present. The prospectus of the meeting was openly circulated in both duchies, and General Manteuffel notified General Gablenz that it was contrary to the treaty of Gastein, and requested him to interfere to prevent it. Gablenz promised to do this, but afterwards permitted the rally to take place on condition that no definite resolutions should be adopted by the assembly. This technical point was adhered to, but several of the speakers made violent attacks on the Prussian government, and the

---

[1] Von Sybel, iv. 291.

meeting dissolved with three rousing cheers for the Duke of Augustenburg.[1]

To Bismarck this was like a challenge to fight. Not only the convention of Gastein had been openly disregarded, but a high Prussian official had been hoodwinked in order to carry out this revolutionary scheme. Bismarck wrote to the Prussian ambassador at Vienna three days later with the request that he should bring his statement to the notice of Francis Joseph: "The Altona meeting has been held under the protection of the Austrian double-eagle, and has been permitted to make exactly the same attacks upon Prussia that the Frankfort Confederate Diet ventured to make, and on account of which the free city received a rebuke from Austria. Prussia cannot suffer Holstein to become in this way a home of revolutionary sentiments, nor that pledge to deteriorate which was confidently placed in Austria's hands at the Gastein treaty. Such occurrences as these," continued the despatch, "cannot help weakening and subverting that feeling which his Majesty has long and fondly cherished,—the conviction that the two German powers naturally belong together."

The manner in which Mensdorff treated this frank and manly despatch was characteristic of Austrian diplomacy. He represented to Werther, the Prussian ambassador, that he was greatly concerned at the Altona incident, was dissatisfied with the conduct of Gablenz, and had already sent a reproof to him for his action on that occasion. Having administered this sop to William I., a week later he sent a despatch to Bismarck which contained the following statement:

"Prussia has, in making her complaint about the Altona meeting, evidently forgotten that it was her own government that once rejected the proposal of Austria to bring forward in the Confederation a motion prohibiting all such meetings throughout Germany. Austria recognizes her duty only so far as to preserve the substance of the treaty undiminished. Moreover, the conduct of the Austrian government in Holstein depends only upon its own promptings, etc.

The same independence is also recognized and conceded to the royal Prussian government in Schleswig."

This asserted in substance that while Francis Joseph expected Prussia to respect the convention of Gastein, he intended to administer the affairs of Holstein according to the understanding of the Frankfort convention of 1864, or, practically, in any manner that suited his interest. The despatch was at once an assertion of the Gastein treaty and a repudiation of it, and proves conclusively that if the convention was a temporary makeshift on the part of Bismarck, it was not considered more seriously by the Austrian government. If Bismarck had been intriguing in Holstein, Mensdorff was quite ready to meet him half-way in that line of business. We do not hear of any complaint of Bismarck in this controversy, and it is quite possible that the petition of the Holstein nobility was a mere offset to the incipient stages of the Augustenburg agitation. General Manteuffel, whose character, in spite of his name, vies with that of Von Moltke, governed Schleswig in an exceptional manner, and if there was a party to the Gastein convention who wished for peace, and sincerely desired to observe it, it was the old King William I. Men of his time of life are not inclined to go to war, and his reluctance to do so is admitted by Bismarck himself.

What an opportunity this would have been for Cavour! But Cavour was sleeping in dull, cold marble, and his successor, the wily La Marmora, was a man of a different stamp. He played fast and loose with Bismarck, and, feeling himself indispensable, tried to obtain more than the lion's share. Bismarck would hear of no claim beyond Venetia for Italy as the reward of a successful campaign; the Italian Tyrol was not to be thought of. Then La Marmora intrigued at the Austrian court, hoping to frighten Francis Joseph by the threat of a Prussian alliance. Then the Roumanian revolution occurred, and he advised with Louis Napoleon as to the possibility of an exchange of Venetia for Roumania on the part of Austria. Napoleon thought this might be possible, and issued a circular note to the powers; but here the Tsar Alexander interfered and set down his foot that the thing should not be done,—he would first go to war. Bismarck was well aware of all this, endured it, and worried through it all as a lawyer does with a lucrative but unreliable client; and when La Marmora discovered at length that he could not have his cake and eat it too, he came round to Bismarck's position ; and on April 8, 1866, an offensive and defensive alliance between the Prussian and Italian governments was signed by Bismarck and the Italian envoy at Berlin. This may be considered the commencement of the war between Prussia and Austria.

CHAPTER VI

NEGOTIATIONS with Italy involved also negotiations with Napoleon III., whom Bismarck might otherwise have left as much out of his account as he did the English ministry. There was a perpetual alliance between the Italian and French governments, and Victor Emmanuel held to it with a chivalrous fidelity which shames the diplomacy of his premier. He would take no step forward without asking Napoleon's advice, so that consulting the French oracle came to be like consulting the oracle of Delphi. As a consequence every move on the Berlin chess-board which affected the government at Florence produced an almost immediate countermove at Paris. According to all accounts Napoleon was amiability itself; he approved of the cession of Venetia to Italy, and the retention of the two duchies by Prussia, without suggesting any special compensation for France and himself; but Bismarck was too well acquainted with Louis Napoleon to place any great confidence in this. On one occasion Napoleon hinted to Baron Goltz, the Prussian envoy, that a slight consideration for his good-will would be acceptable, and Goltz explained to him the difficulty of changing the German frontier, though a matter immaterial to Prussia, on account of the strong national sentiment in Germany, and Napoleon replied, "You have done your country a great service in clearing up any misunderstandings in that respect." Bismarck's despatch to Goltz of February 20 speaks, at all events, in no uncertain tone:

"Although I quite agree with your Excellency that after a rupture with Austria had already taken place we could hardly secure the support of France upon other than very onerous conditions, yet it seems to me as difficult as it would be dangerous to take such

118

measures as might induce the emperor to make a declaration that would in any way offer us certain guarantee. If the views of the emperor are to be looked upon as a definite factor in our political calculations, they must be formulated with due authority. We cannot be satisfied with promises that are simply morally binding; and even if the emperor could be induced to declare in definite form his possible intentions, it would be only with the understanding that the king would also be willing to do the same."[1]

This shows conclusively that up to that date no territorial bargain had been transacted with Napoleon III.; nor is there any evidence that one was made afterwards. Bismarck's last interview with the "disinterested friend" was at Biarritz the preceding October, and in his lengthy report of it to the king there is not a definite statement of Napoleon's that any one can take hold of, except a plain disavowal of any intention to take possession of Belgium.

Louis Napoleon does not appear in Bismarck's report either as a sagacious man or a person of much force. He afterwards, however, volunteered a shrewd suggestion that the Schleswig-Holstein problem was not a sufficient excuse to place before the world for going to war with Austria; that the Prussian government should appear to be actuated by a more important principle. This placed Bismarck in the position of a man who is obliged to show his hand in order to prevent distrust, and who, if he committed himself, would either be obliged to adhere to some specified plan or incur the odium of a broken agreement. His reply was, that the Prussian government desired a reorganization of German affairs which would make Germany independent of the Austrian empire and Austrian influence; that he wished to form a confederation of the North German states, with their military affairs in the control of Prussia, and a South German confederation, with Bavaria for its military leader. Such a plan was well adapted to secure the French emperor's approval, for Bavaria had been the ally of Napoleon I. and Louis XIV.; her proclivities were antagonistic to Prussia, and the Frankfort confederation would

---

[1] Von Sybel, iv. 82.

be replaced by three distinct political unities. Bismarck, however, was better informed in regard to the internal affairs of Bavaria, and had reason to believe that in a national emergency he could count on the support of her government.

Although the French minister of foreign affairs, Drouyn de l'Huys, had informed Baron Goltz that France required no compensation worth mentioning, yet when the treaty of the alliance between Italy and Prussia had been signed, Napoleon began to fear that the latter might derive too good a bargain from it. The forces on either side were very nearly equal, and if the Prussians were better soldiers than the Austrians, the Austrians were better than the Italians; but the geographical position of Austria placed that country between two fires, and he may have remembered, also, that the Prussian troops were armed with breech-loading rifles, a weapon in which he himself had great confidence. He therefore reopened the negotiations with La Marmora in regard to a peaceable cession of Venetia, which he thought might now be obtained, in return for the withdrawal of Italy from the Prussian alliance. He believed that in this way Prussia, also, might be forced to cede Silesia to Austria, and be compensated for this severe loss by the annexation of Schleswig and Holstein. As it was certain that William I. would never give up Silesia without a bitter struggle, this plan evidently included an alliance between France and Austria for that purpose, the result of which, it was anticipated, would be a crushing defeat for Prussia and the loss of her territory on the west bank of the Rhine. Fortunately for both Italy and Prussia, there was a king behind La Marmora who had never yet broken his word, and who considered a political alliance as a sacred obligation. La Marmora replied accordingly that he considered it a matter of duty and national honor not to break loose from Prussia, especially as the Prussian government was preparing for war, and had declared to the powers that it would invade Austria if Austria attacked Italy. Victor Emmanuel maintained the same position, even after the offer of Venetia had been made, without taking Silesia into consideration. Such was the difference between

these two sovereigns; but the plan of Napoleon was a chimerical one, and might have finally resulted in the union of South Germany with Prussia against France, as in 1870.

Before the war began there was still another slight pacific ruffle on the troubled waters of German diplomacy. Baron Gablenz, a brother of General Gablenz, and a member of the Berlin Chamber of Deputies, thought he had hit upon a plan for solving the Schleswig-Holstein question and preventing the impending conflict. It was, in brief, that the two duchies should be formed into a state under the authority of a Prussian prince; that Prussia should pay five million thalers for the harbor of Kiel, and the duchies twenty millions more for a war compensation; that Austria should have the supreme command of the South German troops, and Prussia of the North German forces.[1] This would seem to be the most sensible course yet suggested, and General Gablenz advised his brother to submit it to Count Mensdorff. Thus fortified, Baron Gablenz went to Vienna to consult Mensdorff, who promised that the Austrian cabinet would consider his proposition seriously if he would first obtain the King of Prussia's approval. The baron hurried back to Berlin. It was the 1st of May, and eighty thousand Austrian troops were already assembled on the frontier of Silesia. Bismarck had no hopes of peace, but he spoke favorably of Gablenz's plan to William I., who cordially approved it. Gablenz returned to Mensdorff, who this time referred him to Francis Joseph himself. "There must be some reasons why these satisfactory propositions were not made before they could be no longer of service," said the politic emperor, and there the matter ended. Could better proof be obtained of the unwillingness of the Austrian court to come to a reasonable agreement?[2]

Amid all this wilderness of barren and unprofitable diplomacy, there is one voice that sounds clear and true,—the

---

[1] Von Sybel, iv. 247.

[2] Von Beust says (Memoirs, i. 324), "Although Mensdorff severely condemned all the despatches that aggravated the situation and prepared the war, he was weak enough to sign them."

voice of Bismarck. He occasionally hedges in his statements, as a diplomat may, but they are always worth having,
and more often he goes frankly and directly to the point.
Take, for instance, this passage from his directions to Baron
Goltz in regard to a possible arrangement with Napoleon III.:

"The lack of honesty towards Austria, of which France would
possess the means of convicting us at any moment, would not only
cost us the confidence of Austria for a long time to come, but would
as well bring upon us the condemnation of the people and the
governments throughout Germany. It would excite great distrust
of us in the mind of England, who would see herself indirectly
threatened through us upon that side where she is fond of counting
upon our help in the event of a great conflict. It would also cool
down our relations with Russia. We should be isolated from the
other powers and dependent upon France alone." [1]

It was no cynic of human nature like the Edinburgh reviewer that wrote such a statement, but one who knew that
the only sound basis of politics, as of mercantile affairs, is
honesty and mutual confidence. His photograph, taken at
this time, gives the impression of a determined, clear-sighted,
and veracious man. The cautious crow's-foot in the corner
of his eye shows that he is capable of dissimulation, but the
manly expression forbids our mistaking him for a trickster.
One element, at least, we can always eliminate from Bismarck's
motives, and that is personal ambition. He admits, in one
of his letters, that he is sometimes swayed by personal feeling, but this admission is in his favor. If a man has personal
ambition he shows it as a boy, either in his studies, his exercise, or in a desire to perform exceptional feats. We hear of
nothing like this in Bismarck's youth. He was always interested in politics, and often wearied his boon companions at
Kniephof with long dissertations on political subjects; but
though, as one of the landed gentry, his entrance into political
life was an easy one, he made no effort in that direction until
the public excitement in 1847 roused 'him to unusual exer-

tion. When his king called him, he answered, " I am ready;" but in his letters he always speaks with the same nonchalance of his appointment to the Diet at Frankfort, his mission to St. Petersburg, and, finally, his elevation to the highest position in the state. He does not appear to have cared for money, except to supply the needs of his family, and his life at Schönhausen and Varzin was that of a quiet country gentleman.

I have always held this opinion of Bismarck, and I was greatly pleased to find it confirmed by the statement of Baron Von der Pfordten, the wisest of Bavarian ministers, in 1866, and the one man outside of Prussia who seems to have understood the Berlin sphinx. Although an opponent of Bismarck to a certain extent, he could not help respecting him. " They make a great mistake," he said to Prince Reuss, " who attribute personal ambition to Bismarck. He is the incarnation of the Prussian state. He is no opponent of Austria on principle; on the contrary, he would be glad to join hands with her, but always on the condition that she will not forever be placing obstacles in the way of a justifiable Prussian policy. This is a thoroughly German idea, and just for this reason I place confidence in that man who is its chief representative." [1] Von der Pfordten had listened to Bismarck's discussion of the German problem, and believed in his plans; and this kernel of Prussian sentiment in Bavaria at that time is significant, and proved of great importance in the events that followed.

Such was the judgment of an enlightened Bavarian, and we can place it beside the action of a mean, bigoted Communist. As compared with the first portion of the nineteenth century, the latter half has shown a decided tendency to social demoralization. James Russell Lowell was confident that he perceived it, in both Europe and America, twenty-five years ago. He judged of it by the literature which people were reading, and from the conversation of people whom he met. It has shown itself in various ways, but in none so distinctly

---

[1] Despatch of Prince Reuss, April 10, 1866.

as in the tendency to assassination. During the eighteenth century and the first half of the nineteenth assassination was hardly known. There were two attempts on the life of Napoleon, which is not surprising, considering the excitement of those times ; but since 1850 two Presidents of the United States and a President of the French Republic, as well as a number of minor officials, have been assassinated, and attempts have been made on the life of almost every sovereign in Europe. Such a condition of affairs was never known before in Christian countries, not even during the sixteenth century. In fact, the men who perpetrated these outrages were not Christians, but atheists, the natural product of the atheistic philosophy of the present day. It is the result of infinite self-conceit, of a man becoming a god unto himself. Such were the characters of Wilkes Booth and Guiteau, though they did not belong to the Communists. To assassinate a Caligula or a Commodus, monsters of depravity, is honorable ; but he who assassinates a man of good character like the Tsar Alexander, because he represents a different set of political principles from the assassin, becomes a Caligula himself. The Nihilists are the *cobras* of modern society.

Charles Cohen, the would-be assassin of Bismarck, has been spoken of as a high-minded but fanatical youth ; but I can discover nothing in him but a base and degraded soul, the fit companion of Booth and Ravaillac. He belonged to the Internationals, and no doubt was urged on to the business. So much may be said in extenuation for his crime. It was on the 7th of May, 1866, that he came up behind Bismarck on the Unter den Linden and fired two shots at him. One of these went through Bismarck's coat, and the other may have missed him as he turned round. He sprang at Cohen, but before he could reach him the latter fired another shot, which is supposed to have glanced off Bismarck's ribs. He fired once or twice again while he was in Bismarck's clutches, and yet Bismarck escaped without even a troublesome wound. It was reported in Vienna that Bismarck was protected by a shirt of mail, and if so, he showed remarkable foresight ; but his friends have denied this, though the fact was no discredit to him. Cohen had provided himself with a dose of poison, which he swallowed soon after being taken to prison. Bismarck's escape seemed miraculous, and did much to establish popular confidence in him, while the Prussian people realized how nearly they had lost so valuable a man. There were few persons of note in Berlin who did not call to congratulate him that evening.

The startling sensation which went through Europe at the criminal attempt of this ruffian soon subsided in the exciting events that followed. La Marmora's reply to Napoleon III. was politely received, but its effect must have been irritating to an exceptional degree; for it placed the emperor in the position of a man who had been caught cheating at cards. Neither was the news from Berlin such as to afford him consolation. As Bismarck saw the game before him more and more clearly, he became more confident and obdurate. Benedetti, who had become celebrated as Louis Napoleon's man of business, wrote to him in May from Berlin that the chief obstacle to an understanding was the sentiment of the whole Prussian nation, which firmly opposed surrender of the smallest portion of German soil, either their own or of any other state. "I know of no one," he wrote, " besides Count Bismarck, that has any idea of the possibility that the cession of territory to France might lie in the interests of Prussia, and even he would consent only to a change that would more or less improve the line of the frontier." Bismarck was wise enough to be willing to make a small sacrifice for the sake of a great good; but this public sentiment in regard to the inviolability of German territory is another evidence of the strong current that was running in favor of German national unity.

Napoleon had now been foiled by his own weapons, and the "disinterested friend" determined to play a bolder and more reckless game. Emissaries from Pius IX., who was now becoming greatly alarmed for the States of the Church, were at work with the empress, and Eugénie gave her feminine opinion that in case of Italian success there was grave danger that the influence of Victor Emmanuel would supplant that of her husband in " the orient." At the same time an incident occurred which greatly assisted in facilitating Napoleon's sudden change of base. Thiers, the French Warwick, who undid Louis Philippe, made a speech in the French assembly which might be characterized as the essence of political meanness. He denounced the alliance between Prussia and Italy as likely to strengthen both nations; France had the first position in European affairs, and the way for France to be strong was to keep other nations weak. Italian unity was as dangerous as German unity would be. The aim of Prussia evidently lay in the direction of German consolidation. It was the duty of the French government to prevent Italy from taking part in the cursed war which was then approaching.

Louis Napoleon has never been credited with such a cynical statement as this, and, in truth, his previous policy had been of a much more liberal character; but if he had instigated Thiers's speech it could not have better served his purpose. The applause from the opposition benches was drowned by the supporters of the government, and this declaration of French superiority was telegraphed all over the world. In order to attest the project he had been fostering so zealously, Napoleon now proposed a peace congress to settle the affairs of Germany in a manner agreeable to other nations. He communicated his plan to Lord Clarendon, the English foreign minister, who, as party feeling in London was running strong against Prussia, readily assented to it.[1] Alexander and Victor Emmanuel also expressed their assent, and it may seem surprising that Bismarck should have done so; but there was nothing he would have liked better at this time than to expose the political programme of Austria in contrast with his own before a congress of the great powers. Exactly how the congress was expected to rearrange German affairs remains in doubt. Napoleon must have sketched out a plan of some kind for Clarendon and La Marmora. It is certain that Italy would not have consented to it without the cession of

---

[1] It was at this time that the New York *Nation* spoke of Bismarck as the most reckless political gambler that ever sat at the helm of state, and predicted that he would be duped by Napoleon III.,—a reflection of English public opinion.

Venetia, and equally certain that Austria would have required compensation for this. That Napoleon proposed to have Silesia restored to Austria, and Prussia compensated with the kingdom of Saxony, is a Prussian supposition, which still requires confirmation. The Austrian reply to the circular note was characteristic; it was that Austria would take part in the congress only on condition that none of the powers represented should be expected to cede territory which had been guaranteed by existing treaties. This was, of course, a nullification of the original project, and killed it dead.[1] No wonder if Count Belcredi, the successor of Mensdorff, dreaded to face Bismarck before an international congress.

It was now the last of May, and trade in Germany was at a stand-still. The political atmosphere was sultry and oppressive, like the death-like calm which precedes the tornado. People wished the war would begin, rather than remain in this state of suspense. Von Moltke argued that every day's delay was to the advantage of Austria, but certain diplomatic formalities had to be gone through with before the challenge to arms was made. It is amusing to read at this stage of proceedings how each party tried to cast the responsibility of hostilities on the other. Neither wished to appear before the world as the aggressor. " Hypocrisy," said Wendell Phillips, " is the homage which vice pays to virtue." In the seventeenth century princes and cabinets did not trouble themselves much about such formalities, and Louis XIV. marched his troops into Strasburg without a day's warning. As a matter of fact, the war was the result of a mutual understanding, and its responsibility went back to the first Frankfort Diet after the revolution of 1848. The true responsibility of it rested with Prince Schwarzenberg and his imperial pupil. It had been gradually coming on ever since Bismarck had asked the Austrian delegate for a light for his cigar,—a light which at length produced a terrible conflagration.

Louis Napoleon cuts a sorrowful figure during these last

---

[1] Von Beust says Austria declined the congress proposed by Napoleon III., or, what amounted to the same thing, accepted it with such restrictions that it never came to pass. Memoirs, i. 290.

days of peace. His intrigues at the court of Vienna were incessant, but the exact form which they took will never be known. Baron Goltz discovered that interviews between Napoleon and the Austrian envoy at Paris were of daily occurrence, and it was reported to Bismarck from Rome that the French ambassador was as frequent a visitor at the Vatican. At the same time the Duke of Saxe-Coburg also showed Bismarck a letter from Count Belcredi, in which it was stated that Francis Joseph had arrived at a complete understanding with Napoleon III., and if Prussia went to war she would have to deal not only with Austria but with France. Professor Müller says, " It is uncertain what Napoleon was to acquire in accordance with this carefully guarded treaty, but it is not likely that Austria, which has not scrupled in times gone by to sacrifice German territory, would have hesitated to cede the left bank of the Rhine, if by so doing she could defeat her hated rival." [1] Von Sybel's statement, that finally Prince Napoleon telegraphed to the King of Italy that Bismarck had made a secret agreement with Francis Joseph—a telegram which Victor Emmanuel immediately reported to Count Usedorn at Berlin, and which Bismarck pronounced an infernal lie—is by no means incredible, but needs to be supported by documentary evidence.[2]

It is interesting to note the successive steps by which Prussia and Austria reached a collision. On June 1 Belcredi appealed to the Diet at Frankfort for a final settlement of the Schleswig-Holstein question. Bismarck then declared that this was contrary to the Gastein convention, and an order was sent to Manteuffel to march his troops into Holstein and form a government there in conjunction with the Austrian commander, according to the *status* previous to Gastein. Gablenz refused to co-operate with Manteuffel and retired to Altona. Manteuffel marched in with twenty thousand men and established a government of his own, and Bismarck issued a circular to the German princes, a far-reaching act of statesmanship,

---

[1] Müller's Political History, p. 331.
[2] Von Sybel, iv. 473.

in which he outlined the proposition of a German national union, based on popular suffrage, with Prussia for its military leader. In regard to this circular he wrote to the Duke of Saxe-Coburg:

" The propositions contained in the outline are in no case exhaustive, but are the results of the necessary consideration of various influences with which a compromise must be made, *intra muros et extra.* But if we can bring even these to their actual realization, then one portion, at least, will be accomplished of the task of rendering harmless that net of historical boundaries which runs through Germany; and it is unfair to expect that one generation or one man, even my most gracious sovereign, should in a day make good what generations of our ancestors have in the course of centuries spoiled."

The essence of Bismarck's plan consisted of the following points:

."Exclusion of Austria; creation of a confederate marine; division of the military command, Prussia taking the north and Bavaria the south; a parliament to be elected by the people on the basis of a universal suffrage, and which should have the functions already specified above and sharply defined; and, finally, the regulations of the future relations with German Austria by means of a special treaty." [1]

The present organization of Germany was established sub-stantially on this basis.

At that time, however, it was a revolutionary act. On the 11th of June the Austrian delegate moved in the Diet at Frankfort that the whole army of the confederation should be mobilized in order to bring Prussia to terms, and on the 14th the Diet, by a vote of nine to six, declared war against Prussia. The only princes who supported Prussia in this emergency were the Dukes of Oldenburg, Mecklenburg, and of the Saxon duchies and Luxemburg; but the free cities also, except Frankfort, took the same side, and the people of North

---

[1] Von Sybel, iv. 484.

Germany showed their political tendencies in an unmistakable manner. The chambers of Cassel, Nassau, and Darmstadt refused to appropriate money for the campaign. In the Hanover assembly a resolution was passed in favor of neutrality, and the people of Leipsic petitioned the King of Saxony to follow a similar course. Bismarck issued a manifesto to the governments of Saxony, Hanover, Cassel, and Nassau, promising them, if they would dismiss their forces and remain at peace, that their rights and the integrity of their territories would be respected.[1]

The war of 1866 closely resembled in its political bearing the war which had just been finished in the United States. In both instances the nucleus of strife originated in the political fallacy that a sovereignty can exist within a sovereignty. Even Abraham Lincoln, who denied the right of secession and was always true to his principles, spoke in 1859 of Massachusetts as "a sovereign State." Four years of bloody warfare were required to knock that notion in the head. "Sovereignty," said Bismarck afterwards in the German Reichstag, "is a unit and must remain a unit,—the sovereignty of law." The Austrian motion in the Diet for the mobilization of forces was, in fact, unconstitutional. It properly required a committee of investigation to inquire into the facts of the case and make a report on the subject before it could be legally adopted; but it was part of Bismarck's strategy to allow it to pass with a simple protestation on the part of Prussia, for he was right glad to have the old confederate government place itself on record in that way.

There is a story which came to me through a Prussian naval officer that on the evening of June 15, 1866, Bismarck was at a small party in Berlin, when a royal messenger entered and delivered a letter to him. As he was writing the reply a young lady said to him, "Let me read, Count Bismarck, what important thing you are writing," and he covered the paper with his hand. When the messenger had left the room Bis-

---

[1] This should be borne in mind in connection with Bismarck's course of procedure after the war was finished.

marck rose and said quietly to the company, " I trust it is for the best, but to-morrow we fight." [1]

An investigation of the genesis of war in civilized countries might prove a more profitable study than the present discussion of free trade and protection. Von Holst has done something towards it in his elaborate analysis of the slavery question in America. Generally speaking, wars are sent to mankind for their political sins, and, as a rule, it is the right that conquers, though, as in private families, the innocent suffer with the guilty. It must be admitted that the wars which have taken place since 1855, with the exception of the Servia-Bulgarian and Greco-Turkish wars, have been greatly to the advantage of civilization. If we consider the ancient world, it is evident from the victories of Pyrrhus over the Romans, even such as they were, that if the Greeks had not degenerated after that time they would not have become the tributaries of Rome. If the Italians had remained as brave as they were in the time of Marius, it is not likely that their country would have been overrun by Goths and Vandals. The Saxons were conquered by the Normans because they had become sluggish and effeminate; and if the Poles had possessed an efficient government, with a well-disciplined army, in the last century, it is not probable that their country would have been divided up among neighboring states. The Prussian idea is that it does every man good to be a soldier; and Sumner's theory that a first-rate military organization tends to promote warfare between nations is not supported by facts. Two vigorous rival nations like the French and English, always likely to misunderstand each other, cannot exist side by side without some sort of military organization; and if one increases it, the other must do so likewise. The army of Frederick the Great maintained peace in Europe for thirty years, a longer period than had ever been known before. War is, after all, not so very much worse than peace. A week in one of our largest city hospitals is nearly equal to

---

[1] According to Hesekiel, Bismarck received the royal order in his own garden about midnight.

a battle-field; and the fishermen who are drowned every year, the railway navvies who are killed, and the other casualties in dangerous employments constitute a startling sum total. It is said that in China men and women throw themselves into the rivers every night to avoid starvation. People rarely starve to death in prosperous America, but thousands lose their lives every year in the effort to gain a living. War takes away from men the fear of death, and every one who dies makes room for some other in this crowded world, and the life of a soldier is better than that in a cotton-mill.

> "He alone deserves his freedom and his life
> Who daily conquers it in strife." [1]

What Garibaldi was to Cavour, Von Moltke was to Bismarck. Without Bismarck the most famous general of his time might never have been heard of beyond the limits of Germany; but without Von Moltke, Bismarck might never have accomplished those great plans which continually urged him onward. Among military inventors Von Moltke stands next to Napoleon and Frederick, and it is admitted that both as a strategist and as a tactician he has never been surpassed. No other general except Napoleon has won such decisive victories, and even the hero of Austerlitz might have been surprised at the capture of an army of one hundred and thirty thousand men. Whether he could have accomplished such feats as Wellington at Waterloo, Frederick at Leuthen, or Napoleon in his Italian campaigns, cannot be determined, for he never found himself placed in like emergencies.

Von Moltke had not at this time developed that system of tactics for which he will always be remembered,—a method of deploying troops so as to capture his adversary, as it were, in a net. The strategy of his campaign in 1866 can best be appreciated by considering the complications which it involved, and the absolute certainty with which his dispositions effected their purpose. He had six different armies to deal with, varying from twenty thousand to two hundred and fifty

---

[1] Faust, Part ii., Act v.

thousand men. The main Austrian army, under General Benedek, was extended from Cracow to the right bank of the Elbe, in Bohemia. Prince Clam-Gallas protected the valley of the Iser, a branch of the Elbe, with a force of sixty thousand men, much too weak for the purpose. The Bavarian army of forty-five thousand men was mobilized on the Danube. The Darmstadt-Nassau-Würtemberg army of nearly fifty thousand men occupied the valley of the Main; and the Hanoverian army of twenty thousand men threatened Brandenburg on the west. Within seven weeks after the declaration of war these enormous forces were either captured or dispersed by the Prussian troops.

Moltke's first object was to corner the Hanoverian army and render it innocuous. He conjectured that its commander would endeavor to form a junction with the Austrians, and, having the advantage in celerity, directed a force of ten thousand men to Eisenach, to take possession of the route to Bavaria. A similar force was directed from the Rhine against Hesse-Cassel, which served the double purpose of capturing the obstinate old Elector and preventing a junction between the Hanoverians and the army on the Main. General Falkenstein, with a single army corps, marched up the Main, defeated the army of the confederation, and drove it back into Würtemberg. Another Prussian army corps marched into Saxony, and, having taken possession of Dresden and Leipsic, proceeded to operate against the forces in Bavaria, apparently with orders to avoid an engagement, if possible. Although Von der Pfordten considered Austria an essential ingredient in German nationality to counterbalance Prussia, the Bavarian government acted at this time in a rather indecisive manner, and evidently preferred to avoid a collision with Prussia, if possible.

Von Moltke also judged correctly that General Benedek would remain on the defensive. His plan of campaign has been compared to the Waterloo campaign, but it is more like that of Marengo. Following in the steps of Frederick the Great, he directed Prince Frederick Charles, with the right wing and centre of the main Prussian army, to enter Bohemia from the north, while the crown prince with the left wing marched parallel to it on the east side of the Giant Mountains. According to this plan, in case General Benedek should invade Silesia it was expected that the crown prince's army would be able to sustain the attack until Prince Frederick Charles should come to his rescue. This, however, was not considered likely; and if the Austrian forces remained in Bohemia they would be obliged to concentrate somewhere on the line of the Elbe, in which case the crown prince would fall upon their flank, as Desaix did at Marengo. Such a plan, if carried out successfully, would prove fatal to the Austrian cause.

The numbers engaged on each side were nearly equal,— that is, about two hundred and fifty thousand men. On the 27th of June Prince Frederick Charles entered Bohemia. There was a slight conflict at Hünerwasser, and a pretty stiff battle at Münchengrätz with Clam-Gallas, in both of which the Prussians were successful. The battles of Nachod, Skalitz, Burkersdorf, and Schweinschädel were gallantly won by Prussian generals of division, but General Gablenz defeated the Prussians at Trautenau. He might have defeated them again at Burkersdorf but for an unfortunate despatch to retreat from General Benedek. It does not require much knowledge of military affairs to realize the immense mischief which such orders might occasion. General Benedek was a splendid fighter, and was credited with having saved the Austrian army from a rout at Solferino. He was given the chief command in 1866 according to a popular demand, but it is stated that he did not consider himself fitted for the position. In contrast with his categorical method let us compare the following extract from Von Moltke's directions to the crown prince and Prince Frederick Charles :

"If the initiative is taken on our part an occasion may easily arise for attacking the enemy in separate bodies with superior numbers, and for following up the victory in another direction from that assigned. But the uniting of all the forces for the decisive blow must always be kept in view. The commanders-in-chief must, therefore, from the moment they come face to face with the enemy, act according to their own judgment and the requirements of circumstances; and at the same time they must always consider their relations with the other army associated with them."[1]

Why could not Napoleon have given a similar order to Grouchy in the Waterloo campaign? An American who called on Von Moltke during the siege of Paris found nothing in his room but a table, a chair, and a map of France. It was by this constant simplification that he attained such breadth and clearness in his ideas.

In three days the Prussians had won five battles equal to those of Frederick in the second Silesian war. The Berliners were wild with joy, and Bismarck suddenly became the most popular man in the country. Such is human nature, and such the effect that may always be depended upon as the result of military success. Bismarck had calculated on this only too exactly. Long since, in his consultations with the king, he had said, "We must repose our confidence in the ancient spirit of Prussia,—in its military spirit." William I., Bismarck, and Von Moltke went at once to the scene of action, for they knew that the great crisis had now arrived,—a turning-point in the history of Europe. On the 2d of July they reached the head-quarters of Prince Frederick Charles, near Gitschin, and at a council of war it was decided to attack the Austrians, who were posted beyond Sadowa, on the following day. Communication was established with the crown prince, who promised to reach the field of battle by noon.

The Austrian officers had become satisfied in the recent encounters of the superiority of the needle-gun, and advised General Benedek against continuing the war, but the emperor encouraged Benedek to fight where he stood, and at the same time promised him the support of the army in Italy, which had already defeated the Italians at Custozza on the 24th of June. Benedek had collected over two hundred thousand men between Königgrätz and Sadowa, and held a strong position on a range of hills south of the latter place. He had the advantage of Von Moltke by nearly eighty thousand men,

---

[1] Von Sybel, v. 120.

and he hoped to crush him before the crown prince could arrive on the ground.

The battle of Sadowa, fought on the 3d of July, is an oft-repeated tale. Never since the conflict between Bajazet and Timour had such large forces been opposed to each other, and yet the loss of life was not nearly equal to that at Waterloo, Leipsic, or Gettysburg. The Austrian soldiers, encouraged by the presence of a commander in whom they had confidence, maintained the fight from early morning till one o'clock, and their desperate rushes against the Prussian lines explained the tactics by which Benedek expected to win the game. This was an imitation of the French tactics of 1859, and, like the attack by columns, is wholly ineffectual against repeating fire-arms. Fransecky's division of Branden-burgers and Magdeburgers suffered so severely, however, from these attacks that every seventh man in it was either killed or wounded. Every one has heard of Bismarck's solicitude for the old white-haired king, who sat on his horse like a marble statue, unmindful of the shells which flew screaming past him, and how Bismarck's keen eye was the first to discover the approach of the crown prince's army.

By this time most of Benedek's generals of division were fighting the battle on their own account, and without much regard for the commands of their superior. This was another natural consequence of Schwärzenberg's policy, and there could be no worse condition for an army in which to receive an unexpected attack. The crown prince, as fearless as his father, directed his forces perpendicularly to the Austrian right wing, which was almost immediately thrown into confusion. If Benedek had ordered the retreat at once, and protected it in person at the head of his reserves, he might even then have preserved his army for another battle. Instead of doing this, he wasted his reserves in a vain attempt to recover the captured positions ; so that when the final break came his decimated regiments had no chance to reorganize. The retreat soon became a rout, and full twenty thousand Austrians were taken prisoners. It has been estimated that if the crown prince had followed up his advantage with an energy equal to that of Gneisenau at Waterloo, the greater portion of the Austrian army would have been captured.

The honor of the victory belongs specially to Von Moltke, who planned the movements of both Prussian armies, and held his regiments in hand during the battle like men upon a chess-board; and next to him to General Fransecky, who sustained the severest attacks of the day without asking for the reinforcements which he knew were not to be had. Von Sybel states that the king took command in person; but if he had actually directed the movements of the army, Bismarck would not have warned him against exposing himself to danger. Bismarck, as he tells us himself, went to rest that night under a shed by the roadside.

It was not only a victory of Prussia over Austria, of the needle-gun over the musket, but, as in the time of Frederick the Great, it was a victory of efficient government over misgovernment; of reality over sham; of plain dealing over pretension; of progress over stagnation; of free schools over ignorance; of Protestantism and religious freedom over Catholicism and intolerance; of modern ideas over mediæval traditions; and, one might almost say, of veracity over dissimulation. Among those who were killed on the hills of Sadowa might be recounted the Prussian party of progress, which never, at least, showed its head again conspicuously. Progress was discovered to be in the direction which Bismarck had pointed out, and in the place of the Progressists arose a new party in all parts of Germany, the National Liberals, who gave Bismarck and his plans an enthusiastic support until the great work he had undertaken was fairly accomplished.

In 1808 Napoleon wrote to his brother Joseph, " To win a victory is nothing; to know how to make use of it is everything." Bismarck knew this as well, and he recognized the fact that Sadowa had upset the balance of power in Europe, and that there would be nothing but confusion until it was re-established upon an enduring basis. He realized that his severest struggle had yet to come; that every court in Europe would be filled with jealousy at the advantage which Prussia had gained, and that his work now must be to prevent this from taking the form of a European coalition which would wrest from Prussia her momentary supremacy. To consolidate that power and render it as impregnable as possible was the sufficient labor of a lifetime, and to this he now dedicated himself. The destiny of Prussia, however, was, as we have seen, always associated in his mind with the destiny of Germany as a whole. They were two similar ideas, one of which included the other, and, as with President Lincoln after the war for the Union, the interests of the states that had been subjugated were as serious a concern with him as those of Prussia itself. The statesman who sees deep into the future is not likely to be elated by success, and in the day of triumph Bismarck was the one cool head among those about him, who knew how to restrain the eagerness of friends and guard against the machinations of enemies.

The civilized world was electrified at the news of Sadowa, and Napoleon III. was astounded. He could not have been more so if a mine had exploded in the Tuileries. He had been playing with fire till his fingers were burnt. The opposition in the Chamber of Deputies knew enough of what was transpiring to be aware that he had encouraged Prussia in this bold stroke, and would be sure to fling it in his teeth. Let him turn as he would, the defeat of the Italians and the negotiations with Count Belcredi for the cession of Venetia were the only support he had to grasp at, and this was fragile enough. England was just now occupied with one of her frequent party revolutions, and the Tsar was as imperturbable as a Russian bear. The French Minister of Foreign Affairs is supposed to have advised a bold game of bluff,—a rather dangerous game to play against Bismarck, as Drouyn de l'Huys discovered afterwards to his cost. Count Lavalette, on the contrary, warned Napoleon that his army was in no condition to encounter the victorious Prussians, and that he had better keep on the shady side of fortune.

Bismarck was not surprised, though William I. may have been, on the 5th of July to receive a telegram from Napoleon III. offering his services as a mediator, and requesting, in the interests of European peace and harmony, that they should explain how they proposed to make use of their good fortune. Von Sybel's statement, that the king, on reading this despatch, made a memorandum of the terms of peace with Austria, which agreed substantially with those which were finally adopted, does not accord with Bismarck's own account,—namely, that he was obliged to make his utmost exertions at this time in opposing a project for the annexation of northern Bohemia.[1] It was decided to meet the advances of Napoleon in a friendly spirit, but his interference in German affairs was to be politely discouraged. The king wrote an autograph letter to his dear brother of France, and a despatch was sent to Baron Goltz to observe a respectful but firm attitude towards the French government. Von Beust believes that Napoleon would have pursued a more decisive policy at this critical moment but for a painful malady from which he was suffering, though he admits at the same time that there was a strong party, headed by Prince Napoleon, who were opposed to this.

Meanwhile Venetia had been surrendered to France by the Austrian government, in the hope that Napoleon could use it as a make-weight to detach Italy from the Prussian alliance, and thus enable Francis Joseph to withdraw a hundred thousand soldiers for the defence of Vienna. To the astonishment of both parties concerned, this move produced exactly the opposite effect from what was expected. Victor Emmanuel had lost all confidence in his former ally, and had already decided in his own mind to have nothing more to do with him. In spite of the persuasions of La Marmora, the adroit, facile man to whom the disaster of Custozza had chiefly been owing, the King of Italy sent a prompt declination of the province of Venetia to Napoleon, and ordered his generals to invade Venetia and take every advantage of the fortunate change in affairs.

The truth was that Bismarck, guided by his clear sense of

---

[1] Bismarck wrote: "It is I who have the thankless task of pouring water into the foaming wine, and of pointing out the fact that we do not live alone in Europe, but with three neighbors."

the situation, had fairly turned Italy around on its axis, and the Italians themselves were fully conscious of this. There was some competition in the carrying trade of the Mediterranean between Italy and France, but the antagonism in material affairs was very slight. In what might be called immaterial affairs, however, in regard to the temporal power of the pope, there was broad enough ground for disagreement. Louis Napoleon served a double purpose in sending Oudinot to suppress the Roman republic in 1849; it was for his interest that the republic should be suppressed, and he also won over to his party the strong moral influence of the Catholic clergy. From the earliest times it had been the policy of the popes to keep Italy divided, in order to prevent the growth of any political power which might neutralize their own. The anathemas which Dante hurled at Boniface VII. were succeeded by the cold-blooded analysis of Machiavelli, whom the terrors of the Inquisition could not prevent from attributing the misfortunes of his native country to the temporal power of the popes. It is true that for some centuries the spiritual authority of the popes was the main protection of Italian independence; but this had ceased to be of any avail long before Machiavelli's time, and political intrigue had taken its place. Memories of the grandeur of the Roman empire were still cherished among the Italians, and Mazzini, the Italian apostle of regeneration, had preached that Italy never could be lifted out of the mire except through national unity. Whatever he had been in the past, the pope now appeared as an obstacle to Italian progress, while Bismarck seemed like an agent divinely ordained for the purpose. It was only a Protestant power that could cordially co-operate with the Italian king and his cabinet, and between Prussians and Italians there was neither material rivalry nor mental antagonism. Hegel and other German writers on politics were studied by Italian statesmen during the period of reorganization in 1870, and the influence of German ideas on the present Italian government is plainly perceptible. Italy is the natural ally of Prussia.

Thus the Venetian manœuvre proved a failure. Neither

could Napoleon III. prevent the Prussian army from advancing on Vienna. The Austrian government, emboldened by Napoleon, asked for a truce, but made no offers for peace. Von Moltke pushed aside the army of Benedek, who had been superseded by the Archduke Albert, and besieged it in Olmütz. An attempt to rouse the Hungarians completely failed. They would only come to the support of the government under the guarantee of a state constitution. Finally, when the outposts of the Prussians came within sight of Vienna, the emperor applied to William I. for a cessation of hostilities. Bismarck now desired moderation, but in this wise conclusion he found himself opposed by the king, who considered his terms of peace humiliating to Prussia, while Von Moltke and most of the generals urged an attack on Vienna. William I., however, was finally won over by the crown prince, who suddenly found himself on the same ground as Bismarck, and gave the minister-president a magnanimous support.[1]

---

[1] Bismarck's account of this affair in his Memoirs makes a charming incident, creditable to both, but especially to the crown prince.

CHAPTER VII

BISMARCK ENLARGES PRUSSIA

In the negotiations that followed after Sadowa, the intervention of Napoleon, although it caused Bismarck continual anxiety, was actually of service to him in the way of mitigating the severity of the Prussian conditions. Neither did his cool head neglect the opportunity of notifying the Tsar in regard to passing events. Napoleon's action naturally caused an irritation in St. Petersburg, which was not without its influence in Vienna. Finally, on the 26th of July, the preliminaries were agreed upon at Nicolsburg, though the actual treaty between Prussia and Austria was not signed for more than three weeks later. The indemnity required of Austria—about twenty-five million thalers—was comparatively insignificant, and the Danes in Northern Schleswig were allowed to decide by a free ballot whether they should belong to Denmark or Germany. For the rest, Austria was to withdraw from the German confederation and from all interference in German affairs. Venetia was to be surrendered to Italy, of course, and with it a strip of territory was required to rectify the boundaries of Silesia. Saxony was obliged to pay a small indemnity and place its fortresses in the hands of the King of Prussia. Napoleon was unable to obtain the right for Saxony to join the South German Confederation, which was part of his programme; but he succeeded in preserving for King John his territory intact. Whoever has read Bismarck's memorial to William I. on July 27 must realize that he was the one who is properly to be credited with moderation, and that the opposition against him was such as only a strong man could have overcome.[1]

For the rest, the South German states were required to pay

---

[1] Von Sybel, v. 339.

an indemnity—probably that which Austria was unable to pay—and form a military confederation under the leadership of Bavaria. In regard to Nassau, Hanover, and Cassel, with its obstinate old Elector, Bismarck kept his promised word. The reigning princes were to be deposed and their territories incorporated in Prussia, but the reigning families were to retain their estates, or, as happened in the case of Hanover, receive a monetary compensation. Darmstadt was to be divided into two portions, of which Prussia was to absorb the northerly part. The other North German states were to form a close confederation with Prussia, having the King of Prussia for their military commander.

Thus the two portions of Prussia were united, and the nation as a whole strengthened. We have seen how ineffective the forces of the smaller German states proved during this campaign. In fact, North Germany was to become Prussia, and with a population of nearly thirty-five millions— seven times as great as in the Seven Years' War—it could bid defiance to any power in Europe. The division of Germany into three parts was calculated to remove the apprehensions of Louis Napoleon in regard to the balance of power; though Bismarck foresaw, as he afterwards stated, that South Germany would finally attach itself to the Prussian confederation as a piece of iron is attracted to the magnet. William I. wrote to his nephew, the Tsar, who expressed grave apprehensions lest Bismarck's bold stroke should prove injurious to the monarchical principle, a very manly letter, in which he said:

"I was obliged to regard the sentiments of my people and my army, and to adopt such measures as would insure the country against the return of a state of things similar to that through which we have just passed. To leave to those sovereigns a portion of their territory would have occasioned a dismemberment of the states that would have been more distressing to the inhabitants than anything else.

"You fear a German parliament and revolution. Believe me, nothing has done more harm to monarchical principles in Germany than the existence of these small and powerless dynasties, who prolong their life at the expense of national interest, who perform their duties as sovereigns very unsatisfactorily, and who compromise the reputableness of monarchical principles just as a numerous and indigent nobility bring reproach upon the dignity of the aristocracy. Public opinion is thoroughly convinced that these small monarchies naturally and necessarily stand in opposition to national interests. In the event of a fresh crisis the decadence of national institutions would have occasioned the most serious dangers." [1]

It is interesting to view this subject from the monarchical stand-point, and King William's statement has the cogency of a sincere belief that the work he was doing was for the good of Germany. Bismarck discovered soon after that it was not the monarchical principle which troubled the Tsar so much as the desire to obtain a share for himself in the surprising good fortune of his royal uncle at Berlin.

Great men who act in harmony with universal laws accomplish many things indirectly and unintentionally which are of advantage to the human race. The successors of Alexander the Great established an immense trade between Europe and India which never came to an end until the discovery of the South Cape; and Cæsar's conquest of Gaul may be said to have opened a door for civilization to walk into Northern Europe. So Bismarck's attack on Austria was at least as great an advantage to that empire as to Prussia itself. The defeat at Sadowa was the finest piece of good fortune that had ever happened to Francis Joseph. What advantage to him or to Austria was the Frankfort Diet or the German confederation? No revenues were derived from it, and it gave him no assistance in the Italian war of 1859, while it must have caused him continued anxiety and perplexity. It was merely the advantage of a name and of a certain facility for political intrigue,—two very dubious advantages. The continual change of ministry in the Vienna cabinet from 1859 to 1866 was an outward manifestation of the confusion which reigned within. Austria was placed in a false political posi-

[1] Von Sybel, v. 449.

tion,—like a man who enters politics without any actual talent for them,—and as soon as this came to an end the empire and its rulers suddenly found themselves at peace internally and at harmony with the rest of the world. Bismarck was never more far-sighted than when he told Count Karolyi categorically in 1862 that Austria's centre of gravity was not in Germany, but at Buda-Pesth.

The immediate condition after Sadowa was discouraging enough. The treasury was empty, and the government had no credit. The pay of the highest officers was in arrears, and Von Beust was not even remunerated for the expense of his embassy to Paris. An attempt to borrow several millions from the Catholic Church resulted only in the gratuity of one hundred thousand dollars for the care of wounded soldiers. The affairs of private individuals were not much better than those of the government. An expectation of revolution in Hungary, the insubordination of the Croats, and the Prussian occupation of Bohemia had reduced traffic to its lowest and most inevitable conditions. Force had always been required to hold the empire together, and its discordant elements seemed on the point of disintegration.

In this crisis a wise counsellor came to the assistance of Francis Joseph, and this was King John of Saxony. Educated in an hereditary antagonism to the Prussian government, King John was nevertheless one of the best Germans of his time, and during his life Saxony was in a very flourishing condition; as, for that matter, it still continues to be. He was a king in the old Homeric sense, and it was said of him that he had rather go without his own breakfast than that the meanest of his subjects should suffer for it.[1] He had long been aware of the evils from which Austria was suffering, and knew more about them than Francis Joseph could know. He now went to him, and said, as we may suppose, "I wish to lend you my best man. Von Beust is the right person to bring order for you out of this chaos." What argu-

---

[1] He was often to be seen at the university attending lectures on history and literature, so plainly dressed that only those well acquainted with his face could recognize him.

ments he used on the occasion have not transpired, but no doubt King John added some plain remarks on the necessity of an honest and efficient public service.

It is interesting to notice the transmigration of French liberal ideas to Saxony through the alliance with the first Napoleon, and their further transplantation to Vienna by Von Beust. It was only a Saxon or Bavarian statesman who could have accomplished this in the right way, so opposed was it to all the traditions of Austrian statecraft. We cannot enter here into the details of the complicated but harmonious system which Von Beust evolved out of what might be called the dregs of Metternich. Let it suffice to say that he satisfied the Hungarians with a well-devised local government, and with an equal representation in the Imperial Diet; he pacified the Czechs with a different system, which united them more closely to the central power, and arranged for the Croats and other ignorant Sclavonic tribes a government suited to their intelligence. These different systems he united in a comprehensive government machine, which, considering the diverse materials of which it is composed, has worked in an admirable manner till the present time. In all departments of the state he introduced such economy and efficiency that the Austrian government, from being one of the most corrupt and tyrannical in Europe, became so improved during his ministry that its superior was not to be found among constitutional monarchies. A thorough liberal in religion, he introduced religious toleration, and the Jesuits, who had been expelled by Prince Kaunitz one hundred years before, and had returned again under the dogmatic *régime* of Metternich, were once more sent about their business. In this he was assisted by a popular uprising against priestcraft in general, and the Austrian church became nationalized in the same manner that French Catholicism had been long since.[1]

Thus by Bismarck's diplomacy and Von Moltke's victory Venetia and Italy were liberated; Germany received a consti-

---

[1] An American resident at Innsbruck said to me in 1869, "The day of the priests is done in Austria."

tutional government; Jesuitism was suppressed, and Francis
Joseph permitted to enjoy the remainder of his life in peace
and tranquillity. The Hungarian exiles were recalled, and
Hungary received greater advantages than were demanded in
1848. Bismarck may be credited with having a direct hand
in the liberation of Hungary, for he wrote to Baron Goltz in
regard to Napoleon's offer of mediation that the Hungarian
constitution ought to be one of the conditions of peace.[1]
Whether he did this because it would please the Hungarians,
or because he thought it would weaken Austria and make
her government more dependent on Prussia, must remain a
matter of opinion. There was small room for sentiment in
Bismarck's politics, though we sometimes meet with touches
of it; but he evidently believed in the modern principle that
language and race should decide nationality as far as possible. That the Croats and Galicians should become independent in this manner was plainly impracticable.

During all this time Napoleon III. was twisting and writh-
ing like a man who is trying to escape from some kind of a
trap. After his autocratic intervention on July 5, and his
indignation at the King of Italy on the 8th, he sent for Baron
Goltz on the 11th and talked to him in a pitiful strain of the
services he had rendered the King of Prussia, and of the
friendly feeling he had for him. If Prussia and Italy, he said,
were to persist in their opposition they would expose him to
deep humiliation. However, he did not expect any cession
of territory, but only to have his wishes respected in the conclusion of peace. On the 13th again he notified Goltz that
some cession of territory on the Rhine would be indispensable, perhaps the boundaries of 1814, to efface the memory
of Waterloo. Goltz had been an admirer of the empress, and
she also had an interview with him,—much like a lovers'
quarrel,—in which she argued the case for France with feminine vehemence.[2] The French court was divided into oppos-

---

[1] Von Sybel, v. 288.

[2] The episode of the Prussian secretary of legation at Washington may be
remembered in this connection. Attractiveness to the fair sex is considered one
of the qualifications of a continental envoy.

ing factions, and the emperor, in his frail health, was dragged this and that way by them. Drouyn de l'Huys, bold and confident, imagined himself a second Bismarck, and that he could accomplish great things if he only had free rein. He was supported in this by the empress, who was instigated by the emissaries of the pope; for now that Victor Emmanuel's alliance with France was exchanged for one with a Protestant power, Pius IX. could see plainly that his temporal authority depended on a slight support. On the other side, Lavalette and Prince Napoleon saw the situation more clearly, and greatly dreaded stirring up such adversaries as Bismarck and Von Moltke, whom they recognized for what they really were,—two geniuses, such as only appear once or twice in a century.

Prince Napoleon, the son of Jerome, and the only member of the Bonaparte family who resembled the great Napoleon in appearance, is credited with having shown the white feather at the Crimea, but in the present emergency, and consistently until the surrender at Sedan, he chose a position which showed good political judgment so far as the affairs of France were concerned. He even went so far as to seek an audience with Baron Goltz, and to do what he was able in the way of furthering a speedy settlement between Prussia and Austria.

"'If you do not enter Vienna,' he said, significantly, 'the emperor will willingly favor you in your other conditions.' Then he wrote a memorial to the emperor, in which he said, 'We must expect that if Herr von Bismarck is threatened by France at his back, he will play out his last high card and come forth no longer as a Prussian, but as a German, and will call out the ardent passions of all Germany by proclaiming the imperial constitution of the revolutionary parliament of 1849. In what a position would he thus place us! What would then be our motive for engaging in a war against Prussia and all Germany?'"[1]

It is noteworthy that Bismarck used this same argument to the Tsar Alexander four weeks later. It contains the pith of

---

the matter, and is a rare contrast to Thiers's statement that the way for France to be strong was to keep her neighbors weak. The Parisians might call Prince Napoleon " *Plon-plon*" or whatever they pleased, but there were few among them who showed such good judgment. The French editors kept up a continual clamor at this time, creating as much confusion as possible, instead of allowing the dust to settle so that people could see the political prospect clearly. Newspapers seem occasionally like a necessary evil. The emperor finally agreed to Bismarck's terms of peace, and then, just as they were to be signed, he sent Benedetti to make new demands for territory on the Rhine.

On his return to Berlin, Bismarck went through the ovations customary on such occasions with the stolidity of a noncommissioned officer on parade. He had too many cares on his mind to respond freely to the popular enthusiasm. He had settled accounts with Austria for a time, but France, Italy, and Russia still remained to be considered, as well as the relations of Prussia with the South German states, and the organization of a North German confederation. The manner in which he played off the governments of these countries against one another in the negotiations that followed, and without any real duplicity on his own part, is remarkable enough. He received a donation from the indemnity fund of three hundred thousand thalers, or less than half as much as was voted by the British Parliament to the Duke of Wellington for defeating two of Napoleon's marshals.

Ten days after the conclusion of peace at Nicolsburg, Benedetti appeared in Berlin with a formulated demand from the French government for territory on the Rhine. This was made in writing, and included Rhenish Bavaria, Rhenish Hesse, and the fortress of Mainz, as well as the boundaries of 1814, with a favorable outlook in the direction of Luxemburg for the future.[1] The demand, though imprudent, was not so very unreasonable, since the districts named had for twenty years been included in French territory; but even if

---

[1] Müller's Political History, p. 357.

Bismarck could have persuaded William I. to agree to it, the result must have been a serious antagonism between Prussia and Bavaria, which could only be healed by compensating Bavaria in some other direction. In fact, the Prussian government had no right to surrender Bavarian territory,[1] and that Napoleon should have demanded it was a natural but clumsy blunder, for it placed a card in Bismarck's hand which he could play with telling effect at any future time. In respect to Bismarck's reception of Benedetti, the account given by Von Sybel, who was well acquainted with Bismarck, is more likely to be correct than the brusque treatment attributed to him by others. The laconic " Good, it is war, then," does not form an essential part of Prussian history; neither does the statement that Napoleon would be obliged to go to war in order to save his throne, which would indeed make him appear in a ridiculous light. Benedetti threw out a hint of this kind at the close of the interview, but on his own responsibility, not as coming from Napoleon. Otherwise the interview was a lengthy one, though Bismarck firmly and decisively refused to entertain the French proposals. " If you force us into a war," he said, " we will make peace with Austria and the South German states, and invade France with six hundred thousand men, and we will take Alsace and Lorraine away from you." This was the end of the game of bluff, and also the end of Drouyn de l'Huys's political career. He sent in his resignation a few days after Benedetti's return to Paris, and has never been heard from since.

After this General Manteuffel was despatched to St. Petersburg, in order to smooth down the Russian bear. Manteuffel was a soldier-statesman of the old Prussian school, and much more conservative than Bismarck himself. He was just the man to sympathize with Alexander in his reactionary moods. The Tsar received him rather coolly, and stated that, in spite of his friendliness for King William, he was much displeased

---

[1] Bestowing a piece of the Rhineland on the house of Wittelsbach was a shrewd device in the Congress of Vienna, for it wholly changed the traditional policy of Bavaria.

with Bismarck's revolutionary proceedings. The deposition
of a king and two grand dukes was a dangerous innovation,
aimed directly against the divine right of kings, and calculated to undermine the royal authority in all countries. An
interview with Gortchakoff led to a similar discussion, which
the Russian minister suddenly changed to a conversation on
the peace of Paris and the Russian restrictions on the Black
Sea. Manteuffel judged from this exactly where the shoe
pinched, and sent a telegraphic summary to Bismarck, who
now appeared as firmness itself. "We have agreed," he said,
"to grant favorable conditions to Würtemberg and Darmstadt, out of consideration for Russia, but we can give no
attention to scruples. Pressure from abroad will drive us to
the proclamation of the imperial constitution of 1849. If
there is to be a revolution, we shall prefer to make it ourselves." At the same time he gave Manteuffel to understand
that when the right occasion arose for abrogating the Black
Sea restrictions Prussia would be ready to support her northern
ally. Friendly letters between the king and the Tsar concluded the Russian difficulty.

The South German states had now to be dealt with, and
here the French demands of August 5 served Bismarck as a
two-edged sword. The king wished to annex Bavarian Franconia,—the region from which the Franks formally set out to
conquer Gaul,—but Bismarck was prudently opposed to this,
because it would aggravate the ill feeling of the Bavarians
towards Prussia, and arouse an antagonism which might not
subside for a hundred years. He accordingly used Benedetti's proposals as an argument with William I. in favor of a
more conciliatory policy, and with the Bavarian court for the
purpose of obtaining a military alliance.

The peace preliminaries between Prussia and Austria had
left the South German states wholly independent, but it had
practically left them defenceless, and they now began to realize
this. The Grand Duke of Baden, who was personally friendly
to Prussia, saw plainly enough that Napoleon III. could now
take possession of his country without opposition. No portion of Germany had suffered so much from French invasions

LIFE OF BISMARCK

as Baden, and he applied at once for admission into the
Prussian confederation. Bismarck proved to him that such
a departure would tend to aggravate their relations with
France, and be contrary to the understanding with Austria
and Russia; but he intimated that there was another method
by which the desired result might be attained.

The meeting between Bismarck and Von der Pfordten was
a memorable one. There was no German statesman whom the
Prussian minister respected so much. He explained to Von
der Pfordten the king's ultimatum for Franconia, and for a
war indemnity of thirty million florins. Then he showed him
the proposition of Napoleon III., signed by Drouyn de
l'Huys, for the surrender of Rhenish Bavaria to France, and
offered him his choice between the cession of Franconia and
an offensive and defensive alliance with Prussia. It is easy to
imagine Von der Pfordten's decision, and it is said that the two
prime ministers embraced each other after the German fashion.
The same arrangement was concluded with Baden; and Würtemberg, lying between the two states, followed as a matter of
course. The "puffy" old Duke of Darmstadt, who depended
for his immunity on the friendship of the Tsar, and for his
income from the gambling hells of Hesse-Homburg, was also
brought to a realizing sense of his dependence on Prussia by
Napoleon's proposals of August 5.

This was Bismarck's master-stroke, for it gave William I.
the command of all the German forces, excepting those in
Austria. Von Beust has denounced it in his Memoirs as an
infraction of the peace preliminaries and the treaty of Prague,
which was signed ten days later, without the least suspicion
on the part of the Austrian or French governments of Bismarck's military convention. He compares Bismarck to Macchiavelli, and calls it a piece of unheard-of duplicity. Von
Beust did not realize, apparently, that Napoleon's territorial
demands after the signing of the preliminaries had upset the
political basis on which the peace conditions were grounded;
that if the South German states were in any way dissatisfied
with the conditions of the treaty of Prague, they had sufficient time to enter their protest against them. There was

nothing in the treaty which precluded the South German states from making alliances wherever they could find them; and though the alliance of Prussia differed from other military alliances in placing the South German troops under the command of Prussian officers, this was considered essential, in order that they should be properly instructed in Von Moltke's tactics, and so that the German army could act together as a whole. The best evidence of the success of this policy is that the Crown Prince of Saxony, who fought against Prussia at Sadowa, was soon after placed in command of a whole army corps of the confederation; nor is it credible that Bismarck exerted undue pressure on the South German states in this matter, for in that case their ministers could have easily blocked his game by notifying Louis Napoleon.[1]

The peace of Prague, with whose terms we are already familiar, closed the last scene in this great historical drama.

---

[1] "In 1849 was the time to do what Bismarck did in 1866 in the South German governments,—to treat the Italian states with consideration, but to insist on their binding themselves by treaty to a state of dependence on Austria." — *Von Beust*, i. 361.

CHAPTER VII

THE chief obstacle to parliamentary government in Germany lies in the national characteristic which is called particularism. "Every German," said Bismarck, "has an idea of his own, which he holds on to like a nugget of gold." This prevents their fusing together in political parties, as the English and Americans do, and it is natural that the better educated they are the more prominent this peculiarity appears. The old map of Germany—large states and small states, states separated by other states, and states within states—was a very good picture of the German mind. The tendency of national unity has been to diminish the number of political parties in Germany, but they are still numerous, and their description is bewildering. At the same time the Germans have a national impulse,—an idea of their destiny as a nation,—and this unites them at times, so that they seem to act almost like one man, after which, having accomplished the special work in hand, they relapse into particularism again. This is especially true of the Prussians.

After the peace of Prague, Bismarck found his countrymen in this unified condition. The National Assembly passed his budget with but few dissenting votes, and when a committee from the House waited on the king to announce this fortunate event, his Majesty remarked that he hoped that the preceding disagreement between himself and his people would never happen again. It never has happened since, and this goes far to prove that the era when Bismarck first accepted the presidency was a revolutionary one, a bloodless conflict between the people and their government, in which the government for once was in the right, and exceptional measures were justifiable.

The army appropriations, although somewhat increased,

passed both Houses without difficulty. The Prussian government does not communicate state secrets to the National Assembly, but enough of the attitude of Napoleon was generally known to stir Prussian patriotism to its depths. Great confidence was felt in Bismarck's political wisdom, and the current of popular prejudice was now in his favor, as in the struggle with Austria he was obliged to contend against it.

The National Assembly made short work of the annexation of Cassel, Hanover, Nassau, Lower Darmstadt, and Frankfort; for the conservatives wished to do this in order to strengthen the government's military power, and the opposition because they expected to recruit their ranks with dissatisfied delegates from those states. In this matter Bismarck appeared to great advantage in comparison with a numerous body of members, who advocated the incorporation of all North Germany in the Prussian state, without regard to the fear of God or the opinion of the world at large. Nothing could be more unprincipled than such a proposition, and Bismarck answered it in a telling speech, in the course of which he said: [1]

"So far as our confederate allies are concerned, we have had only few, and those were weak; yet not only our duty, but also wisdom, bids us to keep our word even to the smallest of them. The more unsparingly Prussia shows that she can sweep her enemies from the map of Germany, the more exact must she be in fulfilling her promises to her friends. It is precisely in South Germany that the belief in our political honesty will be of great importance."

The sovereigns of those petty states, of whom William I. wrote to the Tsar that they were as injurious to the monarchical principle as an indigent nobility was to the cause of aristocracy, could not complain that Bismarck had not warned them in time what the consequences would be of giving their support to Austria; but he now proved himself better than his word in offering them a liberal pecuniary compensation for

---

[1] Von Sybel, v. 494.

the loss of their titles and landed estates. The Landtag was indisposed to grant this, though the revenues from the annexed territories would more than compensate for it in the difference between a national system and a provincial system of government, and Bismarck was obliged to exert all the influence he could bring to bear in order to carry the measure through. Great sympathy was felt for the King of Hanover, on account of his blindness; but this treatment was much more considerate than the first Napoleon's had been on similar occasions in disposing of conquered territory.

The organization of the North German confederation, which differed but little from the Prussian state itself, introduced a new element into German politics, that of universal suffrage; and in this Bismarck was opposed not by the Progressists, but by some of his most faithful supporters in the National Assembly. Seven years later Dr. Frederick Kapp, author of "The Hessians in America," and secretary of the Prussian Landtag, spoke of it as the iron chancellor's one serious mistake. Bismarck's belief was that if the laboring classes felt that they had a direct influence in the government, they would be more loyal, patriotic, and contented for it, and would serve to counterbalance the influence of those local politicians who were always looking to sectional advantages. In the old Germanic theory of government the king, the nobility, and the commons were compared to the three sides of a triangle, which mutually support and restrain one another. It was supposed that the nobility and the commons would be sure to restrain the king from extravagant and tyrannical actions; that the king would unite with the commons to restrain the rapacity of the nobles; and that the king and the nobility would be able to prevent popular revolutions. It may have been this mediæval idea to which Bismarck reverted in his mind; but the laboring classes form in reality a fourth division of the body politic, which have to be considered in a different way. The modern world differs essentially from the mediæval in its accumulation of wealth and the consequent opportunity for luxurious living. The tiller of the soil in the Middle Ages might envy the social advantages of the baron, but it was a hopeless envy, for he knew it would be impossible for him to fill the same position. At the present day the case is different: men care little for titles if they can only obtain means for luxurious living and the education of their children. It is this which makes socialism so dangerous at the present time, and will make it more dangerous in the time to come. Thus far Bismarck's suffrage law has not answered his expectations, but its ultimate effect still remains to be unfolded.

The organization of the North German confederation was not a difficult task, since it merely applied the principles of Prussian polity to a few smaller states. Delegates to the North German Reichstag were elected on the 12th of February, 1867, and on the 24th they met together in the king's palace at Berlin, where William I. opened the assembly with a congratulatory speech full of confidence in the future of Germany, and with great expectations of German civilization. A number of unfriendly delegates from Saxony, Hanover, and Darmstadt made this legislative body more difficult to deal with than the Prussian Landtag had proved to be, but after seven weeks' discussion the government constitution was adopted with a few simple changes, and the assembly dissolved.

In the general congratulations of this period we hear of only one dissatisfied person, and that was the Crown Prince of Prussia. From being a firm adherent of constitutional methods during the storm and stress of Schleswig-Holstein, he suddenly changed his tone and now appeared as the advocate of arbitrary power. He informed Bismarck that there were too many kings in Germany,—his father was the only real king,—and the others ought to be reduced to the dignity of grand dukes. When Bismarck suggested that it might be difficult to persuade them to agree to this, he replied that they must be made to agree to it.[1] Bismarck may have concluded that the crown prince's duties as commander of the second army did not give him sufficient occupation.

---

[1] Von Sybel, however, does not give his authority for this conversation, though it agrees with a later statement in the crown prince's diary.

LIFE OF BISMARCK

After all other affairs had been satisfactorily arranged, a peculiar difficulty arose in respect to the settlement with Saxony. On the occasion of Von Beust's retirement from the Saxon ministry King John wrote him a cordial and gracious letter of regret, expressing his appreciation of Von Beust's long service in the Saxon government, and of his valuable assistance during the perilous period through which the state had lately passed. This letter Von Beust afterwards injudiciously published in Vienna, where it served to make him popular, but at the same time aroused a hostile feeling to King John at the Prussian court. Von Beust had been the ablest and most outspoken of the opponents of Prussia at the Frankfort Diet, and this letter was considered in the light of an incendiary document calculated to excite ill feeling between Prussia and the South German states. The King of Saxony was, therefore, called to account for it, and bluntly informed by Bismarck that he should consider himself fortunate not to share the fate of the King of Hanover. As the irritation excited by Von Beust's letter subsided after a time; as the Prussian demands were also mitigated; and as King John had public opinion everywhere on his side, the negotiations were finally concluded by Bismarck with the payment of a moderate indemnity and the transfer of the Saxon fortresses.

THE LUXEMBURG INTRIGUE.

Napoleon III. realized, after the refusal of his demand for more territory in August, that Bismarck was not the man to be caught with chaff or intimidated by threats. He saw plainly enough that if he was to obtain any portion of Rhenish Prussia or Bavaria he would have to do it by force of arms. He began at once to reorganize the French army, and recalled the troops which were supporting Maximilian in Mexico. Meanwhile a design occurred to him, or to his counsellors, by which he might make an entering wedge into Prussian territory by a little expenditure of French gold. The duchy of Luxemburg, situated between Lorraine and Rhenish Prussia, belonged by hereditary right to the King of Holland, but as a part of the German confederation it had since 1849 been garrisoned by Prussian troops. Napoleon now thought of purchasing the King of Holland's right, if the Prussian government would only agree to withdraw its garrison, and then Benedetti was again despatched to Berlin to sound Bismarck on the subject.

There are conflicting statements in regard to the negotiations which followed. Professor Müller affirms that Bismarck treated the proposal in a dilatory manner,—that is, he deferred it from time to time by such pretexts as are customary in diplomatic circles. Benedetti afterwards claimed that he drew up a treaty, at Bismarck's dictation, between Prussia and France, which included the purchase of Luxemburg from the King of Holland, and the consolidation of Belgium with France, in return for an offensive and defensive alliance. If Benedetti allowed himself to be fooled in this manner he was a most unskilful ambassador, for the possession of Belgium by Napoleon would have irritated the British government very greatly, and have alarmed the King of Holland still more. The latter would hardly be inclined to yield his rights in Luxemburg to a power whom he would be obliged to face on the Rhine and Scheldt. This was supplementing Luxemburg with a right which would be likely to defeat the project, and it is certain that if Bismarck agreed to it at any time, the fact was not mentioned by the King of Holland in the subsequent negotiations. The approval of his sovereign was a side-door through which Bismarck could always retreat from any temporary agreement. It is by no means improbable that Benedetti afterwards made up the story about Belgium in order to excite prejudice against Prussia in Holland and England; but, as the case stands now, there is no way of determining anything about it. Napoleon's adherents, and a number of German writers also, have always insisted that Benedetti was brutally deceived.

The action of the Prussian government, as soon as the matter came before the world, was prompt and decisive enough. In February, 1867, the subject was communicated to the King of Holland by the French ambassador, and he at once agreed to the proposition, provided Napoleon would guarantee his country against Prussian encroachment. This was also for Napoleon's interest, and as Benedetti had given out the impression in Paris that Bismarck was ready to fall into line, Baron Goltz was notified that if Prussia would withdraw the troops which garrisoned Luxemburg the existing tension between the two governments might be considered at an end.

Bismarck, however, promptly and decisively declined to do this, and a resolution introduced into the North German Reichstag to the effect that neither Luxemburg nor any other German territory should be ceded to a foreign power was carried through with enthusiasm. How dangerous the game was which Napoleon was playing may be judged from the fact that a strong party in Berlin, with Von Moltke at its head, advocated war with France as the only effectual method of stopping the political machinations from that quarter. Bismarck, however, saw another method of playing check to Napoleon again, and considered it too soon after the Austrian campaign to depend on the cordial support of the South German states.

Between these two parties the king finally decided in favor of peace. That he should have been averse to war at his time of life is not surprising, though he no doubt considered peace the wiser course.

The convention of great powers which decided the political relations of Belgium and Holland in 1839 had guaranteed in that treaty the independence of Luxemburg. Bismarck was aware of this, and he now appealed to the governments of Austria, Russia, and Great Britain to carry out its provisions. This speedily resulted in a conference at London, to which Napoleon III. and the King of Holland were invited, nor could they decline to send representatives. The French envoy argued that Prussia had already violated the treaty by maintaining a garrison in Luxemburg; but the conference finally decided that the King of Holland had no right to dispose of the duchy as if it were his own personal property, and William I. was requested to withdraw his troops from it, which was accordingly done. Von Beust's attempt at a compromise, by proposing that the strip of French territory, from five to ten miles in width, which was ceded to Belgium after Waterloo, should be restored to France, only served to arouse great indignation among the Belgians. The neutrality of Belgium was guaranteed for the future, but Luxemburg was permitted to enter into the Zollverein, or German customs union.

This was in May, 1867, and Louis Napoleon had been outwitted three times within ten months. The French court was furious, and Napoleon III. openly declared that Count Bismarck had hocussed him. Why he should make such a confession, for which no one would be likely to pity him, can only be explained by his wishing to excite the Parisians to a higher pitch of animosity against Prussia. However, the international exposition, which was designed to attract public attention from the mistakes of 1866, and give the appearance of external magnificence to the hollow shell of the Second Empire, was now coming on, and Napoleon was obliged to repress his resentment until after that had passed. All the crowned heads of Europe must be invited to it, as well as their prime ministers, and such a love-feast as they must have had there does not often happen in this world.

It was more like a battle-field than a love-feast. They were all more or less in danger of assassination, and no one knew this better than Bismarck. It has been affirmed that he did not wish to go, not so much from fear of death as from the chance of having his plans all brought to naught by the stray bullet of a fanatic. Then the idea of making himself agreeable to a man whom he cordially despised, like the French emperor, must have been highly distasteful to him. The whole business was full of pretence and hypocrisy,—a grand piece of political clap-trap. No one would suspect Napoleon of conniving at unlawful machinations against the persons of his enemies, but it was not impossible that some desperate Bonapartist might try to immortalize himself in that manner. The lot fell, however, to the Tsar Alexander, who was shot at and missed, by a Polish exile, while riding in the procession,—an event not likely to startle him into a more favorable policy towards French annexation on the Rhine. Bismarck rode beside Gortchakoff in the procession, and had ample opportunities to discuss points of mutual interest in the policy of their respective governments.

The secret arrangement between William and Alexander has never been revealed, and probably never will be, but the fact that such was made, some time between 1867 and 1870, is not to be questioned. It is referred to indefinitely in Hesekiel's biography of Bismarck, which was published previous to the Franco-German war, and referred to by Alexander in the telegram sent to William I. on hearing of the Austro-German alliance, " Your Majesty seems to have forgotten the promises of 1870." Dr. Frederick Kapp said in 1873,[1] " Bismarck's great move which upset Napoleon's calculations was the bargain he made with Gortchakoff. He said, ' If you will leave us to deal with France now, we will show you a good turn in the time that is coming.' " This mutual arrangement was carried out to perfection, so that Von Beust, though he noticed Gortchakoff's coolness towards him and Napoleon, was even led to believe that Russia was favorable to an alliance between France and Austria. The Tsar had no objections against setting a trap for the author of the Crimean War to fall into, provided this also agreed with the interests of the Russian empire; but if he was to serve as a protector to Prussia in the war, he expected recompense for it. In what shape was he to receive this ?

It could not have been simply a revocation of the Black Sea restrictions. That by itself would not have been enough. Von Beust asks, " Why should the Tsar depend on Prussia for a revocation of the treaty of Paris, when Austria offered to arrange this for him in 1867 ?" The reason is plainly because Austria could not bid high enough for the Tsar's friendship. Alexander was not a Solomon, but he was too wise to join a coalition against Prussia, which would finally result to his own disadvantage. No wonder that Gortchakoff

---

[1] In conversation with the writer.

was cool towards Von Beust. It is clear from Dr. Kapp's remark that in 1873 Bismarck's debt to the Tsar had not yet been liquidated in spite of the Black Sea reversion. Alexander has been popularly credited with being a peace-loving Tsar, but it was natural that he should desire to regain the ground which his father had lost; also, perhaps, to liberate the Christian states which are situated between the Balkans and the Danube from Turkish rule. It would not have been for Austria's interest to encourage this programme. It was Louis Napoleon's fatal delusion that he could persuade Alexander to withdraw from the Prussian alliance.

BUILDING THE REICH.

Bismarck returned to Berlin after the exposition to take up his work again of strengthening the German confederation. His policy now was a defensive one; to establish a central government for the German people which should not only rest on a firm basis, but prove advantageous and give satisfaction to the component parts of this extensive system. This was his first principle, and his second was to avoid foreign complications. At what time he became interested in the writings of Alexander Hamilton is uncertain, but it is known that he held them in very high estimation, and had a professorship established in one or more German universities, for instruction in the federative principle of government, as elaborated by that rare American genius. It is even affirmed by his friends that Bismarck considered Hamilton the greatest statesman of the last hundred years; and it is certain that the federal principle is the only one by which national unity can be made to harmonize with local and sectional interests. We may begin to appreciate the debt which we owe to Hamilton in America, when we consider that both Germany and Austria have been reconstructed, and in a manner regenerated, by the principles which he enunciated. France and Italy, being homogeneous nations, do not require its application, but who can doubt that Gladstone would have succeeded better in dealing with the Irish question if he had been willing to accept a lesson from statesmen on this side the Atlantic?[1]

Bismarck, like a good architect, did not attempt to build his edifice too rapidly. For this reason he had left the Schleswig-Holstein question still open until a favorable moment should come for its final settlement. It will be remembered that by a provision of the treaty of Prague the people of North Schleswig were permitted to decide by a majority vote whether they should belong to Denmark or to Prussia. The question was not a very important one, for the province is small and its inhabitants chiefly farmers. There seems to have been all through this period a peculiar obstinacy in the Danish government, which was the cause of serious losses to the state,—in the present instance, with the Copenhagen cabinet refusing to accede to Bismarck's proposition that the voting should take place under the auspices of a mixed Prussian and Danish commission. The Danish government insisted that the people of North Schleswig could do their own voting without any assistance from Prussia; to which Bismarck coolly replied that the voting should not take place except under well-regulated conditions.[2]

This gave the French emperor another opportunity to interfere,—in behalf of the oppressed Danes. He was politely informed, however, that the stipulations of the peace of Prague only concerned Prussia and Austria, and that there was no occasion for his taking further interest in the subject.

Bismarck's next move was to conclude a commercial treaty with the South German states. After the first excitement of Sadowa and the military alliance, a reaction had set in at Munich and Stuttgart against Prussia. The Bavarian nobility

---

[1] Dr. Kapp once said, "I look upon Hamilton as a greater statesman than Bismarck. When I first went to New York I wanted to know about American politics, and I was advised to read Jefferson; but I soon found that all those Tammany fellows were quoting Jefferson, so then I changed to Hamilton, and then I discovered where the United States government came from." Jefferson was always opposed to centralization.

[2] Which side was right in this discussion is uncertain, for we do not know the Danish account of it; but Bismarck's demand would seem to have been reasonable.

were connected by marriage and other social ties—always a powerful factor in political organizations—with the Austrian nobility and gentry. At the same time the priests, acting under orders from the Vatican, started up an anti-Prussian agitation among the common people, so that Americans travelling in Bavaria were surprised at the violent antipathy to the North German confederation, not knowing the source from whence it arose. It was natural that the appointment of Prussian officers to important commands in the military service should give offence; though this was indispensable if the army was to be reorganized in an efficient manner. Von der Pfordten, who always remained faithful to what he considered the true interests of Germany, and who had among other trials the giddy young king to deal with, found it difficult to maintain his ground.

In Baden, on the other hand, there was an active movement favorable to Prussia, and Bismarck found no difficulty in having the whole army of the Palatinate placed under the command of a Prussian general, who was only responsible to the Grand Duke. He likewise obtained the appointment of a Prussian professor at Heidelberg to lecture on the French Revolution, the wars of Napoleon, and the federal system of government as applied to national unity. In Würtemberg public sentiment was like the man who could not agree with his neighbors. The Swabians were always at odds with the Bavarians, but disliked the Prussians even more. Situated close to Switzerland, they had imbibed much of the spirit of the freedom-loving mountaineer,—an influence plainly perceptible in the verses of their national poet, Schiller. They were, perhaps, less favorably inclined towards the Prussians out of opposition to the people of Baden, and this feeling extended as well to the nobility and to the government. According to the treaty of Prague the South German states were permitted to form a confederation of their own, if they preferred to do so, and Von der Pfordten made some tentative negotiations with this end in view. It was found, however, that Baden much preferred to join the North German confederation, and that the Würtembergers were quite as reluctant to place their military force at the disposal of a Bavarian general. Professor Müller, himself a Würtemberger, says:

"A confederation embracing not more than eight or nine millions, and set between three great powers, would be unable to stand on its own feet and pursue an independent policy. It would be sure to become the sport of foreign intrigue,—now begging favors in Paris or Vienna, now asking succor from Berlin, and disappearing with the first storm that swept the face of Central Europe."

It was openly declared in the Würtemberg assembly that if the kingdom was to be coalesced with any political body it should be with a strong power like Prussia, and not with a weak one like Bavaria. There was good sense in this, such as any one could understand, and it showed the inevitable tendency in which German politics were drifting.

Bismarck perceived that events were taking such a shape as he would like to have them, but he knew that time was required to ripen this movement in the South German governments, and that any decided interference on his part might only result in the gathering of green fruit. Meanwhile he had a cure in hand for the unsettled condition of their affairs, and this was a commercial treaty. The three inland states, separated by hundreds of miles from the sea, were obliged to depend on their neighbors for the transportation of imports. Baden could obtain this traffic through France, but likewise possessed the power of exacting a duty from the other two. Bavaria could import through Austria, but by a longer route, and necessarily with more expense. Bismarck could obviate this difficulty by conferring on the South German states the same advantages of the Zollverein enjoyed by the North German confederation. Already on June 3 he had held a conference with Von der Pfordten, Varnbuler, and the Baden minister at Berlin, in which he proposed the adoption of uniform measures for imports and the regulation of national custom-houses for all the German states excepting Austria. Such an advantageous measure was eagerly snapped at, and on Bismarck's return from Paris it was agreed that the southern states should send delegates to the North German parliament, in number according to the ratio of their population, who should vote on all commercial questions which came before the house, but not on political questions.

Here was German national unity established in respect to military service and commercial rights, and yet it could not be said that the peace of Prague had been violated or that the South German states had not acted of their own free will. To constitute Germany a nation there only remained to empower the representatives of Würtemberg, Bavaria, and Baden with full authority to vote on all subjects that came before the Reichstag, and to give the formality of a title to the whole. The French might growl at this, and the Bavarian nobility howl at Bismarck, but every merchant and shopkeeper in Munich and Stuttgart was now a Prussian at heart, and the industrial classes of South Germany were rapidly forming a solid phalanx to resist foreign interference. The industrial interests of these states did not differ essentially from those of Prussia, but in the old Frankfort Diet, with delegates appointed by the sovereigns, there was less opportunity for a free expression of opinion.

The elections in 1867 showed a cordial endorsement of Bismarck's policy. The Conservatives retained their usual strength in Prussia, while the opposition lost more than thirty seats, which were mostly won by the National Liberals, and it was noticed that the representatives from the annexed districts of Hanover, Cassel, and Schleswig-Holstein belonged nearly all to this new party. With three legislative bodies, the Prussian Landtag, the North German Reichstag, and the National Customs Union, to deal with, Bismarck had his hands more than full of legislative business, and how he could have carried it through seems wonderful enough.

This second North German Reichstag might be compared with the earlier sessions of the American Congress, before partisan spirit and trade politics had debased and cheapened our legislative currency. It was composed for the most part of patriotic men, who gave their time and strength for the good of their country, and who met together to establish, in all sincerity, the foundation of a new era in German history. Nevertheless it was rather a difficult legislative body to deal with for this very reason. Von Beust considered the English and Belgian the only successful parliamentary governments in Europe, because in those countries there are two political parties, either of which is ready and able at any time to assume the management of public affairs. In the German, Austrian, and Italian parliaments such parties do not exist, for they would have no opportunity to assume the direction of affairs. As they have no opportunity for executive action, so there is no party discipline,—little or no subordination of the individual. The more high-minded men are, the less willing they are to subordinate their opinions to the judgment of others, and the more likely to resent external interference as an infringement of personal liberty. The earnest desire of the Reichstag of 1868 to do their work in the most thorough and effective manner resulted in a continuous crossfire of amendments and counter-amendments to every measure which was proposed, and this not only seriously impeded the progress of public business, but sometimes resulted in perverting the character of the legislation in such a way as to defeat the very object for which it was intended. There was a constant tendency, especially among the National Liberals, for parties to resolve themselves into separate groups, and the smaller the group the more uncompromising and difficult to reason with. It was only a Bismarck or a Gladstone that could finally have succeeded in dealing with such a political body; the latter by his oratorical skill and rare tact in harmonizing conflicting elements, and the former through his logical understanding of the situation and his inflexible determination to make others perceive this also. Bismarck was the Olympian schoolmaster of the Reichstag.

One of the first questions which came before the North German assembly was a measure in regard to the deposed King of Hanover, who was well known to be making use of the gratuity of the Prussian government to support a Hanoverian legion in France with the funds he had thus been supplied with, and his adherents could congratulate themselves on the fact that Prussia was providing them with the means to make war against the North German confederation. Bismarck had inquired of Queen Victoria, who very properly took an interest in the fortunes of her relative,what sum would be sufficient for the exiled king to live on an equality with an English prince, and she had replied that a hundred thousand pounds a year would be enough.[1] Bismarck had exceeded this somewhat, but prudently had retained in the Prussian exchequer the principal from which this income was derived. Besides the support of a body of troops in France, it was notorious that certain German newspapers were subsidized by the ex-king to stir up an agitation against the new confederation.

Bismarck, in his appeal to the Prussian Landtag for funds to remunerate the deposed sovereigns, had laid special stress on the point that their acceptance of the money would give to the transaction the legal character of a bargain, which would be likely to invalidate any future claims they might make to their former possessions. The King of Hanover, however, after receiving the gratuity, declined to make any formal renunciation of his sovereignty; but Queen Victoria, in the English negotiations on the subject, with great good sense, held to Bismarck's position, declaring that this was of little consequence, since, by accepting the money, he would be bound in honor not to interfere with the North German confederation. Duke Adolph, of Nassau, who had received nine million thalers in return for the confiscation of his territory, accepted the conditions under which it was offered to him and gave the Prussian government no further trouble.

The behavior of the King of Hanover, on the contrary, placed Bismarck in a peculiar position. As the Reichstag was not in session at the time the convention with Queen Victoria was concluded, the Minister of Finance had taken the required funds from a loan authorized in 1866 for army expenditures; and it was necessary now to obtain the sanction

---

[1] August Belmont once stated that he did not know how he could spend more than a hundred thousand dollars a year, and Froude said, " There are millionaires in New York who have the income of an English prince, but they are by no means so extravagant."

of this act by a vote of the Reichstag. In the face of the Hanoverian legion it was rather difficult to do this. There were complaints of ministerial arbitrariness, a breach of trust, and misplaced confidence, without allowing for the exceptional conditions under which the transaction had taken place. The government was in a position not unlike that of a man who has made purchases with borrowed money and is unable to repay it. Bismarck made as little as possible of the Hanoverian legion, and enlarged on the advantage to Germany of appearing before the great powers in a magnanimous light; so that, with the help of the Hanoverians and Schleswig-Holsteiners, the bill was finally passed.

It was not long, however, before the same subject came up again. The inimical proceedings of the King of Hanover had been placed beyond question, and Bismarck wished the treaty with him to be reversed, and the income which had been guaranteed in it divided between a secret-service fund and a fund for a local assembly in Hanover for the transaction of business peculiar to that province. These two measures were introduced separately, and met with vigorous opposition on all sides. The National Liberals supported the confiscation, but wished to have the property of the King of Hanover turned over to the Prussian state for the amelioration of taxes. The Conservatives, on the other hand, objected to the Hanoverian state assembly as a luxury that would only be enjoyed by that province, whereas the various provinces of the old kingdom of Prussia possessed no such advantage. Dr. Windhorst, the Hanoverian clerical, denounced the confiscation of King George's funds as a violation of the sacred rights of monarchy.

The Liberals, however, found satisfaction in the advocacy of a state assembly, as they foresaw it would make an entering wedge in the direction of local self-government, and they finally concluded that this was more important than the question of a secret-service fund. The Conservatives, to whom the favor of royalty was as a second nature, were brought to terms by William I., who realized as well as Bismarck the advantage at that moment of conciliating the Hanoverians, who may be said to constitute the heart of Germany. In this way both bills were finally passed; but Bismarck incurred the displeasure of the Conservatives, who considered him, as political parties are apt to do in such cases, as trying to curry favor with the Liberals, and as having intrigued against them with the king. His two principal speeches on the Hanover question were soon afterwards translated into English, and there is not much eloquence in them, but a cogent, logical statement of the case in hand. " No motive," he said in the last of them, "except personal ambition could have induced a king whose dominions separated the two portions of Prussia, and whose good will it was therefore for the interest of our government to conciliate, to join hands with the enemies of Prussia."

The constitution of the North German confederation had been framed with rather too exalted a view of human nature. It was supposed that the true representatives of the German people would always behave and act like gentlemen, and, while there was no rule by which a member of the Reichstag could be suspended, as in the House of Commons, for unseemly conduct or improper language, it was expressly provided, under Article LXXXIV., that members of neither house should be called to account for their votes or for any expression of opinion. Von Sybel says, " The idea prevailed that within the circle of the nation's representatives the public humiliation consequent upon the call to order following upon a breach of decorum would be an all-sufficient means to insure justice and propriety of behavior."[1] Truly, it is important in politics to consider the ideal, for without that there can be no sure progress; but it is equally important to remember that human nature changes but little from one generation to another, and is at best a variable and uncertain commodity.

An illustration of this had already arisen in the preceding session. A deputy named Twesten in the present parliament had criticised with unmeasured severity the Prussian police

---

[1] Von Sybel, vi. 344.

and courts of justice; and another deputy named Frentzel, one of the remaining Progressists, had brought serious charges against the chief of the Königsberg police. In both instances these gentlemen had indulged in plenty of loud-voiced rhetoric without producing any sufficient testimony to substantiate their statements, and Count Lippe, the minister of justice, brought a legal action against them for libel on the government. The two deputies were tried before the Superior Court, and were acquitted on the ground that Article LXXXIV. permitted full expression of opinion in the assembly; but on appeal to the Supreme Court this judgment was reversed, and a decision rendered of the highest importance in its definition of the right and limitation in freedom of speech. It was held by the Supreme Bench that an *opinion* could only be construed in the sense of a *process of reasoning*, and that mere vague assertions, unsupported by documentary evidence, could not properly form an opinion, and might be held as reprehensible in a parliament as in a court-room. This marks the exact difference between freedom of opinion and license of speech, a point which people often find it difficult to determine.

The immediate consequence was, however, that the Chamber of Deputies passed a resolution declaring that the proceedings of the Supreme Court were unconstitutional, and protested against their validity. Count Lippe on his part entered a protest against this action as an infringement on the supreme tribunal of the land, and a conflict between the Landtag and the Supreme Court ensued, which continued till near the close of the session. The court's decision had excited great popular indignation, and was made use of as an electioneering argument. In November, 1867, Lasker introduced a bill requiring that the legal construction of Article LXXXIV. should be accepted as unrestricted freedom of speech, which was passed by a narrow majority in the Landtag, but defeated in the upper chamber. Bismarck, however, considered it best in this instance to take the popular side. The sentence of Twesten and Frentzel, which had been two years' imprisonment, was reduced to a small fine, and the point at issue permitted to remain in abeyance. The Landtag showed a patriotic spirit in passing appropriations for the army, and for those novel expenditures which are required for the establishment of a new governmental system.

THE BREWING OF THE STORM

Old Marshal Niel was intrusted by Napoleon with the reorganization of the French army, which he effected in rather too antiquated a manner. The infantry were armed with the chassepot rifle, which proved to be a better weapon than the needle-gun, but their tactics were not adapted to the use of it. Marshal Niel adhered to the old Napoleonic methods, which the French naturally supposed could not be improved on. He did not consider sufficiently the influence which modern inventions, especially the improvement in fire-arms, might have on them. He did not recognize that heavy-armed cavalry, such as was so effective under the command of Murat, could no longer make a sustained charge against the firing of modern projectiles; and he either retained or introduced a complicated series of evolutions, quite at variance with the principle asserted by Frederick the Great, that nothing which is not simple is of any use in war. He established large central depots of military stores, which were found inconvenient when the war finally came, and caused delay by creating a traffic blockade on the railways. It was at this time that the world began to hear something of a deadly machine invented by the French emperor himself, which was expected to surpass all others in its destructive effect on ranks of infantry.

Metternich's policy was dogmatic, Bismarck's rational, and Louis Napoleon's empirical. Dogmatic politics, starting on a basis of things as they are, always succeed most easily for a time, but finally, as they are not suited to the progressive wants of mankind, end in revolution. A rational policy is the only sound one,—a policy based on a knowledge of human nature and progressive development,—but involves the necessity of a perpetual conflict between the different classes of society,—the governing and the governed,—such as we meet with in the history of Rome before the time of Marius, and in England since the time of James II. This is the proper and healthy condition for a nation to continue in; and though it sometimes approaches to a social revolution, it is really the best preventive against revolutions. The struggle between the centrifugal and the centripetal forces of society keeps the body politic in a healthy condition, and affords room for those popular impulses to expand in, which finally take the form of national progress. An empirical policy, which is neither consistent with any set of political dogmas nor allows sufficient scope for popular movements, necessarily results in a series of makeshifts. It is like leaping one ditch after another, and, though it may succeed with skilful management for a time, it is sure to end at last in complete and utter ruin.

The failure of the second French empire was inherent in the condition of the French people. For the last hundred years France has been the head centre of the liberal movement in Europe; but France is still a Catholic country. There is a political contradiction in this, which has resulted in intermittent revolutions. Catholicism belonged to the earlier mediæval period, when ignorance was the rule and education the rare exception, and it still continues well suited to the intellectual capacity of ignorant persons. The invention of printing necessarily brought with it a more enlightened and spiritual faith. There is an element of progress in the Church of Rome, but it is too slow and too much embarrassed by old traditions to keep pace with the march of events. An educated man in a Catholic country, therefore, finds himself in a position of outward antagonism to his inner life, and if he breaks through this he finds himself in that element of disbelief which we call scepticism. Either condition is weakening intellectually, and places him at a disadvantage with the man who has a real faith which he can express freely in outward action. This is the reason why French literature in the nineteenth century compares so unfavorably with English and German literature. The average Frenchman of to-day is either a philosophical materialist or a lukewarm Romanist, just as either his mental tone or external conditions happen to decide for him.

It is true that the French take their religion very lightly, but, while this affords them an opportunity for intellectual progress, it has a decidedly weakening effect on character. The Gallic race is light-hearted and cheerful. In many phases of life the French appear to great advantage beside their more stolid neighbors in England and Germany; but light-heartedness is not inconsistent with profound religious feeling. Of all the sects of Protestants, the Huguenots were the most impassioned, and the strong religious convictions of their opponents are indelibly expressed in the sermons of Bossuet and the poetry of Racine. It was this moral and intellectual intensity which brought about the grand epoch in French literature, and produced those noble old Frenchmen of whom Lafayette was one of the last examples. What a change to the time when the funeral of Victor Hugo, the Dickens of French novelists, was made a public orgy in the streets of Paris!

This contradiction is illustrated to perfection in Louis Napoleon's Italian policy. Beaconsfield affirmed in his last novel that during Garibaldi's invasion of the papal states Napoleon's inclination was really on the side of the insurgents; and it is known that he was for some time wavering in his decision. Yet he suppressed the Roman revolution of 1848 in order to obtain the support of the French Ultramontanes, though in doing so he offended his former confederates and risked assassination by the Orsini bomb. Then in 1859 he undertook the campaign in Lombardy in the interest of French liberalism. In 1868 again he defended the pope against Garibaldi, and compelled the Italians, in order to realize their aspiration for national unity, to seek the alliance of a Protestant power. On the other hand, in order to gratify the frivolity of his subjects, which arises from their lack of religious seriousness, he was obliged to make a continual effort in the way of scenic diversion. He was continually afraid of being outvoted in the Chamber of Deputies, of revolution, and assassination. During the last seven years of his reign Louis Napoleon was in the position of a man who is riding two horses, which may separate at any time and let him fall between them. Benedetti spoke seriously enough to Bismarck when he said, on the 5th of August, 1866, " There is too much danger that if Napoleon does not obtain proper compensation it will cost him his throne."

While strengthening the internal condition of his kingdom, and preparing himself for a contingency towards which events were rapidly drifting him, Napoleon looked abroad for the possibility for an alliance which might serve him when the final struggle came. The British government, weakened by internal dissensions and always loath to take an interest where the ultimate advantage might accrue in a large measure to another country, he knew well enough would give him no assistance. He had a permanent defensive and offensive alliance with Victor Emmanuel, but the sentiment of the Italian people was turning against him, and of all governments in Europe at this time the Italian was the one most dependent on popular support. He had mortally offended Francis Joseph, but still he hoped that self-interest and hatred of Bismarck might counterbalance the grudge of Solferino at the Austrian court. He therefore attempted to build up an Austro-Italian alliance out of such poor material as was still left to him,—a doubtful undertaking, and a crazy structure to depend on if he succeeded in erecting it.

Von Beust is here of great value to us, for, though he sometimes hedges like Bismarck in his assertions, and tries to give a favorable Austrian color to them, the sound character of the man is beyond question. Already during the Luxemburg difficulty the Duc de Gramont had proposed an alliance to him in case of war with Prussia, with the offer of Silesia or an equivalent in South Germany. He says:

"I replied by pointing out that the emperor, having millions of German subjects, could not make an alliance for the purpose of diminishing German territory. I cannot recollect whether I repeated in this despatch the idea which I have repeatedly expressed to the Duc de Gramont, and to which he alludes in his answer of January, 1873, but I remember the idea itself very distinctly. It could not be our task to attack Germany any more than it is our duty to protect her. The field of action to which our interests pointed, and where all the races in the empire could fight without aversion, was the East." [1]

This reply must have been as unpleasant to the Duc de Gramont as some of Bismarck's replies were to the French emperor. Von Beust had a number of reasons for this declination, of which the first and foremost was the character of Napoleon himself. "We had to consider a double danger," he says, "when considering such a proposition,—the possibility of Napoleon coming to an agreement with Prussia at our cost, and his leaving us to enjoy the evil effects of his alliance." Then, Von Beust did not like the idea of having his internal reforms suspended, and perhaps thwarted altogether, by the exigencies and perhaps catastrophes of a colossal war. In the third place, it was doubtful if the Hungarians, who were now *quasi* independent, would support a coalition against Bismarck, whom they naturally looked upon as their best friend. Moreover, the agitation in the Danubian principalities, which had commenced with the assassination of the Prince of Roumania, appeared to be on the increase, and was a source of grave anxiety to the Vienna cabinet.

In August Napoleon and Gramont made a visit to Francis Joseph at Salzburg to condole with him on the murder of his brother Maximilian by those Mexican devils, and it is noteworthy that the imperial party was severely hissed at the railway station of Augsburg, in Bavaria, on their way thither. This ought to have been a note of warning to Napoleon as significant of the disposition of the people of South Germany. To a more alert mind than his it would have been sufficient to change the whole current of his policy, but he knew that the Bavarian nobility were on his side, and neglected to consider the effect of Bismarck's popular elections. Augsburg is the financial centre of Southern Germany, and it was Bismarck's Zollverein from which the hisses originated.

Maximilian was in a measure Louis Napoleon's victim,

---

[1] Von Beust's Memoirs, ii. 172.

though he finally lost his life through an excess of chivalrous devotion to his Mexican adherents. The meeting, therefore, could not have been a very cordial one. Francis Joseph
had reason to be pleased with the removal of his brother to a
distant scene of action, but he showed true fraternal feeling
and deep concern at the approach of his unhappy fate. It is
not likely, therefore, that there was more than a formal discussion of politics at Salzburg, though Prussian government
organs undoubtedly made the most of the meeting there.
Von Beust says:

" We arrived at the conclusion that it was our joint task to observe minutely the stipulations of the peace of Prague, but to avoid
on both sides any interference in German affairs. It was especially
agreed that France should refrain from any measures or manifestation of a threatening nature, while Austria should limit herself to
preserving the sympathies of South Germany by developing a
liberal and truly constitutional system." [1]

This amounted to nothing more, apparently, than leaving
things as they were. In the following October, when Francis
Joseph visited the Paris Exposition, Von Beust had an interview with the Prussian envoy, and they agreed in thinking
that the best means of avoiding a collision with France
" would be to consolidate South Germany so as to present a
united front to the foreigner." Between the two evils of as-
sisting Napoleon or remaining outside the German confederation the Austrian emperor evidently preferred the latter.

In the summer of 1868 Napoleon renewed his proposals for
a Franco-Austro-Italian alliance. The discussion of the subject was protracted for more than a year, and the most that
the Austrian government was willing to admit was that in
case of complications with Russia, and Prussia's giving Russia
countenance and support, Austria would be willing and ready
to take part with France in a war against Germany; but such
an unequal conflict as that might prove had no charm for
Napoleon III.

---

[1] Von Beust's Memoirs, ii. 36.

Old political stagers predicted that the campaign of 1866 would have its reflection in a number of small insurrections in various parts of Europe, and so it proved. The Panslavic agitation continued to seethe and ferment, but did not come to the surface of events till ten years later. The Cretan insurrection began in the winter of 1867, and Garibaldi's invasion of the papal territory took place the following summer.

The first of these was so favorable to the interests of Prussia that we might almost suspect that Bismarck had instigated it, though he could only have done so through the mediation of the Russian court. It would be interesting to know what he thought about the Cretans and Turkish affairs in general, but he gave no more sign than the Speaker of the House of Commons does in regard to the subject of debate. However, he readily agreed with the British ministry in favoring a friendly attitude towards the Cretans at Constantinople; but Napoleon followed the example of Austria in taking an opposite course, which practically left the Sultan to act as he pleased.

The first six months of 1867 in Italy proved an anxious period for both Bismarck and Napoleon. The sudden acquisition of Venetia, against all expectation, had filled the Italians with an enthusiastic longing for their ancient capital, but Prussia could do nothing for them in that direction. The nation was not in a condition to cope with France, and its acquisition depended on either the good-will of Napoleon or such an internal condition of French affairs as to render his interference impossible. This latter alternative does not appear to have occurred to Victor Emmanuel's counsellors, and there were those among them who were willing to join in an attack upon Prussia if Napoleon would only permit them to march into Rome.[1] It is doubtful if the king would ever have consented to this, and the pressure of events soon turned the political current in the opposite direction. Ratazzi, who had succeeded La Marmora, informed Napoleon that the situation was critical, and that he feared the patriotic ardor of

---

the Italians would soon find an outlet in one way or another. Napoleon felt himself in the same position, and attempted to effect a compromise with Pius IX., but met with such an obstinate refusal that for a time he allowed matters to take their natural course. In Florence the uncertainty of opinion was so great that two ministries resigned in less than four months.

The natural course of events in Italy meant—Garibaldi. Rome was his game, and he was ready to spring upon it as soon as the leash which held him was loosened. An invasion of the states of the Church by his "sons of freedom" followed as a matter of course, and it is said that Napoleon was never so distracted in his mind as on this occasion. He gave orders and countermanded them a number of times, but finally decided to support the pope. The battle of Mentana followed, and Garibaldi's forces were dispersed by the effective use of the chassepot, but the same fusillade killed Napoleon's influence in Italy. The French alliance continued as an empty form, but it was worse than nothing, for it served to encourage an expectation which could never be realized. The chassepot, however, had done its whole duty, and the superiority of the Prussians at Sadowa was now fully explained.

The continued interference of France in the affairs of so many other nations had now aroused a general feeling of exasperation at European courts, and Napoleon's attempt to shift the responsibility of the pope's temporal authority from his own shoulders by a conference of the powers met with small favor, and finally died a lingering death amid great volumes of diplomatic correspondence. The sympathy in England, both Tory and Liberal, was with the Italian government. Von Beust, having a controversy with the pope himself over the *concordat*, had no desire to increase the pope's influence by strengthening his position, and Bismarck was non-committal. In the summer of 1868, as Marshal Niel represented to Napoleon that it was folly to make war on Prussia without a substantial ally, the emperor bestirred himself again to bring about the triple alliance with Austria and Italy, but Von Beust had his hands full without attempting to pull Napoleon's chestnuts out of the fire, and Victor Emmanuel, though expressing the most cordial sentiments towards his imperial friend and benefactor, would only join the proposed alliance on terms which were a practical nullification of it. These were that the French garrison should be withdrawn from Rome, and the possession of the Italian Tyrol guaranteed in case of a successful termination of the war. Napoleon must have perceived from this only too clearly what he had to expect from Victor Emmanuel.

In this perplexity, and, as it were, grasping at straws, he turned to Isabella, the disreputable Queen of Spain. The influence of the pope in European politics would never have been one-half of what it actually has been if it were not for the influence of the priests on queens and empresses. Isabella, who governed by means of one of the most tyrannical of prime ministers, was no doubt informed by him that it would be impossible to drag her impoverished country into a war with Germany, but that there would be no difficulty in providing for the protection of Pius IX. with forty thousand Spanish bayonets. This would have relieved Napoleon from further embarrassment in that direction, and enabled him to add the troops in Rome to his effective force upon the Rhine; but the covenant had been no sooner agreed upon, in September, 1868, when suddenly the Spanish revolution took place; the queen and her minister, Gonzalez Bravo, were defeated at the battle of Alcolea, and Isabella obliged to fly for succor to the man who had expected assistance from her. Such a bugaboo had Bismarck become to the French people that he was accused by the Parisian journals of having instigated and abetted this Spanish revolution; though he was opposed to revolutions on principle, and the compact between Napoleon and Isabella was not discovered till many years afterwards.[1]

It is noteworthy that, although Napoleon III. professed to be the champion of popular rights and the principle of nationality, all the popular movements of this period, excepting the campaign of 1859, were unfavorable to him, and equally to the advantage of Bismarck, who never pretended anything of the

---

[1] Von Sybel, vi. 411; also Meding's Memoirs, iii. 360.

sort. The conclusion is unavoidable that Bismarck was acting in harmony with the laws of nature, or human nature,
and that Louis Napoleon was contending against them. The
condition of France in 1868 is a fair example of the result of
a government based, like that of Napoleon I., on prestige and
popularity. When Marshal Niel, a genuine old soldier, attempted to reorganize the French army, he found such opposition to his plans, both in the Chamber of Deputies and
among his colleagues, that it became simply an impossible
task. The French people believed that they had only to rise
up in their might, as they did in 1793, and demolish the Prussians. Thiers, Favre, and other opponents of the government,
who had attacked Napoleon in the Chambers for permitting
Bismarck to build up a strong German power, were now as
vehemently opposed to granting appropriations for an increase
of the army, while the newspapers of both parties maintained
a continuous clamor against the odious Prussians. It is supposed also that Marshal Niel's colleagues in the ministry secretly undermined his efforts to create a strong military
establishment for fear of the ascendency which this might
give him. The consequence was that the appropriations were
largely reduced, and a force of three hundred thousand men
was the most the marshal could report to Napoleon at the
close of the year.

Sparta, Rome, and Prussia are the three military nations
of history,—that is, as compared with others. Napoleon
I. made France a nation of soldiers during his time, but after
Waterloo this came to an end. Frederick the Great so organized the Prussians during his reign that with seven millions
of population he was able to maintain himself and preserve
the peace in Europe for thirty years.[1] Scharnhorst originated
the present Prussian military system, which has been developed not only into the most effective but the most equitable
that has ever been devised. It was a decided improvement
on the French system of the First Empire, and it was evi-

---

[1] He wrote to the King of France, " Not a shot is fired on the continent
without my permission."

dently what upset Napoleon's calculations in 1813. Every able-bodied youth at the age of eighteen is obliged to report himself to the authorities for service. The sons of counts and barons are obliged to do this, the same as common peasants. Wealthy young men, however, are permitted the advantage of serving for only two years if they will contribute to their own maintenance during the time. As all others serve for four years, this is not abstractly just, but probably, on the whole, better for the state. At the expiration of four years they go into the Landwehr, or reserves, and are required to drill six weeks each year for six years longer. The officers are to a large extent taken from the titled classes, and are required to be highly educated men, so that a refined *esprit du corps* is preserved in the profession. In the autumn the soldiers are relieved from discipline, and take part in gathering the crops.

Although a large army is always something of a burden to a nation, the German system certainly has a number of advantages. It trains up young men in the most healthy and orderly of all modes of life just at the time when they are liable to contract idle and dissipated habits, so that it may even be affirmed that the time devoted to their country in this way is no loss, but doubled or even trebled in the average duration of German life. It also effects an unconstrained intercourse between the different classes of society, by which the higher are induced to respect the more humble, and the less educated to acquire something of the culture of those who have been more fortunate ; and, as Von Moltke discovered, it teaches them all to speak good Hanoverian German, so that dialects and provincialisms are now dying out.

If we now contrast this with the Napoleonic system, it is easy to foresee—if we did not already know it—the issue of the impending struggle between France and Prussia. The French army was recruited by the old method of conscription, and the unfortunate persons enrolled in this manner were obliged to serve from ten to fifteen years. Those who had the means to purchase a substitute were certain to do so, and thus the real burden fell almost entirely upon the laboring classes. The system was just and fair only in the sense that a lottery is just and fair. There are no braver soldiers than the French; but a man's devotion to his country will always be more or less influenced by the way in which he is treated by his country,—if we except such rare instances as Aristides and Mazzini. The more prosperous classes were supposed to be organized into a national militia; but, though the service was made obligatory, various ways were discovered of escaping from it, and Marshal Niel found his most difficult obstacle in attempting to give a sufficient consistency to the National Guard, so that it might serve to garrison the fortresses. The young aristocrats of Paris stubbornly objected to anything like discipline, and ridiculed the Prussians as Bismarck's drudges, low-bred fellows who ate with their knives. There was actually more equality in monarchical Germany than in democratic Paris.[1] The average intelligence of the French army officers was also of a lower grade than the German. There was not, perhaps, so much favoritism in the appointments as there was formerly in the English army, but there had been numerous promotions for bravery on the field of battle which went much beyond the actual deserts of the individual. French generals were captured in the campaign of 1870 so ignorant that they could not write their names.

THE ROUMANIAN QUESTION.

How easily a person in Bismarck's position accomplishes what he undertakes, if he only comprehends the situation, is shown by the *dénoucment* of the Roumanian complication in 1868. After the Roumanian revolution of 1866, Napoleon, of course, wished to increase his prestige by originating the appointment of a prince to fill the vacant throne, and, perhaps to bring Prussia into closer relations with his policy, he pitched upon Prince Charles Anthony, of Hohenzollern-Sigmaringen, a twelfth-century relative of the Prussian king. He was, however, much more nearly connected with Napoleon him-

---

[1] Paris has been republican certainly since 1830. The support of the Second Empire came chiefly from the country districts.

self, since his mother was a princess of the Murat family. He was at the time an officer in the Prussian army, and as such a subject of William I., who disapproved of the appointment as likely to result in political complications, but recognized the young man's right to accept the position if he thought best. Bismarck held the same opinion at first, but, on finding that Austria and England were opposed to it, he changed his mind and advised the prince to accept.

Louis Napoleon's man of business in this affair was a Roumanian named Joan Bratianu, who accordingly obtained a plebiscite of the Roumanian people (after the French fashion) in favor of Prince Charles; and the prince, after being smuggled through Austria in disguise, was seated with *éclat* on his precarious throne. Being a Prussian officer through and through, he naturally wished to introduce the Prussian military system in his principality, and one of the first acts of his government was to negotiate with William I. for forty thousand needle-guns. These, however, could not be had at once, owing to the danger of an attack by France; and meanwhile Bratianu, who was prime minister and a brilliant but visionary man, had evolved a scheme of his own for enlarging the boundaries of Roumania in imitation of Garibaldi's conquest of Naples. Incendiary movements, of which Prince Charles must have been entirely innocent, were set on foot on the borders of Bulgaria and Transylvania. It is possible that these may have been instigated at the Russian court, but that Bismarck could have had nothing to do with them is evident from the events which followed. About the same time a consignment of needle-guns, which had been forwarded through Russia in order not to attract the attention of Von Beust, were discovered by Austrian spies. Von Beust immediately notified Napoleon, who informed the Gladstone ministry, and a great howl was raised over this fresh instance of Bismarck's insidious machinations.

The howling of the French press did not trouble Bismarck, for he knew that the louder they howled the stronger and more deep-rooted would become the sentiment for national unity among the German people; but when the Hungarian press began to complain of the faithlessness of their Prussian allies, and to talk about the integrity of the empire of the Danube, he recognized that the right time for intervention had come. He directed the Prussian minister at Bucharest, on the 22d of November, 1868, to demand of Prince Charles the immediate dismissal of the Bratianu ministry, and when this was complied with the whole disturbance came suddenly to an end. Whatever may be said or thought about the agitation on the Bulgarian border, it is incredible that Bismarck should have intended to irritate the Hungarians, or the Tsar to offend Francis Joseph, by the disorders in Transylvania. Bismarck recognized the true origin of the difficulty and removed it with a stroke of his pen.

The Cretan revolution had now been dragging along for a year with hopeless prospects, and there was danger that Greece would become involved in the struggle to its own ruin. Von Beust would have liked much to have had it suppressed, but his hands were tied for the time being, and he could only influence the French cabinet in the same direction. Gladstone had favored the Cretans, and Bismarck was not unfriendly to them; but the latter now saw that of two great calamities one was sure to happen,—either Greece itself would be crushed by the Turkish army, which was assembled on the borders of Thessaly, or that there would be an Oriental convulsion like that of 1854. He accordingly laid the case before Alexander, and persuaded him to see it in its true light. He then proposed to Napoleon and the Sultan, a European conference for a pacific solution of the problem. This all parties concerned readily agreed to, and with it closed the year 1868.

CHAPTER IX

THE FRANCO-GERMAN WAR

FRENCH authorities are altogether silent on the subject, but it is well known in Germany and Spain that the proposition to place Prince Leopold of Hohenzollern on the Spanish throne originated in the summer of 1869. It was Salazar, a Spanish minister of the provisional government, who first made the proposal, and Dr. Busch gives a circumstantial account of an interview on the subject between Benedetti and Bismarck, wherein the former pointed out the critical situation of affairs which might result from it; in reply to which Bismarck made a counter-proposition, which must have pleased Benedetti still less. He suggested that Prince Frederick Charles, nephew to William I., and one of the ablest generals in Europe, would make a more suitable candidate, if only his religion did not interfere to prevent it. Unemployed princes have been commonly ready and willing enough to change their religion for the sake of a throne; but Benedetti did not suggest this, and there was otherwise a grim humor in Bismarck's proposition which he may have laughed at afterwards himself. If there was a man in Europe who could discipline the Spaniards and train them up in the way they should go, it was the red Frederick; and if the Cortes had offered him the Spanish throne, it is safe to presume he would either have done this or died in the attempt.

It is rather suspicious that about this same time Marshal Niel submitted to Napoleon III. the plan of a campaign for the invasion of Germany. According to the statement that has been made of this plan the French army was to follow the line of the Main, and having once defeated the forces opposed to it the left wing was to unite with a division from Holland, which was expected to join in this raid for conquest; the centre was to instigate a revolution in Hanover and Hesse,

and the right wing was to detach Würtemberg and Bavaria
from the Prussian alliance. This was a bold design, but one
which could have succeeded only through exceptional good
fortune. The probability is that, even if successful in their
first attack, the French invading divisions would have been
overpowered by the Prussian reserves, for it was part of Von
Moltke's strategy to retain his best troops for such an emergency. Whether it was intended to act upon this plan at once
we do not know, for Marshal Niel died on August 13, and his
successor, General Lebœuf, made wholly different arrangements.

Prince Leopold, like Prince Charles Anthony, was more
closely connected with the Bonaparte family than with the
royal family of Prussia, but he was also an officer in the
Prussian army, and considered William I. as his liege lord
and the head of the house. In the autumn of 1869 he was
first interrogated by Salazar in regard to accepting the Spanish throne, and, after a consultation with King William, declined the offer. William I. was always strongly opposed to
it or to any measure which would have a tendency to promote
a war with France. Underneath the documents in the national
archives, and such confidential letters as have been preserved,
there is always an undercurrent in national diplomacy which
never comes to the surface. It is possible that Napoleon III.
suggested the candidacy of Prince Leopold, in order to set
him up as a man of straw, to serve as a pretext in the way he
finally did ; or it is possible that the nomination was instigated
by Bismarck in order to establish a strong position in the rear
of France, which might at least serve to divert the enemy's
attention. Much more likely is it that Serrano, Salazar, and
the other Spanish leaders, having become thoroughly sick of
the Bourbon and Hapsburg families, had concluded to apply
for a scion of royalty from a house that had long since proved
its virtue, intelligence, and capacity for government. The attempt to establish another Bonaparte dynasty in Spain would
have been injudicious for a number of reasons, especially since
the intriguing resident of the Tuileries would then have a
continual excuse for interfering in the affairs of the Spanish

government. With respect to Germany no such complications would be likely to result. There were neither conflicting interests nor allied interests between the two countries, and Leopold on the throne of Philip II. would have been as far removed from Prussian influence as it was possible to be on the continent of Europe.

Another incident in this rather uneventful year was the reaction against Prussia in Bavaria and Würtemberg. The greatest of statesmen cannot alter the character of human nature, and the haughty bearing of Prussian officers in those countries produced an effect like that of the first Napoleon's subordinates in the Confederation of the Rhine. There was great rejoicing in Munich when a Prussian captain, for once, became intoxicated and disgraced himself generally. The Jesuits took advantage of this to increase the agitation as much as possible, and Bavarian newspapers were loud-voiced in their protestations against Prussian tyranny and their desire for French intervention. In Würtemberg the ebb-tide was so strong that not one National Liberal was elected to the German Customs Union.

This only served, however, to mislead Louis Napoleon, who made the common mistake of supposing that a majority of votes, and the opinions of editors, represent the real political force of a country. There is quite likely to be in such cases among the more influential men a reserved opinion which holds a steady and determined course, while the popular excitement foams itself away without producing any definite result. Von der Pfordten and Varnbüler knew all the time on which side their true interests lay, and realized as well the strong clutch which Bismarck had upon their governments. While the chambers at Stuttgardt resounded with the eloquence of anti-Nationalists, Von Suckow, the Würtemberg chief of staff, was quietly arranging in Berlin the course which he and his forces should pursue to make a junction with Von Moltke in case of a French invasion. In Baden the enthusiasm rose to such a pitch that it caused Bismarck no slight anxiety, lest the excitable Germans of the Palatinate, who are really Burgundians, should bring on a collision with

France through an excess of patriotism. For the second time he was obliged to decline the request made by the Baden minister for permission to join the North German confederation, and the vote of the chambers for an exceptional appropriation of two million florins to introduce the Prussian military system was treated by Parisian journals as if it had been an open declaration of war. In the North German Reichstag Lasker introduced a bill for the purpose of bringing all the jurisdiction of German citizens within the province of legislative authority, and, surprising as it may seem, this extravagant proposition, which would have placed even the judges of the courts at the mercy of political parties, passed the lower house, but was rejected by the Bundesrath. A bill to establish a central board of jurisdiction for mercantile affairs passed both houses, but, in opposition to Bismarck's wishes, who preferred to have it located in Berlin, the Reichstag decided to establish it at Leipsic. Thus it appears that the minister-president could not always have his own way, even when his influence was at its highest ascendency.

That Bismarck still earnestly wished to remain at peace with France is evident from a peculiar little piece of diplomacy which seems like rather small business for so great a man, but which, nevertheless, must be admitted to have been intended for the public good. He dictated a letter to Dr. Busch with directions that it should be published in a paper at Cologne, as pretending to emanate from a Parisian liberal. Similar letters were published in the New York *Tribune* about the same time, so that we may judge that it did not misrepresent the liberal feeling and opinion in 'France. A French professor, visiting in America in the summer of 1868, said, "They are all for fight in Paris, and Napoleon encourages it, because he hopes in that way to get rid of the National Assembly." In this letter Bismarck said:

" The urgent desire of every sincere supporter of constitutionalism in France may be thus summed up: Let us have no new diversion abroad just now, no new phenomenon cropping up in the foreign political horizon, which may be turned to account not as a

real motive, but as a pretext for howling down the youthful existence of constitutionalism in France, or for turning public attention
to foreign complications. The emperor, as we believe, is in
earnest with his experiment, but the people in his immediate
entourage and the tools he uses—who are all greedily yearning for
some event that may give them a chance of diverting the emperor
from a groove they hold in abomination—are very numerous, and,
in virtue of the roots they have struck into his eighteen years past,
much more powerful than people fancy abroad. Whosoever has
constitutional development at heart can now only wish most earnestly that no change may take place in the foreign relations of
France which may in any way lead to the reaction wished for by
the opponents of any and every constitution in France.''

After the surrender at Sedan, Napoleon always asserted
that he had been forced into the war; and though Bismarck
remarked that the emperor was not so innocent as he pretended, there can be little doubt that during this later stage
of the French mania he would have been glad to resist the
current of public opinion and court intrigue, if he had been
able to do so. Looked at from this side, one can feel a good
deal of commiseration for him; but it was the inevitable result
of a habit which had become chronic with him to meddle in
the affairs of other countries. He had sown the wind, and
now the tornado was coming. Who could tell what course it
would take? and Louis Napoleon realized only too acutely
how powerless he was to control the forces which he had
conjured up.

The state of public feeling in 1870 may be best estimated
by the irritation that was caused in Paris by the appropriation
of five million thalers by the German Reichstag towards
boring the St. Gothard tunnel, which would give Germany
direct communication with Italy, independent of France or
Austria. Bismarck was quick to perceive the advantage of
this for the future interests of his country, and that it would
be equally certain to withdraw large traffic from the Mont
Cenis tunnel of Napoleon; but not less than six or seven
years would be required for its completion, and who could
tell what political changes might take place within that time?

Nevertheless, it was looked upon as another of Bismarck's insidious designs, to which there seemed to be no limit. When the British Parliament was opened in the spring of 1870, Gladstone, in the name of the queen, congratulated the nation that the prospects of peace were never more favorable for Europe than at that moment. Napoleon sent a similar message to the Chamber of Deputies at Paris. What else could they say? In France and Germany there was such deep-seated unrest that even the sound of a church-bell seemed to every man like a call to arms. If the beating of a drum was heard in the Boulevard des Italiens, every man dropped his work and ran to the sidewalk. The political atmosphere was sultry; yet the sun might continue to rise and set in peace, as it had done for so long.

What pretext Napoleon would have found for commencing hostilities but for the Spanish candidature cannot even be imagined. It would have been more honest for him to have sent a declaration to William I.,—" Luxemburg or war;" but he wished to have an apparent justification, no matter how slight it might be, to place before the world. There have been numerous accounts of this important transaction, but they all come to much the same result. It is certain that the Spanish throne was offered to Prince Leopold twice at least before he accepted it, and that King William earnestly endeavored to persuade him to relinquish the idea; but, as in the case of the Prince of Roumania, he felt that he had no right to go beyond this. In General Hazen's invaluable book,[1] " The School and the Army in Germany and France," there is a verbal statement by Bismarck himself, which in this connection is of great interest, since it brings the man so vividly before us. Generals Sheridan, Burnside, and Hazen were commissioned by President Grant to make a report on the Franco-German war; and Sheridan, with the true instinct of military genius, went straight to the Prussian head-quarters. It is now nearly thirty years since his statement was made

---

[1] This is not intended, however, as an endorsement of General Hazen's attacks on General Townsend and the United States Engineer Corps.

to these generals, and, allowing for a slight variation through General Hazen's memory, no evidence has come to light which vitiates any portion of it. Bismarck says nothing in it of the supposed insult to King William by Benedetti, but keeps to the main point, which is, after all, that the French government insisted upon making the candidacy of Prince Leopold a *casus belli* after that candidacy had been revoked and could only be considered a past event. Bismarck saw that what Napoleon wanted was war, and, if so, Napoleon should have it. His firmness, calmness, moderation, and clear-sightedness at this time show forth in bold relief against the frothy ebullition of Napoleon's court. The Empress Eugénie is reported to have exclaimed, " This is my war. With God's help we shall subdue the Protestant Prussians."

The precise order of events, as narrated by Müller, was nearly as follows : On July 4 the French government sent a telegram of inquiry to the foreign office at Berlin, to know what position Prussia would take in regard to the candidacy of Leopold, and a reply was returned that King William had no interest whatever in Spanish affairs. At the same time the Duc de Gramont requested Baron von Werther, who had succeeded Von Goltz at Paris, to inform William I. that Napoleon expected him to prevent Leopold from accepting the Spanish throne. In the Chamber of Deputies, Gramont announced that France would not permit a neighboring nation to upset the European balance of power by uniting two thrones in one royal family. On July 9 Benedetti had an audience with King William at Ems, in which he assumed that Prussia was responsible for the nomination of Prince Leopold, and the king denied any such responsibility or control over the action of the prince. He added,—what must occur to every sensible person,—that it was to the government at Madrid, and not at Berlin, to which Napoleon ought to apply on this subject.[1] It does not appear that this had been thought of at Paris at all. On July 12 the withdrawal of Prince Leopold was announced to the European courts by a despatch from his

---

[1] Dr. Busch, ii. 53.

father's castle at Sigmaringen, and this certainly ought to have removed all pretext for a quarrel between France and Prussia. This it was generally supposed to have done; and Bismarck noticed that Von Moltke's face, which had commenced to brighten with a sort of internal light at the prospect of active service, now became old and wrinkled again.

Louis Napoleon was distracted between doubts and fears, and worried continually, but the war party had the upper hand, and he was carried along like a chip on the tide. The very next day Gramont informed Von Werther that, in order to resume cordial relations with Prussia, it was essential that William I. should make a distinct avowal to Napoleon, to the effect that when he empowered Leopold to accept the Spanish throne he had no intention of doing injury to the interests of France, or to offer any offence to the French nation,—that is, in substance, that William I. should make a public apology for the act of a third person which he had never encouraged. Baron Werther, instead of reporting this message to the king, prudently notified Bismarck in regard to it, and he, with his usual tact, telegraphed the baron to take a short leave of absence. Having been foiled in this direction, the Duc de Gramont, who appears to have managed the whole affair, sent word to Benedetti at Berlin to demand King William's definite approval of Prince Leopold's declination, and to give an assurance that no member of the Hohenzollern family should again become a candidate for the Spanish throne. Benedetti accordingly took the next train to Ems, and went through with this programme in a conspicuous and embarrassing manner. The king, of course, refused to give any pledge for his future action in any matter whatever, and upon Benedetti's requesting a subsequent interview, William I. refused to see him.[1]

---

[1] This is the despatch of the Duc de Gramont to Benedetti in regard to the interview at Ems, according to the statement of Jules Favre, July 17, 1870: " Make a last attempt with the king; tell him that we confine ourselves to asking him to forbid the Prince of Hohenzollern reconsidering this question in the future. The king must say, ' I do forbid it.' And he must authorize you to write to me, or charge his ministers or ambassadors to let me know what he

LIFE OF BISMARCK

This was an insult, and evidently intended for one. To have given such a pledge would have made William I. the vassal of Napoleon, and would have degraded him in the opinion of all Germany. He did not, however, immediately request Benedetti's recall, though the French allege that he insulted Benedetti by not recognizing him at the railway station on leaving Ems. He at once telegraphed to Bismarck, who was with Von Moltke in Berlin.

The king sent a brief account of the interview with Benedetti, and authorized Bismarck to publish a similar statement if the cabinet thought best. Von Moltke and Von Roon, so Dr. Busch states, did not consider the situation a critical one, but Bismarck thought otherwise, for he realized that this publication would make Napoleon III. appear ridiculous before the civilized world. Bismarck's version of it runs as follows:

"Ems, July 13, 1870.—When the intelligence of the hereditary Prince of Hohenzollern's renunciation was communicated by the Spanish to the French government, the French ambassador demanded of his Majesty the King at Ems that the latter should authorize him to telegraph to Paris that his Majesty would pledge himself for all time to come never again to give his consent in case the candidature of Prince Hohenzollern should be renewed. Upon this his Majesty refused to receive the French ambassador again, and sent his aide-de-camp in attendance to tell him that his Majesty had nothing further to communicate to the ambassador."

It has been repeatedly stated that Bismarck gave an intentional force and cogency to his version of the Ems telegram not to be found in the original, and prejudiced writers have made superhuman efforts to hold Bismarck responsible on

says. That will suffice. And, in fact, if the king has no reserve, this will be for him only a secondary question; but for us it is a very important one; the king's word alone can constitute a sufficient guarantee for the future.

"*I have ground for believing that the other cabinets think us just and moderate.*

"*The Emperor Alexander supports us warmly.*"—"Government of the National Defence," p. 253.

LIFE OF BISMARCK

this slender basis for the war of 1870. The telegram from Ems, however, has lately been made public,[1] and a comparison with Bismarck's statement proves that, although the latter was somewhat condensed, he has not swerved a hair's breadth from the sense of the despatch received through Councillor Abeken. William I. evidently desired to consult Bismarck before publishing an account of the interview with Benedetti, but the idea of giving it publicity must have been his own. If he had hesitated before, he now saw clearly that the time for action had arrived. At that moment he and the Prussian people were one.

This publication had the effect which Bismarck expected, and which also was what the French government most desired. All Paris was in an uproar, and the newspapers printed "On to Berlin" in the largest capitals. The final declaration of war was not made, however, till the 19th of July, and the intermediate time was spent by Bismarck in futile negotiations with the English ministry for arbitration, and in a confidential arrangement with Alexander II., who providentially happened to be at Ems in company with King William. The behavior of the British cabinet was simply mercenary, and Bismarck always expressed himself in regard to it in a very decided manner. There can be no doubt that Gladstone himself would have liked to preserve peace, and it would have been much to the honor of England had he done so; but he could not withstand the pressure of the British commercial interest, which forms the strongest element in the English Liberal party. Dr. Kapp said, "We appealed to England to prevent war, but they preferred to let it go on, in order to make money out of it." The British envoy at Berlin was directed to advise the Prussian government to the effect that King William should make a suitable apology to the French Emperor,— little less in itself than an additional insult. This was about what Bismarck anticipated, and he did not concern himself further on the subject.

After all, what cause of complaint had France against the Prussian government? The North German Confederation

[1] Bismarck's Memoirs, ii. 97.

196

contained a population of about thirty millions, and South Germany some fifteen millions more. The population of France was nearly forty millions, including Algeria. What was there, then, for the French to be alarmed at? If the French government had a right to form an alliance with Italy, why should not William I. possess the same right to ally himself with the South German states? In what manner was the German confederation dangerous to French interests or French independence? The *Moniteur* of July 8 said, in an attempted explanation of the French position:

"Our policy towards Spain must be a moderate one, but we are upon quite another footing with Prussia. This power, self-deluded by its first successes, seems to think it can acquire preponderance and even rule throughout Europe. The time has come to put an end to such pretensions. The question must be enlarged; Prince Leopold's renunciation is no longer sufficient. The least we can demand, the least that will now satisfy us, will be the formal recognition and enforcement in word and spirit of the Prague treaty."

Truly this is not a strong statement. It might be asked in this connection how the policy of the Prussian government had differed during the past twenty years from that of the French government. Both had made war upon Austria, and both had formed alliances with Italy. If Prussia had annexed Schleswig-Holstein, France had annexed Savoy. If the Prince of Roumania and the proposed candidate for the Spanish throne were distantly related to the King of Prussia, they were more closely connected with the house of Bonaparte. If Bismarck had interfered with the internal affairs of German states, was not Napoleon perpetually doing the same? One might suppose that two equally balanced powers, side by side on the map of Europe, would be more likely to keep the peace through mutual respect and dread of one another than if one was decidedly more powerful than the other. It is a rare instance when either individuals or nations apply the same rules to themselves which they do to other people, and the French had long since ceased to be capable of this. The oft-repeated principle of Thiers, that if France wished to be strong she must keep her neighbors weak, was captivating to the Parisians.

It is often difficult to distinguish between national vanity and that consciousness of a nation's solidarity which forms the basis of patriotism, for the two merge into each other; but when a people continually speaks of itself as the "first nation of the universe," as the French have done since the time of Louis XIV., we may safely affirm that they have more vanity than self-respect. General Hazen reports that reading-books were discovered in the French school-rooms in which France was plainly declared to be the first of all nations, and represented as the birthplace of all great men, as well as the source of all discoveries and inventions. French children were educated in these notions, so that they became to them like a religion. Thiers's history of the first Napoleon is full of this patriotic glorification, and even Guizot, in his "History of Civilization," does not hesitate to place France above all other countries as the type of what a civilized nation should be. During the campaign of 1870, Bismarck suggested that the different personages, who were responsible for the war and so much bloodshed, should all be brought into court and placed in the prisoner's dock together,—first, the old Napoleon; then M. Thiers, who wrote his history; the Empress Eugénie, the Duc de Gramont, Pius IX., and others. Behind them all, however, might be placed the French habit of self-glorification, which both of the Napoleons had played upon, and which Napoleon III. especially had cultivated as the most efficient means of preserving his popularity. His official newspapers in Paris were not only *claqueurs* for himself, but for the French people also. There is plenty of national vanity in Germany, England, and America; but we do not find statesmen like Bismarck and Gladstone, or historians like Macaulay and Von Sybel, giving utterance to such fulsome adulation as that referred to from Thiers and Guizot.

THE CAMPAIGN OF 1870

In the light of subsequent events, Napoleon III. appears like a self-deluded man rushing upon destruction; but in July,

1870, he counted upon eventualities which might have misled many another. In the first place, he felt a sort of maternal confidence in his own invention,—the *mitrailleuse*,—which was expected to concentrate a more severe fire on some particular point of the enemy's line than any other form of military weapon in existence. With this and the traditional dash of the French soldier he expected to gain a success at the outset, and establish his lines on Prussian territory. He was confident that in that case Austria, Bavaria, and Denmark would fall to and attack his enemy in the rear, while Victor Emmanuel, wishing to be on the winning side, would also lend a helping hand to the vivisection of Prussia. The Bavarian newspapers gave him good reason for this confidence. The *Vaterland* asserted that the Bavarian chambers would not vote a single *gulden* for the mobilization of the army to assist Bismarck in furthering his unrighteous schemes. There was the same popular opposition among the democrats of Würtemberg and the imperialists of Vienna; but Napoleon had not counted on Alexander II. and Von Beust and Von der Pfordten[1] and Von Moltke. He judged by general principles, and was as ignorant of the precise situation in foreign capitals as, according to Bismarck, he was of geography. To the request of the younger Metternich, who was Austrian envoy at Paris, as to what answer he should make to Napoleon's entreaty for an Austrian army of observation in Bohemia, Von Beust replied with such icy coldness as to preclude all possibility of aid from that quarter. Almost simultaneously with the Ems telegram, Von Beust wrote to Metternich:

" I consider it paramountly important that the Emperor Napoleon and his ministers should not entertain the erroneous impression that they can, at their own good pleasure, drag us with them beyond the limits of our engagements, to the disregard of our own vital interests. They make much too bold in talking confidently about a corps of observation, to be stationed by us in Bohemia. The duke has no right whatsoever to count upon any such measure on

---

[1] Von Bray had succeeded Von der Pfordten, but his policy towards Prussia still continued in Bavaria.

our part. All that we have undertaken is not to ally ourselves to any other power without giving France due notice. . . . . It is alleged that Prussia will provoke war unless she will withdraw the Hohenzollern candidature. On this point I will speak quite frankly. If war be inevitable, it is, above all, owing to the attitude assumed by France from the very inception of the difficulty. Her first announcements do not in the least partake of a diplomatic character, but practically constitute a declaration of war against Prussia, couched in terms that have aroused amazement throughout Europe, and justified the conviction that she has made up her mind beforehand to war at any price . . ."

Napoleon III. was like a stock-gambler who is always ready to make friends with his last enemy if he can gain something by it; but Francis Joseph was made in a different mould,—an implacable Hapsburger. He admired and hated Bismarck, but he detested Napoleon. He perhaps recollected the policy of Metternich in 1813, to allow France and the allies to get well into the struggle before he interfered. Napoleon III. remembered that Austria was in the rear of Prussia; but he forgot that Hungary was in the rear of Austria. Von Beust asserts in his Memoirs that Russia exerted no pressure on Austria at this juncture, and there really does not seem to have been much need of it. Von Bray and his colleagues carried his bill for a war credit through the Bavarian chambers, in spite of the Ultramontanes and the *Vaterland* paper. The greatest triumph of Bismarck's policy appeared in Saxony, where the crown prince, who had fought so gallantly against the Prussians at Sadowa, led a whole German army corps to the campaign against France. Private soldiers may sometimes be made to fight against their inclination, but the commanding general must have his precincts swept clean of suspicion. At the same time it was reported to the associated press that Victor Emmanuel had telegraphed to the French government that any *attempt* to assist France in the present emergency could only result in his losing his crown. Napoleon must have left the Tuileries with a heavy heart.

Von Moltke's face grew young again at the prospect of having a crack at the "red legs," as the French soldiers were commonly designated. He was better informed concerning the condition of the French army than Napoleon was, and felt confident of success. The Crown Prince of Prussia says, in his diary, under date of July 15:

" Bismarck informed me that he, with Roon and Moltke, would go with me to Brandenburg to meet the king. On the way he expressed with great clearness and proper seriousness, free from his favorite little jests, his view of the peculiarities of our situation with France, so that it became clear to me that he and Moltke do not desire concessions for the sake of peace, which is already impossible, considering the strength and position of the French army. The king was surprised at our arrival, and during the rest of the journey, after he had heard Bismarck's statement, he had nothing substantial to oppose to the urgency of ordering immediate mobilization."

There can be no question that the crown prince took an active interest in the great events of 1870, and did his full share in what was accomplished at that time. The Reichstag emulated the French assembly in the unanimity with which it voted a war credit of a hundred and twenty million thalers. So do whole nations join in the chase when the dogs of war are let loose.

Professor Müller and General Hazen have both given an erroneous impression of the forces engaged on either side in 1870, by the manner in which they have stated them. The latter expresses his surprise that Napoleon, with armies amounting to three hundred thousand men, should have deliberately waged war against a force of twice that magnitude; while Müller speaks of the number of Germans finally engaged in the conflict as over eleven hundred thousand. Leaving out of account that Napoleon expected that the South German troops would fight with him, instead of against him, the German army at the commencement of hostilities numbered about five hundred thousand men; and as Bazaine's army at Metz numbered one hundred and seventy thousand, and one hundred and twenty-five thousand French soldiers surrendered at Sedan, it is evident that there must have been nearly one hundred thousand more stationed at Paris, Strasburg, and other fortresses, besides the Garde Mobile. During the siege of Paris enormous armies were recruited on the Loire and Rhone, and as at this period of the conflict the Germans were everywhere outnumbered, it seems probable that France finally placed in the field as large, though by no means so well disciplined, a force as her rival.

The first conflict took place at Saarbrücken, on the 2d of August, and is memorable for the melodramatic despatch which Napoleon sent to Eugénie concerning their intrepid boy, whose "coolness under fire made veterans weep." The town was held by a single Prussian regiment, which was driven out by General Frossard's army corps after a hot skirmish. The German victories of Spicheren and Wörth, however, followed on the 4th and 5th instant. Spicheren was a remarkable battle, fought by the colonels of German regiments without any general commander. At Wörth the Crown Prince of Prussia gave MacMahon a crushing defeat, as he well might with an army of a hundred thousand against fifty thousand men. At Vionville [1] Prince Frederick Charles fought a desperate battle against a French army twice as large as his own. At nightfall he remained master of the field, but gained no other advantage. The battle was remarkable for two cavalry charges, one of which was fully equal to the charge of the six hundred at Balaklava. Bismarck's two sons took part in the first charge, and the eldest, Herbert, escaped in a miraculous manner. One bullet struck his watch, another went through his coat, and a third wounded him in the thigh. His brother William came out of this fiery gulf unharmed, and brought with him a wounded comrade, whom he threw upon a horse at the risk of being captured himself. The second charge on the left wing was even more terrible. Out of eight squadrons of cavalry only three returned to the German lines. The rest were left upon the field,—a portion also captured,—but they succeeded in protecting the German flank until reinforcements could arrive.

Von Moltke now concentrated all the force he could bring

---

[1] Also called "Mars la Tour."

together against Metz, and Bazaine took up a strong position similar to Wellington's ground at Waterloo, but covering a much wider extent, with his right wing resting on Metz and his left extending to the village of St. Hubert on the northwest. His effective force numbered about one hundred and forty thousand men, and that of Von Moltke one hundred and seventy-five thousand. The struggle which followed can only be compared to the battles of Borodino and Leipsic, though the losses on either side were not so great. William I. and Bismarck arrived on the ground at noon, and witnessed the engagement. The French Zouaves, who had served in Algeria and stormed the hill at Solferino, declared that they had never seen such fighting as there was at Gravelotte.

The German head-quarters were stationed at Gravelotte, from which the battle has derived its name. The strength of the French position, partially fortified, is supposed to have counterbalanced the advantage of numbers on the German side. Canrobert commanded on the right, Bazaine in the centre, and Frossard on the left.

Von Moltke's plan was first to attack the enemy's right wing, and then, finally, to turn the left wing by a flanking movement, conducted by the Crown Prince of Saxony, with a simultaneous attack on Frossard's front. The movement against Canrobert failed, and the flanking movement occupied so much time that the Berlin guards, who attempted the front attack too soon, were fearfully cut up and obliged to retire. The Prussian cavalry that accompanied them succeeded in breaking the French squares, but suffered as severely as the French squadrons at Wörth. It was considered essential to sacrifice Prussian troops if possible, where sacrifices had to be made, in order to prevent the allied German states from feeling that their soldiers were made use of for Prussia's interest.

Encouraged by his success in repulsing the enemy, Bazaine decided to take the offensive, and late in the afternoon began a well-planned and determined attack on the German centre. The French fought more bravely than in any previous engagement, and for some time the issue of the battle remained in doubt, but they were finally repulsed by drawing together a large number of field-pieces at the critical point. Von Moltke followed this up by an assault on the extreme right and left of the French positions, and, though the attack on Canrobert did not meet with much success, the Crown Prince of Saxony finally captured the most important of Frossard's positions, and by nightfall Bazaine found himself with only one outlet of escape, and that in the direction of Metz. During the night the French abandoned their remaining positions, and the following day retired within the fortress. The German loss at Gravelotte was something over eighteen thousand men, of whom nearly five thousand were killed outright,—an exceptionally large proportion. The French loss was not much over twelve thousand, so that it is evident that they did not fight so bravely here as at Leipsic and Waterloo. Bazaine, although defeated, is admitted to have shown good military skill.

During Bazaine's attack on the Prussian lines both William I. and Bismarck were again in danger, for the former was too much absorbed in watching the course of the battle to consider his personal safety. On the following day Count Herbert was carried on a mattress to his father's quarters, where they made a bed for him on the floor. His wound was painful, but not dangerous. After he had been sent home to recuperate, his father said, " I trust now that I shall be able to save that fellow." He was evidently proud of both his sons, and related to several persons how William had helped a wounded comrade on to a horse and led him from the field. Before the close of the war both the young Bismarcks were promoted to lieutenancies.

Two nephews of Von Moltke were also serving at this time in the ranks. There is no other instance in modern history where the near relatives of such important personages have fought as common soldiers. It is this impartiality which inspires the Prussian people with such confidence in their government.

In the grave rejoicing over this victory at the Prussian head-quarters Bismarck's diplomatic habit never deserted him. He directed Dr. Busch to send a despatch to Berlin as follows :

"In the battle before Metz, August 18, the Saxons distinguished themselves by their usual bravery, and contributed most essentially to the attainment of the object of the German commander. To bring the Saxon army corps into the field very long marches from the right to the extreme left wing had been made the day before, and even on the 18th itself. In spite of these fatigues, they attacked with extraordinary energy, drove the enemy back, and completely fulfilled the duty they were charged with, thus preventing the enemy from escaping towards Thionville. Their losses in these actions amounted to twenty-two hundred men."

Bismarck was evidently desirous to conciliate the Saxons and inspire them with a more national feeling, but the Prussians bore the brunt of the struggle, and the Dresdeners still continued to abuse him for the next ten years.

SEDAN

At the outset of the war Napoleon had extorted a promise from Victor Emmanuel that he would respect the territory of Pius IX. so long as hostilities might continue. After the battle of Wörth, Prince Napoleon was despatched to Italy to obtain assistance on any terms that should be demanded, even if it was the possession of Rome itself. The Italian cabinet, however, could see plainly from this that Napoleon was in a very tight place, and that Rome was practically theirs as soon as they chose to take it. Prince Napoleon was therefore put off with the plea of a pretended consultation with Von Beust. This required several days, and the consequence was that Prince Napoleon was obliged to remain in Italy all winter. If Von Beust had little inclination for a French alliance in July, he had still less in August, with the prospect of another invasion of Bohemia; and the French opposition papers treated Prince Napoleon's embassy as if he had deserted his country in her hour of need, though it was not difficult to imagine the occasion for it.

Bismarck, meanwhile, was *en rapport* with the governments of Great Britain and other powers. He knew of Prince Napoleon's mission and how to counteract it with an equally good offer. After the battle at Gravelotte he sounded the great powers in regard to the annexation of Alsace and Lorraine. He did not expect favorable replies from them at this time, but he wished to inform them what they might look for in case the German successes continued. August 28 he dictated an official letter on the subject to the government organ in Berlin, indicating the policy which William I. and his ministers intended to pursue, and closing with this statement in regard to the restoration of those German provinces which had been treacherously seized on in the seventeenth century:

"He who sincerely desires peace on the continent of Europe, he who wishes that nations should lay down their arms, and that the plough should prevail over the sword, must wish above all that the neighbors of France on the east may secure this position, for France is the only disturber of peace, and will remain so as long as she has the power."

It is doubtful if any one in Germany—and certainly no one in Berlin—imagined that the Alsatians would make any decided objection to this transfer of their nationality. Their names are German, and most of them could speak German. Though they had long been accustomed to French domination, and were French themselves by association, they had at first been greatly incensed at this. To some one[1] who suggested that a slice of France might be added to Rhenish Prussia, Bismarck replied, "We do not want too many Frenchmen in Germany."

Dr. Moritz Busch has given a faithful account of Bismarck's sayings and proceedings during the campaign of 1870, and much of it is instructive and valuable to us. We miss, however, the penetrating force and broad generalization of statement which make the remarks of the first Napoleon so magnetic and impressive. Bismarck is admitted to have been the wiser man of the two, but he was not in a position to speak out his mind so freely. There were some truths which even Napoleon at the height of his power could not venture

---

[1] Name not given, but he must have been an important personage, perhaps self-important.

to speak; but Bismarck was obliged to be doubly cautious, for he had not only the ear of the public on one side, ready to catch up and report whatever he might say, but on the other side the royal family had also to be considered. It was a shrewd statement Von Beust made, that it was generally better for an ambassador to see too little than to see too much.[1] It would not do even for Bismarck to appear to be too knowing, and as a natural consequence he made a practice of disguising his genius in the dress of trivial conversation. He told anecdotes of Humboldt, Metternich, and other past actors on the German stage, amusing enough, but not of exceptional value. General Sheridan, to whom, as an American, he might perhaps have spoken more freely, found him a great talker, but not memorable for bright and characteristic sayings. Bismarck talked about small matters to change the current of his mind and to avoid speaking of more important ones. He acquired this habit at Frankfort in the days of the musty old Diet, and found it useful ever afterwards.

We do not hear of profound reflections on European politics, but we know from Dr. Busch that Bismarck occasionally conversed with him in a higher strain than was his usual wont, and it is just these colloquies, which we should most like to know, that his secretary prudently declines to favor us with. He talked philosophy on his way to the battle of Sedan,[2] as such a man might to prevail over the demon which accompanies extravagant success; and there are other incidents as terse and significant in their way as those recorded of old Dr. Johnson. One such happened just before the battle of Beaumont, while the troops were hurrying forward to take up their allotted positions in the field. Bismarck was giving some directions to Privy Counsellor Abeken, who sent the famous telegram from Ems, and in the midst of his statement Prince Charles of Hohenzollern rode by with

---

[1] In reference to Prince Richard Metternich, who was wholly surprised at the breaking out of the Franco-German war.

[2] Bismarck carried with him to the French campaign a book called "Daily Refreshments for Believing Christians," and he had a clerk in his employ named Engel (angel).

his negro lackey in oriental costume. Abeken followed this phenomenon with his eyes, and failed to hear what Bismarck was saying. The count lost patience and exclaimed, " Listen to what I have to tell you, Mr. Privy Counsellor, and for God's sake let princes be princes. We are talking business here." Then, after he had finished with Abeken, he remarked, " Our old friend is quite carried away if he sees anything belonging to the court; but, after all, I could not do without him." To Bismarck princes evidently were princes, and they were nothing more. The undisguised use which Bismarck made of newspapers, at this and other times, to circulate opinions and statements favorable to his policy was one of his peculiarities; so much the honester and better that it was undisguised.

Von Moltke left Prince Frederick Charles to besiege Metz, and, having united with the crown prince, set forward on the road to Paris. His army had been largely reinforced from Germany, and amounted to more than two hundred thousand men in all. The whole northeast of France was filled with German soldiers. At Verdun, half-way between Metz and Chalons, Von Moltke first heard that the French army was at the north of him, and he considered this move to his advantage, as he could now descend perpendicularly on Mac-Mahon's communications. There were a number of small engagements along the line of the Meuse, in all of which the French were compelled to retreat. On August 30 a French army corps was surprised at breakfast near Beaumont by the German heavy artillery, and, having been severely bombarded, were attacked by German infantry and driven off in great confusion. MacMahon, having thus been already foiled in his plan, withdrew his outposts and concentrated his forces around the fortress of Sedan. The star of the Bonapartes was evidently setting.

This was the worst plan that MacMahon and Napoleon could have pursued. If they had made a precipitate retreat towards Paris a large portion of their army might have been saved. The siege of Paris would have followed as a matter

of course, but its chances of success would have been considerably lessened, and Louis Napoleon would have remained
on his throne, at least until peace was declared. Sedan is a
Vauban fortress, built on rising ground in a valley, and nearly
surrounded by lofty hills. Before the invention of rifle projectiles it was calculated to sustain a siege of a year's duration, but with the improved ordnance of the nineteenth century an enemy can command it from the heights on every side.
Metz was impregnable, but Sedan proved a strategic trap.

The town lies in the centre of a natural amphitheatre,
through which winds the sluggish Meuse to its meeting with
the Sambre, on which Blücher was defeated in 1815. About
the same distance to the southwest is the city of Laon, where
Blücher defeated the first Napoleon. On the 1st of September MacMahon formed his line of battle in the concave order
on a range of low hills behind the fortress and town, his left
wing drawn around to the river, and his right wing stretching
off towards the west. He had blown up the bridge crossing
the river at Sedan, but the Germans, having control of Stenay,
marched down both sides of it, and planted batteries on the
heights to the east and south. William I. and Bismarck, with
a large retinue of princes and officers, took possession of a
stubble-field on a hill about one mile from the town,—a spot
still exhibited to tourists. The king went round to the different groups, saying, " Gentlemen, spread yourselves, and do
not attract the enemy's fire by standing too close together."
Von Moltke and the German staff, with whom was General
Sheridan, occupied a lower position on a declivity nearer the
scene of action. The army of the crown prince was on the
opposite side of the Meuse. As the battle progressed the
German line extended itself continually to the left, and to
withdraw attention from this movement Von Moltke directed
a vigorous attack on the left wing of the enemy. It was
unfortunate for the French that Marshal MacMahon was
wounded early in the engagement; and his successor, General
Wimpfen, does not appear to have understood the character
of this enclosing movement. From the first the French suffered more than the Germans, being exposed to an almost

concentric artillery fire, and it was not until General Wimpfen had repulsed the enemy on his left wing that he seems to have realized the situation his army was in. He then brought forward his least injured regiments on the right for a desperate attempt to break through the cordon of the crown prince. Here he arranged an attack of infantry supported by cavalry at about half-past two P.M. Bismarck, from his standpoint on the eastern side of the Meuse, could see the blue and red lines of the French advancing and falling back again under the destructive fire of the Prussians. Then came the cavalry charges,—a magnificent spectacle. Twice they came on, but never reached the Prussian lines. "The beggars are too weak," cried Sheridan, who had begun to sympathize with the hard position of the French army. The king could see through his field-glass that the ground was covered with the bodies of horses and men.

After this Von Moltke ordered a gradual advance along the whole line, and in the course of an hour the French troops had everywhere fallen back to the immediate vicinity of the town and fortress. This placed them more at the mercy of the German shells than before, so that MacMahon's army was fast becoming a demoralized mob. Then Napoleon, wishing to prevent further bloodshed, ordered a white flag to be raised over the fort, and the firing ceased. "This must be a proud day for you, Mr. Chancellor," remarked one of the foreign *attachés* to Count Bismarck. "I have nothing to do with this," quickly replied the latter; "it is the king and Von Moltke who are to be congratulated here. That the South Germans fight with us, not against us, may be something to my credit, but I have nothing to do with military affairs." When some one inquired if the French emperor was not with the army which was about to surrender, Bismarck said, "I doubt it. Napoleon is not very wise, but he knows too much to be in Sedan." It was not long before an officer arrived to inform the king that Napoleon was in the fortress.

General Wimpfen now appeared with Von Moltke to arrange terms of capitulation. Napoleon wished permission for his troops to march over the Belgian frontier and be disarmed there, but this could not be granted. William I. said, "This is indeed a great success," and gave his two hands to Von Moltke and the crown prince, adding, "I thank you both for what you have contributed towards this victory." He then thanked Bismarck also, and drew him aside for a lengthy conversation, which produced a slight expression of displeasure on the face of the crown prince, more noticeable from the gladness of those around him.[1] The capture of a live emperor, however, was not an every-day occurrence, and required serious diplomatic consideration. How he should be received, how he should be disposed of, and how his capture would affect the relations of Prussia with other governments, were points on which only Bismarck could be consulted. He advised the king to avoid an interview with Napoleon, and that he had better return to Stenay, where he could find more comfortable quarters. Afterwards Bismarck said, that if the emperor were to break his parole and escape over the Belgian frontier it might be quite as well for all parties concerned. From being the first monarch in Europe, Louis Napoleon had suddenly become a white elephant, whom nobody wanted.

Bismarck was awakened at an early hour on September 2 with the information that Napoleon desired a personal interview with him at Donchéry. Mounting his horse, he rode down the hill alone to meet Napoleon, who was in a carriage with three French generals. Bismarck says, "I had a revolver in my belt, and his eye rested on it for a moment." What was Napoleon III. thinking of in that instant? Was it the possibility of suicide? Bismarck took off his hat, though contrary to rule on such occasions, and they went together into a weaver's cottage, a yellow house with white shutters, Venetian blinds on the upper story, and a slated roof. Napoleon was friendly enough, as Bismarck said afterwards; complained that he had been forced into the war; wished for an interview with King William; wished for more favorable terms, which he would negotiate on a political basis. Bis-

---

[1] In one way or another Bismarck was evidently a thorn in the side of the crown prince. No wonder he speaks so frequently of the old monarch's health in the letters to Frau von Bismarck.

marck informed him that the terms of the surrender had been negotiated by Von Moltke, and were not within his province; that the king was at an inconvenient distance, and that as he, Napoleon, was now a prisoner of war, political negotiations could only be carried on with the *de facto* government of France. He assured Napoleon of considerate treatment, and offered him his own lodging for the night.[1]

Napoleon's friendliness may have been owing in a measure to the insults he had received from his own soldiers. He felt now that his life, at least, was safe, and perhaps the wheel of fortune might again turn in his favor. The French prisoners also took their captivity in a light-hearted manner, and the wounded Frenchmen made friends with their companions in the German hospitals.[2]

Bismarck, having disposed of the emperor and sent his secretary to distribute five hundred cigars among wounded soldiers, went in search of his younger son, and suddenly came upon " Count Bill," who was a large, athletic fellow, carrying a French pig in his arms, evidently for the benefit of the mess-room table. On seeing his father he dropped the pig and fell into his arms. Bismarck thought the French officers must have been astonished to behold a German general embracing a private soldier. His son explained that he had found driving a pig very troublesome, and finally concluded that it would be much easier to carry it.

Von Moltke is the only high German official who is reported to have shown a decided elation at the victory of Sedan. He may have felt that his life's work was nearly finished, for serious resistance was no longer to be expected. That he had overcome the enemy, with the advantage of numbers, discipline, and courage on his side, was not sur-

---

[1] This promise was faithfully kept. Napoleon was sent to Wilhelmshohe through Belgium the next day in a close carriage to avoid the humiliation of his being exposed to the gaze of German soldiers. During his confinement in Prussia he was handsomely treated,—very differently from the treatment of Napoleon I.,—and, according to the American opinion, much better than he deserved. W. Müller has made a mistake here; Busch was on the ground.

[2] Dr. Busch, i. 103.

prising, but that all the movements of that vast army should have been directed with such precision, and been so invariably successful, was a record for the future historian which the greatest commanders might have envied him. The first Napoleon himself might have been astonished at the capture of an army of one hundred and twenty thousand men. He went on his Russian campaign with nearly half a million soldiers, and the only advantage he gained over the enemy was the indecisive victory of Borodino. Von Moltke was always the model of what a soldier should be,—as Emerson says,

> "Grave, chaste, contented though retired,
> And of all other men desired."

When some one asked a Prussian officer, many years after these events, why Von Moltke had not been made a prince, as Bismarck was, he replied, "Von Moltke does not care for it himself, and we all feel that it would add nothing to his reputation." He has been compared to Wellington, who was also a man rather difficult to find fault with; but he made war on a grander scale than Wellington, and was more decidedly a man of genius, though perhaps not as forcible a character. That they were both of a reserved temperament does not imply that they were cold-hearted or indifferent to the welfare of their fellow-men. Von Moltke was probably the most popular German of his time.[1] It was not without reason that he was called "the thinker of battles."

---

[1] The writer saw Von Moltke on the floor of the Prussian Landtag in 1873. He was of rather slender build, broad-shouldered but thin, with aquiline features and a much-wrinkled face; eyes like a falcon's. His eyes were supposed to resemble Frederick the Great's; Cæsar also had falcon eyes. He wore silver epaulets and a broad red stripe on his pants. When he saluted an acquaintance he bowed low and came up again very erect.

CHAPTER X

WILLIAM I. and Bismarck looked at each other after Napoleon III. had been transported to Germany. What next? They had not long to wait for news and political changes. The Second Empire had only existed by the support of the army, and now that that was gone, it collapsed like a railway speculation. In the Chamber of Deputies there was the greatest confusion; the rabble of Paris broke into the legislative halls and intimidated the ministry, who requested the establishment of a committee of defence, while the radical leaders demanded the deposition of the Bonaparte dynasty. Finally Gambetta, Favre, and a majority of the assembly left the hall, and, escorted by an immense crowd, held a meeting at the Hôtel de Ville, where a republic was proclaimed and a provisional government constituted, with a committee of public safety and General Trochu for president, an officer whose chief distinction at this time was that he had not been in favor with Napoleon. Thiers prudently declined to serve on this committee, among whose members there were several avowed Socialists. Before these proceedings were concluded the empress had already left the Tuileries and was on her way to England. The committee immediately made arrangements for levying fresh armies,—one in Brittany, another on the Loire, and a third in Provence. Jules Favre, the French compeer of Wendell Phillips, with two others, were appointed on an embassy to confer with Bismarck in regard to an armistice and an honorable peace, if that could be obtained.

Bismarck held the opinion that Victor Emmanuel was ready to sell his soul for Rome, and it is certain that an Italian envoy, Count Vimercati, was in consultation with Napoleon at Metz previous to the battle of Saarbrücken. Victor Emmanuel finally kept his word to both parties in this conflict; and, though after the defeat at Wörth he resisted a strong pressure from the Italian Liberals to take possession of the Eternal City, after Sedan he considered his engagement no longer binding, and accordingly marched in with a sufficient force to overawe Pius IX. Great was the rejoicing of the Roman citizens at the downfall of the priests' temporal power, and a plébiscite, taken immediately afterwards through the States of the Church, resulted in an almost unanimous approval of consolidation with the Italian government. Few more important events than this have taken place during the nineteenth century, and here again we recognize the harmony of Bismarck's policy with the essential needs of his time.

Nevertheless, at the moment Bismarck treated the matter with cool indifference. " We might have done something for the pope," he said, " if he had been willing to do more for us. Nothing for nothing is the only rule that one can act on in such cases." He may have thought at the moment that the Italians were getting more than they deserved, and this feeling must have been increased when Garibaldi, carried off his feet with the name of a republic, landed at Marseilles with a shipload of Carbonari to assist the French in driving the Germans out of their country. A change in the form of government did not make the war less unjustifiable, and Garibaldi, without being aware of it, was now enlisting in the pope's service and doing the pope's work.[1] It was true he may have suspected that on the conclusion of peace the King of Prussia would replace Louis Napoleon on his throne, but Bismarck's attitude towards the government in Paris must have soon dispelled this illusion.

In fact, Bismarck always favored republicanism in France from the first. If, as has been stated, he did so from an expectation that the extravagances of the new government would bring republicanism into disrepute, the result has not answered this calculation;[2] but it is certain that he once said

---

[1] The German hegemony in Europe is still the only support of Italian unity.

[2] One reason may have been to justify King William's proclamation before the battle of Wörth, that he came to make war against the French government, and not the French people.

to Dr. Busch, "I am by temperament a republican, but my belief in God makes me a monarchist," a statement which it is difficult to understand, except by supposing that he considered it prudent to qualify the assertion in some way. He may have heartily wished at times for a German republic of which he could be president, impossible as he knew this to be. At all events, when the German ambassador at Paris advocated the support of a *coup d'état* for the restoration of the Bonapartes, Bismarck set himself firmly against it, although such a change would have been for the interest of Germany as well as the monarchical principle; for nothing could be more improbable than that either Napoleon III. or his son would undertake another campaign on the Rhine. At the present time Germany has more to fear from republican France than it might from a Bourbon or Bonaparte dynasty. Here Bismarck appears again in alliance with the tendencies of his age.

The German army now began to extend its lines towards Paris, and Bismarck issued a circular to the powers, stating the terms on which the king and his ministers were willing to conclude peace,—nothing less than the retrocession of Alsace and Lorraine, or, as the Germans call these provinces, Elsass and Lothringen.

The great powers could make little objection to this, as they would certainly have done the same under like conditions. Considering the success of the German armies, it was looked upon as a modest demand. In like circumstances the first Napoleon would have annexed the half of France. It is known that Bismarck favored this demand, but he was willing to leave out Metz and its surrounding territory for the sake of an earlier agreement, but Von Moltke and the Prussian staff would not hear of this. They considered the fortress of Metz essential to a scientific frontier for Germany. If Bismarck had opposed these terms the result would have been the same. The current of feeling, not only in the army but throughout Prussia, would have been too strong for any one man to resist it.

The provisional government at Paris replied with a manifesto, in which the expression, "not one inch of territory, not one stone of our fortresses," has become proverbial. The idea of dismembering France, even to this extent, had never been dreamed of before, and excited the greatest indignation. It was another illustration of how impossible it was for the French to place themselves in the position of other people. If the Prussians had been defeated in an equally decisive manner they would have been obliged to surrender the left bank of the Rhine as a matter of course. Even if the provisional government had thought best to accede to this sacrifice to prevent further bloodshed, it is not likely that public opinion would have supported it; but there was good reason why Favre, Gambetta, and their associates should desire to continue the war.

Bismarck had reached Ferrières and was quartered on the country residence of the Rothschilds about the middle of September, when Sir Edward Malet, the British envoy at Paris, came to him as an intermediary, and wished to know if the Prussian government would treat with the Paris committee as the *de facto* government of France; and Bismarck's reply was, that he was ready to consider terms of peace with any government that would obtain the substantial support of the French people. This was sufficient guarantee of the republic before the world, and showed that Bismarck had no intention of interfering with the domestic affairs of France.

Jules Favre came to Ferrières on the 19th and 20th of September in order to negotiate an armistice,—presumably to hold elections for the establishment of a new government, but also, doubtless, to gain time for military preparations. Bismarck tried to explain to him that as an armistice would be an advantage to the French, the Germans should also receive corresponding advantages, and suggested the surrender of Strasburg and Toul in return for it; but Favre either could not or would not recognize this fact, and expatiated on the sufferings of his country and the advantage to Germany of a speedy conclusion of the war. He insisted, however, that it was impossible to make territorial concessions to Prussia. Bismarck spoke of Strasburg as the western gate of Germany,

LIFE OF BISMARCK

" the key to their house," and that its possession was essential for the future security of the German nation.

Favre [in his own account]. Then it is Alsace and Lorraine.

Bismarck. I have not spoken of Lorraine; but as for Alsace, I am very decided. We regard it as indispensable for our defence.

Favre. Such a sacrifice would inspire France with sentiments of vengeance and hatred, leading by a fatal necessity to another war. Alsace intends to remain French. She might be ruled, but cannot be assimilated. The province will always be an embarrassment and perhaps a source of weakness to Germany.

Bismarck. I do not deny that; but in any case, even if we treat your nation in a generous manner, she will always be plotting against Germany. Your people will never become reconciled to Sedan any more than they are to Waterloo.

Favre attempted to show Bismarck that he ought to recognize that the progress of industry, the creation of railroads, the interchange and complication of commercial interests, would tend in future to render war more and more improbable. The present war was a severe lesson to France, and all the more so because the French people had been dragged into it against their will. Bismarck, however, denied this, affirming that the French had desired the war and supported the emperor in proclaiming it. Favre's reiteration that the war was the exclusive work of Napoleon III. was promptly denied by Bismarck, and certainly was not a fair statement. Neither was Bismarck mindful of the Duke of Brunswick in 1792, when he declared that Germany never made war upon France. Favre believed that there was but one means of pacifying the French people and of uniting the two nations, by relinquishing the old policy of conquest and military glory, and by adopting that of liberty and the fraternity of nations. In conclusion, Bismarck said:

"I acknowledge that you have always supported the policy you defend to-day; and if I were sure that it were that of France, I would engage the king to withdraw without touching your territory or demanding an obole. And I know so well his generous sentiments that I would guarantee you his acceptance. But you represent the imperceptible minority. You have sprung from a popular disturbance, which may overthrow you to-morrow. We have therefore no guarantee. We should have no more in any government which may succeed you. The evil is in the fickleness and irreflective character of your nation; the remedy is in the material pledge which we have the right to take."

At a second interview, which took place in the Salle de Chasseurs at Haute Maison, Favre pressed the subject of an armistice, but without making any impression on the minister-president. When in the course of his argument he referred to the Prussian victories, and the effect that they had produced in the eyes of the world,—a military glory which might satisfy the most ambitious,—Bismarck interrupted him with,—

"Do not mention that; that is a glory without value to us. It is our interest alone that we consult, and the need of guaranteeing it is so evident that we should be wrong to abandon ourselves to a chimerical hope."

Favre believed that a profound change had taken place in the French nation and in the opinions of the civilized world, —a strong opinion against going to war:

"The majority of the nation will be necessarily drawn by that irresistible current which conducts her towards a new policy and to higher destinies. She will understand that the support of all nations—especially Germany—is indispensable to her; and she will seek it, not by sterile conquests, but by the benefits of work and interchange; and it may be affirmed that if this movement be favored by wise statesmen, war will soon become impossible."

To this Bismarck replied,—

"The question is to find these wise statesmen, and I am convinced that they do not exist in France. You express noble ideas, and if you were master I should be of your opinion, and would treat with you at once; but you are in opposition to the real sentiments of your country, which retains its warlike disposition; and, to speak only of the present, you, as a government, are born of sedition, and you may be overthrown to-morrow by the populace of Paris." [1]

So the conference ended. The interviews have slight historical importance, but Favre's account of them has a rare value for its clear setting forth of Bismarck's plain, straightforward method of dealing. How conspicuous does the virtue of these two men appear in it! How much honester were these two diplomats negotiating for whole provinces than the average business man who has wool to buy or iron to sell! The problem they were dealing with was one of the gravest, and the arguments on either side evince great good sense and historical foresight. Only time can determine which of the two was most nearly right.

Bismarck showed Favre a curious missive which had been sent to Napoleon III. by his empress as a sort of passport for a Bonapartist envoy. It was a photograph of an English sea-port, and underneath was written, "This is a view of Hastings, which I have selected as a residence for my good Louis;" signed "Eugénie." Bismarck did not think well of the emissary, but gave him permission to visit the emperor. Bismarck, in his report to the king of the interview, said:

"I was unable to convince him that conditions which France had obtained from Italy and demanded of Germany, without having been at war with either country,—conditions which France would undoubtedly have imposed upon us had we been vanquished, and which had been the natural outcome of every modern war,—could involve no dishonor to a country conquered after having gallantly defended itself; or that the honor of France differed in any essential respect from that of other countries."

So they parted, to meet again under less favorable auspices for France.

Favre and the provisional government had excellent reasons for not desiring too speedy a termination of the war. Marshal Bazaine was a thorough Bonapartist, and had with him in Metz the only French army that was now of any value.

---

[1] Favre's "Government of the National Defence," chap. iv.

If peace had been concluded at this moment, it is morally certain that he would have marched upon Paris and replaced Napoleon in the Tuileries. To give stability to the new government it was, therefore, necessary that the Committee of Safety should maintain an army of its own and continue the war until either Bazaine surrendered or they became strong enough to withstand the Bonapartist faction.

Neither did Favre and his colleagues count without some chance of success. To besiege a city of two million inhabitants, fortified in the most skilful manner and capable of raising an army of one hundred and fifty thousand men within its walls, was a problem altogether new in military science. Three hundred thousand men would be required to invest it, and half as many to prevent Bazaine from breaking forth from Metz. Then they depended on a general arming of the population, such as had been so successful in the first French revolution. What they neglected to consider was that the soldiers who drove the Duke of Brunswick back to Germany in 1792 were fighting for a great cause; they were filled with the spirit of the time, and the whole French nation was at a white heat. It was now the Germans who had a cause to fight for, and this was as essential to their success as Von Moltke's tactics. The rank and file of Louis Napoleon's army were not the persons who made the conflict, and felt little interest in it. Never since the Seven Years' War had French armies fought so tamely. The Parisian journalists and gay saunterers of the boulevards who had helped to precipitate the conflict were the ones who had least at stake in it. The small peasant proprietors in France knew little of what Bismarck was doing, and cared less. They hated war, and only wished to enjoy the fruits of the earth without interference. Nevertheless, the Committee of Safety was so nearly right that Bismarck confessed to Von Beust three years later that if Bazaine had held out a week longer German affairs would have been in a critical condition. By the 1st of December Germany was almost denuded of able-bodied men, and trade, except for military supplies, was nearly at a standstill. Such mammoth wars cannot be of long duration.

As Favre's mission had come to no result, Thiers was sent
on a circular tour to foreign courts for the purpose of organizing a coalition against Germany. Thiers was the best person that could have been appointed for this purpose, for,
in spite of his national egotism, he was the ablest French
politician of his time,—a skilful and conciliatory negotiator.
However, he met with no success. He found in England, it
is true, a favorable public sentiment,—songs about that wicked
Bismarck were sung in coffee-houses and cheap theatres,—
but as the British government had no army to speak of, there
was not much it could do to assist its Crimean ally. The Tsar
Alexander asked the coldly pertinent question, "What can
you do for us in return?" Neither he nor Victor Emmanuel
could be persuaded that the retrocession of Elsass and Lothringen could in any way disturb the European balance of
power; while Von Beust was still less inclined to place an
army of observation in Bohemia than he had been two months
earlier. Meanwhile Von Moltke had drawn his lines about the
capital, and Paris was besieged. On October 6 Bismarck and
William I. arrived at Versailles; the king was quartered in the
palace of Louis XIV., and Bismarck at the house of Veuve
Jessé. An English M. P., who was residing in Paris and permitted himself to be shut in there, has given an edifying
account of the proceedings he witnessed. The confusion
would seem to have been almost indescribable, and he compares General Trochu to a military professor who understands
theory, but is not a fighter. Large crowds of French men
and women rushed into the city at the last moment, where
they could be of no use except to eat up the supplies and
hasten the famine. It seems as if the Committee of Safety
might have been wise enough to send away those families
who could afford to live in London or elsewhere before the
city was encircled by the German forces.

Bismarck, anticipating that the Paris government would
make what capital they could out of the failure of Favre's
negotiation to prejudice the German interests, addressed a
circular to the powers, in which he summed up the situation
in these terms:

" By refusing to avail itself of the opportunity offered to it to elect a National Assembly (even within the portions of French territory occupied by us) the French government proves its determination to prolong the difficulties, hindering it from effecting an international conclusion of peace, and to close its ears to the voice of the French people."

One effect of this was to excite the Legitimists and Bonapartists with renewed hope that their claims might yet find consideration at the German head-quarters. The crown prince in his diary thus sums up the position of affairs on October 9 :

" Bismarck tells me that Chambord and Ollivier have written to his Majesty. The former wishes that he should comply with the demands of his people, but make no concessions of land ; Ollivier stands for war, but warns against debt ; and both presume to give advice to the conqueror ! St. Cloud in flames. Burnside comes again from Paris, commissioned by the government, which offers proposals without any judgment, hearkens to no suggestions, and carries on the war without plan, holding counsel only with itself. Bazaine wishes his chief of staff to arrange treaties of a military-political kind. Bismarck will listen to him, but neither Roon nor Moltke, who, disagreeing with each other, yet object to the reception of communications. Friedrich Charles is opposed to this because he fears the capitulation may be concluded at Versailles. The king will direct the negotiations from Würtemberg so as not to appear in Bavaria's tow. Bismarck keeps watch of the imperial question, advising me that in 1866 he may have failed to realize the strength of the popular impulse in Germany for the imperial title. He is now chiefly apprehensive of too great a display in the way of court splendor, in regard to which I reassured him."

It is clear from this summary that there was not always harmony and agreement in the German camp. We see the crown prince already looking forward to the imperial title and substantially justifying Von Sybel's statement in regard to the kings and dukes in Germany in 1866 ; while Bismarck applies a timely warning to the weak side of the victor of Wörth. If there were five distinct political parties in France, there were also five different commanders-in-chief to the German forces. Somewhat later we hear of a decided coolness between Von Moltke and the crown prince in regard to military operations before Paris. Fortunately, everything came to be decided at last by the old monarch, and he finally followed Bismarck's advice.

General Burnside had offered to serve as mediator in the interest of the French republic, and Bismarck, who liked Americans on account of their frankness and business-like methods, readily agreed to this. He was accordingly escorted to Paris under a white flag, and remained there two days, but returned without accomplishing anything. Burnside described the condition of affairs there in terms similar to the besieged M. P., and he did not hesitate to express the opinion that it was of no use attempting to reason with such people. The real difficulty was that he had undertaken the office of peace-maker too early in the season; but it is evident that he considered that the German claims were not unreasonable. Gambetta had gone off in a balloon to organize the army of the Loire, from which grand results were expected. A note was received from Earl Granville—a faint echo of Thiers's visit to London—entreating King William to bring the horrors of war to a close as speedily as possible, and was bluntly answered by Bismarck to the effect that there was no place for sentiment in politics.

If Jules Favre had consented to Bismarck's proposal in regard to an armistice, the French cause would have lost nothing by it, for Toul surrendered three days later, and Strasburg followed suit at the end of a week, after a bombardment of three days. How Bazaine was informed of MacMahon's advance on the line of the Meuse remains a mystery; but he made a vigorous attempt to escape from Metz at that time, which was frustrated by the activity of Frederick Charles, though with heavy losses on both sides. Bismarck complained at dinner that the Red Prince was not sufficiently considerate of the lives of his soldiers. It is doubtful if Bazaine made any effort to escape after the dethronement of Napoleon; and the reference in the crown prince's diary to an audience with Bazaine's chief of staff clearly refers to some political negotiation, which was, however, strangled in its birth. An army of one hundred and eighty thousand men could not hold out forever in a besieged fortress, and Von Moltke calculated exactly the length of time they would be able to do this. On the 27th of October, Bazaine, Canrobert, and Lebœuf surrendered with six hundred cannon, besides the guns on the fortress; the heaviest capitulation recorded in history. That Bazaine behaved with comparative indifference towards the French cause after the battle of Sedan cannot be denied; but whether the result would have been different if he had made successive attempts to escape from the German blockade is doubtful. In all probability, by acting as he did he saved the lives of thousands of brave men. After peace was concluded, however, he was made a scapegoat of and condemned to death for treasonable practices towards a republic which at that time certainly had no real existence. His sentence was commuted by President MacMahon to exile for a term of years.

WILLIAM AS EMPEROR

That Bismarck should take advantage of these signal successes to strengthen the position of William I. in Germany was to have been expected. He felt now that he held the South German states in the hollow of his hand, and could accomplish whatever the king and his ministers considered best; but there is nothing more remarkable in the life of this world-statesman than his readiness to seize an opportunity when it suddenly presented itself to him, and the cautious, gradual manner which he adopted at other times to gain his ends. His prediction, made years since, that the North German confederation once formed, the South German states would gravitate to it as inevitably as iron to the magnet, was now to be fulfilled; but he did not wish to artificially hasten an event which he foresaw would take place in the due course of nature. In spite of the popular enthusiasm which is aroused by a victory like Sedan, he knew that the least attempt to exert a pressure on Würtemberg or Bavaria would not only

excite anti-Prussian agitation there, but would create a permanent ill feeling in those states, and an evil reproach towards the
king and himself in other countries. The crown prince was
equally desirous of attaining this end; and we may suppose
that his interest in German national unity was a fairly unselfish
one; but he did not, like Bismarck, see over the whole ground,
and he feared that the grand opportunity might pass by without achieving the due result. From the last of October until
December, 1870, we find continual references to this subject in
the crown prince's diary, which proves that the matter was
under discussion at the German head-quarters for several
weeks before definite action was taken.

The discussion would seem to have been concerning the
organization of an upper house of parliament, and that the
crown prince, from his English education and proclivities,
favored something like the House of Lords, without realizing
the political weakness and comparative uselessness of that
venerable body. It may have been that the King of Saxony
and others wished for such a collective union of princes, so as
to maintain their dignity nearer to an equality with William I.
Bismarck, however, did not want personages of that sort
staying in Berlin; besides which, the presidency of such an
assembly would have been a severe burden to the aged king.
Neither did he believe in the imitation of foreign political
machinery. Every country, in his opinion, should have its
own style of government.

On the 1st of November the crown prince speaks of a conference between the ministers of the smaller German states
for the purpose of winning over Bavaria to the scheme of a
German empire, with responsible delegates for the states, or
else a House of Lords; but he says, "It has come to no result, because Bray, the Bavarian envoy, asserts that all these
questions will have to be discussed with Count Delbrück at
Munich." Bavaria was evidently the chief and only remaining obstacle to the completion of this plan.

What the king's views were on this subject we have no
means of ascertaining further than this: The crown prince
says, October 27:

"The king told Regenbach yesterday that he looks upon the North German situation as requiring a change and revision, and has declared himself generally favorable in regard to the question of the empire. As Bismarck cannot leave here, people are of the opinion that the German Reichstag had better be called here. Then the power of impressions would work; and if, besides, the congress of princes would join in with the same session, as is now much desired by me, then the German cause would be helped at a blow."

Again the crown prince writes, November 16:

"Talked with Bismarck about the German question. He wants to come to a decision, but expounds the difficulties with a shrug of his shoulders,—What can be done with the South Germans? Do I wish that they should be threatened? I answered, 'Yes, indeed, there is no danger at all if we are fair and imperious; you will see that I am right in maintaining that you are not as yet, by any means, sufficiently aware of your power.' Bismarck seriously deprecates any threatening,[1] and thinks if we went to extreme measures we might drive Bavaria into the arms of Austria. 'We shall have to leave the imperial question to work itself out of its own free will.' I replied that I was well acquainted with that method of procedure, but that, representing the future as I do, I could not regard the matter with indifference; that it would not be necessary to use brute force to prevent Bavaria and Würtemberg from uniting themselves to Austria."

There is no reason why we should blame the crown prince for his attitude on the South German question, except so far as it appears inconsistent with respect to his professions of liberalism and government according to law and order during the Schleswig-Holstein muddle. No great nation has ever been organized without the use of force in some direction. We may have supposed that the United States was an exception to this, until we were undeceived in 1861. There was no serious disagreement between Bismarck and the crown prince, as the partisans of both have sometimes tried to prove;

---

[1] One of Bismarck's sayings was, "If you want to make a bargain, never threaten."

it was only a question of the right time and method; and here Bismarck appears in decided advantage to his would-be rival. If there was opposition anywhere to the founding of a new German empire, it came from the Prussian Particularists, who foresaw that the admission of the South German states would diminish their influence, and perhaps from the old king, who dreaded the infusion of Bavarian Catholics and Würtemberg democrats.

The real difficulty in dealing with Bavaria in this emergency originated not in Munich, but in Rome. Since the occupation of the latter city by Victor Emmanuel, Pius IX. and Antonelli had been in a state of exasperation beyond the faculty of speech either to express or describe; and since they could discover no way to escape from their own difficulties, they were determined to make as much trouble for Bismarck and the King of Prussia as they possibly could. There is no engine for such work like the priesthood, and perhaps it was fortunate that the young King of Bavaria had no queen for the Jesuits to play upon; but they exerted themselves to arouse the Bavarians to the danger which threatened the true faith from the prospect of having their country under the control of a Protestant emperor, and they started a lively anti-German agitation in Elsass and Lothringen. This went so far that the Bavarian ministry feared a popular uprising in Munich, which, with their whole army employed in France, would have been a dangerous problem to deal with. Prussian interference would have been only too likely to kindle this into a flame, and it was from his better information of existing conditions that Bismarck could answer the crown prince with so much confidence.

Two months later, after the empire had been established and William had been crowned emperor in Versailles, it was generally reported in English newspapers, and echoed in many American ones, that the Crown Prince of Prussia was opposed to the new political order in Germany, and would have much preferred to have his father remain simply King of Prussia at the head of the North German confederation. This is an excellent example of the growth of the modern *mythus*.

Although English gentlemen have always confessed that the national organization of Germany was an advantage to Great Britain and conducive to the general peace of Europe, a large allowance of national vanity was aroused by the surprising victories of Gravelotte and Sedan and the formidable growth of this neighboring power. As the crown prince was Victoria's son-in-law, it was considered essential for the credit of the English royal family that he should be represented as having no direct agency in such high-handed proceedings. All newspaper editors are by no means to be considered untruthful; but when one of the brotherhood imagines such a *canard* as this, others naturally copy it, and the correspondents of leading newspapers were not slow to transport such valuable information to America. Now they are trying to prove that it was the crown prince rather than Bismarck who laid the corner-stone of the new German empire, since Germany is the main support of England's Eastern policy.

THE TSAR CLAIMS HIS REWARD

On or about October 30, Prince Gortchakoff cast a diplomatic bomb-shell among European potentates by issuing a circular to the effect that, since the Franco-German war had materially changed the political status of Europe, Russia did not consider the clause in the treaty of Paris which restricted her from a free navigation of the Black Sea was longer obligatory on her government. The true reason was that the French government was no longer able to enforce the treaty of Paris, and the British government, left to itself, would not be likely to attempt it. This had evidently been agreed upon at Ems, for Bismarck is admitted to have said, on hearing it, "The fools have begun a month too early;" and the crown prince reports that his father was greatly disturbed by it. In fact, Gortchakoff had chosen the most critical moment in the affairs of the Germans to assert the Russian claim, and it was as much a surprise to Bismarck as it was to the British Cabinet or to the unutterable Turk. It was, in fact, the moment when the Prussian government would be most dependent on Russia's friendliness; and if Gladstone had been a

match in diplomacy for Bismarck, and had acted in a bold
and decisive manner, thirty days later the German forces
might possibly have been encamped again before the Rhineland. Gladstone, however, was pacific, indisposed to foreign
intervention, and indecisive. He commissioned Lord Odo
Russell, a sort of English Polonius, to wait on Bismarck and
protest against the action of Russia. Von Beust thought that
Lord Russell was the most unsuitable envoy he could have
selected, and that if an inflexible, determined Englishman had
been sent in his place something would have been accomplished. Sir Odo Russell is said to have been an admirer of
Bismarck, and by this time there was no diplomat in Europe
who did not dread an audience with the Prussian colossus.
The interview was pleasant enough, with an effusion of amiability on both sides, but resulted in nothing.

Bismarck knew how to suit himself to his man. Treaties
were, after all, only good so long as they could be enforced.
The Black Sea clause was a mean and petty restriction on
Russia and of no real advantage to any other power. It was
unreasonable that a nation should not have the right to protect the shipping on its own coast. Such a restriction must
come to an end sooner or later, and it had already endured
for fifteen years. He could not believe that England would
go to war on a question which concerned her material interests so little. Besides, the British government was not prepared for war. As for any future aggrandizement of Russia,
that would concern Germany quite as much as it would England. He advised a European conference in order to give the
Black Sea clause a dignified burial. There was not much
that Lord Russell could say against this, and the suggestion
of an Anglo-German alliance against Russia had a hopeful
sound.[1]

Alexander and Gortchakoff may have feared that the German successes would make Bismarck too independent, but
they clearly made a mistake by interfering with him when his

---

[1] The crown prince writes, December 6, "Odo Russell says that Bismarck is
favorable to an alliance with England."

hands were full. This showed Bismarck what he might expect from them in the future, and it would have been more for their interest in the long run if they had trusted him as Francis Joseph and Andrassy afterwards trusted him. There is no evidence that Bismarck ever betrayed the confidence of man or woman, though during the siege of Paris the French newspapers published the most infamous libels against him. " It is fortunate," he remarked, " that they do not know about the little house in my garden." He talked at dinner of the war between Poland and Prussia in the time of the Great Elector, which might have resulted in the conquest of Poland but for the interference of Holland. " Poland," he said, " might have played the same part in Prussian affairs which Hungary had in Austrian;" and this would certainly have been far better for the Poles than their present situation. He remarked to the crown prince, " I wish your Royal Highness would study the Polish language," to which the latter replied that he had already had enough of such studies.

The capitulation of Metz was a severe blow to the Paris Committee of Safety, and immediately afterwards Thiers, having returned from his foreign expedition, requested a consultation with Bismarck in regard to an armistice. He was accordingly conducted to the domicile of Madame Jessé, and Bismarck immediately asked him if he was provided with full and necessary powers for the negotiation. When Thiers expressed surprise at such a question, Bismarck informed him that news had already been received of a revolution within the city since he had left it. Thiers was evidently startled, and Bismarck judged from this how unstable the state of affairs was in Paris.

In a general circular of November 8 Bismarck said:[1]

" I proposed to him to fix the relative positions of both armies, as they stood on the day of signing the armistice, by the line of demarcation; to suspend hostilities for a month, and during that time to accomplish the elections and the constitution of a National

----

[1] Our Chancellor, p. 72.

LIFE OF BISMARCK

Assembly. . . . With respect to the elections in Elsass I was able to assure him that we would not insist upon any stipulation calling in question the restoration of the German departments to France before the conclusion of peace, nor would we haul any inhabitant of those departments over the coals for having represented his compatriots in a French National Assembly. I was amazed when he rejected these proposals, and declared that he could only agree to an armistice if it should include a thorough provisioning of Paris. I replied that this would involve a military concession, so far exceeding the *status quo* and every reasonable expectation, that I must ask him what equivalent, if any, he was in a position to offer for it.''

The situation of France was a peculiar one. The country was without a legitimate government, and could only obtain one through an armistice; and yet an armistice would afford the French such advantages as no enemy in the field could possibly agree to. Thiers was entirely right in saying that a German possession of the forts would be a capitulation within an armistice. If the whole negotiation was a stratagem of the French in order to gain time, who can blame them? The endurance of the Parisians was heroic, and they were not yet prepared to yield to the conqueror. The army of the Loire was still in position, and much was expected of a second army which General Bourbaki was organizing on the frontier of Switzerland, and with which he intended to invade Germany.

About the middle of November Bismarck and the crown prince came pretty close to a quarrel. The latter says:

"Bismarck thought the expression of my opinions must have an injurious effect on the imperial question. In his judgment the crown prince ought not to utter such opinions. I take a most decided stand against having my mouth sealed in this manner, especially with regard to questions like this of the future. I looked upon it as a duty to leave no one in doubt in regard to my opinion; furthermore, nobody except his Majesty himself can give me any directions in regard to what I may talk about or not. Perhaps they take the ground that I am not yet old enough to have my own opinion. Bismarck declared that if I gave him orders, he would treat me accordingly. Against this I protested, because I had no orders to give him. Whereupon he said, as far as he was concerned, he would gladly make room for any other person whom I considered better fitted to carry on the matter than himself, but until then he must hold fast to those principles which accorded with the result of his experience and of his best understanding. Then we came to questions of particulars. I remarked that perhaps I had become a little excited, but one could not expect me to be indifferent at a turning-point in the history of the world."

Here we have a view behind the scenes,—an insight into those family jars of the Hohenzollerns of which much has been said and so little is known. There was evidently a constant internal struggle going on; or, if not constant, at least intermittent, like that of Richelieu with Louis XIII. This vigorous conflict of opinion only indicates a vigorous intellectual life. Bismarck and the crown prince had the same end in view, but wished to reach it by different ways, and each thought that his road was the only safe one. Such controversies are common enough in all human affairs, from the direction of a household to the management of an empire.

The policy of Bavaria toward other German states had always been mean and provincial. A Bavarian who married a wife from any other German state could not bring her to his home without paying a heavy duty on his feminine importation. The King of Würtemberg had complained to Bismarck two years previously that the railway fare between Munich and Stuttgart was so arranged as to impose a tax on those of his subjects who wished to visit the Bavarian capital. If Bavaria entered the new German empire these petty sources of local emolument would have to be dispensed with; and the Bavarians strongly objected to being taxed for a German navy, since as an inland community they would derive only an indirect advantage from it. November 29 Dr. Busch says, "In the afternoon I sent off another article on the convention with Bavaria; a grudging dissatisfaction seems to be the prevailing mood there." There was also opposition on the Prussian side, which irritated Bismarck, although he declared he was not surprised at it. "They are out of humor," he said, "because certain officials, who will have to conduct themselves in all respects according to our laws, will wear the Bavarian uniform. . . . They would have us wait a long while. If we put off we allow time for our enemies to come in and sow tares among our wheat. They want more uniformity,—if they would only think of five years back and what they would have been satisfied with then." Something, it is true, had been conceded to Bavaria, chiefly in matters of form and uniform, in order to bring the state fairly within the German fold; but was not this better than the use of force or intimidation?

A brief review of the Bavarian negotiations will explain the difficulty of Bismarck's position in regard to them, as well as the cause of the crown prince's irritation. The last of September Bismarck commissioned the Prussian minister Delbrück to proceed to Munich and hold a trial conference with King Louis's ministry on the imperial question. Much to Delbrück's astonishment, the Bavarians designated eighty particulars in which they wished the constitution of the North German confederation changed before Bavaria could enter it. They wished an independent administration of the army, their own legislation in regard to the judiciary, complete independence of their railway system, an absolute veto on constitutional changes, and exemption from taxes for the support of a navy. Such conditions had never been heard of before, and seemed to preclude the necessity of further negotiation.

However, Bismarck was not discouraged; he saw that he had begun at the wrong end, and took another direction. A month later he invited the ministers of Baden, Würtemberg, and Darmstadt to a conference at Versailles, and when the Bavarian ministers were informed of this they expressed a desire to be present also. At the conference, however, they found themselves in a minority, for the other states cared little for most of the Bavarian exceptions. It was plain to them that if all other states had the right to a constitutional veto there would never be any constitutional changes. Von Bray, who had succeeded Von der Pfordten as premier to King Louis, finally yielded this point, but the conference came to an end without definite result.

Three weeks later there was a conference at Versailles with the Darmstadt, Baden, and Würtemberg ministers, to which apparently Von Bray was not invited. This time the obstinacy of the Würtemberg assembly prevented a conclusion, but terms were agreed upon to the satisfaction of the Würtemberg ministers, who dissolved the assembly and ordered a fresh election. On November 15 Baden and Darmstadt signified their assent to enter the national federation on the same terms as the Saxon duchies. Finally the Bavarians, finding the current too strong for them, came to an agreement with Bismarck the last of November, after several days of very hard talking. Bavaria retained her diplomatic service, the management of her military establishment, postal, telegraph, and railroad lines; besides which a most important compromise was that the united votes of Bavaria, Saxony, and Würtemberg in the Reichstag should constitute a veto on any proposed change of the national constitution. There were other minor exceptions, but the eighty objective points were reduced to less than a dozen. Würtemberg was admitted with similar privileges in regard to the post, railroads, and telegraph lines, and a new assembly, in which the demagogues were left out, ratified the Versailles convention at once. Could there have been a finer illustration of Richelieu's grand maxim, " First, all methods to conciliate "?

This brought the crown prince's troubles to a close for the present. After an interview with his royal father and Bismarck, on December 3 he wrote:

"As he left the room Bismarck and I shook hands. This day finds the emperor and the empire irrevocably fixed. Now are the sixty-five years of long interregnum and dreadful emperorless time past. This grand title is a surety in itself, for which we might thank the Grand Duke of Baden,[1] who has spared no trouble. Rüggenbach is sent by Bismarck to Berlin."

---

[1] The grand duke may not have realized that this would result in Bismarck's driving the gambling-hells out of Baden.

LIFE OF BISMARCK

It was sixty-five years since the first Napoleon had compelled the Emperor Francis to change his title from Germany to Austria, but the office had been practically in abeyance since the peace of Westphalia in 1648. The first German empire, which began after the death of Charlemagne, was ruled by the finest race of monarchs of whom history can boast, ending with Frederick II., to whom both pope and Saracen were obliged to bend the knee. The present German empire is constituted in a wholly different manner from its predecessor, and is substantially a new form of government, similar to that of constitutional Austria, which antedated it but four years. Nothing now remained to complete its establishment but the coronation of William I.

When King Leopold of Belgium wrote a letter of congratulation to the crown prince on the fortunate conclusion of the imperial question, the latter magnanimously showed it to Bismarck, who expressed himself in a highly appreciative manner over its contents, and requested him in his answer to refer to the advantage which a strong Germany would be to Belgium, and the protection which a strong Germany would afford the Belgians against France. "Founding the empire," however, began in 1866, or, one might say, on April 1, 1815.

General Bourbaki, having assembled an army of more than a hundred and twenty thousand men about Lyons, including the remnant of De Paladine's force, early in January decided to take the offensive, and marched northward, driving General Werder before him towards Belfort. His plan seemed to be to relieve the siege of Belfort, and then cut the Prussian communications with Germany; perhaps, also, to invade the Rhineland. General Werder took up a strong position at the south of Belfort and applied to Von Moltke for reinforcements. General Manteuffel was despatched to his assistance with two army corps, in whose ranks was Count William von Bismarck, now promoted to a lieutenancy for bravery on the field of battle. He had fought at Sedan and done his duty in the siege of Paris, and was now entering on his last campaign.

Before Manteuffel could arrive, Bourbaki attacked Werder,

January 15, and was repulsed. General Werder's army consisted of only about forty thousand men, but he held his ground against Bourbaki three days in succession. The losses of the French were not heavy, and General Bourbaki, a noble type of the old French soldier, was so much discouraged at the conduct of his troops that he attempted suicide.

On November 30 General Trochu had arranged for a grand sortie on the side of Paris towards Fontainebleau. General Ducrot attacked the German lines with not less than fifty thousand men, but after an engagement of several hours was obliged to retreat with heavy loss. After this there was more than a month of inactivity, when a series of desperate sorties were attempted during the middle of January, but all without effect. These were timed in concert with Bourbaki's advance on Belfort, and after his defeat there the Parisians settled down to face starvation and the inevitable. When, on the 21st, a second socialist uprising had to be suppressed, the Committee of Safety realized that their time had come. On January 8 Von Moltke had commenced his bombardment of the city,—mainly for moral effect,—but so solidly built were the blocks on Napoleon's boulevards that in the better portion of Paris it was even less effectual than he anticipated, and the fires which it caused in the Latin Quarter were easily extinguished. The Tuileries and Louvre were not damaged, and would seem to have been purposely avoided.[1]

THE CORONATION AT VERSAILLES

The new German empire was announced to the various governments of Europe, January 1, 1871, without waiting for the sanction of the Bavarian legislature, since that of the king and his ministers had already been obtained. In mediæval Germany the emperor had always been chosen by electoral princes of the larger states, with a tendency to hereditary

---

[1] The building to which the Venus of Melos had been removed for safety was afterwards set on fire during the Commune, and the statue was preserved as if by a miracle.

succession so long as the imperial family produced first-rate men. After the time of Charles V. the title had become hereditary in the house of Hapsburg, but it also became little more than a title. Bismarck had taken advantage of this fact to make the position hereditary in the Prussian family, which certainly was no more than prudent, and in order to clinch the business at both ends he wished to have the confirmation come from the representatives of the people as well as from the princes. A vote to this effect, therefore, was obtained from the North German Reichstag, not without a good deal of declamatory opposition from the Prussian Particularists, the Saxons, and the Ultramontanes.

The chief objection to the new title seemed to be that it would afford William I. an increase of authority, which might prove dangerous to the personal liberty of German citizens, although there is practically no real difference between the authority of a king and of an emperor. The difference always consists in the manner in which their authority is limited. Louis XIV. was a more absolute ruler than Napoleon I. Emperor, *Imperator;* Kaiser, *Cæsar;* and Prince, *Princeps Senatus*, were all derived from the titles of Augustus, but no German emperor from Henry the Fowler onward possessed the unlicensed power of the Cæsars. In the character of their authority they resembled more closely the Henrys and Edwards. *King* is of German derivation, and its origin is lost in the prehistoric twilight of the German forests. English monarchy is the best representative of it, but Napoleon cheapened the title by conferring it on the electoral princes of Saxony and Bavaria. It was now essential that the King of Prussia, as the chief executive of United Germany, should be endowed with an exceptional distinction, and what could be more appropriate than the name of Kaiser? His authority as emperor, however, never equalled that which he had exercised (or Bismarck for him) during the previous five years; nor did it much exceed the authority of President Lincoln during the Civil War.[1]

---

[1] It was characteristic of King William's plain good sense that he at first objected to the imperial title, which he spoke of as a fancy-dress affair, and it was

The time for the coronation was fixed for the 18th of January, an anniversary of the day when the first King of Prussia was crowned in 1701. It was his contribution in soldiers and money to the war against Louis XIV, by which he obtained that elevation; and Prince Eugene, foreseeing its ultimate effect on Austrian affairs, declared that the man who suggested it ought to have been hanged. Now the successor of Frederick was to receive a still further elevation through a war with France, in the very hall of Louis XIV.,—the Hall of Mirrors, intended purposely to give an infinite reflection to the magnificence of the grand monarch. Louis XIV. never dreamed what a use his showy palace would come to. Certainly it never saw a more distinguished gathering than the present, considering the princes, generals, and foreign ambassadors who were assembled there; not supernumeraries in uniform, but men of genuine ability, who had earned their right to surround Emperor William by dignified public service. There were, besides, two men of genius there,—Bismarck and Moltke,—conspicuous above all others, whose names will be spoken so long as German or English lasts.

The crown prince's account of the ceremony has rather a critical tone. The Prussian court chaplain, in his opening prayer, referred to the German spoliation by Louis XIV., the theft of Strasburg and the sacking of Worms, and the final retribution which had attended these unhallowed deeds. The crown prince did not find this in good taste, nor was he better pleased with Bismarck's reading the proclamation to the German people in his "monotonous, business-like manner." William I. read a congratulatory address to the sovereigns and representatives; and then the coronation took place, and the Duke of Baden called out, "Long live his Imperial Majesty, the Emperor William!"

---

only through the united efforts of Bismarck, the Crown Prince of Prussia, and the King of Bavaria that he was finally persuaded to agree to it. Even after this he had a stubborn controversy with Bismarck as to whether his title should be Emperor of Germany or, as the latter preferred, Emperor of the Germans. Bismarck supported his argument by producing a thaler of Frederick the Great on which was the legend *Rex Borussorum.*

The two Fredericks were created field marshals of the empire, a title of more value since it occurs but rarely in Prussian history as compared with the French custom. Napoleon I. made it much too common, conferring it on officers of inferior merit like Grouchy and Suchet. Bismarck about this time received the honorary distinction of lieutenant-general.

The London conference on the Black Sea clause had opened the day previous. Bismarck seems to have given the subject little attention; but we find an entry in Dr. Busch's diary, a short time before, to the effect that the Prussian delegate was to support the claims of Russia with all his might. As Bismarck's influence was now at its height, and as Francis Joseph and Victor Emmanuel were very much afraid of what he might do next, the British government found itself in a minority of one, and allowed the question to subside as quietly as possible.

CONCLUSION OF PEACE

The bombardment of Paris lasted two weeks before the white flag appeared announcing the capitulation. Trains of supplies had been prepared in Germany for the benefit of its starving citizens before the catastrophe came, and Bismarck feared that the knowledge of this might encourage the Parisians to prolong their ordeal, but it was the revolt of the Communists which finally broke the camel's back. On January 23 [1] Favre appeared at Versailles with request for an armistice, which, however, was as unreasonable as the previous one. He wished for permission to have the regular troops march out with honors of war and retire to the Loire, where Gambetta was again organizing fresh levies. This, of course, could not be granted, and a long, fruitless discussion ensued, lasting the best portion of five days. Bismarck said of him afterwards, "Favre is a good talker, and his sentences are well balanced, but he is not the man to effect a favorable bargain, not even to sell a horse." In order to find out more

---

[1] The crown prince says on the 24th.

exactly as to the condition of affairs in Paris, he said to Favre, " We know the situation in Paris better than you do, who have only been there a few days; there are still provisions in the city for three weeks more." By the surprise on Favre's face Bismarck perceived that this was not the case.

The bombardment continued all the time while Favre and Bismarck were arguing at Versailles. Finally, on the 28th, it was agreed that there should be an armistice for three weeks, during which time elections should be held for delegates to a national convention, with authority to make a permanent peace and decide all questions appertaining thereto. The army in Paris was to be surrendered to Emperor William, with the exception of one division, who were to retain their arms for the preservation of order, and the German forces were to occupy the forts. Besides this, the city of Paris was compelled to pay a war contribution of two hundred million francs. The surrender and the occupation of the forts took place the following day, while provision trains rushed into Paris from all directions. The crown prince states that Favre ate like a wolf.

Gambetta's behavior in this crisis was indicative of the peculiar mental condition of the average French mind, as it had been fostered by the political writing of Thiers and the imperial adulation of Louis Napoleon. Although he had seen the armies which he had conjured up, as Bismarck said, with a stamp of his foot, dissipated like smoke, and every fortress, as well as the capital, was now in the possession of the enemy, he still refused to believe that the war was over and that further resistance was useless. The French army and government had ceased to exist, and yet he still had faith that in some miraculous manner his country might yet be delivered from the Germans. He opposed the armistice with all the force of his untiring energy, and when he failed to produce an effect in this direction he endeavored to turn the elections to account by supporting such candidates as might persuade the convention to continue the war at all hazards. Nothing could be more unpatriotic than such a course, and yet Gambetta always believed that he was the one person in France who lived for his country and for her alone. The last of January he published a manifesto on his own responsibility, declaring that no persons who had held office or had in any way been connected with the government of Napoleon III. would be eligible to vote at the coming elections. Bismarck protested against this, or any other measures which would interfere with the free expression of public opinion; and, as the national committee also objected to it, Gambetta resigned. It has been supposed that his course at this time was dictated by personal ambition,—a desire to preserve his popularity at the expense of his colleagues, who would have to bear the odium of the capitulation,—and this is the natural way to look at it; but it is quite as likely to have arisen from the same infatuation which had led his countrymen into this unequal conflict. Thiers, Favre, Gambetta, and Rochefort formed a descending series in French republicanism, if the last can properly be called a republican.

The elections were held on February 8, and four days later the national convention met at Bordeaux and declared almost unanimously for peace and republicanism,—as two years previously the French people had declared for the continuation of the empire. On the 17th Thiers was elected temporary president of the republic, and on the 21st, with Favre and Picquard, he proceeded to Versailles to conclude terms of peace with Bismarck.

It must have been with gloomy forebodings that these three gentlemen made their way to the mansion of Veuve Jessé, but Bismarck's demand exceeded even their worst anticipations. Strasburg, Metz, and Belfort must be given up with adjacent territory, and in addition France must pay a war indemnity of six thousand million francs. Such a demand had to be fought out so long as words and arguments would last, and Thiers and Favre were just the men to do this. On the other hand, Bismarck had France completely in his power, and, so to speak, held the long end of the lever. The limitation to this was that he was really as desirous of concluding peace as his opponents, and he also knew that there is an element of desperation in the French character which always has to be considered in critical emergencies. It must have been a severe ordeal for all concerned. It is nervous business bargaining for a house, and when it comes to a question of thousands of millions of dollars the strain is, to say the least, herculean.

The discussion was conducted in French, and the fine language was all on the side of Thiers & Co., but the facts were mainly with Bismarck. When they urged that the war was not of their making, he replied, " Yes; but you continued it, and could have obtained better terms after Sedan." When Thiers called it a veritable spoliation, he was reminded of the terms which Napoleon exacted of Prussia in 1806 and remained inexorable, although the weeping queen, mother of William I., fell on her knees before him.[1] It was true that Napoleon had never exacted such a colossal sum of money, but he had systematically fleeced Prussia for six years, so that her wealthiest merchants were reduced to poverty. Bismarck had not based his calculations on guess-work, but had a prepared table of statistics on hand in order to prove that the revenues of France were quite equal to the provision of such a sum. Finally he declared, in reply to Thiers's eloquent protest that France might be ruined but would never consent to a dishonorable peace, " If you persist in prolonging the war four or five years, the German government will annex France."

A more potent argument, perhaps, was the threat to reinstate Napoleon with the two hundred thousand French soldiers who were then imprisoned in Germany. We may wonder that Bismarck consented to continue this discussion. Lord Nelson's method on such occasions was to place his watch on the table, and give the opposite party an hour for silent reflection on the subject; but Bismarck was not so domineering as that. Exacting he certainly was, but he liked to base all his actions on logical grounds, and to satisfy his

---

[1] Thiers could not be ignorant of this, for he had written a graphic account of it. She was avenged by her own son.

opponents that whatever he did he considered right. Finally he brought the conference to a conclusion in a highly adroit manner. The French commissioners had protested vigorously against a triumphal entry into Paris, and so, when Bismarck perceived that they had reached the last ditch of despair, he offered them the choice between a triumphal entry and taking off a milliard of francs with Belfort from the conditions of peace. The offer was snapped at eagerly, for the triumphal entry really amounted to nothing, and, after an eloquent epilogue on the buried glory of France, the bargain was clinched at five milliard francs, with Alsace and Lorraine.

Von Beust allows Thiers the credit of having saved Belfort and reducing the war indemnity, and something may be accredited to the tenacity with which he conducted the negotiation, but it is more probable that Bismarck put these items on before he took them off, as men usually ask more for an object of barter than they are willing and ready to accept. One does not altogether like Bismarck's small tricks and stratagems, but the charitable way to consider them is as a part of his profession as a diplomat rather than as belonging to the man. They do not differ essentially from the deceptions which doctors practise for the benefit of their patients. Referring to this interview, Favre afterwards said of him, " Bismarck is a political man of business, and on such a scale as it is difficult to imagine."

The peace preliminaries were signed at Versailles on February 26, and the French commissioners at once returned to Bordeaux, where the national convention ratified it by a relative vote of five to one. As Bismarck knew that the payment of such an immense sum would only be secured under compulsion, he made the new government agree to an occupation of French territory by German forces until it was liquidated,— an evacuation of territory to take place according to the partial payments which should be made. This was another expensive burden on the French people, but there was no help for it. On March 1 a select army corps was reviewed by Emperor William and afterwards marched through Paris, with the emperor, Bismarck, Moltke, the crown prince, and other high officers. It was like a city of the dead; the blinds and shutters were everywhere closed, and not a Frenchman was to be seen in the streets, except here and there a stray vender of supplies. It gave the private soldiers, however, an opportunity to view this wonderful city, which in its way is without a rival, and to many of them it would be the only chance they would ever have. During the following week as many battalions as possible were entertained by their officers in a similar manner. The emperor signed the treaty of peace at Versailles the following day, and on the 17th was again in Berlin.

The French will never forgive Bismarck for the severe terms of this treaty, and he has been liberally blamed for it in England and America. If our civil war cost the United States government three million dollars a day, it is not probable that the French campaign cost the German governments at a higher rate. If greater forces were employed in it, the cost of labor and materials must have been relatively smaller. Half of the five milliard francs, therefore, must have been intended to cover the loss in killed and wounded, and should properly have gone to them or their families. It is to be feared that this was not the case to the extent to which it might have been. What is abstractly right in particular instances often has to give way to what is judicious. It was Favre's finest argument at the conference, as previously at Haute Maison, that to conclude an enduring peace it was necessary to agree upon terms which the vanquished party should consider reasonable.

Bismarck did not believe in this. You may, perhaps, expect magnanimity from an individual if you know your man, but from a large number of men it is useless to think of it. In the second Silesian war, when Frederick the Great was attacked by Austria and Saxony and defeated his enemies in four decisive engagements, he replied to their commissioners, "I want nothing of you but peace," trusting in this way to escape future coalitions against him. Yet he was obliged not long afterwards to contend against the whole continent of

LIFE OF BISMARCK

Europe,—the hardest piece of work that man ever succeeded in. On the other hand, the first Napoleon's practice of weakening his enemies by taking territory from them is supposed to have been the proximate cause of his downfall. It is often difficult to choose between the danger of doing too much and that of letting slip a favorable opportunity. The practice of abstracting territory as one of the penalties of warfare is not confined to Europe : there are precedents for it in both North and South America. It is well known that Bismarck's own judgment favored the establishment of a frontier in a nearly straight line from Luxemburg to Switzerland, but Von Moltke insisted on Metz (which can only be compared to Gibraltar and Ehrenbreitstein) as equal in value to three army corps. Bismarck had a very strong pressure behind him,—an exultant army and an ambitious court. It was in his nature to conceive and carry out grand designs, yet if he could have been satisfied himself and satisfied others with the cession of Elsass and an indemnity of three milliard francs, it might have been less expensive for Prussia in the long run. The possession of Elsass and Lothringen has cost the German government not less than fifty million thalers in the military establishment which it entails.

The French at least should feel indebted to Bismarck for relieving them of Louis Napoleon. To whom else can we attribute the demoralized condition of the French army which was so conspicuous at Vionville and Sedan,—the army which in 1855 had so heroically stormed Sebastopol, and behind this there must have been the same tendency in the French people, from whom the army was taken ? Whatever may be the virtues of the Bonapartes, their line of policy is not the one by which the French nation can rise to a higher civilization than that of the First Empire. The French people are now at liberty for the first time in history to work out their destiny according to their own judgment, and the person whom they have to thank for this above all others is Otto von Bismarck. A meddlesome Metternich or Beaconsfield would have restored the Bonapartes or Bourbons, and compelled France to accept another term of monarchy.

CHAPTER XI

PRUSSIA is really the most peaceable of the great powers of Europe. This becomes evident when we compare the different campaigns undertaken by the Prussian government during the past century with those of other countries. Counting from 1798, the French have had full twenty years of warfare, and Great Britain about the same, if we consider such small affairs as the Ashantee war and the Egyptian campaign in the way of fractions. Russia has had fourteen years of war; Austria, twelve; the United States of America, nine, including the numerous Indian wars; and Prussia, seven years of warfare. Italy and Spain have been treated too much like footballs between other nations to enter into this computation. Many of these wars have been inevitable, and could not have been avoided, so far as we can judge from a candid estimate of the facts concerning them; but Great Britain could certainly have escaped from the War of 1812, and France from the War of 1870. It is difficult to determine whether the English or French are the more pugnacious people, but they certainly lead all others in that respect.

Grim old Manteuffel was left in command of the army of occupation, to make sure of the French indemnity, with about one hundred and fifty thousand men, and the rest of the German forces returned to their own firesides as quietly and methodically as they had come. To the French they were like an army of locusts; but the manner in which they went back to their daily avocations, as if nothing great or remarkable had happened in the mean time, is very pleasing, not to say poetic. Senator Wilson, of Massachusetts, was present when some twenty thousand men were mustered out of service at Munich, and was delighted with the sober, orderly manner in which they dispersed; not crowding the sidewalks or filling up the streets with idle groups, though the beer-gardens were unusually well attended, and every musician that could be found was in request for them.

The war was over, but whether peace was at hand Bismarck did not feel sure. It seemed as if the era of prosperity had arrived for Prussia; but there is a Spanish proverb, " Beware of smooth water," which men of the wiser sort always bear in mind. He knew the inflammable condition in which he had left the French people, with an improvised and untried government and inexperienced rulers, who pretended always to act in conformity with the popular will. It was one of his few maxims that the unexpected may happen in France at any time; and, sure enough, it did in less than two weeks, to the astonishment of mankind. Overcome with the exertions of the last six months, Bismarck had only reached his country residence when the first news from the Paris Commune followed close upon him.

All the world was startled, and especially America. Powerful revolutionary elements and extensive secret organizations were known to exist in Europe from Poland to Portugal; but it was generally supposed that their object was the subjugation of tyrants, that they were chiefly enemies of the monarchical order, and if they once attained republican governments they would be contented. In the Paris revolution of March 17, 1871, there was plain evidence that the object of these associations was not republicanism, but the abolition of the Roman law, the system of jurisprudence which has held society together since the dark ages. It was an attack on the very existence of government, on the possession of property and all individual rights, on education and superior culture. To name it in a single phrase, it was barbarism let loose. This was the character by which it declared itself, and the moment it selected was the one above all others inimical to republicanism and liberal institutions. It was at once predicted in political circles that the result of the Commune would be the restoration of the Bourbons, and it came very near to this shortly afterwards. It is not to be doubted that the Commune greatly strengthened the cause of monarchy in Europe, and that the antagonism to communism is now the strongest support of kings and emperors.

The proceedings of the Paris revolutionists were worthy of such a cause. Thiers had contended in the peace stipulations at Versailles that a division of the National Guard should retain their arms, and the far-sighted Moltke protested against this. The result was now perceived in the fusion of the National Guard with the communists. Two generals of the regular army whom they captured were condemned and shot, after the fashion of 1793. The Socialists plundered the churches, forced loans from the banks, insurance companies, and millionaires, burned down the Tuileries, and imprisoned the priests, against whom they seemed to have a particular spite. The final murder of Archbishop Darboy and his companions requires no comment. It was from this class of irreconcilables to civilization that Charles Cohen emanated, the would-be assassin of Bismarck in the spring of 1866, and numerous other assassins and inhuman monsters have emanated from it since. The Internationals were not all Communists, however, but contained many stanch Republicans and high-minded men. There were wheels within wheels in the society, and its membership included a wide range of political theory and belief.

The Paris revolution must have been in preparation for a number of years. According to Disraeli, the secret societies promised to Napoleon III. the continuance of his reign and the succession of his son if he would only leave Rome to Garibaldi, but he did not do this. An International named Linton, an English engraver, came to America in 1868, to obtain recruits for a conspiracy against the French emperor. He persuaded Wendell Phillips to become an associate member of the fraternity, and even Charles Sumner had some connection with the Internationals at an earlier time. It was the Mazzini wing of the society which Sumner affiliated with, but after the Commune in 1871 he disclaimed all further connection with them.

The government at Versailles appealed to Bismarck for assistance, and, though he preserved his attitude of non-inter-

LIFE OF BISMARCK

ference, he hastened the liberation of a large body of French soldiers captured at Sedan, considering it only right that their country should have the benefit of their services. These, being troops of the regular line and chiefly Bonapartists, could be depended on not to fraternize with the insurgents; and Marshal MacMahon, having repulsed two attacks of the Communists before the arrival of this re-enforcement, stormed the forts about Paris and finally entered the city on May 21. The Communists were driven from one barricade to another, and a large body of them, who had taken refuge in the church of the Madeleine, were all bayoneted by the infuriated soldiers of Napoleon. Fifty thousand more were taken prisoners, and the streets of Paris ran with blood.

Bismarck, although there was nothing he hated like socialism, saw that in this outbreak there was more justification than even a republican might suppose. In a semi-official statement, published the last of April, he said:

" It is communism of the grossest description which has tempted from fifteen to twenty thousand released criminals and other scum and dregs of modern society to lend their aid to these champions of cataclysm. In this revolution, however, bad as it is, may be detected a movement founded upon reason and supported by orderly and intelligent social elements,—viz., the effort to obtain a sensible municipal organization, and to emancipate the commons from vexatious and unnecessary state tutelage, an effort finding its explanation in French history, and its exact converse in Haussmann's tyrannical proceedings, so injurious to the Paris municipality. Were the Parisians endowed with a municipal constitution like that possessed by the Prussian cities ever since the days of Hardenberg, many practical thinkers in Paris who now hold aloof from the Versailles government would be satisfied, and no longer support the revolution by passive resistance."

Haussmann the Alsatian was Louis Napoleon's prefect of the Seine, and it is to be feared that in his remodelling of the Paris boulevards he often proceeded in a tyrannical and unfair manner with respect to the property of persons who stood in the way of his improvements.

LIFE OF BISMARCK

It was a momentous occasion, the first opening of parliament for united Germany on March 21, 1871. The address from the throne was brief, dignified, and modest. The emperor said :

"On seeing you for the first time after the glorious but hard struggle which Germany has successfully accomplished for her independence, the German Diet assembled round me, my first impulse is to offer my humble thanks unto God for all important successes with which His grace has crowned the faithful unanimity of the German allies, the heroic courage and the excellent discipline of our troops, and the self-denying devotion of the German nation.

"We have accomplished that which since the time of our fathers has been the universal aim for Germany,—the union and its organic formation, the safeguarding of our frontiers, the independence of the development of our national laws.

"Although hidden, the consciousness of its unity was ever alive in the German nation; it burst its shell in the moment of enthusiasm in which the entire nation arose to the defence of their threatened Fatherland, and cut its name in indelible characters on the battle-fields of France as a nation resolved to be and remain one people.

"The spirit that lives in the German people, and that penetrates its culture and civilization, as well as the constitution of the empire and the structure of its army, preserve Germany in the midst of successes from any temptation to misuse the power gained by her unity. The respect which Germany claims for her own independence she is fully prepared to accord to the independence of all other states and nations, the weak as well as the strong. The new Germany that has come forth from the fiery ordeal of the present war will be *a reliable surety for the peace of Europe, being sufficiently powerful and self-conscious to reserve for herself the ordering of her own affairs as an exclusive but at the same time fully sufficient and satisfactory heritage.*" [1] . . .

The announcement that Bismarck was created a prince[2] and

---

[1] Bismarck's Speeches, v. 7.

[2] Readers of Bismarck's Memoirs will remember that he wished to decline this title, and went to the *Schloss* in Berlin for that purpose, but at the top of the

251

chancellor of the new empire was received with more enthusiasm than the title of count and field-marshal general which was bestowed on Von Moltke, for it was felt that the latter had not been rewarded equal to his deserts. No shade of envy or disappointment, however, could be detected on the face of the old veteran, who was as cool-headed in the hour of success as on the field of battle. He had done his work, and he must have been conscious that he had earned an enviable place in the world's history, and not in that of Germany alone. From this time forth he avoided ovations and all other demonstrations in his honor,—an unostentatious hero. As for the sincerity of the emperor's pacific intentions, twenty-eight years of continued peace and prosperity in Europe ought to have sufficiently proved it. Sensational news and magazine writers maintained a perpetual clamor in regard to the danger of the German military power and the malign intentions of Bismarck, until he and Marshal Moltke both became too old to take the field,—and it is wonderful how much of this was believed; but the world finally concluded that William I. and his ministers knew their own interests too well to run the risk, by grasping too much, of losing any portion of what they had already gained.

The government had a large majority in this Reichstag and could have accomplished almost anything that Bismarck considered expedient, but the chancellor now showed his strength in his moderation. He had no intention of tinkering the political machine until he discovered how well it would run, and where the weak spots in it actually were. A fund of two hundred and forty million thalers, or nearly one-fifth of the war indemnity, was set apart for the benefit of wounded and disabled soldiers, as well as for the widows of those who had fallen in the campaign; four million thalers were distributed among the more deserving veterans, and four millions were divided among the most distinguished generals. Prince Frederick Charles, Manteuffel, and Von Roon received

---

royal staircase he was met by the whole imperial family; William I. embraced him, and he felt that it would be positively ungracious to oppose his wishes.

three hundred thousand thalers apiece, and it may be fairly said that they deserved it. Bismarck himself was rewarded by his sovereign with estates in Holstein valued at nearly a million thalers.

This Reichstag seemed almost like a symposium of sages, but its perfect harmony was somewhat ruffled by an astonishing resolution, offered by the Catholic members, that it was the duty of Emperor William to interfere in behalf of the pope and drive Victor Emmanuel out of Rome. This motion was brought up on March 30, and was closely followed by a demand of the Polish members of Posen for Polish independence. Bismarck perceived that the two movements were closely connected, and conjectured rightly that they both originated from the Vatican. It was the first premonitary cloud, small as a man's hand, of the approaching storm. Bismarck replied to the Polish resolution:

"You, gentlemen, are really no people : you represent no people ; you have no people backing you,—you are backed by nothing but your fictions and illusions, one of which is that you were elected by the Polish people into the Reichstag in order to represent the interests of the Catholic Church, and if you do this whenever the interests of the Catholic Church are at stake you meet the expectations of your electors. But a mandate to represent the Polish people or the Polish nationality has been given you by no man, and least of all by the people of Posen and Western Prussia. I do not share your fiction that the Polish rule was good and not bad. I wish to be impartial and just, but I can assure you it was truly bad, and therefore it will never return."

What the Poles demanded was nothing less than separation from the German empire, and Bismarck, in his position, could not have spoken otherwise than as he did. Not only was the thing absurd in itself, for the Prussian Poles are too small a community to form an independent political organization, but the inevitable consequence would be that Posen would become the centre of a revolutionary movement which would extend to Russian Poland and produce a coalition of Russia with France. But for the instigation of the priests it is not very probable that the Poles would have thought of this chimerical project, but Bismarck hit the nail exactly when he referred to the Polish members as representing the interests of the Catholic Church. It is true that the old Polish government was one of the worst,—fully as vicious as the French government of the eighteenth century,—but there is no reason why a reunited Poland should not obtain a government as just and liberal as that of France at the present time. A reunited Poland, however, would mean the disruption of the Russian Empire, for which at present there is no vestige of hope.

In reply to the request of Dr. Windhorst and other Clericals for material aid and comfort to the pope, it was considered sufficient to substitute a resolution to the effect that the present German Empire was not identical with that of Frederick Barbarossa, and that the day of interference in internal affairs of other countries had passed by, "never to return, it was to be hoped, under any form or pretext." The vote by which this resolution was carried—243 to 63—not only indicated the strength of the Clerical party in the Reichstag, but the comparative numbers of Protestants and Catholics in the empire. Dr. Windhorst then moved the insertion in the imperial constitution of the three liberal principles of the Prussian constitution,—complete independence of the church, freedom of the press, and the right to hold public meetings ; but, as this was evidently intended to place the Catholic Church beyond the sphere of government supervision, it was also defeated. Bismarck evidently intended to have a Protestant empire.

Unlimited success always has its effect. Emperor William and his chancellor did not lose their balance politically, as many predicted they would, but the victories of Sedan and Gravelotte produced an aggressive Teutonism which lasted five or six years, and resulted in some peculiar manifestations. The Berlin hatters consulted together to introduce a German national hat, intended to supersede the French *chapeau*, which has become the dress-hat of all civilized countries, but their attempt ended in a miserable failure. It was also currently reported that Bismarck attempted to make German the language of diplomatic correspondence, and with as little success. A communication in German to the British ministry was returned to him. France, although conquered, still remained France, and Paris still continued the centre of good taste and fashion, because the world felt confidence in French judgment so far as dress and behavior are concerned. To the feminine world, at least, Paris had become an oracle—a religion of the toilet—which it would require centuries to overthrow. The French language also had superseded Latin as the universal tongue, not from the supremacy of Louis XIV., but because it was the most convenient language for communication between the different European nations. Everybody knew more or less French, because France was in a central position between Spain, England, Germany, and Italy. French became the language of diplomacy by the principle of natural selection, and it was as impossible to change this as to move Mont Blanc. Berlin, however, had become the political centre of Europe, and it remained to be seen what would be the consequences thereof.

THE FRANKFORT CONVENTION

Alsace and Lorraine were not annexed to Prussia directly, but placed under military government for the time being as imperial fiefs. It might have been supposed that Alsace would have been united with Baden, but the people of the Palatinate were as much opposed to this as the Alsatians were to being separated from France. It would have joined two states together of nearly equal size, but of different religion and antagonistic in all political respects. Representative government under such conditions would be practically impossible; and if Lorraine had been added the people of Baden would have found themselves continually outvoted in their state assembly by their two unfriendly neighbors. The formation of the annexed provinces into fiefs was looked on as a concession by Prussia to the German Union. Bismarck did not consider it prudent that they should possess local autonomy, but they were, of course, represented in the Reichs-

tag, and their delegates lost no time in protesting against
their separation from France. This action was anticipated,
and failed to excite a ruffle on the surface of legislative affairs. But they soon began to agitate in a more serious
manner.

France could hardly be said to have had a regular government until Thiers was chosen president of the republic on the
last day of August, 1871, and it is not to be wondered at that
the Versailles organization managed affairs in a rather irregular and uncertain manner. It is not surprising that the needful supplies for supporting the German army of occupation
were not forthcoming in suitable quantity; but the French
commissioners, who were occupied at Brussels with the German representatives in reducing the preliminaries of Versailles
to a sound legal condition, showed a disposition to evasion
and postponement which did not augur well for a speedy conclusion, and the people of the annexed provinces had begun
to complain of an unfair discrimination against them in their
dealings on the other side of the border. This was all natural enough, but required serious attention, and Bismarck
accordingly seized the opportune moment before the Commune was crushed to summon Favre, the French foreign
minister, to an interview at Frankfort, and there, in the ancient
seat of the Frankish nation and the former capital of mediæval Germany, the final settlement between the two countries
was effected.

A few days later Bismarck made a report of this meeting
to the Reichstag, in which, after specifying the details of the
conference, he said:

"When I went to Frankfort I did not hope to settle matters
finally, but to obtain an abridgment of the terms fixed for payment of the war indemnity and an improvement in the nature of
the guarantees for that payment. But, in the prospect of a definitive settlement which became manifest at Frankfort, I recognized an
enormous advantage to both countries concerned therein, being
convinced that such an arrangement will not only materially lighten
the military burdens Germany has hitherto had to bear, but will

contribute in no inconsiderable measure to the consolidation of affairs in France. . . . This settlement will probably not please everybody, but I think it realizes all that we could demand from France in reason, and conformably to the traditions connected with transactions of this class. We have secured our frontiers by territorial annexation ; we have, so far as is humanly possible, insured payment of our war indemnity. I feel confident that the present French government intends to carry out the treaty honestly." [1]

His tribute to the character of the French government was well deserved. The affairs of France were never so wisely administered as by Favre and Thiers, and their overthrow was little to the credit of that restless and changeable people.

The Reichstag had adjourned on the 14th of June, and on the 15th there was a triumphal procession in Berlin such as reminds us of the days of Pompey and Cæsar, though there were no captives present to humiliate the vanquished foe. It was a triumph of rejoicing unmixed with vengeance.

A chosen corps of forty-five thousand men, selected from the different armies of Germany, were mustered in the Tempelhof field, where the emperor appeared at eleven A.M., accompanied by his ministers, generals, and princes of the royal family, to take command of the procession. He was followed by a brilliant cavalcade, in which the different royal and princely houses of Germany were represented, and after this came the carriages of the Empress Augusta, the crown princess, and other queens and princesses. The emperor led the procession at the head of the guard to the Brandenburg gate, where he encountered sixty beautiful young ladies, dressed in blue and white, representing the large and small political divisions of Germany, who presented him with a laurel wreath of gold in the name of the United Fatherland.

Thence the procession was conducted by the emperor through the Unter den Linden, which was spanned by five triumphal arches, adorned with trophies of the war, while the sidewalks were lined with captured pieces of ordnance. The emperor rode a dark brown horse of great beauty, and sat as erect and looked as vigorous as any man in the procession; but Bismarck, in his white cuirassier's uniform, was the objective point of every eye, and no man knew better how to carry himself in a dignified manner. The stately courtesy of the empress, who bowed repeatedly to the enthusiastic crowd, was contrasted with the more gracious manner of the crown princess, who had been brought up in a less military and more democratic country. In front of the French hotel the procession halted and a deputation of officers brought forward the eagles and standards taken from the French and presented them to the emperor with appropriate ceremonies. When they reached the end of the avenue the emperor and his suite took up a position by the statue of Blücher, while the procession marched past for the space of two hours. He then crossed the Schloss-brücke leading to the palace and unveiled the statue of his father, Frederick William II., in whose reign Prussia had been conquered by the French and afterwards recovered her independence. The ceremony included music by the royal band, an address by the emperor, and speeches by Bismarck, Von Moltke, and others,—altogether a tasteful and impressive ceremony.

The unprecedented success of the French campaign and the sudden rise of Prussia to the first position in European affairs was viewed with no slight jealousy by England and Russia, but created great rejoicing in Italy and Hungary. There was no longer danger of French regiments being seen at Rome; no more fear that Hungarian independence would become the dream of a day, as in 1848. Francis Joseph, who was really the football of the age he lived in, found himself as dependent on the Hungarians as he formerly supposed Germany dependent on him, and he was willing to accept this fact for the sake of peace and harmony after so many troubles and disasters. Bismarck, writing from Hungary in 1852, mentioned meeting the Austrian emperor, and of being pleased with him. It has been said that he also liked Bismarck, and it is certain that from this time forward he followed Bismarck's advice with an implicit confidence that proved much to his advantage.

The Tsar of Russia passed through Berlin in the summer of 1871 on his way to Ems, and held a satisfactory consultation with William I. Francis Joseph must also be conferred with to secure the peace of Europe on an enduring basis, but for him to come to Berlin might have had the appearance of too exacting a requirement; so William I. graciously offered to meet his imperial brother at Salzburg in Upper Austria. Bismarck and Von Beust accompanied their respective sovereigns, and held, no doubt, a highly edifying conference; but little of their conversation has ever been revealed to the public. The Paris Commune, however, was a phenomenon which must have occupied their attention, and Bismarck is supposed to have made the most of this argument to bring the three imperial powers into a closer and more sympathetic relation. The evident danger to all governments from those secret societies, whose object strikes at the root of civilization itself, was the most serious problem of the future. All monarchical governments especially should cultivate peaceful relations to avoid public censure and disarm the imputations of these invisible enemies to law and order. There was, in fact, at this time the shadow of a second Holy Alliance passing over Europe; but it proved to be nothing more than a shadow, and Bismarck was too far-sighted to attempt the revival of a political organization with which the name of Metternich would always be connected. One consequence of the Salzburg meeting was the retirement of Von Beust in the following autumn, and the appointment of Count Potocki as Austrian premier in his place. His previous antagonism to Bismarck rendered it impossible for Von Beust, in spite of his invaluable services to the state, to take the lead in a policy of reconciliation towards Prussia. He may have requested this himself, and Francis Joseph sent him to the court of St. James, where he found ready listeners to his animadversions against the German chancellor. That his removal was suggested by Bismarck is not at all probable. Such a decided change of policy required a change of ministers to make it effectual, and Potocki was soon succeeded by Count Andrassy, the first Hungarian premier to rule the Empire of the Danube, who was the right man to carry out the Salzburg programme. He was in all respects Von Beust's equal, even if Louis Napoleon had not spoken of him as a "caged eagle," and he appears to have been the one statesman of his time whom Bismarck thoroughly respected.

FRENCH AFFAIRS

Thiers was finally elected President of the French Republic on the last day of August, and his first serious effort was an attempt to arrange with Bismarck for the evacuation of French territory by anticipating the payment of the war indemnity. Bismarck was ready to meet him half-way on such a question, and expressed a desire to do anything he could to facilitate the establishment of order and tranquillity under the new government. Germany could not accept French securities in return for the indemnity to any large amount, because in that case it would depend on the good-will of the French people whether the securities were finally redeemed; but if the bankers would exchange French *rentes* for other securities there would certainly be no objection. The Rothschilds and other bankers assured Thiers that this could be done, and the French government accordingly advertised for a loan of two and a half milliards (five hundred million dollars), and over seven milliards were subscribed, or more than enough to extinguish the whole indemnity. This was not accomplished, however, until 1873; but by this policy Thiers relieved France of the burden of supporting fifty thousand German troops. There were other reasons why the Germans should evacuate France as soon as possible.

There is no better evidence that the campaign of 1870 was a popular war on the French side than the spiteful feeling that has endured so long towards their gallant opponents. There was no such bitterness in Germany towards Napoleon I., and it is difficult to find an unfavorable criticism of him among German writers. The French went to war for glory, and got the worst of it, and might have learned wisdom from the lesson. Instead of doing so, however, they immediately commenced preparations for a war of revenge. This belligerent

spirit manifested itself in the autumn of 1871 by the murder
of a German soldier at Melun and another at Paris. The
cases were so clear that Bismarck trusted the trial of the assassins to French jurisdiction, which resulted in their acquittal
amid a chorus of approbation from the more ordinary class
of French newspapers. Under some conditions such a fla-
gitious proceeding might have resulted in a renewal of hostilities; but Bismarck contented himself with notifying President Thiers that in the future, if the perpetration of such
crimes was not duly punished, French hostages would be
exacted and further reprisals inflicted. If the classes to which
judges and barristers belonged were not above such bitterness of feeling, the German government would be obliged to
take rigorous measures for the protection of their citizens in
the occupied departments.[1] Thiers accordingly issued a proclamation to the French people on December 7, in which he
said, "To those who may believe that killing a foreigner is
not murder, I may observe that they are abominably in error."
The Empress Augusta ingenuously wrote to Guizot to advise
her how the French animosity towards the Germans might be
ameliorated. No doubt it might have been ameliorated by
a heavy reduction of the war indemnity and the retrocession of Metz; but this plan does not seem to have occurred
to the newly created empress. The letter occasioned a good
deal of comment; so that Count Henry von Arnim, the German envoy at Paris, sent a despatch to Bismarck concerning
it, and also in regard to the troubles of German residents in
Paris, who were suffering a kind of small persecution on account of their nationality.

Bismarck replied that, with all respect to the empress, he did
not consider any attempt to appease the wrath of the French
people would be likely to succeed, and, as for the German
residents on French soil, they were at liberty to return to
their own country, and must take their chances if they remained.

---

[1] Our Chancellor, ii. 80. I cannot learn that these villains were finally punished at all.

This certainly was not a narrow or supersensitive view of the situation, and later reports indicated that the complainants were chiefly German Jews, who had gone to Paris on speculation and to escape military service; so that they were suffering not for their patriotism, but from their pronunciation.

THE KULTURKAMPF BEGINS

The spiritual strength of Protestantism consists in its liberty of conscience, which allows every man to think for himself, and, though this has its small evils, it is far better than the religious despotism of the Church of Rome; but in this also lies the political weakness of Protestantism. It is strange how little sympathy was felt by English and American Protestants for the German struggle against papal infallibility between 1871 and 1882. It was a long-continued, harassing conflict, and caused Bismarck more trouble than Francis Joseph or Louis Napoleon had. It has been called in Germany the Kulturkampf, or religious battle.

The dogma of infallibility was intended to place the authority of the pope above all civil authority, and was directly aimed against the Italian government. That it would produce a conflict with the civil authorities must have been foreseen, but what advantage the Church of Rome was to gain by this the most impartial judges could not determine. The obstinacy of priests is proverbial, and little as their spiritual weapons avail them against the scepticism of the nineteenth century, their defensive armor is as invulnerable now as it was in the twelfth century. Like the Greek Capaneus, they can be buried for a time, but cannot be destroyed.

In Italy the dogma proved of very slight effect. The people were so heartily on the side of national unity that it could hardly find an entering wedge anywhere. Of all civilized cities there were none in which the pope was less respected than his own capital. The king of Italy had already been excommunicated with but trifling inconvenience to himself or the government, and the pope might continue this down to his most petty officials without its attracting serious attention. The distinction between civil and religious marriages continued, without producing any worse consequences than a few youthful and perhaps unprincipled divorces.

In Switzerland, however, the dogma created a fierce tumult between the Protestant and Catholic cantons, and in South America a number of violent revolutions were occasioned by it with various results. In Ecuador the Clerical party was triumphant, while in Brazil the reaction against the Church was so energetic and the clergy so tenacious of its rights that the Supreme Court finally imprisoned the archbishop—buried like Capaneus—for four years. In the old, unconstitutional Prussia of Frederick and his descendants the pope could not have accomplished much, but in constitutional Germany the Catholics, by uniting with the Poles, Saxons, and other malcontents, could cause the government a good deal of annoyance, and this Pius IX. was determined they should do. There was practically little to be gained by it, but revenge is sweet, even to a pontiff. It was to be a campaign of obstacles.

There is only one step from papal infallibility to the worship of man as a god,—from the High Pontiff to the Grand Lama. Bismarck informed the crown prince, during all the pressing business of the French campaign, that he intended to make a stand against infallibility.[1] What he would have done if the conflict had not been forced on him is not very evident, but he perhaps foresaw that it would be forced on him. "Sovereignty," he said, "is a unit, and there could not be two sovereignties in Germany." It was not long before this question was brought to a crucial test. The first three months of peace had not closed when the Catholic Bishop Krementz of Ermland excommunicated one of the subordinates of his diocese for refusing to subscribe to the new dogma. This in a Catholic community was a serious matter to the subordinate priest, and an infringement of the principle of religious liberty which had continued in Prussia for nearly a hundred and fifty years. Emperor William was very much disgusted at it, and still more indignant when the Archbishop

---

[1] The crown prince's diary, November, 1870.

of Cologne suspended a number of professors at Bonn for the same reason. This was not only persecution, but in direct contravention to Prussian law, and the more inexcusable since it was only through the liberality of the Prussian government that the university at Bonn was permitted to exist. Not only the German government but public opinion, even among a large portion of Catholics, was mightily stirred up at such a tyrannical procedure.

While the Ecumenical Council was in session the Prussian envoy at the Vatican had warned Bismarck of the course events were taking, and suggested the appointment of a lay representative to confer with Pius IX. and endeavor to restrain him before the Rubicon was passed; but Bismarck knew Pius IX. too well to make the attempt. "We should only obtain a rebuff," he said, "and weaken our cause before we were fairly in the field." Now he acted with his customary promptness, and on July 8 issued a decree abolishing the Catholic department of public worship in the ministry. This was a summary proceeding and was freely criticised; but this branch of the government jurisdiction was filled mainly with Ultramontanes, and Bismarck foresaw that it would continue to be an obstacle between the public and any laws which the Reichstag might enact on this question. It also served as a case of *lex talionis;* for if the professors at Bonn were to be deposed the Catholics serving under the government would also lose their places. The almost infinite wealth of the Roman Church, however, prevented this from having much effect.

As the priests in Bavaria and other Catholic communities preached sermons exciting their parishioners against the government and urging them to vote for Clerical candidates, the Reichstag passed a law in December that this should be considered insurrectionary talk, and its authors be held responsible according to the penal code. The Bavarian government supported this bill, and, in fact, the condition of affairs in Bavaria was a smaller duplication of that in Prussia. The Bishop of Strasburg was one of the first to suffer under this law. His attacks on the government were so violent and uncompromising that he was banished from the empire. The conflict, however, was like fighting a swarm of mosquitoes, for where one irreconcilable papist was disposed of two or three others appeared in his place. The mock-heroic is such an easy part to play that there will always be found plenty to attempt it when the opportunity presents itself. The self-imposed imprisonment of Pius IX. served as an example for his dark-robed followers to imitate.

Bismarck's next card was a trump, and a high one. Ever since the foundation of the Prussian monarchy, and of many other German states, all schools, public and private, had been under the jurisdiction of the church. The universities were independent, but in primary and secondary instruction the courses of study and the text-books in use were under the supervision of the clergy. This, of course, gave them great influence over the minds of the young, and a change in this direction would affect the future of all Germany. By a sweeping measure in January, 1872, this jurisdiction was transferred from the church to the state,—making the board of school inspectors a government appointment in both Protestant and Catholic communities. At the same time the religious instructors connected with the schools were not to be interfered with, so long as they avoided the obnoxious dogma and made no attempt to prejudice their youthful hearers against the German government. When the bill for this purpose was introduced in the German Reichstag it produced the most profound sensation that had been known since the capitulation of Paris. Dr. Windhorst instantly recognized its importance, and exerted himself in opposition to it with an energy and determination equal to Bismarck's own, and in power of invective he went far beyond him. Never had Windhorst displayed such resources; never had the keen blade of his scimitar flashed so brilliantly. The act was revolutionary,—it would penetrate to every German home; would overturn all traditions of German education; would strike at the root of moral instruction. What would Germany be like in the next century with such violent changes and innovations?

There were others who considered the measure revolutionary, but a revolution too long delayed and now most needful and salutary. Bismarck was on hand to defend his bill, which he did in his usual clear-cut, business-like manner. The fine speeches were all on the side of clerical independence and the rights of minorities, but the votes were on the side of Bismarck.

Having proved to Pius IX. and Antonelli what he had power to accomplish, Bismarck now adopted a more pacific policy, and evinced his desire to ameliorate the situation by the appointment of Cardinal Hohenlohe as special ambassador to the Vatican, where Germany had only been represented before by a simple legate or *chargé d'affaires*. The Hohenlohe family of Germany is, like the Orloff family in Russia, bred to the diplomatic service for generations. Until the present epoch they have never risen to high distinction, but they have grown time-honored, both in the service of Prussia and of Bavaria. If there was a person in Germany who could have been selected with any expectation of success as a mediator between Emperor William and Pius IX., it was Cardinal Hohenlohe. His loyalty to the state was unquestionable, and as the first Catholic appointment of the kind from a Protestant government he ought to have been acceptable to the pope. Pius IX., however, was soured beyond the help of antiseptics, and he was determined to continue the selfish warfare, although there was nothing he could gain by it except the mean satisfaction of causing petty annoyances.

On April 25, 1872, Von Derinthal, the German *chargé d'affaires* at Rome, reported the appointment of Cardinal Hohenlohe to Antonelli, and announced the expectation of his early arrival. As no reply was received to this communication, Von Derinthal was directed to make inquiries of the Jesuit cardinal as to the cause of his silence. Antonelli replied that, though the pope was not insensible to the good intentions of the emperor, he was nevertheless, under existing circumstances, obliged to decline the acceptance of so important a mission. Great indignation was expressed at this in Berlin and other German capitals, and a motion was immediately made in the Reichstag to strike out from the schedule the appropriation for the *chargé d'affaires* at the Vatican. On May 14 Bismarck made a speech in the Reichstag in opposition to this motion, which has become historical. He said, *inter alia:*

"I hardly believe that with the existing ruling sentiments of the Catholic Church an envoy of the German empire could, by most skilful diplomacy or by persuasion, exert any influence; that he would be capable of modifying the attitude taken by his Holiness the Pope towards us in temporal matters. According to recently expressed and publicly promulgated dogmas of the Catholic Church, I do not think it possible for a temporal power to attain to a *concordat* without this temporal power being effaced to a degree and in a way which the German Empire, at least, cannot accept. Fear not; to Canossa we shall *not* go, neither bodily nor mentally.

"I had hoped that by the choice of an envoy who had full confidence from both sides on account of his love of truth and his trustworthiness, and on account of his conciliatory disposition,—I had hoped that the choice of such an envoy as his Majesty the Emperor had made, in the person of a noted prince of the church, would be welcome in Rome; that it would be conceived as a pledge of our peaceful, friendly sentiments, that it might be used as a means of coming to an understanding. . . . My regret at this refusal is exceedingly great; but I am not justified in giving this regret the form of an irritation, for the government owes our Catholic fellow-citizens an untiring search for those paths in which the boundary-line between clerical and temporal power, so absolutely necessary to us in the interest of peace, might be found in a manner least inclined to cause ill-feeling. Therefore, I shall not be discouraged by this occurrence, but continue in trying to persuade his Majesty the Emperor to find a representative of the empire for Rome who enjoys the confidence of both powers, if not in an equal measure, at least to a degree sufficient for his calling. That this task has been rendered exceedingly difficult by recent events can hardly be denied."

Even the Clericals could not withhold their admiration for Bismarck's calm, dispassionate wisdom, and the more enthusiastic Liberals were obliged to admit the superiority of his judgment. He again repeated his determination never to

admit any claim of the Church of Rome that a law passed
by the Reichstag should not be binding on every German
citizen. The motion for striking out was then rejected by
a heavy majority. The expression, "We are not going to
Canossa," became as proverbial as the earlier expression, "By
no means sufficient"; and though much of the anti-papal
legislation was afterwards retracted, it cannot fairly be said
that Bismarck ever went to Canossa any more than Canossa
came to him.[1]

Afterwards the Jesuits still remained to be dealt with.
Antonelli was the chief adviser of Pius IX., and diplomatic
opinion made him responsible for a large share of the pope's
deviltry; but there were other substantial reasons. Within
the last fifteen years the number of convents in Germany had
increased from sixty-nine to eight hundred and twenty-six,
and the number of persons immured in them from nine hundred and seventy-six to something like ten thousand. This
withdrawal of so many efficient helpers from the community,
and a large proportion of young women among them, was
looked upon as a national evil, and generally attributed to the
influence of the Jesuits. Huge petitions from all parts of Germany were presented to the Reichstag, praying for the expatriation of the order of Jesus; and it is noteworthy that on
these, besides other distinguished names, was that of Prince
Hohenlohe of Bavaria, the brother of Cardinal Hohenlohe
who had lately been refused as ambassador to the Vatican.

The question was debated on May 15, and a resolution
drawn up jointly by a body of conservative and liberal members was adopted petitioning the chancellor for the expulsion
of the Jesuits. The petition desired Prince Bismarck, firstly,
to take measures that peace and concord among the various
churches of the empire should be preserved; and, secondly,
that a bill be introduced for the purpose of regulating all religious orders, congregations, and the like, to decide whether
they should be admitted, and on what terms, special consid-

---

[1] Canossa, a town in Lombardy, where the Emperor Henry IV. abased himself
before Gregory VII.,—the greater Gregory, and most powerful of all the popes.

eration being taken in this matter to the behavior of the order of the Jesuits. In accordance with this resolution the Federal Council, on June 11, adopted a bill authorizing the police authorities to forbid members of the society of Jesuits from residing in any part of the German empire, even if they possessed rights as native Germans. At the first reading of the bill the federal commissioner, Friedberg, declared that the law was only provisional, and necessitated by the dangerous opposition of the order of Jesus to the state. At a meeting of the leaders of the various parties in the Reichstag, with the exception of the Clericals, a substitute for the government bill was agreed upon, to the effect that members of the order of Jesuits, if foreigners, should be expelled from the empire; but if native Germans they might remain on certain conditions, and by changing their residence to places designated by the government. This substitute was finally adopted by a hundred and thirty-one against ninety-three votes.

A few days later, when a German Catholic delegation at Rome waited on Pius IX. to assure him of their unfailing allegiance, the pope complained of the persecution of the Catholic Church in Germany in bitter and aggressive language, finally concluding with the words which were generally reported, " Be trustful and united, for some stone will surely fall to shatter the heel of this Colossus." [1] This was imprudent, to say the best of it, for it easily might be interpreted as an invitation to rid the world of his opponent by unlawful means, and so it seems to have been interpreted. It also showed plainly that the Catholic party were getting the worst of this war of legal measures which they had inaugurated. The Bishop of Ermland was one of the first to feel the weight of the anti-Catholic laws. He persisted in excommunicating all those who did not subscribe to the doctrine of infallibility, and in consequence his salary was stopped by the government. He entered a suit for arrears, but lost his case and was obliged to depend for his living on the slender munificence of the Vatican.

---

[1] Müller's Political History, p. 500.

CHAPTER XII

THIERS remained president of the French Republic from August, 1871, until May 24, 1873, and he did much to raise his country from the gulf of despair into which it had been plunged by the suicidal folly of Gramont and Napoleon III. His appointments were judicious and gave satisfaction; he elevated the character of the foreign service; he was a skilful financier, and helped to lighten the severe burden of the war indemnity. In a little more than two years the last regiment of the army of occupation was recalled from French territory, a great relief to both parties concerned. Thiers advocated the adoption of a protective tariff, which stimulated industry, effaced the ravages of war, and gave a kind of prosperity and prestige to the new republic. Unhappily, he felt too confident of his position, and had no suspicion how short-lived his ascendancy would prove to be. Von Beust came to see him from London for a consultation on the peace of Europe, and remarked to him on the strength of the opposition in the French Chamber of Deputies. "Yes," replied Thiers, "they sometimes make disturbances, but I have only to do so," holding up his finger. It occurred to Von Beust that Thiers might have made the same remark to a less friendly and prudent person than himself.

This self-complacency may have helped to bring about his downfall, but there was also a deeper reason. France had not yet become republican at heart. As the brilliant monographist, Arsène Houssaye, wrote at the time, the French Republic derived its support from a combination of Legitimists, Orleanists, and Bonapartists. The monarchical reaction had set in again, and the elections for 1873 were strongly in Napoleon's favor. Strange as it may seem, Thiers was repeatedly outvoted in the Chamber of Deputies, and finally sent in his resignation, in a confident belief that it would not be accepted. On the contrary, it was accepted, and Marshal MacMahon, still faithful in spirit to the old emperor, was chosen in his place. It is thought that if Thiers had dissolved the Chambers and appealed to the public for support, a new election might have sustained him in his place; and MacMahon afterwards made precisely the same mistake in his struggle against Gambetta.

Napoleon III. did not remain idle at Chiselhurst, nor had he given up hope of returning to his uncle's throne. His situation was convenient for loyal Bonapartists, who came and went continually from France. Finally, in the autumn of 1872, a definite plan was arranged for a second *coup d'état*, no doubt with the connivance of President MacMahon. In order to accomplish this it would be necessary for the emperor to appear on horseback, and unfortunately his physical condition was such that a dangerous surgical operation was necessary before he could attempt it. The operation was undertaken on January 9, and Napoleon expired under the influence of the chloroform.[1]

This left the Bonapartists without a leader until the prince imperial should be more advanced towards manhood, and it strengthened the two Bourbon factions in a corresponding degree. The Count of Chambord was the Legitimists' heir to the throne, and the Count of Paris was the nearest living relative of Louis Philippe. Neither of them was a man of exceptional ability nor especially popular; but the tide was running in their favor, and if one or the other could be persuaded to resign his claim it was likely that France would again become a monarchy. The idea of this was acceptable to Emperor William and the other hereditary monarchs of Europe, including Queen Victoria; but Bismarck did not favor it, and it is supposed that he had frequent discussions on the subject with his sovereign, who finally yielded his opinion to Bis-

---

[1] Von Beust even fixes the date, March 20, on which Napoleon III. intended to imitate his uncle's return from Elba. He says, " Great hopes were then entertained of a Napoleonic restoration, as I saw during my occasional visits to Chiselhurst." Memoirs, ii. 195.

marck's superior wisdom. The German ambassador at Paris, however, Count Henry von Arnim, was an enthusiastic monarchist, and, having been sounded by the Bonapartists shortly before Napoleon's death, notified Bismarck of the fact, adding a decisive opinion of his own approval of the movement.[1] This in itself was exceeding the customary bounds of an envoy's authority, for it was not Von Arnim's place to judge of what measures the home government should adopt. Bismarck, however, replied to him in a temperate manner, and endeavored to persuade him that the interests of Germany were not likely to be improved by any change from the prudent and pacific policy of Thiers. His argument did not seem to produce any effect on Von Arnim, who continued to discuss the matter and reiterate his first position. At the same time Bismarck became satisfied that Von Arnim was carrying on a correspondence on this subject with some one at the Prussian court independently of the foreign office.

Bismarck found more difficulty in obtaining suitable ambassadors for the foreign service than Von Moltke did in his selection of subordinate generals for the army. Dr. Busch's report of his chief's commentaries on some of them is more amusing than complimentary. Baron Goltz, who figured at Paris during the campaign of 1866, was always flirting, so Bismarck said, first, with the Queen of Portugal, and afterward with Eugénie herself; and, though this was creditable to his powers of attraction, it was not exactly what Bismarck wanted of him. Von Arnim, while legate at the Vatican, had troubled his superior with such freedom of advice as was hardly in place from a subordinate officer. His despatches from Paris were composed in a similar tone of self-confidence, which may have caused Bismarck to suspect that in opposing Von Arnim he had also to deal with a power behind him. Who it was that encouraged the count in this business to show such a bold front has never yet come to light, but

---

[1] Even recently it was stated in an American magazine that from the beginning of Von Arnim's career he "developed strong radical opinions, and was bitterly opposed to the growing influence and conservative policy of Bismarck."

suspicion naturally points towards the crown prince. It is possible, however, that Von Arnim was aware of a difference in opinion between the emperor and Bismarck in regard to republicanism in France, and hoped, by taking the emperor's side, to widen the breach, bring himself prominently into favor, and supplant Bismarck when his master had become dissatisfied with him. Among the long list of opponents whom Bismarck may be said to have tumbled from their horses in this grand political tournament, there was no other so vainly ambitious, so unscrupulous of his means, and who so well deserved his fate as Henry von Arnim.[1]

This, however, is anticipating events. From the time of MacMahon's accession to the presidency, Von Arnim paid no more attention to Bismarck's directions than a spoiled child does to those of his parents. It was not long, therefore, before Bismarck informed him that it was his business to take orders, and not criticise the home government. This resulted in a letter from Von Arnim to the emperor, complaining that Bismarck placed him, metaphorically, in a strait-jacket, and did not allow him such freedom of judgment or action as an envoy or plenipotentiary was always supposed to possess. That this letter did not result in his immediate recall is ample evidence that Von Arnim was not acting alone, but was the confederate, if not the instrument, of more powerful parties at court. The difficulty of Bismarck's position in this emergency cannot be overestimated. If there had been a flaw anywhere in the magnanimous nature of the old emperor for jealousy to enter in, Bismarck would have gone under like Von Stein before him, and as Chatham did after the Seven Years' War. He was compelled to endure, in the most critical and important position of the foreign service, a subordinate who deliberately opposed his policy and who evidently intended to become his rival. The Bismarck who had revolutionized Austria and crushed Louis Napoleon was to be balked by this "young gilded serpent," as Richelieu called

---

[1] There is an excellent account of this intrigue in Holtzendorff's Rechtsgutachten.

the giddy favorite of Louis XIII. To the emperor, who sent for him, Bismarck opened his mind concerning Von Arnim with customary frankness. He may have found William I. more than half inclined to side with Von Arnim's opinion. At all events, it was agreed that Von Arnim should not be removed for the present, but that Bismarck should await the development of events.

The transition from the prudent and peaceable administration of Thiers to the energetic but less experienced Mac-Mahon was not favorable to the interests of Germany, and it was doubly irritating to Bismarck that his representative in Paris not only would not be persuaded of this, but had actually assisted in bringing it to pass. The tendency to sudden changes in French politics was of itself a source of insecurity to Germany and a danger to the peace of Europe; and with a disorderly Chamber of Deputies, a fanatical clergy behind that, and a Bonapartist general at top, the prospect of a continued peace did not look favorable. As the monarchical movement strengthened during the summer, Von Arnim became bolder and more combative. He believed the tide was running in his favor, and there can be little doubt that he received equal encouragement from Berlin. The evacuation treaty, which had been commenced by Thiers and left unfinished at his resignation, was so delayed and neglected by Von Arnim that Bismarck was obliged to attend to the case himself with the help of the French ambassador at Berlin; and now it appeared that the whole of Thiers's communication on the subject had not been reported by Von Arnim to Bismarck the preceding winter, as it should have been. Any other foreign envoy would have been immediately superseded.

The emperor sent for Von Arnim to return to Berlin and explain himself, and, according to the latter's account of the interview, William I. was not, on the whole, displeased with his statement, while he admitted that Bismarck had serious faults which made him difficult to deal with. The truth of this statement is questionable, but it is certain that the emperor was conciliatory, and advised Von Arnim to call on Bismarck in a friendly spirit. Whatever spirit he may have been in at the time was quickly knocked out of him by the savage attack that Bismarck made. The wrath of many months, bottled up like champagne, burst forth in a torrent of vindictive eloquence which swept everything before it.[1] After the first surprise, Von Arnim, who was a man of real ability, defended himself stoutly,—stemmed the torrent, as it were,— and finally persuaded Bismarck that they should lay their case together before the emperor. We can almost admire Von Arnim for the determined manner with which he sustained his position, unstable as it was, against the strongest will and before the most powerful monarch in Europe. Bismarck impeached Von Arnim's veracity, and the latter returned the compliment in round terms. If the emperor's confidence in Bismarck remained unshaken, he nevertheless concluded to give Von Arnim the benefit of a case not proven. Perhaps he also wished to have it said that he did not always follow Bismarck's judgment. The Iron Chancellor was obliged to accept a reconciliation, and Von Arnim returned to Paris with the admonition to be more prudent in the future. What a position for the autocrat of Europe to be placed in! Truly, Bismarck was a much-enduring man.

Von Arnim now hurried onward to his fate like a ship that is driven on the rocks by a storm. The monarchical movement in France ripened by the magnanimous withdrawal of the Count of Paris in favor of the Legitimist candidate, to whom the National Assembly finally offered the crown, only to discover that they had set up a fool for all men to gaze at.[2] The Count of Chambord would accept the proffered honor only on condition that the French would serve under the white flag of his ancestors, and that he was not to be circumscribed by constitutional forms. It was this foolish letter of Chambord's which upset Von Arnim's plans, and perhaps saved Bismarck for Germany. It left the monarchical movement stranded on a bar, and produced a revulsion of feeling among the French people, who now realized from what an empty figure-head they

---

[1] Arnim's " Pro Nihilo."
[2] This is what Minister Bancroft called him at the time.

had escaped. Louis XV. did not deal a more severe blow
at royalty. The Prussian court saw clearly now that Bismarck was justified in the course he had pursued towards
the French republic; but Von Arnim did not see it, and continued as stiff-necked as ever. All this time the Kulturkampf was raging, and a number of French ecclesiastics on
the borders of Elsass and Lothringen were preaching incendiary harangues against the Protestant Germans and their
heathen emperor. It was the business of the German ambassador to notify the chancellor of this, but he failed to do so,
and the information came to Bismarck from other sources.
When Von Arnim was directed to confer with President Mac-
Mahon on the subject he is reported to have replied that he
did not consider it of sufficient importance. How far it is
best to interfere in such matters is always a question of judgment, but Bismarck believed that incendiary harangues and
sensational newspaper articles caused a great deal of mischief.
In this case it was part of the same struggle that he was fighting in Germany, and the relation of the two countries was too
critical at this time to leave much of a margin for theoretical
politics.

Bismarck accordingly applied to the French envoy at Berlin,
M. de Gontaud-Biron, who appears to have been a sensible
person and well adapted to his difficult position, to convey a
remonstrance to President MacMahon in regard to the inimical behavior of the French ecclesiastics, but MacMahon,
requiring the support of the Ultramontanes, and being aware
that the German ambassador was opposed to Bismarck's
action, declined to interfere. This, however, was the first step
towards Von Arnim's downfall, for the German emperor's
sympathies were heartily enlisted in the conflict with Pius
IX., and he had no intention of yielding an inch on that question. Bismarck accordingly returned to the attack, and, finding that he had French law on his side, pressed the case so
energetically that in January, 1874, he issued a circular note
to the great powers, dwelling on the serious danger that evidently existed of a renewal of the conflict between France
and Germany, and intimating broadly that in such case the

authorities at Berlin would not wait until the enemy was better prepared for it than at present. Diplomats had learned by this time to know that Bismarck meant what he said and never threatened in vain. To his enemies he had come to appear like a veritable bogie, or limb of Lucifer. President MacMahon recognized the crisis and bowed his head to it. The incendiary bishops were threatened with suspension in case they continued their warlike counsels, and the Ultramontane movement was thus held in check for the time being.

The exasperation of the French people, however, soon expressed itself in a new direction. Previous to 1871 it had been customary to commission envoys from the French court to all the more important German states, and these positions served as comfortable sinecures to the impecunious dependents of Napoleon, but after the establishment of German unity these missions naturally came to an end for the smaller states with the exception of Bavaria. It was now proposed (winter of 1874) in the French Chamber of Deputies that diplomatic relations should be renewed with Saxony and the South German states. This would have served as a fine entering wedge for French intrigue, and was, in fact, a blow aimed directly at German national unity. It was Von Arnim's business to have protested against it at once; but, instead of doing so, he wrote to Bismarck for instructions as to how he should proceed. Such a case indicates little more than a sulky disposition, but, as it happened, it capped the climax. The truth was that, now the monarchical problem was out of sight, Von Arnim had lost much of his former importance. The emperor now agreed with Bismarck, and on March 12 Von Arnim was superseded by Prince Hohenlohe and directed to report at Constantinople.[1]

"Whom the gods would destroy they first make mad." Henry Von Arnim's subsequent behavior can only be accounted for by a blind rage which overpowered all judgment.

---

[1] Bismarck had provided Von Arnim with seven thousand thalers from the "reptile fund" to subsidize French newspapers in the German interest, but he was satisfied that Von Arnim had used this money to subsidize German newspapers against himself.

He carried off from the embassy at Paris a large number of state documents, which might either have compromised his previous transactions there, or such as he thought might aid him in fighting out his quarrel with the chancellor. He also supplied a news correspondent of the Vienna *Press*, an old Catholic-Metternich organ, with material for an attack on Bismarck's Roman Church policy, in which it was compared to a disadvantage with the advice proposed by Von Arnim while Prussian legate at Rome. This was published in time to prevent Von Arnim's departure for the Turkish capital, and created a lively sensation throughout Germany and Austria. Bismarck at once divined its authorship, and though Von Arnim denied any connection with it he was at once retired from the diplomatic service. It was an act of treacherous insubordination which even the kindly old emperor could not overlook.

Worse consequences were soon to follow. Hohenlohe, who has since become chancellor himself, was more of a Prussian than a prince; he had no intention of doing his work as ambassador by halves, and he soon reported from Paris in regard to the missing documents. This was a case of theft, quite as much as if Von Arnim had stolen government bonds; but he does not seem to have realized the fact. Perhaps he supposed that his social position and powerful friends at court would shield him from the customary penalties of Prussian law. When the missing documents were demanded he returned a portion, but evidently not the whole number. Bismarck had a search-warrant issued; Von Arnim's house at Stettin was ransacked, and, as other government papers were found in his effects, he was arrested and brought to jail in Berlin.

At this a general outcry was raised throughout France and England. Before the proper explanation could be offered it was looked upon as Bismarck's high-handed tyranny, and Disraeli congratulated a small audience, the following evening in London, that they did not live in a country where domiciliary visits were possible. His speech was, of course, reported to the press, and Bismarck telegraphed to London the next day to know if the English premier's remarks were intended to have a personal application, to which Disraeli replied meekly enough that he had no thought of such a thing,—to the great amusement of the opposition. The Anglo-American public was still more astonished to learn that Von Arnim's offence was for intriguing *in favor of* monarchy.'

His imprisonment only lasted a few days, for the condition of his health was so delicate that it was feared the confinement would prove fatal to him. His trial, which took place in December, was looked forward to with great expectation by Bismarck's enemies, for it was supposed that all the dubious tricks and underhand methods by which the chancellor gained his ends would now be revealed. They were, however, doomed to grievous disappointment. Von Arnim did bring some unpleasant charges against him, but they were unsubstantiated, and even if true would not seriously compromise him. On the other hand, the letter to the Vienna *Press* was traced directly to Von Arnim's apartments in Paris. His unpatriotic policy and selfish ambition were paraded before the court in perhaps too sensational colors; while Bismarck's character went up ten degrees in the public estimation; for it clearly appeared that he had endured much and patiently, and was really a disinterested statesman whose country's welfare was the magnetic needle which guided his course through storm and darkness. William Müller says, "The most weighty despatches were read and published, and the world had another opportunity to admire the consistency and far-sightedness of the chancellor's national policy." One fact was elicited, however, which must have caused him some uneasiness, and that was the plans he had already laid in regard to the election of a successor to Pius IX. The trial concluded on the 19th of December, and Von Arnim was sentenced to three months' imprisonment, which seems rather a light penalty when it is considered that two centuries earlier he would certainly have been decapitated.

Bismarck considered the punishment too light, and appealed from the decision of the Superior Court to the High Chamber

---

' This at least was the commencement of it.

of Justice. Von Arnim also appealed, but prudently took himself out of the way before the decision of the second tribunal, on October 20, 1875, which increased his sentence from three to nine months; after which a charge of high treason was brought against him, and, as he refused to appear before the court, he was sentenced to five years' imprisonment. He lived for some time in Switzerland, where he published tracts and books in self-defence, and afterwards went to Vienna. He died at Nice, strangely enough on April 19, 1881, a man of ruined reputation and an illustration of Wolsey's warning to Cromwell, "Let all the ends thou aimst at be thy country's, thy God's, and truth's." Of all the incidents of Bismarck's life his conflict with Von Arnim has the most strongly dramatic character, and if we could only know what went on behind the scenes,—Bismarck's struggle with the emperor, and the influence that was brought to bear on the other side, —it would be far more interesting than it is now, seen from the external side. Some Schiller of the future, perhaps, will place it on the German stage. It was the last, if not the first, "intrigue" against Bismarck during the reign of William I., and it is not surprising that no others followed it.

THE MAY LAWS

Meanwhile the Kulturkampf was dragging on its wearisome existence, with a good deal of animosity and hard feeling on both sides, but with little real injury to any one concerned in it. Political intrigue is the natural element of the Vatican, and a priest enjoys his obstinacy as an athlete does his exercise. Neither is it likely that Bismarck and Dr. Falk suffered more severely; and the conflict aroused an interest in religious subjects in Germany such as had not been felt since the Thirty Years' War. The breach between the Emperor William and Pius IX. widened continually. In December of 1872 the pope referred to Bismarck and the emperor, before a meeting of cardinals, in such opprobrious language that the German legate at the Vatican, who duly reported the circumstance, was at once recalled. Such action between two civil governments would have been tantamount to a declaration of war,

but Bismarck was the only person in real danger, and whether
he realized this or not, he kept straight on his course, like the
knight in Dürer's picture, though death and the devil stalked
behind him.

Early in the new year Dr. Falk had introduced a bill in the
Reichstag containing a number of laws for the better regulation
of Catholic institutions in Germany. They occasioned a long
and spirited discussion, and were finally enacted in the month
of May, from which they derived their well-known title. As
the original document is lengthy and legal in form, we will
content ourselves here with an abstract statement of them.

The first of the May Laws placed a limitation on the penalties
imposed by Catholic ecclesiastics on the members of their diocese
or parish. It permitted them to regulate the conditions of membership in the church, and also to dismiss members who had in-
fringed on the laws of religious government; but it withheld all
right of jurisdiction over the property, freedom, or reputation of a
German citizen, or of taking any action whatever affecting his civil
rights. This was especially designed to prevent intimidation or
undue influence in regard to voting at elections.

The second measure was intended to control the training and
education of the clergy, and provided that neither priest nor bishop
should be installed unless he were a graduate of a German gymnasium, and had studied three years at a German university. After
this he might study at the College of the Propaganda in Rome if he
chose; but he must first become a German by education and by
habit of thought. The second law also provided a board of inspectors for all religious seminaries and monastic institutions, and placed
them under the direct guardianship of the civil government. It required the Catholic bishops to give previous notification to the government of the appointment of priests to particular parishes, or of
their transference from one parish to another, and it forbade appointments or changes without the approval of the state inspectors.

The third law was intended for the protection of Catholic dis-
senters, so that the same freedom of opinion might be encouraged
within the fold of the Church of Rome as now exists in all Protestant communities. A dissenter was only required to express his
difference of belief before a local court of law to obtain protection
in his new position.

The fourth measure was intended to provide against all secret and arbitrary forms of punishment, especially corporeal chastisement, and placed all monastic institutions under the supervision of inspectors for this purpose.

Surely there was nothing very terrible in this. It seems like a fair and judicious measure, not of a coercive character, but intended to guarantee the same freedom of thought, right of individual opinion, and unrestricted action in the clerical profession which prevails in other professions. A similar code had long existed in Würtemberg and some other German states. Compared with the religious code of Sweden, or that of England in the eighteenth century, it was liberality itself. According to the traditional custom of the Church of Rome, Catholic boys, especially of indigent parents, are marked for the priesthood while still at the gymnasia, and hurried or coaxed into the College of the Propaganda at Rome before they are old enough to realize the difference it is going to make to them. Their studies are, of course, all directed to a single end; they have no debating societies, hear no arguments on opposite sides of a question, know nothing of the free discussion which takes place in Protestant universities, and thus their whole intellectual life becomes a piece of cast-iron dogmatism. No progress is possible in a religion constituted in this manner, and if it once began the whole fabric would fall to pieces. Catholic priests are often sympathetic, warm-hearted, and practically helpful men, but the higher mental qualities are stultified in them. Bismarck and Dr. Falk struck at the root of the matter, and if their plan could be carried out in all Catholic communities the supremacy of the pope over the minds of his followers would soon come to an end. They wished to have all citizens of the empire become Germans before they became anything else. No wonder the May Laws raised a storm in which, as Æschylus says, " The heavens were embroiled with the deep."

These laws were debated in the Reichstag until the 27th of February, when the final vote was taken on them. Just before this was done Bismarck addressed the assembly in favor of the bill.

The returns of the last elections had not been so favorable to the government as previously, and though the Clericals were still in a weak minority, they, as well as the Social Democrats, had gained a number of seats. As this fact was made the most of in debate by Dr. Windhorst and Lasker, Bismarck recalled to their minds that he had predicted as much, the year before, and considered it likely that they might gain still more ground. The reason for it was to be looked for in the distrust and difference of opinion between the Conservatives and the National Liberals. "There can be no decisive political action without *confidence*, and confidence is a delicate plant; if it is once destroyed it will not soon sprout again. The supporters of the government, though united in their opposition to the usurpation of the pope, are divided among themselves, and hence become a prey to decomposition." He then said:

"The gentleman who spoke last has further followed the same tactics taken up by the opponents of this bill in the other house, that is, to give these bills a confessional—I would say, a clerical character. The question which we are treating becomes, in my opinion, falsified, and the light in which we look at the same is false, if we treat the same from the confessional or clerical point of view. It is essentially political; it is not, as our Catholic fellow-citizens are made to believe, the contest of a Protestant dynasty against the Catholic Church,—it is not a contest between faith and infidelity. It is the ancient contest of power, which is as old as the human race; the contest of power between kingship and priesthood; a contest of power that is much more ancient than the appearance of our Saviour in this world; the contest of power in which Agamemnon engaged at Aulis against his seers, which there cost him his daughter and prevented the Greek ships from sailing; the contest of power that impregnated the German history of the Middle Ages up to the decomposition of the German Empire, known as the conflict of the popes with the emperors, which found its climax in that the last representative of the illustrious Swabian imperial lineage died on the scaffold under the axe of a French conqueror, and that this same French conqueror was in league with the pope then reigning. We have been very close to an analogous solution of this same situation, only applied to the customs of our

LIFE OF BISMARCK

own time. If the French war of conquest, the outbreak of which
coincided with the publication of the Vatican decrees, had been
crowned by success, I do not know what one might have been able
to report of the *gesta Dei per Francos* even within domains of the
church.

*   *   *   *   *   *   *   *

"Also in the conflicts of the popish power it has not always been
the case that just Catholic powers were the exclusive allies of the
pope ; neither have the priests always stood by his side. Cardinals
have been the state-ministers of great powers at a time when these
powers followed a strongly anti-papistical policy, even to pronounced violence.

"The question is, here, the defending of the state. The question is, the limitation of priestly by monarchical government, and
this limitation must be such that the state can assert itself at the
same time. For 'in the kingdom of this earth' it is the state which
rules and which has the precedence." [1]

Bismarck's interpretation of Iphigenia at Aulis is not to be
found in Greek mythologies, but it is plausible and probable.
There was no doubt a conflict between the temporal and the
priestly power at that time, caused, perhaps, by some slight
or displeasure which the augurs had incurred from Agamemnon. Unfortunate is the nation in which priestcraft or any
traditional religious formalism gains the ascendancy ; all the
higher forms of intellectual life are crushed out of the people,
and progress in civilization is no longer possible. India is
an example of such a country, and formerly, also, Egypt.
Two thousand years before Christ only the Jews could compare with the Hindoos in their lofty religious thought and
grand conception of a supreme being ; but the whole political
power of India was permitted to merge in the priesthood,
an inflexible system of caste was established, life became a
traditional, unprogressive routine, and the Brahmans, with
their fine intellectual heads and close kinship to European
nations, are no wiser to-day than in the time of Moses. So
it would have been in modern Europe but for the reformation
of Luther and Calvin, and so it was largely in Spain, Italy,

---

[1] Bismarck's Speeches, Reclam ed., v. 251.

284

and Portugal from that time until the revolution of 1789. It was an after-skirmish of this old battle that Bismarck was fighting.

The chief measures of the May Laws were passed at this date by a strong majority, but were amended at various times afterwards, and the question of civil and religious marriages was brought up the following month. It was considered necessary to introduce this separately, because Bismarck had formerly placed himself on record against it in the debates on the North German constitution of 1868. It is even stated that he now placed himself in opposition to it, and was over-ruled by Dr. Falk and his associates in the ministry. However that may have been, either he was prostrated by the severe strain of business or, as his opponents declared, was *schul-krank*, because he did not wish to have his sudden change of base continually hurled at him in argument. The latter is likely enough, although there is sufficient difference between the action of such a law in Protestant and Catholic commu-nities—since it is impossible to place the highest Protestant prelate in the position of the pope—to justify such an altera-tion of opinion. The people who prefer a contradiction in form to an agreement in fact are always sufficiently numerous to have made it unpleasant for Bismarck to face this discus-sion, and the government would also have suffered a certain loss of prestige in the eyes of the vulgar, so that it was quite as well that he should not be present during the debate. The Italian application of the law has already been referred to. It was found necessary there in order to prevent acts of illegally appointed priests from having a public validity, and there was no reason why the same application should not be made in Germany.

The bill was passed without Bismarck's assistance, and with the other measures previously agreed upon was approved by the emperor on the 1st of May. It was first necessary, how-ever, to change the Prussian constitution in regard to civil marriages; and here the chief difficulty was encountered in the Prussian House of Peers, always more conservative than the Landtag or the Reichstag, whose members were only too

ready to make changes that would suit the requirements of
the moment, without much consideration for the future. The
vote was taken on April 24, and Bismarck in his explanatory
speech aptly compared his change of policy to the action of a
man who has been compelled by circumstances to lay aside a
peaceful demeanor and adopt a belligerent one.

The Church of Rome has always been the enemy of
national consolidation, and its intrigues for this purpose were
older than the order of the Jesuits. Francis Newman takes
notice that it was not long after the formation of European
countries into solid nationalities with effective central governments that Protestantism appeared. The priests and the
socialists were now Bismarck's two enemies, and the manner
in which he finally played off one against the other was an
ingenious piece of statecraft which cannot be too much admired. The constitutional amendment on civil marriages was
passed, but not without a general expression of regret that
such a measure should have become necessary.

THE ASSASSIN KULLMAN

The stone which Pius IX. had predicted and desired to fall
on the heel of Bismarck took the form of a pistol-bullet, at
Kissingen, in July of this year. The self-appointed avenger
of Catholic wrongs was a cooper of Magdeburg named Edward Kullman, a man possessed of an idea until it had become
a personal devil. He was only twenty-one years old, a youth
of good conduct and reputation, but at that impressionable
age much given to the society of priests and religious exercises. The prince was riding in a half-open carriage on
July 13 through the crowded streets of the watering-place,
when a man in priestly habiliments placed himself as if by
accident in front of the horses, so that the driver reined them
in. Simultaneously Kullman advanced, and fired a shot at
Bismarck's head. At the same instant Bismarck was raising
his hand to make a salute, and the bullet just nicked his
wrist without doing further injury. Kullman probably aimed
at his head from the popular impression that Bismarck always

wore a shirt of mail under his military coat,[1] and this reputation no doubt preserved Bismarck's life; for, though he
may have taken such a precaution at one time, it is not likely
that he always continued it.

Kullman was instantly seized, but in the public anxiety for
the chancellor, his confederate, whether a priest or not, appears to have escaped.[2] After Bismarck had returned to his
hotel he sent for Kullman and cross-examined him. The
latter made no secret of the object of his crime, and an investigation at Magdeburg soon implicated a priest named Stöhrmann, who suddenly died before the plot could be traced any
further. In the sixteenth century this would have been accounted for by a mandate from the Vatican, but in our own
time it is more likely to have been a case of suicide. Although this chapter of the Kulturkampf is the darkest episode in the biography of Pius IX., there is no sufficient reason
for believing that he would deliberately plan an assassination.
Kullman was tried at Würzburg and condemned to fourteen
years' imprisonment,—a sentence which seems hardly severe
enough. As a matter of security he ought to have been imprisoned during the rest of Bismarck's life. In Prussia death
is the penalty for an attempt to assassinate members of the
royal family, and so it should be everywhere for the highest
officers of state, such as presidents, cabinet ministers, and
field-marshals. It is no ordinary crime, but high treason of
the blackest description.

A cold shudder ran through Germany at Kullman's attempt, and there was scarcely a Protestant church where
prayers and thanks for the chancellor's safety were not offered
the following Sabbath. The act was, of course, injurious to
the pope's cause, and even converted a large number of Ultramontanes into honest, patriotic Germans. The Clerical party
endeavored to counteract this feeling by stigmatizing Kullman as a half-deranged crank, who was not altogether respon-

---

[1] There was also a belief that he wore a coat of plaited linen of many thick-
nesses which no bullet could penetrate.

[2] At least I have not been able to find an account of his arrest or trial.

sible for his act ; but the Magdeburgers, who have good reason for their strong Protestantism, testified contrary to this, and his connection with a large Catholic society and the influence of the priest Stöhrmann were soon proved beyond question. The weapon that he used was traced to the man from whom he bought it, and was found to have been purchased during the Clerical agitation of the previous year. The sudden death of Stöhrmann added to the public sensation, and attached to the event the character of a dark and hidden mystery.

Bismarck cannot be blamed after this for withdrawing the German legate from the Vatican, and ordering a strict enforcement of the laws against revolutionary sermons and libellous publications. Incendiary language and personal calumny are the powder and ball of the assassin's revolver. Among others who were indicted under his special orders was a Silesian priest named Majunke, formerly editor of the *Volkszeitel*, a furious Catholic publication, who was also a member of the Reichstag. Surprising as it may seem, Majunke succeeded in escaping arrest, and, trusting to the protection of those " sacred precincts," appeared in his seat when the Reichstag was convened in the following December. It was now that the Social Democrats, and especially Lasker, who was really a German Rochefort, showed their true colors by supporting the Clericals in their hour of disgrace. A committee appointed to consider Majunke's case reported that the indictment against him was well grounded, and that the judgment of the court of a year's imprisonment ought to be enforced ; but Lasker succeeded in carrying a motion by a small majority which substantially declared that members of the Reichstag were superior to the civil laws, and could only be judged and punished by their own associates. This was practically the same as the pope's doctrine of infallibility, and it is an indication of a tendency of our time which goes to maintain that legislative bodies exist by divine right, and that their decisions are equally inviolable.

How disheartening this must have been to Bismarck! He was in constant danger of assassination, and yet this body of men, who were supposed to represent the sentiment and feeling of united Germany,—the Germany which he had created, —refused him the only relief from this grievous oppression which he knew how to obtain. A man who had been condemned under laws created by the Reichstag could, nevertheless, escape punishment, and continue to beard him in the legislative halls so long as his superstitious constituents chose to send him there. Never before had his language to the popular assembly been so scathing, so scornful. It was like Scipio's reply to the senate when he was accused of peculation. His words were like burning coals, and those who saw the expression of his face never forgot it.

He left the chamber abruptly and waited on the emperor with the information that he had been outvoted and was willing to resign. William I., however, refused to consider this as a possibility, and, though almost as indignant as Bismarck, advised him to take no further notice of the difficulty. Bismarck's absence from the chamber at the next meeting attracted attention, and a rumor of his retirement was circulated, causing no slight uneasiness, among both the Conservatives and the National Liberals. It was now the latter who came forward in his support with a resolution of special confidence in the "wisdom, uprightness, and patriotism of the chancellor," which Deputy Benningsen supported with such a vigorous speech that even Dr. Windhorst was effectually silenced by it. Legislative bodies are even more unwilling than individuals to confess that they have made a mistake, but the resolution was passed by a union of all parties excepting the Clericals, Poles, and Socialists.

The German Catholic bishops held a convention at Fulda and agreed upon a series of resolutions, which were forwarded to the ministry, protesting against the May Laws as unjust, inhuman, sacrilegious, and contrary to canon law. Dr. Falk replied to this with a request that they should submit regular reports of the condition of their parishes and all their proceedings to his bureau. The bishops were enjoined against the installation of priests without previous notification to the government. There were some who might have obeyed this order but for fear of being dispossessed themselves by the

Vatican council. The unfortunate bishops were really under a cross-fire. They declared that they were not able to comply with Dr. Falk's demands, and would be obliged to resist them to the extremity of persecution. Dr. Falk's persecution, however, went no further than to declare the acts of such installed priests illegal, and to suspend the payment of salaries due them from the government. Hundreds of parishes soon became vacant of their officiating clergy, but the parishioners did not appear to suffer much from this, and the government reaped the benefit of the suspended salaries. When Joseph II. abolished capital punishment in Austria the number of murders increased so alarmingly that he found himself obliged to restore the death-penalty ; but we do not hear of an increase of crime or vice in the Catholic portions of Prussia during what has been termed Bismarck's Diocletian period. What might have resulted if this order of affairs had continued for a whole generation, it would hardly be safe to predict.

The severest case under the operation of the May Laws was that of Archbishop Ledochowski of Posen, who was at once a prelate and a Polish count. In order to make amends for the deficit in the exchequer in his diocese, he made an importunate and successful endeavor to raise contributions in all the parishes under his dominion. As this was an onerous burden on the Poles, for the funds were mostly derived from the superstitious peasants, Dr. Falk requested him to discontinue it, and, as he still persisted, Dr. Falk suspended him. As Ledochowski lived in a community that was determined to protect him, he defied the German government, and actually succeeded in protracting his case by a series of ingenious legal make-shifts for nearly seven months before he was finally brought into court under a criminal indictment and sentenced to four years' imprisonment. Among the accusations against him he was charged with having attempted to exclude the study of the German language from the schools in his diocese, and the police discovered that he was in active correspondence with certain Russian Poles who were under suspicion of hatching a new revolution. Pius IX. sent him a cardinal's hat for consolation in his confinement and to show his contempt for German jurisprudence. The Archbishop of Cologne and the bishops of Treves and Paderborn were all imprisoned for short terms for contumacious behavior,—no severe trial for a common priest, but hard lines for a luxurious bishop. A bishop who had been excommunicated by the pope for refusing to support the infallibility dogma was restored to his diocese by Dr. Falk.

The anti-infallibility Catholics under the lead of Dr. Döllinger formed themselves into a separate party called the Old Catholics, with the professed intention of reforming their church and restoring it to the purity and simplicity of the early Christians. Although not a large fraction of their own sect, they gave the German government a strong moral support, and the adherents of the pope quite as much trouble, at the elections.

What was Pius IX. going to do about this? In the preceding August (1873) he had written a most imprudent letter to Emperor William, in which he took for granted that there was a difference of opinion between him and his ministers on the Catholic question, and trusted that he would be sufficiently resolute to adhere to his convictions, and to dispense with the services of those who wished to lead him into controversial pitfalls and unfriendly relations with the See of Rome. What advantage the pope and Antonelli expected to gain from this manœuvre, especially after their declination to receive Cardinal Hohenlohe at the Vatican, it is difficult to comprehend, and its ultimate effect was merely to cause Pius IX. to appear ridiculous. The emperor replied in September that he and his ministry were altogether in harmony in regard to the policy that was being pursued on the dogma of infallibility, and designated the Roman Catholic clergy as the originators of the quarrel, since they had distinctly refused to render obedience to the laws and constitution of the German empire; nor could he consider the pope in any respect as a mediator between him and the Christian religion. The correspondence was made public, greatly to the pope's annoyance; and the absurdity of presuming that the stout old emperor had been acting under the pressure of unfair influence was manifest to everybody.

After Kullman's attempt to assassinate Bismarck the Vatican council prudently went under cover, and the chief interest of the time centred in the prosecution of the Archbishop of Posen, when it was discovered Pius IX. had named Ledochowski to be primate of Poland,—a revolutionary movement, in view of the fact that no such state as Poland existed. The revolutionary intentions of the Vatican were so carelessly concealed that a document in evidence of them from the pope's nuncio at Munich came into Bismarck's possession, and was exposed by him in the Reichstag during the debate on Paul Majunke.

The agitation in Belgium reached such a pitch that Bismarck found himself obliged to interfere, and notified the Belgian government that a stop must be placed to such inflammatory proceedings, which might even endanger the peace of Europe. At first the King of Belgium, relying on the protection of Great Britain, was inclined to disregard this admonition; but a notification from Disraeli, who was even more opposed to Catholicism than Gladstone, caused an alteration in his cabinet councils, and the requisite orders were issued; and though not enforced with proper strictness, they served indifferently to reform the evil.

After the commencement of the new year the pope took courage again, and on February 5, 1875, published an encyclic letter to his bishops, declaring the May Laws invalid with regard to his adherents; forbade all faithful followers, both clergy and laity, from rendering them obedience; and ordered a bull of excommunication against Dr. Döllinger, Bishop Reinkens, and the whole sect of the Old Catholic clergy. In the twelfth century this edict might have produced a terrible effect, but it could do little harm in the nineteenth, especially under a Protestant government. However, it was considered injudicious that so much seed of incipient rebellion should be sown broadcast without receiving some check and supervision from the government; and as the Ultramontane organ *Germania* published at this time an atrocious editorial, in which assassins were made to appear conspicuously to the advantage of what were called the oppressors of the faithful, Bismarck and Dr. Falk contrived together three new enactments, as a supplement to the May Laws, of a still more sweeping character.

The first of these was an extension of the law against government salaries being paid to priests who had been installed contrary to the civil regulations. It provided for a stoppage of salary to all ecclesiastics who were unwilling to subscribe implicit obedience to the May Laws and take an oath to support the government.

The second law was intended for the expurgation of monasteries and cloisters; and it provided that all such establishments should be closed and their inmates expelled unless they were willing to take the oath of allegiance to the German government. The Sisters of Mercy, however, were exempted from this regulation, as serviceable and harmless members of society.

The third law was intended to reconstruct such Catholic parishes as had become disintegrated, and to afford them an opportunity of managing their own affairs,—very much after the American fashion; though it was provided that this should take place under the supervision of government inspectors. Bills were also passed securing to the Old Catholics continued use and occupation of their churches and church property.

Supplementary laws were found necessary to prevent priests who had been turned out of their parishes by the government from returning and performing the functions of their office in an illegal manner, and also for the administration of property belonging to the Church in dioceses left vacant by the expatriation of bishops. In the former case moderate terms of imprisonment were adjudicated, and in the latter commissioners were appointed to care for the property and account for its income in a scrupulous manner until bishops should be appointed who could receive the sanction of the ministry. Various additions were made to the May Laws from time to time, but these are the substance of them. The fierceness of the debate in the Reichstag on this occasion may readily be imagined. Mud-throwing was common, and everything that could be raked up against Bismarck, just and unjust, true and improbable, from his college days to the malicious inventions of the Paris journalists, was made full use of. The socialistic Lasker made himself particularly conspicuous in this dirty work. At the same time Bismarck received abundant assurances of encouragement and support from all parts of Germany, including Bavaria and Rhenish Prussia. A warfare of pamphlets was carried on continually, and cartoons published representing infallibility as an ugly serpent, into which a St. George in the likeness of Bismarck was thrusting his spear. That there were honest convictions on the other side, much endurance, and a praiseworthy dignity to be recognized in the behavior of the priests, is not to be denied. It was at least a bloodless warfare, and even the sufferings of Archbishop Ledochowski and others, who were imprisoned for the glory of Pius IX., cannot properly be estimated at a high rate.

These enactments were passed and approved by the emperor in the spring of 1875, and made a grand clearing out of Catholicism from the greater portion of Germany. Bismarck, like the morning sun, had swept the dark shadows across the horizon. Whether he had slain the python of infallibility still remained to be proved, for such monsters have a rare faculty of coming to life after remaining for long periods in a torpid condition, and it is even said of common snakes that their tails never die till after sunset. He knew that his own life was constantly in danger, but he went straight on, like an ocean steamer through storm and fog. To a certain extent the whole community was in a state of siege, and this he knew could not endure forever. The event from which he chiefly apprehended relief was the death of Pius IX., which now could not be delayed many years. Without the least pretence of concealment he agitated the question of the next pontifical election, and advised the Christian courts of Europe to take such measures in regard to it that a repetition of the present evil might not occur.

The King of Bavaria and his ministry supported Bismarck

in the Kulturkampf to a degree which plainly shows that the question was not one of Protestantism *versus* Catholicism so much as it was of church against state. The elections in 1874 for the Bavarian legislature resulted in a loss to the Ultramontanes, though they still preserved a slight majority in the House. They nevertheless adopted an address to the throne, in which they requested the dismissal of the patriotic ministry and the formation of a cabinet to support the policy of Pius IX.; but the king was not to be moved, and gave the committee from the House to understand that their majority was too small to dictate the policy of Bavaria. At the same time he signified to the ministry that he was entirely satisfied with their position with regard to the Kulturkampf, and assured them of his entire confidence in their management of affairs. This was in November, and one month earlier Emperor William had made a visit to Victor Emmanuel in Rome itself, where he was received with an enthusiasm which in the pope's opinion was near akin to madness.

THE SPANISH REPUBLIC

After the withdrawal of the Hohenzollern candidacy the crown of Spain was offered by the Cortes to Amadeo, the second son of Victor Emmanuel, and this plan of uniting the interests of Spain and Italy by a royal family bond would seem to have been a judicious one. Amadeo, however, found the Spanish throne a most uncomfortable position. The whole country was divided into factions, whose leaders were continually conspiring together to make difficulties for him, and the behavior of the Spanish nobility, always noted for their arrogance, called *soberbia*, was unfriendly and disagreeable. After enduring these tribulations for nearly two years, Amadeo concluded that a princely life in Italy was preferable to a royal life in Spain, and tendered his resignation. This left the monarchical party in the vocative. They had tried every experiment that had offered itself. Castelar, the finest orator in Europe,[1] now led the Republicans to victory, which was

---

[1] According to Sumner's estimate.

not difficult in the demoralized state of the opposition. The
political condition of Spain, however, or the temperament of
the people, is not suited to republicanism, and Castelar had no
sooner become president than he found it necessary to usurp
the authority of a dictator. How reluctant he was to do this
those who knew him can testify. He was a high-minded
patriot, and by no means a sentimentalist; but in the confused
turmoil of Spanish affairs the wisest judgment might have
been at fault. He looked to republicanism as one chance
among others; but republicanism strengthened the hands of
the Carlists, who were the Ultramontanes of Spain. The
guerilla warfare which the Carlists had been carrying on in
the northern provinces now assumed a formidable aspect, and
on December 9 they gained a decisive victory over General
Loma and captured a large number of prisoners.

Among the captives there was a German officer named
Schmidt, who was serving as war correspondent for the German press. In violation of all rules of warfare and humanity
this man was shot by the Carlist general, with many others,
to the great indignation of the German people, who were in
no mood, after their late victories, to feel resigned to such an
outrage. As the Carlists were rebels and beyond the direct
reach of diplomacy, Bismarck found other ways by which he
could make his power felt. Castelar was succeeded by Marshal Serrano as president of the immature republic, which was
not yet recognized by foreign courts. To give stability to
the government at Madrid and weaken the position of the
Carlists, Bismarck proposed to the powers that the Spanish.
republic should be accepted as a *de facto* government. All
agreed to this, with the exception of France and Russia. The
Tsar was sufficiently disgusted with the French republic, and
MacMahon's relation with the Ultramontanes was such that
he was equally afraid of displeasing them and of irritating
Bismarck; so that the curious spectacle presented itself of a
monarchy endorsing a republic, and of a republic supporting
monarchical claims. Not only did the French administration
give moral encouragement to the Carlists, but large quantities
of arms and other war material were being furnished to Don

Carlos by his French sympathizers. As soon, however, as Serrano's government had been recognized by Great Britain, Germany, and Italy, this traffic became contrary to international law, and Bismarck notified the French president that it must come to an end. MacMahon, who was always a well-meaning man, and as desirous as Thiers of the public good, had no objection to this so long as he could give a satisfactory excuse for it. At the same time two German ships of war were despatched to the Bay of Biscay, in order to cut off the supplies of the Carlists in that direction, and it was not long before France also recognized the government at Madrid.

Unfortunately the republic could not support itself in Spain even with foreign assistance. Almost on the last day of December General Campos proclaimed Alfonso, the son of Queen Isabella, at the time a pupil of seventeen years in a French school, to be king of Spain. His example was immediately followed by the other generals serving under Serrano, who accordingly resigned the presidency with a good grace. Two weeks later the unfortunate boy was crowned in Madrid as Alfonso XII. Don Carlos, after struggling obstinately against fate during the spring and summer of 1875, finally crossed the French frontier with a remnant of two thousand men. Although the murder of Captain Schmidt was never avenged, Don Carlos's chances were materially injured by it, and something at least had been gained towards enforcing respect for German citizenship in foreign countries. Germany, for the last hundred years or more, had really been the first nation in Europe,—the nation which produced the greatest men and the finest art,—and yet it had been habitual for English, French, and even Italians to speak of Germans in a tone of condescension, if not of contempt.

THE RIOT AT SALONICA

Bismarck's next interference in behalf of the rights of German citizens placed him side by side with President MacMahon. On May 6, 1876, the French and German consuls at Salonica were murdered by a fanatical mob of Mohammedans for interfering to prevent a young Christian woman from embracing the faith of Islam. It is always difficult to reach the true condition of such affairs, so conflicting are the accounts in regard to them, and whether undue pressure was exerted on the mind of this young girl it is now impossible to determine. The Turks live in a state of sluggish animosity towards their Christian neighbors, which is generally harmless enough, but which may at the slightest irritation madden them to the most desperate deeds. They have learned to tolerate the Christian faith as a political necessity, but they resent the least interference with their own creed with a fury that passes all bounds. If the missionaries make converts of Mohammedans by the Christian method, the Turks retaliate by making converts according to their own method,—that is, at the sword's point. The Turkish mind is so constituted that this seems to them perfectly fair and reasonable. It may have been injudicious for the French and German consuls to interfere with the ceremonies in the mosque, but their murder was no less an outrage of international right.

Bismarck and MacMahon acted in concert. A Franco-German fleet was despatched to Salonica, and the Sultan received a peremptory demand for satisfaction. The customary method of treating such claims of justice at the Ottoman court has been to make unlimited professions with small performance of the same. Real or imaginary obstacles are brought into play, all of which the foreign ambassador has to discover some method of removing, until the time has passed by when anything like justice can be obtained, and only some pitiful compromise is possible. By what persuasion Bismarck succeeded in having his demands enforced in a prompt and effective manner has never transpired, but it is certain that Abdul Aziz acted in this·instance with exceptional alacrity. A Turco-European commission was appointed and proceeded at once to Salonica, where a number of the leading rioters were seized, convicted, and hanged, while many others were condemned to milder punishments, which the German ambassador was directed to see were properly enforced. Even indemnities in money for the families

of the murdered consuls were obtained, though with somewhat more difficulty.

A WAR SCARE

During the spring and summer of 1875 suspicious rumors
were in the air of another war between France and Germany,
and the frog-and-insect chorus on the political Brocken set up
a constantly repeated refrain of "that demoniacal Bismarck,"
who was again going to water the valleys of Europe with
blood. The origin of this appears to have come from the
constantly increasing military preparations of the French government. The Prussian military system had been introduced
into France, and this enabled the nation to maintain a force
twice as great as that with which Napoleon III. went to war
in 1870. Such an army, well drilled, and with competent
general officers, would not have been an unfair match for the
German military machine, and the fact naturally attracted
attention in Berlin, and the question was asked in the impe-
perial cabinet, "Whither is this armament tending?" The
influence of Gambetta was constantly increasing in France,—
a rash, impetuous man, full of what is called the spirit of the
age, and who had proved in 1870 to be not less remarkable
for his organizing ability than for his unwillingness to recognize accomplished facts.[1] There could be no more appropriate or more dangerous leader for a popular war of revenge
against Germany. French newspapers, periodicals, and books
were never more belligerent than at this time, and the same
spirit expressed itself in the fine arts, so that during the next
ten years a large number of French paintings were produced
representing battle-scenes in which the Germans were always
defeated,—and these, too, the work of excellent artists. Meanwhile President MacMahon, who had no intention himself of
going to war a second time for French glory, was organizing
a fine army for Gambetta's purpose,—if only it should fall
into his hands. MacMahon recognized the superiority of

---

[1] Manteuffel expressed his opinion in 1872 that Thiers would be succeeded
by Gambetta, Gambetta by the Commune, and the Commune by a military
despotism.

Von Moltke, and had no desire to try conclusions with him again.

At the same time an intrigue was on foot to unite the Ultramontanes of France, Austria, and Italy in an alliance against Germany. The plan was impracticable in itself, unless a revolution could be effected in Austria first of all. If that could be accomplished it was expected that MacMahon and Francis Joseph would shake hands, and that Victor Emmanuel, finding himself between two fires, and that the chances were turning against Bismarck, would feel obliged to fall into line. The current in Austria, however, was now running in the opposite direction. Public opinion in Vienna, which had always counted for something, and now counted for much more, was fairly expressed by the citizen who knelt on the sidewalk to embrace Von Beust's knees for having delivered Austria from the *concordat ;* yet liberalism had gone a pretty fair length in Austria since the battle of Sadowa, and there were many to predict that a conservative reaction was at hand, as it always comes in time. That it did not come sooner in Austria was mainly owing to the wisdom and conciliatory policy of Bismarck in 1871. The Hungarians are Protestant to the backbone, and now, with the Prussian military system to support their rights, they had no intention of bowing before Catholic mandates from Vienna. The triumph of Pius IX. in Austria must have resulted in civil war.

This movement could not escape the notice of the lynx-eyed chancellor and he took his measures accordingly, but of the consultations that were held over it only a few significant words from Bismarck have survived. The Berlin *Post*, a semi-official organ, was first to sound the note of alarm, in an editorial which was ascribed to the government, though this was afterwards denied. It was mainly an echo of Bismarck's threat to the French government the year before. It called attention to the belligerent tone of French publications and the unprecedented increase of the French army. "If there is going to be a war of revenge," said the *Post*, "the sooner it comes the better for Germany."

This statement created quite a sensation in the political

centres of Europe, which was not much allayed by Bismarck's explanation in the Reichstag a few days later. The present attitude of the French, he admitted, was a threatening one, and would have to be seriously considered. He did not regret the editorial in the *Post*, and wished other nations to take notice of the situation. How long were these attacks on Germany to continue? The French also would do well to consider what might be the effect of a second defeat by the German forces. President MacMahon, who really wished for peace as much as Emperor William did, and was more afraid of his own people than he was of the Germans, appealed to London and St. Petersburg for intervention in behalf of France, and the Parisian journals suddenly changed their tone to a cry for help against the insatiable monster Bismarck. Even Gambetta went under cover, and the Chamber of Deputies became as quiet as an audience at a theatre. There was more occasion for this than perhaps many of them imagined.

In the spring of 1893, after Bismarck had left public life, he made a brief statement which shows that at this time there was a strong war party at Berlin, including Von Moltke, Manteuffel, Prince Frederick Charles, and perhaps other high officials, which Bismarck was obliged to resist and repress at the same time that he made use of the war scare to intimidate the French. It must be admitted that this was a difficult position even for a great statesman to be placed in, and the result of it was that he received the credit of belligerent intentions which properly belonged to others. "I was obliged," he said in 1893, "to protest to the emperor against the interference of the German staff in the affairs of the foreign office." Von Moltke always talked in favor of war,—as Bismarck said, it was his business,—and it is presumable that he thought if there was to be a war of revenge it had better come while he was still equal to the command of the German army, and it could be fought by veterans, instead of under new generals and with untried soldiers. It is not to be wondered at that he should have felt so, but the far-reaching consequences of such a collision were better understood by Bismarck than by himself. In fact, Bismarck had now arranged the map of Europe exactly as he wished to have it, and not on any account would he hazard the chance of having it readjusted again.

It was this consideration also that caused anxiety at St. Petersburg and London. The efficiency of the German military machine was perhaps overestimated at this time. It was considered almost irresistible, and the prospect of a second conquest of France, with consequent loss of more French territory, was not one which either Alexander or Victoria liked to contemplate. If Germany became too strong to be interfered with, the annexation of Holland was not improbable, and such a combination of land and naval power would threaten the independence of Great Britain itself. The Tsar likewise was beginning to think that the agreement with his Prussian uncle at Ems in 1870 was resulting too favorably for German interests. MacMahon's special envoys to Disraeli and Gortchakoff were well received, and the two premiers promised to give the French government active support so long as it persevered in a pacific policy. The French president was only too ready to do this, while Bismarck, for reasons already stated, was obliged to preserve an aggressive attitude; and so it happened that Disraeli and Alexander obtained the credit of preserving the peace of Europe and protecting France from the ambitious designs of the German chancellor;[1] although it is more than probable that the source of this political tension originated in the Vatican and was directed against Prussia.

---

[1] Bismarck said in the Reichstag in 1888: "My Russian colleague, Prince Gortchakoff, first evinced in 1875 an inclination more friendly to France than towards us, and employed artificial means to gain popularity there,—trying to make the world believe that we had some vague notion of attacking France, and that it was his especial merit to have preserved France from this danger."— Speemann's "Bismarck's Speeches," xvi. 160.

CHAPTER XIII

THE most serious trouble with Turkish finances is that there is no limitation to the drafts for the sultan's personal expenses. Abdul Aziz was always extravagant, and had no consideration for bad harvests. In 1874 there was a very short crop in Bosnia and Herzegovina, and at the same time the sultan gave orders to the tax collectors that they must fill up his empty treasury at the risk of their lives. The consequences of this might have been foreseen by any one except a sultan. The collectors' demands were excessive, and finding a deficit in Bosnia and Herzegovina they carried off everything that they could find. Many families fled with what they could take with them in their wagons to the neighboring Austrian provinces. Those who resisted were beaten or imprisoned. A deputation of the wealthier citizens waited on the Turkish pasha, or governor of the provinces, who gave the customary pledges of reform, which he had no intention of fulfilling. A report, circulated, perhaps, by Russian agents, that the Austrian government had proposed to purchase Bosnia and Herzegovina, set the provinces ablaze. It is often said that a man will give all he has for his life; and this, perhaps, is true with regard to individuals, but not where masses of men and their families are concerned. Assured of the assistance of the Montenegrins, who in their Balkan Switzerland have defied the Turks for centuries, the people of these narrow provinces entered on a desperate conflict with the whole Turkish empire. They succeeded in raising an army of from twelve to fifteen thousand men, and drove back the first Turkish contingent that was sent to subdue them. When, however, Raouf Pasha advanced against them with a greatly superior force, they retired to the mountainous districts and maintained a guerilla warfare during the winter and spring of 1875.

Here was a serious problem for England, Austria, and Russia, but especially for Austria. Whatever good-will Andrassy might feel towards the persecuted subjects of Abdul Aziz, he was obliged to recognize the fact that the interests of the Austrian empire were nearly identical with those of the Turkish government. Austria might have long since swept Turkey into the Bosphorus, but for the impossibility of organizing a government at Constantinople that would prove an effective barrier either to the return of the sultan or to Russian ambition. The old Greek empire fell to pieces from the lack of true national feeling; and to attempt to revive it would be like the Jews' returning to Jerusalem. The Slavonic races have not yet shown the least capacity for self-government, and are, besides, antipathetic towards the Hungarians, who, having obtained local autonomy, objected in a determined manner to their further introduction in the empire. Even Von Beust, the most liberal of Austrian premiers, has stated that in his opinion if Abdul Aziz had crushed out the insurrection in Herzegovina at once, it would have been better for all parties concerned.

In Russia the sympathy for their suffering coreligionists was lively and ardent. The government newspapers of St. Petersburg treated the question in a diplomatic manner, but evidently in a firm belief that the time had come to put an end to the atrocities in the Balkan states, while less official publications fairly clamored for the intercession of the Tsar. Fervent prayers were delivered in the churches that the God of battles might give aid and victory to the insurgents, and subscriptions were raised from Finland to the Crimea in aid of their destitute families.[1] In Great Britain there was an apprehension fully equal to that in Austria. Nobody wanted another Crimean War, and it was doubtful if the queen and Disraeli would be supported by the general public in bringing

---

[1] Chiefly, however, from the poorer classes, so that the aggregate was not so very much.

about another Inkerman or Balaklava. In this, at least, Disraeli was confident: that the British fleet could prevent the Russians from taking possession of Constantinople. Beyond that there was diplomacy, in which he believed himself to be more of an expert than afterwards appeared. At the same time his old rival Gladstone was waiting in readiness to take advantage of any mistakes he might make. His position was not a comfortable one, and the path before him was beset with difficulties.

European politics now revolved about Germany. The prestige of the Prussian military machine did not surpass Bismarck's reputation for sound judgment and political foresight. Nothing of importance was likely to be undertaken without his first being consulted. It was not presumed that he could mould Gortchakoff and Andrassy to his will, but if he said to them, "Only thus far it is prudent to go," it was not considered likely that they would exceed his limit. The London *Times* no doubt asserted too much when it declared that Bismarck by one word could prevent the Russian army from crossing the Danube, but there was no question that he could recall it from the Balkan provinces whenever he thought best to do so. He watched passing events with the eye of an expert who knows from old practice when the time has come to take a hand in them. It is doubtful if he shared Von Beust's opinion, but, as he often confessed, his chief interest in foreign affairs was, what advantage or disadvantage might result to Germany. He did not wish to have the Tsar take possession of Constantinople, but neither did he propose to interfere with the Russian government in behalf of Great Britain. As already suggested, there may have been a previous understanding in regard to this very occasion. At all events, he is known to have expressed himself in a friendly way towards Russia at the time, and to have considered the cause of the Slavonic states a just one. If he foresaw or calculated the ultimate effect of the insurrection in the Balkans, he must have been far-sighted indeed.

It was Andrassy's place to take the initiative, as representing the power which was most directly compromised by the Balkan disturbances, and the one which could least be suspected of self-interest. For Bismarck to have done this would have had the appearance of unreasonable interference, and Gort-chakoff might be supposed to act from interested motives. The guerilla warfare had continued through the spring and summer without decisive results; and when, late in August, the ambassadors of the three powers went to Abdul Aziz with a joint note of intervention, the sultan promised everything and performed nothing. The schedule he agreed to, if carried out, might have resulted in an idyllic mixture of despotism and democracy; but he issued one firman after another, and neither Turk nor Christian paid any heed to them. Accordingly, on the last of January, 1876, Andrassy sent a definite demand to the sultan, specifying five essential points of reform,—complete religious freedom, the introduction of a European tax system, the application of the revenue of Bosnia and Herzegovina for a term of years to restoring prosperity in the provinces, the establishment of a commission to supervise the condition of the country farmers, and of a mixed commission to supervise the execution of reforms. This was accepted by the Turkish government, and a proclamation issued promising the rebels a safe return to their homes if they would lay down their arms; but the insurgents refused to do this unless the great powers would guarantee their personal safety and also the administration of the reforms. Procrastination and the memory of broken pledges were the two best allies of the sultan; but he was soon found to have another ally, and one that caused all parties concerned a great deal of trouble.

The behavior of the English Tory government at this crisis was not only injudicious, but a disgrace to the name of civilization. Repeated editorials in the London *Times* argued that the only security for British interests was a prompt suppression of the revolt in such a manner that it would not be likely to occur again; or, in the language of Machiavelli, to deal the insurgents such heavy blows that they could not well be repaid. It would seem as if the Turks required little encouragement in this direction; but it was well known in

Berlin that Disraeli encouraged the sultan in his treacherous
course, and even persuaded Andrassy in the spring of 1876
to set a patrol on his frontiers to prevent the defeated insurgents from crossing, and to close Austrian charitable establishments against the refugees; so that he succeeded for a
time in disturbing the cordial relations between the three emperors. Disraeli, with characteristic cynicism, admitted that
the Bosnians and Herzegovinians were greatly to be pitied,
but said that the peace of Europe could only be preserved
by crushing them to the earth. He did not believe that the
Turkish nature was accessible to reform, and the mildest degree of independence for the Balkan states would only prove
a stepping-stone to Russian aggression. This policy proved
a failure from the start, and resulted in the death of Abdul
Aziz as well as the overthrow of the Tory party.

It was the counterpart of Louis Napoleon's policy in 1870,
a desperate venture which could only succeed by quickness
and good fortune. Unhappily for Disraeli and Lord Derby,
the rebellion was not to be crushed in a week or a month.
Mukhtar Pasha marched into Herzegovina with a considerable army in March, 1876, and offered the rebels two weeks
in which to make their submission. His promises were generous, but nobody trusted them; and before the fortnight had
expired a subsidiary revolution broke out in Turkish Croatia,
and a force of fourteen thousand men sent to suppress it was
defeated. As the armistice came to an end without result,
Mukhtar Pasha marched through the Dugar Pass, where he
was beset on all sides, and compelled to retreat again with
heavy losses. No doubt there were Montenegrins present in
these engagements, but the prince of Montenegro had thus
far preserved an attitude of fair neutrality, although thousands
of Bosnians and Herzegovinians had taken refuge in his
country and were being supported by the inhabitants. Mukhtar Pasha, in order to excuse his defeat, represented that he
was attacked by a large force of Montenegrins, and the consequence was that the sultan prepared an invasion of that
country also. The Turks established a fortified camp on the
borders of Servia, and in less than four months after Disraeli's

cynical statement in the House of Commons the insurrection had spread over a territory seven hundred miles in extent. The most terrible consequences followed in Bulgaria, where the Turkish government had since 1855 practised a regular system of extirpation of the native population and the colonization of the country with bands of Tartars, who lived by a discreet system of plundering. A revolt broke out there on May Day; and as the available forces of the sultan were employed in other directions, the Turkish governor ordered a general arming of the Mohammedan population, who, being under no military control, fell upon the Christians, robbing and murdering indiscriminately, without regard to age or sex. The atrocities committed at Batak, described by a correspondent of the London *Daily News*, sent a thrill of horror through Great Britain, and came close to upsetting the Tory ministry. The number of sufferers in the Bulgarian massacre has been estimated as high as a hundred thousand, and, though that may be an exaggeration, it was without question one of the most awful atrocities in history. We hear so much of " our enlightened era" that it is difficult to realize that such horrors continue to take place and are permitted in Christian Europe. In the time of Frederick Barbarossa an army of knights would soon have been gathered on the Danube that would have retaliated for every Christian life which had been taken. ·

The Bulgarian massacre was the finishing stroke to Abdul Aziz. The ablest of his advisers perceived that he had made a mistake, and the withdrawal of Disraeli's support, which was necessitated by public opinion in England, proved fatal to him. It was also believed that in spite of the financial dearth—many of the highest officers being in long arrears for their salaries—the sultan had immense sums of money stored away in his palace. There was a sudden revolution among the viziers, and Abdul Aziz was deposed. Several millions in gold coin were recovered to the treasury, and a few days later he mysteriously died in the kiosk of Top-Capu, where he had been confined. It was given out that he had committed suicide, but it is quite credible that he was disposed of after the oriental fashion. In his death he was comparable to Nero; nor was his life much better.

When the standard of rebellion was raised in Bulgaria Bismarck saw that the time had come for a definite policy. He proposed a conference at Berlin to Gortchakoff and Andrassy, and the proposition was accepted. By uniting with Great Britain and Austria at this time, Bismarck might have postponed the independence of the Balkan states for fifty years or more. Whatever his motives may have been, he certainly acted in the cause of humanity, and played the part of a true statesman. Andrassy meanwhile had discovered of what light stuff Disraeli was made, and returned to Bismarck's lead with increased confidence. Only two days before the massacre at Batak the three ministers held a meeting and drew up a statement based on Andrassy's previous note. This was agreed upon and approved by the three emperors. A truce of two months was to be proclaimed in order to confer with the insurgents on disputed points, the execution of the reforms was to be superintended by the consuls of the great powers, and an international fleet was to take possession of the Bosphorus as moral support to the consuls. If this failed to produce the desired result, armed intervention should ensue. The plan was approved by the French and Italian governments, but rejected by Disraeli, though he was already aware of the Bulgarian outrages, and in his nonchalant manner had denied all knowledge of them when questioned in the House of Commons. The Tory newspapers congratulated their readers that Bismarck was not, after all, the autocrat of Europe. Andrassy, however, informed the Austro-Hungarian Parliament on May 18 that the conference had resulted in a complete unanimity of the three emperors in regard to the Turkish question, and in a resolve on their part to renew their present agreement from time to time.[1] Disraeli's communication of this circular to the Turkish government, with the expression of an unfavorable opinion on it, was a piece of trickery not unlike Louis Napoleon's.[2] His Eastern policy

---

[1] Our Chancellor, ii. 122.   [2] Müller's Political History, p. 512.

might be compared to a man who was trying to prop up a falling house with a barber's pole.

When this became known in St. Petersburg the peace-loving Tsar was furious. Bismarck, in his place, might have said, as he did of the Augustenburger, " Thank goodness for it;" but Alexander was not so far-sighted. " To have everything spoiled by that fortune-hunting Jew!" For every one could see that by treating the circular of the great powers with such levity Disraeli encouraged the Turks to make the utmost resistance, and it is only fair to hold him responsible in some measure for the events which followed. On June 27 Prince Milan of Servia declared war on the sultan, and on July 2 Prince Nikita of Montenegro followed his example. Their combined forces amounted to over one hundred thousand men, but the Servian army was mainly composed of volunteers not sufficiently well trained for operations in the open field. The most active sympathy was manifested in Russia for the cause of the two princes. It is not permitted to hold public meetings in the dominions of the Tsar, but the war was supported in the churches as a holy cause; collections were taken up, hospital stores were provided by cities and towns, and even ladies of quality volunteered their services with army surgeons to do duty in the hospitals.

While the Montenegrins were successful and held their ground in a number of small encounters, the Servian general trusted too much to the enthusiasm of his soldiers. The Turkish army outnumbered the united forces of the insurgents, and was continually increased by the addition of troops drawn from Asia and Egypt, and with recruits who were attracted by the report of fabulous treasures discovered in the palace of Abdul Aziz. On July 14 the Servians were repulsed and obliged to retreat, and on August 5 they were defeated in a pitched battle at Knyazebec, but continued to contest the invasion of their country step by step in an obstinate and courageous manner. Failing to receive the expected succor from Russia, and finding himself hard pressed, by the middle of September Prince Milan begged of the Turkish commander an armistice, which was readily granted him. As soon as negotiations for peace commenced, however, disagreements arose again between the Turkish government and the Russian ambassador, who insisted on compensation to those sufferers in the Bulgarian massacres who still lived to receive it, and punishment for those who were chiefly accountable for them. As usual, the sultan attempted to shirk the responsibility of direct interference by the execution of a few bashi-bazouks. Disraeli was also obliged to support the Russian demands in this instance as a sop to English public opinion, and the British envoy warned Sultan Murad that in the event of a war with Russia he would be obliged to contend alone; but the new sultan possessed neither force nor intellect, and could do nothing to stem the current of events.

The Tsar Alexander appears more prominently than Gortchakoff in dealing with the Balkan question, and always appears to advantage. Early in November he was interviewed by Lord Augustus Loftus, and expressed himself on the subject with a plainness and sincerity to which subsequent events have testified. The Porte, he declared, by a series of manœuvres had frustrated all Europe's efforts to terminate the war and secure general peace, and that if the other powers chose to put up with such behavior, he could not reconcile it with Russian honor, dignity, and interests to do so any longer. It is plain that he pledged his word to Lord Loftus that he had no design upon Constantinople, and that if he found it necessary to occupy Bulgaria he would only do so until suitable guarantees of local autonomy had been given. He declared that he had made the same proposal to all the powers; that he had suggested the occupation of Bosnia by Austria, and that Great Britain should make a naval demonstration before Constantinople. Alexander then specified his demands of the sultan to be an armistice for Servia and Montenegro, a conference to decide what reforms were practicable and requisite for the Christian provinces, and adequate guarantees from the sultan that the reforms should be carried out in earnest. That the Tsar and Bismarck were acting in concert in this crisis is evident from a statement made by the latter at a dinner-party in Berlin, only three weeks later, in which he said:

"Germany's duty, before all, is to maintain peace within her own borders. If war should take place between Russia and Turkey they will both become tired of it in course of time, and then the mediation of Germany will be more likely to prove effectual. It would be inexpedient to give Russia advice just at present. Such a step would put the Russian nation out of temper, which would be more prejudicial to us than a passing difference with any government. It is unlikely that England will go to war with Russia."

Alexander's proposition was fair enough to have satisfied any one except the sceptical Disraeli. He may have been right in not trusting the Russians any more than he could help, but it was fortunate for Austria that he was not in Andrassy's position. The irritation caused by these events in England was taken note of by the German people in their quiet way, and contrasted with the public feeling there in 1870. Queen Victoria was very much distressed, and exerted herself in a laudable manner in the interest of peace, though, with such a will-o'-the wisp as Disraeli to guide her, her efforts were no more than a vain beating of the air. She sent her secretary, Colonel Wellesley, to the Tsar on a secret mission which has never been properly explained. She also wrote a number of letters to Bismarck imploring him to make use of his great authority for the benefit of England. British influence was also brought to bear on the crown prince, and Bismarck had the same struggle to contend with in the palace which had happened so often before,[1]—this time not a difficult one, however, for the personal regard of William for Alexander had increased rather than diminished since the Franco-German war. The Turk had one other ally in Europe and only one,—Pius IX. The *Voice of Truth*, a semi-official publication of the Vatican, printed an editorial to prove that the Mohammedan rule was to be preferred before the ascendancy of the Greek cross. The head of the Catholic Church would

---

[1] *Our Chancellor*, ii. 127.

seem to have been stony-hearted so far as the suffering of human beings was concerned.

On December 5 the Socialist leader, Eugene Richter, interrogated Bismarck in regard to the presumed support that Russia was receiving from the German government, and received the following reply :

"If, at an ill-timed moment, you put a spoke in the wheel of a power which happens to be in difficulties, it is quite possible that you may upset the coach, but the driver will have noticed who it was that inserted the spoke. The previous speaker, like many other people, labors under the error that Russia is just now soliciting great favors and services at our hands. This is by no means the case. He has hinted that Russia is bent upon conquest and territorial annexations. We have the Emperor Alexander's solemn assurance that he will refrain from the one and the other. Russia asks us for nothing that we can bargain about ; she only seeks our co-operation in a peaceable conference, with an object which is ours as well as hers,—namely, the safeguarding of the Porte's Christian subjects against the treatment which is incompatible with existing European legal conditions, and upon the abolition of which Europe is entirely at one, although she has not yet hit upon the right way of giving effect to her unanimity. It would appear that, should the conference prove fruitless, Russia will very shortly proceed on her own account to obtain by force that which the Porte refuses to concede peaceably. Even in that case Russia asks nothing from us but neutrality, which it is in our interest to observe."

The conferences between the Turkish government and the envoys of the great powers continued at Constantinople from the middle of December until the middle of January, 1877, without coming to any favorable issue, and perhaps it was not intended that they should. It does not appear that the Turks were encouraged at this time by English support, but the war party had gained the ascendancy and the old Moslem element had become thoroughly stirred up. On January 20 the Tsar issued a circular note to the effect that the continual refusal of the Turkish government to consider the claims and wishes of Europe could no longer be disregarded. The Christian nations of Europe were dishonored by it, and the only remedy

now possible consisted in an appeal to arms. At this Victoria
is credited with having written a spirited letter to Emperor
William, in which she designated him and his chancellor
as chiefly responsible for the approaching war.

We wonder if Emperor William replied that he had also
appealed to her government to prevent a war which was a
much more serious matter to Germany than the Balkan question was to England, and had received in reply the advice to
humiliate himself to Louis Napoleon. Let us suppose that
William I. and Bismarck had permitted Victoria and the
crown prince to determine their policy in this crisis; what
would have happened? Two consequences were possible,—
either the Russo-Turkish war would have been prevented,
and the population of the Balkan states have been relegated
to a worse than African slavery, or Russia would have formed
an immediate alliance with France, and carried out her programme as before, on condition of a combined attack against
Germany in the near future. In either case Germany would
have become the chief sufferer, and would have fallen from
the first position in Europe to the tributary one of 1854.
Emperor William would have been obliged either to make
war, in case of the Tsar's refusal to accept an authoritative
mediation, or to expose his own weakness before the whole
of Europe. The result proved that there was no such great
danger to British interests as Disraeli imagined, and that Bismarck understood perfectly the elements he was dealing with,
and how to bring the Turkish problem to a fortunate issue.
It was not until April 24 that the Russian forces passed the
Danube and invaded Bulgaria. The slow progress which was
made after this, however, did not compare favorably with Von
Moltke's rapid and decisive advance in 1870. The army of
the Danube was commanded by princes of the royal blood;
but they were not princes like the two Fredericks, and after
they had met with a bloody repulse south of the Balkans, the
Tsar began fairly to realize this. General Todleben, the
venerable defender of Sebastopol, was given the chief command early in December, and took advantage of an imprudent
advance of the Turkish right wing to isolate it in the Bal-

kans, where its commander, Osman Pasha, was soon compelled to surrender with forty thousand men. On January 20 he captured Adrianople and opened the road to the Ottoman capital, and the following day the London *Daily News* published a statement to the effect that Turkey as a military power no longer existed.

This sudden collapse of the Ottoman empire produced great consternation at Westminster. A large fleet of ironclads was already posted at the Dardanelles; British regiments were ordered from India to the Levant, and Disraeli despatched an ultimatum to Gortchakoff threatening war in case the Russian forces occupied Constantinople. There is no evidence that Alexander intended to do this in contravention to the pledge given to Lord Loftus at Livonia. The Russian army paused at Adrianople; Andrassy conferred with Bismarck, and proposed a European congress to meet at Berlin. Bismarck now appeared as the mediator between these great antagonists. It was he who persuaded Gortchakoff and Disraeli to submit their opposing claims to European arbitration. The Turk was powerless, and could be disposed of as the great powers considered best.

To bring Disraeli and Gortchakoff together was not a simple task, for they represented the most aggressive element in their respective nationalities. The Turkish government had concluded a provisional treaty with Russia on March 3 at San Stephano, and this gave the Russians such advantages as both Disraeli and Andrassy declared were incompatible with the peace of Europe. The war indemnity of fourteen hundred thousand roubles was not so important, since it was quite unlikely to be paid; but the extension of Bulgaria from Roumania to the boundaries of ancient Thessaly, to be occupied by an army of fifty thousand men, would place Constantinople in continual danger from any sudden uprisal of the Greeks and Macedonians. Disraeli was decidedly of this opinion, and the Hungarian traveller Vámbéry wrote lettters and articles on the subject for English periodicals. Indignation meetings were held at Buda-Pesth, and there was a corresponding agitation for Russia in the Slavic provinces of

Austria. Andrassy steered his course between these dangerous rocks like a skilful pilot, and succeeded in preserving
Austrian neutrality without threats or bombast. It was at
this time that Bismarck said of Andrassy in the Reichstag:

"Our relations to Austria are characterized by frankness and
mutual confidence, which is a remarkable fact, considering what
took place in former times, when other political parties in Austria
were more powerful than they are now. This is not only the case
between the two monarchs and the two governments; no, I am
proud to say that my personal relations to Count Andrassy are of
so friendly a character as to permit him to put any question openly
to me in the interest of Austria, and to feel as certain that I will
answer it truthfully, as I do that he tells me nothing but the truth
with respect to Austria's intentions."

The Clericals, of course, sympathized with Turkey, and Dr.
Windhorst had questioned Bismarck sharply with regard to
his sacrifice of German interests by a continued informal alliance with Russia; in this instance German interests and Austrian interests were identical. To which Bismarck replied as
above, and also assured the doctor that there was a perfect
understanding between Count Andrassy and himself, which
did not require Windhorst's oversight or mediation. The easy
good humor of Bismarck's speeches at this time indicates
that he was well satisfied with what was taking place, and
felt himself master of the situation.

The posture of affairs in April appeared more warlike than
before, and Bismarck exerted himself energetically to persuade Alexander to mitigate the conditions of peace, and the
English cabinet to be more willing to accept accomplished
facts. In this good service he was greatly assisted by Count
Schouvaloff, who belonged to the moderate Slavonic party
in Russia, and who acted as a mediator between Bismarck,
Alexander, and Lord Salisbury, whose advent in the English
ministry at this juncture was fortunate for all concerned. The
last of May Schouvaloff and Salisbury signed an agreement
to the effect that the clauses in the treaty of San Stephano
which had become a bone of contention should be left to the

Berlin congress, for which Bismarck immediately issued invitations to all the powers.

As usual, Bismarck was requested to explain his policy in the Reichstag, which he did in the following felicitous manner:

"I do not picture to myself a peace mediator playing the part of an arbitrator, and repeating, 'It must be thus, or thus,' when the whole power of Germany stands behind to enforce my statement; but a more modest one, something like that of an honest broker who really wants to transact business. We are in the position to save any power entertaining secret wishes from the embarrassment of encountering refusal, or even a disagreeable rejoinder, from its opponent in the congress. If we are equally friendly with both parties, we can first sound one and tell the other, 'Don't do this or that, but try to manage it thus!' I have had many years' experience in these matters, and have often observed that in discussions between two people the thread is frequently dropped, and each party feels bashfully disinclined to pick it up. If a third party be present he can do so without hesitation, and even bring the other two together again if they have parted ill-humoredly. That is the part I want to play."

The modest, intelligent simplicity of such a statement disarms criticism, for it seems too much even to praise it; and Bismarck was known henceforth as the "honest broker" among the diplomats of Europe. If he began his course as a statesman with a sword in his hand, he now carried an olive-branch and wielded it no less effectively.

The congress met on June 13 in Bismarck's own dwelling, the Radziwill Palace, in Berlin, and continued its sessions exactly one month. Bismarck presided and played the part of honest broker in and out of its sessions. Gortchakoff may not have expected such an obstinate resistance as he encountered to the Russian demands. The natural tendency of all men to unite against an individual who proves himself too strong for them also applies to nations, and it is only necessary to look at the map of Europe to recognize its application in the present instance. There was an excellent opportunity for French intrigue at the Congress of Berlin, which Waddington, the French envoy, was perhaps too high-minded to take advantage of. If he did not oppose the claims of Russia, he certainly neglected to support them in an outspoken manner. The tendency to an alliance between Austria, Germany, and Great Britain was evident from the first; but in spite of that Disraeli was found the most difficult plenipotentiary to deal with.[1] In his case the proverbial diffi-culty was exemplified of making a bargain with a Jew, and it was essential, besides, that he should return to England with flying colors for the sake of the Tory party, which had been weakening ever since the massacre at Batak; but the current of affairs was now in his favor. Bessarabia was restored to Russia, and the other Christian states became autonomous, with the exception of Bosnia and Herzegovina, which were placed in the care of the Austrian government for a term of years,—an indefinite term, apparently. Servia and Bul-garia were both enlarged in the interest of Christianity, and Batoum was made a free port. The only direct advantage which Russia had obtained from the war, at a sacrifice of seventy thousand men, was Kars and adjacent territory, Bess-arabia, and an uncertain indemnity, which could not be com-pared with the compensation that Prussia derived from the campaign of 1870. Gortchakoff was very much disgusted at this; but the Tsar kept the promise he had made to Lord Loftus, and did not go beyond the scheme he laid down at Livonia.

At the close of the conference *Punch* published a humorous cartoon of Bismarck and Disraeli, viewing each other across a table, and underneath this Bizzy was represented saying, "Do you know, I doubt if our friend the Turk will more than half like this arrangement;" to which Dizzy replies, "Ah, yes, that is possible, but we must *educate him up to it*,"—referring to the sentimental talk in the House of Commons in regard to educating the Turks to a sense of moral responsibility. It

---

[1] Bismarck even states that he went to Disraeli's bedside at midnight in order to obtain his assent to agreements concluded between the other envoys.

would be quite as practicable to train up cougars for sheep-dogs.

This, after all, was the truth of the matter. The English cabinet had been insisting for two years past that the dismemberment of Turkey would be a political monstrosity, the thought of which was not to be tolerated, and Disraeli had declared at a London dinner that "in such a righteous cause the cost of one, two, or three campaigns, in men and money," was not to be considered.[1] Yet this was what the Berlin Congress had accomplished, and what Disraeli subscribed his name to. He returned to England with a flourish of trumpets, and Victoria made him Lord Beaconsfield for work that had really been performed by Bismarck and Andrassy; after which he plunged into the most chimerical political adventures, and led his party to defeat at the next general election. The purchase of the Suez Canal was sensible and practical, but Beaconsfield's scheme of a railroad through Mesopotamia, and his treaty with the Ameer of Herat almost bordered on political lunacy. Bismarck shook his head at the Afghanistan adventure, and remarked that treaties with half-civilized nations were worse than useless,—one must either conquer them or let them alone.

Gortchakoff returned to St. Petersburg with a feeling of dissatisfaction that never left him. He had perhaps pictured to himself reviving the former ascendancy of Russia during the Holy Alliance, and did not realize the difference between the times of Alexander I. and of Alexander II. Bismarck may have preserved Russia from a war with England and Austria, but Gortchakoff did not realize this. The cordial feeling which continued between the two emperors did not extend to their ministers. Bismarck expressed himself afterwards as holding Gortchakoff in slight esteem, either as a man or a statesman. The *Journal de St.-Pétersbourg*, the *Golos*, and other Russian newspapers soon began to attack the policy of

---

[1] Wilhelm Müller says that Disraeli's policy was "oriental" in more senses than one. History, p. 510. It was in fact oriental in its geography, its ferocity, and its extravagance.

the German empire, and hinted broadly at the possibility of
a French alliance. Austria and Count Andrassy came in for
their share of this splenetic humor. The Tsar had supported
Germany during the war in 1870, and the opposition to Gortchakoff at the Berlin congress was treated, of course, as base
ingratitude. It is true enough that Russia was not permitted
the full swing in 1878 that Germany may be said to have enjoyed in 1871, and the accruing advantages of the war with
Turkey were not equal to those which Prussia obtained in the
war with France; but the question may be asked whether
Bismarck could have effected more favorable results for Russia
if he had attempted to do so. The solution of the Turkish
problem was, if anything, more difficult than the creation of
German nationality,—so diverse and antagonistic were the
elements of which it was composed,—and if it was not settled
by the Berlin congress in a wholly ideal manner, it was certainly settled in a more satisfactory manner than any one
could have expected two years before, and the peace and contentment of the Christian provinces since that time is good
testimony in its favor. As Gladstone replied to his old antagonist, "A cordon of independent states is a much stronger
barrier to Russian aggression than the hollow shell of the old
Turkish Empire." For Bulgaria and Servia to come under
the yoke of the Russian despotism would be only a less misfortune than their reconquest by the Turks, and their inhabitants were well aware of this. Humanity, as Bismarck stated
in the Reichstag, had been well served, and Turkey was the
only power that could reasonably complain.

Looked at from all sides the settlement of the Turkish
problem was one of the most ingenious pieces of statecraft.
The Russian press was particularly exasperated at the transfer of Bosnia and Herzegovina to Austria,[1] for by this means
Bismarck achieved a three-fold advantage. The presence of
an Austrian army corps in this entering-wedge of the Bal-

---

[1] According to Bismarck, this was the result of a previous agreement between
Alexander and Francis Joseph before the commencement of hostilities. Memoirs, ii. 235.

kans would serve to discourage local insurrections and rash
political movements; a short route was secured from Hungary to Constantinople by which an Austrian force could
reach the Bosphorus before the Russians might be able to
pass the Balkans; and the loss of Austrian territory by the war
of 1866 was in a great measure repaired.' At the same time
the possession of Bessarabia and the independence of Bulgaria had given Russia an advantage at the mouth of the
Danube which could not but have a permanent effect on the
policy of Austria, and this effect proved in the sequel to be
greatly to the advantage of Germany. Bismarck's master-
stroke, however, was his suggestion to M. Waddington that
the French government should take possession of Tunis as
their share in the general distribution of prizes. This was
done shortly afterwards, but it produced an amount of irritation in Italy which French politicians had not counted upon.
The Parisian journalists discovered too late that Bismarck's
object was to produce an antagonism in Rome against France,
and that the possession of Tunis was paid for in an Austro-
German-Italian alliance. Bismarck had remodelled Europe
after his own fashion, and had buttressed Germany about like
a strong castle. Austria, however, gained the most decided
advantage, for, next to Turkey, it was the power most seriously imperilled by the Russian victories; and it was something more than an amiable formality which led Count Andrassy to propose a vote of thanks to Bismarck, previous to
the adjournment of the congress, for the wisdom and untiring
energy with which he had directed its proceedings and influenced its members in the work of pacification; to which Bismarck replied in a gracious and complimentary spirit.

' Andrassy had a hard struggle to reduce these provinces to an orderly condition after two years of continuous revolution, but the equitable manner in which
he treated all parties, Christians and infidel alike, has been greatly com-
mended.

CHAPTER XIV

SOCIALISM AND THE TARIFF

DURING the last month of 1877 it was well known that
Pius IX. could not live much longer. He had been one of
the youngest popes ever elected to the papal see, and he had
occupied the chair of St. Peter, which he acquired in a literal
sense, longer than any other, but his reign had happened in
unfavorable times, to which his naturally amiable and kindly
disposition was not suited. That he was still possessed of a
forgiving spirit towards his enemies appeared at the sudden
death of Victor Emmanuel on January 9, 1878. " Victor,"
he said, " was not bad at heart, but he was surrounded by evil
counsellors. But he will have a good bath,—yes, yes, he
will have a good bath, and then he will come out all right."
A vivid description of the good bath referred to will be found
in Dante's " Purgatorio," ¹ and in Victor Emmanuel's case it
would come to several centuries of purification by fire. In
less than a month Pius followed after the King of Italy, and
Cardinal Pecci was chosen pope by a vote of forty-five to
eighteen, adopting the title of Leo XIII.

This election was a quiet revolution in the Catholic Church,
for Pecci had always acted in a half-concealed antagonism to
Pius IX. He had been Bishop of Perugia, and a favorite
with the predecessor of Pius, and it was expected that he
would adopt a more conciliatory policy than had prevailed of
late in the Vatican councils. Whether Bismarck had exercised any influence in his election, or whose Bismarck's candidate may have been, has not been revealed, but Francis
Joseph, the King of Belgium, and even the French government took a lively interest in the selection of a pope, and
probably all had something to say on the subject. Those

---

¹ Purgatorio, canto xxvi.

who expected to see Leo XIII. reconciled immediately to the
German emperor and the May Laws repealed by the Reichstag without delay were soon undeceived. Great bodies move
slowly, and though the new pope made friendly advances to
William and Alexander, they were such as signified little
beyond a desire to live as peaceably as the present situation
of affairs would permit.

Leo issued an encyclic letter on April 21 in which he renewed and confirmed all protests of his predecessor against
the deprivation of his temporal dominion and against every
infringement of the rights properly belonging to the Church
of Rome. This was a dignified assertion of a position the
church had assumed, and which the pontiff could not wholly
escape from. He wrote to the Emperor of Germany at the
same time, expressing the utmost good-will, and suggesting
for the promotion of peace and harmony an alteration, though
not the repeal, of the May Laws. William I. never answered
this letter, for the buckshot of Nobeling had laid him at the
door of death; but Leo, upon hearing of this catastrophe,
joined the other potentates of Europe in a despatch expressing the keenest solicitude and sympathy for his condition.
The crown prince was now acting as regent, and between him
and Bismarck there was for once no difference of opinion. He
answered the pope's letter of condolence, and at the same time
replied to his previous communication in regard to the May
Laws. His statement was clear, simple, and emphatic. With
all good-will to the Church of Rome and its highest representative, the regent could see no alternative other than the
supremacy of the empire and the strict enforcement of its
laws. However, a change of policy soon became evident.
The form remained the same, but the animating spirit was
different. There was no longer a German envoy at the Vatican, but diplomatic relations still continued between the pope
and the Bavarian government. When Bismarck went to Kissingen in July it was noticed that he had a number of interviews with the papal nuncio from Munich. No external results followed upon these consultations, but to the shrewder
sort it was apparent that both parties were heartily tired of

the contest, and would be glad of an opportunity to escape from the continuation of it. Although the May Laws remained nominally in force, there was continually less occasion for the application of them, and it is supposed that in many instances the opposition to them passed unheeded where this did not attract public attention. Subsequent events would seem to indicate that there was some kind of an understanding between Bismarck and the pope's nuncio at Kissingen.

It was now that the slumbering volcano of socialism, or, as it is called in Germany, social democracy, suddenly became active beneath the German soil, manifesting itself in a most surprising manner. On the 11th of May, 1878, while the emperor was driving in an open carriage in the Unter den Linden, a tinker from Leipsic named Hödel fired two shots at him from the sidewalk, neither of which took effect. Hödel was immediately arrested, and ultimately executed.

Hödel was not a typical Socialist, but rather a vagabond, like Guiteau, who, having been exposed for fraudulent practices, wished to distinguish himself by some desperate act which he supposed would win the applause of suffering humanity. He had, however, belonged to two Socialist organizations, and professed that his object was to rid the earth of a tyrant. Why he should have considered William I. in the light of a tyrant, while Germany was enjoying a period of peace and prosperity, and its government had no aggressive policy except towards the Roman Catholics, it is difficult to comprehend; but at this same time there were Germans in America who talked against Emperor William with a blind bitterness like negrophobia. A German newspaper published in New York never ceased its vituperation of him, and did not hesitate to declare that the Reign of Terror was preferable to a peaceable condition of society under the existing laws. Carl Schurz, the representative German of America, was described as a traitor to two hemispheres. Only two months later a riot of foreign workmen broke out on the Pennsylvania Railroad, which could only be suppressed by a regiment of United States regulars. It was a wide-spread conspiracy, not directed against monarchical government or any particular kind of government, but against the right of individuals to hold and inherit property.

Bismarck had not expected that Germany would escape from this French mania, but he was surprised at the sudden form in which it appeared. He had looked for a general uprising of the laboring classes in Berlin and other portions of Germany, and this would probably have happened if they had been organized into militia by themselves, as they had been at Paris. If William was less than an emperor to his chancellor, he was more than a friend, and Hödel's criminal attempt was like a blow which stung Bismarck to action. Something must be done; but what? How was this invisible hydra to be reached and dealt with? His health was never so miserable as at this period of his life; for he was now sixty-three, and feeling the influence of old age upon him. Von Beust had proposed to him at Salzburg to organize an anti-international society, independent of governments, which would serve to inculcate such doctrines as might counteract the influence of those chimerical and impracticable theories from which the Socialists distilled their peculiar mental poison. Some attempt had been made at this in Berlin, and what had been the consequence? Irony of ironies: Hödel was an associate of this very society at the time he made his attempt!

"Bismarck," says Von Beust, "agreed that the governments on their side would have to introduce more stringent laws against such revolutionary societies, against communistic undertakings with a criminal intent, such as arson, and against speeches in defence or glorification of communism. Prince Bismarck recommended that a committee should be formed to investigate this question, and to this I agreed, under the proviso that one of the subjects referred to it for consideration should be the condition of the working classes, with a view to its being ameliorated in a constitutional manner."[1] This memorandum formed the basis of Bismarck's subsequent

---

[1] Memoirs, ii. 273.

policy towards the Socialists: first, government repression, especially for incendiary speeches and publications, and, secondly, an attempt to ameliorate the condition of the laboring classes. He had never been a believer in absolute freedom of speech, and thought the Prussians had too much liberty in that respect. He now saw plainly that assassins like Cohen and Hödel were little more responsible for their own acts than the weapons they used. Socialist publications and photographs of Socialist agitators were found upon Hödel's person. It was the rhetoricians who stirred up unbalanced and misanthropic individuals to these desperate attempts.[1] For the government to permit such revolutionary talk and licentious language was a libel on all freedom. There must be a limit in such matters as in all other mundane affairs; and the first point to be considered was the emperor's safety. Bismarck drafted the sketch of a law, making it a penal offence to use inflammatory language in regard to the emperor in any public manner; and also a law to restrict the right of holding public meetings to such as were convened by the better class of citizens. Not feeling equal to an exertion which included so much personal feeling, Bismarck sent the sketch of his laws to the Bundesrath, where all constitutional changes had to be entered, and delegated Von Moltke, whose personal feeling in the case was equally strong, to undertake its passage in the Reichstag; but there, to his surprise and to that of many others, all parties, except the Conservatives, united against the law. The National Liberals deserted Bismarck in a body, an act of treachery, as he considered it, which warned him in regard to the future. Von Moltke's simple, unpretending argument, delivered with all the earnestness of a soldier on the battle-field, failed to produce any effect on the serried ranks of the opposition. Absolute freedom of speech and the right of all classes to hold public meetings had been won in the street-fights of 1848, and was not to be relinquished.

---

[1] So Guiteau admitted on his trial,—that during the month while he was lying in wait for President Garfield he fed upon the editorials of certain newspapers which were violently opposed to the policy of the administration.

The assertion of the Clericals, that the tendency to anarchy was the natural outgrowth of the suspension of religious exercises in so many German parishes, was silenced by the retort that even if such an argument could apply to Hödel, whose parents were Protestants, it certainly could not apply to Kullman; but the chamber was fairly drowned with the floods of Lasker's eloquence in regard to "the rights of man" and "the meaning of the nineteenth century."

Lasker was very close to a Socialist himself, and the Conservatives thought that he would not have regretted it if Hödel's shots had taken effect. The bill was defeated by an exceptionally large majority. One would think that the Reichstag might have taken some action for the better security of their chief magistrate. If Bismarck's measures were considered too stringent, it would seem as if the National Liberals might have introduced a substitute of some kind.

This result so disheartened Bismarck that he contemplated resigning, and declared openly that he would no longer serve so ungrateful a public. It of course encouraged the Socialists, and may have contributed to the subsequent attempt at assassination on the 2d of June. Dr. Charles Nobeling, a philologist and a disagreeable egotist, believed that he could improve on Hödel's method, which it was easy to see had small chance of success unless the assassin were a practised marksman. Nobeling was a fine shot with a fowling-piece, and could hit swallows on the wing. He was well educated, but had lived rather a vagrant life, and was known in all his haunts for the aggressiveness of his socialism. He had lately visited among the Internationals at London, and it was believed that they had encouraged him to make this desperate attempt. The emperor took no special pains to protect himself after Hödel's miscarriage, and could be seen driving on the Unter den Linden at regular hours. Nobeling obtained a room on the first story of a dwelling-house, and, waiting until William I. drove by, fired two charges of buckshot at him in rapid succession. In the excitement of the moment, however, he neglected to allow for the declination, and this saved the em-

peror's life. The buckshot riddled the helmet,—Müller says
it looked like a sieve,—and inflicted a good many scalp
wounds, but did not penetrate the skull. William was driven
back to his palace almost insensible, but was able to say, as
they laid him on his bed, " I cannot understand why people
are always shooting at me." [1] The crowd on the Unter den
Linden, where army officers are always promenading, rushed
into the house where Nobeling was concealed, and, seizing
upon a man whom they supposed to be the offender, came
near tearing him to pieces before his innocence could be
proved. Others who saw the window from which the shot
was fired broke into Nobeling's room and attempted to arrest
him; but the criminal made a desperate struggle, and after
inflicting severe injuries on those nearest him, gave himself
a wound with a dagger which eventually ended his life.

The news went all over Berlin in a twinkling, and the
greatest excitement prevailed. An immense crowd collected
about the royal palace, and stood there silently and respectfully waiting for information of the emperor's condition.
When at length the surgeons reported that his wounds,
though serious, were not necessarily fatal, there was a general feeling of relief. Every one spoke of the strength of the
emperor's constitution, the regularity of his exercise, and his
hardy, vigorous, and virtuous life. These were certainly in
his favor; but the doctors found the next day that the feeling
of discouragement that had taken possession of him was more
dangerous than the gunshot wounds. He had done everything he had known how to do for his people, and this was
his return for it. The two attempts to assassinate Bismarck
had a definite object, but what advantage could any one expect
from removing *him* from the world?

Bismarck was still at Varzin and the crown prince in
London, where the hisses of the Internationals served as a
premonition of Nobeling's crime. Both came at once, and
their strengthening presence revived William's courage, so
that in a few days the Prussian people were rejoiced to learn

that he was convalescent. The greatest indignation was expressed all over Germany at the outrage, and Bismarck, like a man heated through with indignation, dissolved the Reichstag and ordered a new election. Even such an event could not obliterate old party lines, but there was a large increase in the number of Conservatives; and the Social Democrats, who hastened to disclaim all connection with Nobeling, were reduced to nine members, six of whom were from Frenchified Saxony. The Conservatives were still in a minority, but the National Liberals had changed their minds, and many of them had been replaced by men of a more loyal spirit. They would not agree to all that Bismarck desired, but they were willing to adopt a compromise measure, which it was hoped would provide for the better security of the emperor and his chancellor. The chief articles in the anti-socialist law were, firstly, empowering the government to dissolve all societies which were considered dangerous, confiscate all revolutionary publications, and enable the police to interfere with the proceedings of public meetings whenever these showed a dangerous tendency; secondly, to expel from their residences or banish all persons whose proceedings were of an obnoxious character; and thirdly, to make all opprobrious language in regard to the emperor, or even severe criticism, a criminal offence. The Reichstag met on the 9th of September, so that the deputies had sufficient time to act on these measures with calm nerves and cool heads. They were severe and despotic remedies, but it was a case for severity. Socialism was a political monstrosity, which in Bismarck's opinion would have to be treated as Hercules dealt with the hydra. Yet it was not without a *ratio essendi* in the inequality of fortune, the hardships of poverty, and the terrible power which wealth gives its possessor. These would have to be considered, as well as the danger which menaced civilization from its impracticable theories. On September 17 Bismarck reviewed the subject in a temperate and masterly manner, admitting, in the course of his address, that there had been a time when he felt a certain sympathy with socialism, but he could not feel that any longer. He said, in explanation of this:

"The change took place in me long ago, at that moment when either Representative Bebel or Liebknecht—certainly one of the two —represented in a pathetic appeal the French Commune as a model of political institutions, and openly professed himself a disciple of the creed of these murderers and incendiaries. From that time onward I have felt the heavy weight which the conviction of the presence of this danger carries with it. I had meanwhile been absent, owing to sickness or war ; but that appeal to the Commune was a ray of light that was thrown on the matter, and from that moment onward I have known the social-democratic element to be an enemy against whom the state and society had to stand on guard in self-defence. The attempts which I have made in this line at different stages of the legislature are known, and the members of the Reichstag will not fail to remember them. You know, also, that I have not succeeded in carrying out the same ; on the contrary, a great many reproaches have been directed against me on that account ; but from that moment I have never been remiss in my opposition to social democracy. Nor do I believe my endeavors to have been in vain, although they may sometimes appear so. We Germans have no need of resorting to such extreme measures as were used in France in 1871, though France has ceased to be the chief seat of Socialism, and now takes a stand which our government, no less than society, need not be altogether dissatisfied with. What has wrought the change in France, convincing people they have been wholly in the wrong? By no other method than this,—by resorting to forcible means, such as I would not recommend you to imitate . . . Surely, gentlemen, if we are compelled to live under the tyranny of a set of murderers, life ceases to be worth living, and I trust that the Reichstag—that we—will stand by the government, by the emperor, who asks for protection for his own person, for his Prussian subjects, and his German countrymen. It is quite possible that for this occasion, perhaps, some of us may become the victims of murderous assaults ; but let any one to whom this happens bear in mind that he dies on the field of honor for the good—for the great good—of the Fatherland."

The anti-socialist measures, somewhat modified by the amendments of the Liberals, were enacted for a term of four years and a half, but they were enacted again in 1883, and afterwards in 1887 ; so that public opinion in Germany evidently considered them necessary and justifiable. The doc-

trinaires cried out against them as "empirical makeshifts."
"Persecution is the seed of the church," they said, and predicted that now Bismarck would be strangled in his own
coil; but they were not aware that Protestantism had formerly been eradicated from Belgium and Bohemia by unfavorable legislation. It is not easy to decide, even now, exactly the
effect of the anti-socialist laws. They did not eradicate Socialism, for it continued to increase for the following twelve
years, and since then it would seem to have decreased. It
appears, however, to have placed the Socialists on their good
behavior, and given the movement a slightly different direction. There were no more attempts at the life of the emperor
or of other high officials, which is probably what Bismarck
cared for most. Prosecutions under the laws were not numerous, and caused little sensation. They did not arouse the
excitement and animosity of the Kulturkampf laws. A number of the most inveterate of the offenders anticipated their
sentences by emigrating to America, where they filled the air
with outcries against the tyranny of Emperor William, and
finally wound up their career—at least, some of them—on an
Illinois scaffold ten years later. Lasker came across the
ocean about the same time, and added the force of his argument to the odium of these reprobates. If the German government was in any respect more despotic at that time, or is
so now, than it was in 1871, it is the Socialists and not Bismarck who are accountable for this. Bismarck called the
thing by its right name when he declared that it would be
intolerable to live under the tyranny of such men as the Socialists. Nobeling died in prison, but Hödel was hung; and
it is noteworthy that this was the first criminal execution at
Berlin for seven years. What other metropolis can show the
like of that?[1]

The best justification of the anti-socialist laws at this distance is the fact that they have been three times re-enacted
by the Reichstag, at intervals previously agreed upon, when
there was no public excitement such as consecrated their

---

[1] General Grant approved of Hödel's execution.

origin, and at times when Bismarck's influence over the popular chamber was less than it had been formerly. The law to provide for persons talking and writing against the emperor was intended to have the effect of what Berlin doctors call *moralisches* chloroform,—that is, the mild administration of chloroform so as to keep the patient quiet for a few minutes without quite taking away his senses. It was not intended to prevent candid, dispassionate criticism of the government, but to mitigate personal attacks and hot-tempered denunciations against the chief magistrate and those most nearly connected with him ; such as are only too common in all countries where freedom of speech prevails. No person has ever been prosecuted under the law for talking in a reasonable and civil manner, and very few for any description of talking. Bismarck may have shown himself rather too sensitive in prosecuting Mommsen, the historian, for accusing him of having " dispossessed the Prussian crown," a rather serious charge when taken in its literal meaning, but the prosecution was discontinued, and was perhaps never intended for more than a threat. The editor who insinuated that the letters of assassination with which Bismarck was threatened were written at his own dictation certainly deserved his punishment ; for meanness and calumny could go no further, considering the attempts of Kullman and Nobeling. Apart from the assassination of emperors and presidents, indiscriminate falsification is an evil which future statesmen will have to deal with in a most energetic manner, if civilization is not to be utterly corrupted and destroyed by it. When all races of men become so morally perverted that they must be fed continually on partisan lies, like spoiled children on candy, and the truth is hateful in their ears ; then their course lies downward, and the muse of history turns away from them with averted face, for their history will no longer be worth recording.

It will be remembered in this connection that when Bismarck began to manage the Kniephof estate he issued an order that his tenants should attend to the necessary work on their own grounds before they did their work for him. If all land-owners and capitalists were to act on a similar principle it would perhaps be the best remedy for Socialism that could be devised. Bismarck was the same in 1878 that he had been in 1844, and he believed that no methods of repression would be of avail without some attempt to ameliorate the condition of the laboring classes.

He had already made some tentative proposals in the direction of an insurance fund for aged and disabled working-men or their families. The royal family had made large bequests for this purpose, but even an emperor could not fill such a gulf as this subject opened up. Bismarck's favorite device of making a monopoly of tobacco, and devoting the proceeds wholly for the benefit of persons who worked for five hundred thalers a year or less, did not succeed in passing the Reichstag. The Liberals and Progressists, who represented the mercantile and salaried classes, always opposed measures of this description, on the ground that they would interfere with the laws of supply and demand. Unfortunately, humanity sometimes has to interfere to prevent the demands of capital from crushing out the lives of men and women by overwork. Where and to what extent governments should interfere with the affairs of the business community is always a matter of judgment, and no rule can be scientifically devised for it. It is an intricate question, and one on which there will always be a difference of opinion; but it has often been found necessary to limit the number of hours for employees in certain branches of industry, and this, at least, is sufficient to establish the principle of legislative interference.

FREE TRADE AND PROTECTION

The French indemnity, the Kulturkampf, the Oriental question, and the Socialists had so occupied Bismarck since 1871 that he found little leisure to attend to the industrial and commercial interests of the empire, and these had continued in the same routine condition as during the North German confederation without much effort for change being made by any political party or particular faction. He had, however, meanwhile, taken notice of some facts which seemed to him to have a peculiar significance, and now that he had bottled up

the Socialists, as well as such gaseous creatures might be,
with untiring diligence he devoted himself to the material interests of his country. On Christmas evening, 1878, it was
reported to the Associated Press that Bismarck had entertained his friends at the Radziwill Palace with a lengthy dis-
sertation on political economy. He had noticed the surprising prosperity of France after the German evacuation,
and he rightly ascribed it to President Thiers's protective
tariff. He referred also to the United States of America,
which was then entering on an era of astonishing material
growth; referred to the comparatively depressed condition of
English trade, and concluded from these instances that the
countries which had remained open were growing poor, and
those which were closed up by a wall of custom-houses were
becoming rich. He also produced a logical formula which
he had worked out on this new subject, and showed a most
surprising amount of knowledge of facts and details, all of
which had been the result of a few months' study. His first
principle of political economy was that every nation should
do its own work, so far as possible. The report that Bismarck had become a protectionist startled large classes of
people in Germany, and the business world generally.

What political economists commonly leave out of their calculations is the moral element. For instance, in the case of
an irredeemable currency they estimate that a depreciation
will take place in proportion to the excess that is issued; but
experience has proven that this is not the case, for the value
of the currency will always depend chiefly on the credit of
the government and the expectation of its final redemption.
At the time of General Lee's surrender gold was at a premium
in the United States of over one hundred per cent., and in two
days it fell more than fifty per cent., although the volume of
paper money in the country had not changed in an appre-
ciable degree. So Ricardo's theory of rents was found not
to work on our western prairies, for immigration skipped
over certain districts because the resident population was not
found congenial by the new-comers. On this account many
of the finest lands still remain unoccupied. So it might be

said generally of free trade that it leaves out the moral element. The greed of corporations is proverbial, and the law
is obliged to step in to prevent capital from exercising too
despotic a power. Free trade would work very well if all the
civilized world was ruled by a single government. Then the
wool-growers would gravitate to those countries where wool
could be raised to the best advantage, and manufactories
would spring up where climate and water-power were combined to the best advantage. This is the case to a certain
extent at present, but the principle of nationality steps in to
interfere with its evolution. Every nation is obliged to act as
a unit, and to consider its interests irrespective of all others.
There is a constant struggle for existence among nations, as
there is among species of animals. Wool may be grown
better and cheaper in South Africa than it is in Germany, but
the money expended in raising it there is a direct benefit to
South Africa, and if it is sold to Germany that takes so much
from the " Fatherland" for the advantage of a foreign country.
The statement that every nation should do its own work is a
significant one. Every nation on the continent is obliged to
maintain its population as near a maximum as possible for
military purposes, and the question for its government is always, how are its laboring classes to be kept from starving?
If they earn good wages the community is prosperous, but
if the reverse, trade languishes. The funds of a millionaire,
unless invested mainly in industrial enterprises, are a burden
to the community in which he resides. If he spends more
than a fixed amount it is likely to be in foreign countries; but
if the farmers have good crops and get good prices for them
they immediately make purchases, and all the wheels of trade
are set in motion. The manner in which wealth is divided in
a state or nation is more important than the sum total thereof.
After fifty years of free trade the English farmer is poorer
than he was before.

The conflict between free trade and protection, or between
a low tariff and a high one, is at the root a conflict between
buyers and sellers. Those who have goods to sell wish to
obtain as high a price as possible, while those who consume

the goods and live on a fixed income, or, like professional men, are not producers in any way, are equally desirous for low prices. Now, any one can see that placing a duty on any imported article which is also produced in a country will raise the price of it by limiting the supply; and it is equally natural to suppose that by removing the duty the price may be expected to decline again.

As the class of consumers who are not in business for themselves greatly exceeds those who are, we should expect that in any industrial community the free-traders would have a large majority; but this is not the case. The large army of store-clerks live, it is true, on a fixed salary, but the continuation of that salary depends on the general prosperity of the community. If hard times arrive they become anxious lest their salaries may be reduced, or even of losing their positions. Thus their employer's interests become their own, and unless they are in the service of importers they are pretty certain to vote the protective ticket. Lawyers, doctors, and professional non-producers are likely to be influenced in the same way, though not to the same extent; for when money is scarce there is always less litigation, and physicians find it more difficult to collect their charges. Even the farmer will be affected in this manner, because when business is good people are always more willing to pay fair prices for eggs, butter, and summer vegetables. The general influence, therefore, in an industrial community will be in favor of protection so long as protection stimulates industry, and this would probably be the case in England, also, if England were not governed so completely by its commercial interest. If, however, the protection of home industries is carried to an extreme, those industries tend to become more profitable in proportion to others than they should be, and the tariff becomes a tax, for the benefit of those engaged in them, upon all the rest of the community.

If the pudding is to be judged by the eating, free trade cannot be considered a success. It is rather too sweeping a generalization. It originated as a political war-cry to relieve Great Britain of the oppressive duties on breadstuffs, which were intended for the benefit of the landed gentry; and so long as a number of other nations adopted it, as England possessed the carrying trade of the world,' it was greatly to the advantage of British interests; but it is doubtful if it is so now. France and Germany have returned to a protective system, and show no present indication of a desire for change. The English provinces, Canada and Australia, demanded protection as soon as they obtained power to legislate on their own affairs, and it was one of the principal demands of the Irish home-rule movement. This tendency of nations is a much stronger argument than the penny pamphlets of the Cobden Club. It is a mistake to suppose free trade is a political principle. Neither is there good reason for believing that universal free trade would have the effect of preventing wars between the nations of the earth. Nations lose their temper like individuals, and when they once get to the fighting point considerations of material interest are thrown to the winds.

Bismarck had already attempted in 1876 to make tobacco a government monopoly, but he could not persuade the Reichstag to agree with him; and they were probably right enough in this, for, although such an authority would have been judiciously wielded during Bismarck's term of office, it might easily have been abused by his successors. Tobacco, though originally a luxury, has long since acquired the character of a necessity to the working-man, and the comfort of his pipe at the close of the day is as essential to him as the roof over his head. Bismarck, however, believed that his countrymen smoked too much, and also drank too much lager, so that not long after this he issued an address to them on the subject, in the hope that it might induce them to become more temperate.

He gave the German people three months to think over and discuss the tariff question before it was brought up in the Reichstag, and this afforded occupation for many a news-

---

' A legacy from the wars of Napoleon.

writer and magazine contributor. The academic class attacked him at once, and not only denied any advantage in the proposed change, but questioned the sincerity of Bismarck's motives. His object evidently was to conciliate the Conservatives and the landed interest. The cry went abroad that Bismarck had deserted the National Liberals and was coquetting with the Clerical party. All the strongholds of Catholicism—Bavaria, Posen, and the Rhineland—were agricultural districts, which would be benefited by Bismarck's proposed duty on corn; and it was also noticed that almost simultaneously with the proposal of his new tariff in the Reichstag, Dr. Falk resigned from the Ministry of Public Worship. This indicated a decided change in Bismarck's Catholic policy; and he retorted to the National Liberals that if they were unwilling to follow him he must seek new allies where he could find them. There was no need of supposing him insincere in this; and if he had wished to conciliate the Conservatives and Clericals, he might have found a more direct means of doing so than by changing the tariff. Political economy is eminently a practical science, and men who have spent their whole lives in lecturing or hearing recitations are not the best qualified to express an opinion on it.

Low prices are for the interest of the professional class, so far as they depend upon a fixed salary; and it is easy enough to figure out results on paper which in their practical application fail to come to the same conclusion, on account of some factor which has been left out of consideration.[1]

There had never been actual free trade in Germany, nor had there been since 1815 any very high protection. Since 1848 the tendency of Prussia had been in the direction of lower duties, while raw materials were mostly admitted free of duty, and the duties on manufactured articles varied according to circumstances, without any definite system. No attempt had been made by any minister of finance to sys-

---

[1] One factor almost invariably omitted is the excessive productiveness of machinery. Manufacturers combining together can maintain a certain price in their own country and throw a large surplus at a lower rate on to foreign markets.

tematize the tariff, nor had the government made any opposition to the will of the majority as expressed in the Landtag. This continued through the period of the North German confederation until the war with France, after which the influx of gold produced a rise of prices and prosperity for those who were in active business, though not advantageous for people living on a fixed income. This came to an end soon after the French payments ceased, and, as the French tariff had now closed one avenue to English exportation, Germany became the particular centre to which foreign imports gravitated, and the consequence was a general depression of German industry. At the same time the nation was burdened with a number of irregular taxes, of which the matriculary assessments were the most unpopular; and these had been adopted, according to the confession of the Minister of Finance, as temporary expedients.

Bismarck believed that both of these evils could be remedied at a single blow; and it is significant that he should have taken the initiative in this matter, and should have carried through the reform almost on his own shoulders. His plan was to place a moderate protective duty on all materials of commerce, except such as could not be raised or produced in Germany. He did not believe in free raw material any more than in free broadcloth, though the duties on manufactured articles would have to be higher in proportion in order to protect the manufacturer at all. He showed good judgment both in advertising the question a sufficient time in advance, and in not bringing it before the country previous to a general election, so that the deputies who acted on it might come to the subject as unprejudiced as possible. It was not until the middle of April that he introduced his measure, when a storm of facts and figures broke upon him, enough to weary the stoutest brain and puzzle the clearest intellect. There is no other subject in which such contradictory results can be obtained from the most reliable statistics, and the opposition had come prepared for the purpose in a truly German and thoroughgoing manner. Changes of tariff have the effect for the immediate time of transferring money from the pockets of one

class of persons to those of another, and there were few deputies present who did not feel this more or less ; so that it was
not only a national question, but a strongly personal one.
The debates were protracted and acrimonious. The proposed
measure was treated as if it were a return to the dark ages.
The prosperity of England was called to mind, together with
the fact that wages were higher there than in protected
France. The Liberals feared that it would make the government too independent of the popular will. However, a large
body of the Liberals, led by Benningsen, were inclined to
favor the measure to a certain extent, though Lasker and the
extremists were bitterly opposed to it.

Bismarck believed that the more thorough the discussion of
the subject the better the public would be satisfied with the
final decision. He interfered little in the debate, and it was
not until May 2 that he brought forward his own argument
in a moderate, conciliatory speech, which quite surprised those
who had expected that he would attempt to carry through
his bill by main force and hard talking. After referring to
the matriculary assessments as a form of taxation not much
better than financial anarchy, which made the government
a kind of dunning creditor such as must necessarily cause
great irritation, he presented the main points of his statement in the following summary :

" There is still another objection that I must raise against our
present legislation, and this is one of the most important, which is
likely to occupy us more in our discussions than the purely financial
part of the matter will do,—namely, that the present arrangement
of our indirect taxation does not provide for our home industry that
amount of protection which can be provided for it without in any
way injuring our general interests.

" I do not care to enter here into any general discussion on free
trade. Up to this time we all have been protectionists, even the
greatest free-traders that we have amongst us, for no one has till now
expressed a desire to go below the tariff which is in force to-day ;
and this tariff is essentially a moderately protective one, and the
bill which we are submitting is also moderately protective. What
we ask is a moderate protection of home labor. We are remote

from a system of prohibition such as exists in the majority of neighboring states. . . .

"Surely we cannot expect Germany to be ever the dupe of honest conviction. Through the wide-open doors of our importation we have thus far served as a reservoir for the over-production of all foreign countries. Articles that have come from abroad appear to us to have a somewhat higher value than those of domestic origin; and the flooding of Germany with the over-production of other countries must have, as it seems to me, a most depressing influence on our prices and on the development of our industry. Let us, therefore, close our doors and erect higher barriers, such as we here propose to you; and let us take such necessary steps that the German market at least—the market where German good-nature is now being taken advantage of—shall be preserved for German industry.

"The question of a large export trade is always somewhat precarious. No new countries can be discovered; the globe has been circumnavigated, and we cannot find any more important nations to purchase our goods from us. A commercial treaty is a sign of friendship between nations; but the question for the economist is, what is included in it? One might always ask in such cases, 'Which party is going to be cheated?' As a rule, one will always be a victim, although the treaty may last for years before this is discovered. I do not refer here to our own treaties, but would remind you of those concluded between France and England, in which both parties now claim to have been deceived. What I wish to remind you of is the fact that our taxing machinery is not within the power of the government to the same extent as in neighboring countries. The levying and administrating of taxes is with us entirely *publici juris*, the right of the people, and no permissible deviation from the definition of the law can at any time take place with us; while with our neighbors—France not excepted, although France resembles us closely enough—the power of the officials is such that there the administration of the law can be considerably interfered with." [1]

It was said of this argument by the doctrinaires that Bismarck had judged the subject too much from the stand-point of his foreign policy; that he had introduced foreign politics

---

[1] Bismarck's Speeches, Speemann's ed., xvii. 81.

into political economy; and that this was to have been expected from the nature of his genius and the mental methods he had been accustomed to. On the contrary, it was the breadth of his experience and his large way of looking at all subjects which enabled him to see the industrial conditions of his country in their true relations. The claim of specialists that they alone are capable of judging of matters within their own departments is one of the plagues of the century. That a man can only understand a subject by spending his whole life in the study of it is a delusion. It would be much more correct to say, as has been often said in regard to languages, that he who knows but one subject knows none. If an art critic is to judge of an historical painting, he must not only be acquainted with the technicalities of the school to which it belongs, but he must have a fine sense of color, an eye for form, a knowledge of history and philosophy, and, above all, an insight into human nature like that of the dramatic poet; and this last can only be obtained by a wide experience in human affairs. A statesman who has to legislate on the tariff must be well read in history as well as political economy. He must understand international politics, and in what way his proposed measures are likely to be affected by them, or *vice versa*. He must also understand human nature, or how men are likely to act under given conditions. Free-trade doctrinaires might continue to argue the ultimate advantages of every nation's doing the work which it could do best; but the return of France to a protective policy had wholly subverted the basis on which such calculations were made. They reasoned in regard to Germany as if it were an isolated nation which could not be affected by the laws and tariffs of other countries. Bismarck reasoned as if Germany were a member of a large family whose individuals were bound by ties of relationship and habits of co-operation, so that the proceedings of any one of them would be certain to affect, to some extent, the conduct of the others. Abstract principles always have to be modified in their practical application.

Bismarck's tariff was a very moderate one, few of the duties exceeding thirty per cent. *ad valorem*, and the average being little over twenty per cent. The discussion of the subject lasted until the end of July, when the new tariff was passed by nearly a two-thirds majority. Bismarck's foresight in introducing this measure to the Reichstag before it could be acted upon by a popular vote was justified by the elections in 1880, in which the government met with a signal defeat. The various parties and their numbers represented in the election of that year are worth considering as an example of the confused condition of German politics. The Conservatives carried seventy-six seats; the Clericals, one hundred and seven; National Liberals, forty-three; Secessionists, forty-seven; Progressists, sixty-eight; Socialists, twelve; Poles, eighteen; Alsatians, fifteen. From such an heterogeneous body of legislators almost anything might be expected. The Secessionists pretended to be a new party, but they were really Socialists in disguise, with Lasker among them, and the Progressists were not much better.

Bismarck paid no attention to this unfavorable composition of the Reichstag. The new tariff had been enacted, and the majority of the opposition was not strong enough even to carry through a revision of it. He again recurred to his tobacco monopoly, to a state insurance fund for laborers, and for elections every four years instead of every two years. These measures were introduced in a message from the emperor. Bismarck was complained of for attempting to screen himself behind the imperial personality, and William I. replied to this in a second rescript, in which he asserted his own responsibility for the policy of the government. Public opinion, however, did not like the measures any better for this; they were considered reactionary and intended to strengthen the imperial authority, and make it more independent of the popular will. Bismarck informed the deputies that if they did not like his programme the measures could go over to another Reichstag, and the whole session was consumed in fruitless discussion and parliamentary wrangling. Meanwhile, the new tariff was accomplishing what its supporters anticipated for it. New manufactories were being constructed, industry stimulated, and the laboring classes obtained slightly better remuneration for their work. On the other hand, annual salaries were not raised to correspond with this change, so that even the large body of government officials were very much dissatisfied with it. The dissatisfaction in Great Britain was more open and pronounced. The unpleasant feeling towards Germany occasioned by the Danish war and the battle of Sedan had been passing away under the influence of the Kulturkampf and the Congress of Berlin, and now here was a protective tariff, and the doors of the only large nation in Europe which had remained open to English manufacturers were closed. The ill effects of this were soon perceptible in Manchester and Birmingham. The tide turned again, and Bismarck became more of a bogie than ever. A newspaper warfare against him commenced which did not subside so long as he remained in power, and even such a high-toned weekly as the *Spectator* kept up a running scream against him which was re-echoed in America.[1]

THE AUSTRO-GERMAN ALLIANCE

Bismarck again astonished the world in 1879 by a diplomatic triumph of the first magnitude, and this was nothing less than turning the Austrian empire round upon its base. Political combinations had become with him a matter of tact rather than thought, as Napoleon confessed his movements were on the battle-field, and he may have felt this approaching change during the Berlin Congress. The difficulty was to make others feel it and see it as he did. Is it possible that he foresaw this culmination of his life's work in his lenient treatment of Austria after the battle of Sadowa?

It is not to be supposed that the Russian complaints against Bismarck were altogether groundless. He had kept his agreement with the Tsar so far as he could consistently with German interests, but not to the extent which Alexander expected. Even if a definite programme is sketched out beforehand, results are sure to differ from expectations, and circumstances alter cases. The irritation which commenced at the Berlin

---

[1] Echoed by Protestant protectionist newspapers like the New York *Tribune* and the Boston *Advertiser*.

Congress was considerably aggravated by subsequent events at Constantinople. It soon came to be reported that a large number of Prussian officers had entered the Turkish service, that Prussian tactics were being adopted in the sultan's army, and that German councils and influence had superseded English councils and influence. This was natural enough, for the Sublime Porte, after his defeat in the Balkans, desired to reorganize his army after the best pattern of the time, and there was no law which could prevent German officers from resigning their commissions and leaving their country if they chose to do so. The pay of a German line officer was little more than enough to keep him in clothes and tobacco, whereas in the service of the Porte he would be able to lay up a competency. In Russia this would not have been permitted, for the Tsar's government claims an absolute control over the life and property of its citizens, so that it is impossible to leave the country without special permission to do so. Beyond this, the Turkish envoy to the Congress at Berlin had returned with a strong impression of Bismarck's sagacity and political influence; and Bismarck, on his side, had expressed a very friendly feeling towards the Turkish government. Now that the Balkan question had been settled in just the right way, he was as anxious as the sultan himself that it should not be unsettled again; and to further this purpose Bismarck was not unwilling to give the sultan a little moral encouragement, so that the evil tendency to excess which always follows upon a prosperous issue should not lead the Christian states of Turkey into extravagant political movements.

It was even more for the interest of Austria that peace should be kept between the Balkans and the Danube; but it was not for the interest of Russia,—at least, not in the opinion of the Panslavists, who now were in the ascendancy. Panslavism is as dangerous for the Slavs outside of Russia as it is for Austria; but it is one of the tendencies of the time towards the union of all people of kindred race and tongue. Thus the *rapprochement* of Austria and Germany was a consequence of the Russo-Turkish war, but it might never have exceeded a mutual understanding between the two powers if it had not been for the imprudence of Alexander and Gortchakoff. In 1888 Bismarck made an explanation in the Reichstag of the causes which led to the changed relations between Russia and Germany, in the course of which he said:

"I had the feeling at the time of the Berlin Congress of having rendered such services to Russia as have seldom been rendered by a minister to a foreign power. Judge, therefore, of my surprise and disappointment at perceiving how a kind of newspaper war gradually began in St. Petersburg, in which German policy was attacked, and suspicion was cast on me personally in regard to my intentions. These attacks increased during the following year till 1879 they grew into a strong demand for a pressure that we were to exercise on Austria, in matters which did not admit of our interfering with Austrian rights. I could not lend my hand to that, for if we allowed Austria to be estranged, we would necessarily become dependent on Russia if we did not wish to become quite isolated in Europe. Would such dependence have been bearable?" [1]

In a letter of September 10, 1879, Bismarck explained the Russian complication to his faithful friend and admirer, the King of Bavaria, and from this we cull the following extract:

"Russian policy has remained unquiet, unpacific; Panslavistic chauvinism has gained increasing influence over the mind of the Tsar Alexander, and the serious (as, alas! it seems) disgrace of Count Schouvaloff has accompanied the Tsar's censure of the count's work,—the Berlin Congress. The leading minister, in so far as such a minister there is at present in Russia, is the war minister Milutin. At his demand, the peace, in which Russia is threatened by no one, has yet been followed by the mighty preparations which, notwithstanding the financial sacrifice involved in the war, have raised the peace-footing of the Russian army by 560,000 men, and the footing of the army of the west, which is kept ready for active service, by about 400,000 men. These preparations can only be intended as a menace to Austria or Germany, and the military establishments in the Kingdom of Poland correspond to such a design. The war minister has also, in the presence of the tech-

---

nical commissions, unreservedly declared that Russia must prepare for a war 'with Europe.'

"In this situation of affairs Russia, in the course of the last few weeks, has presented to us demands which amount to nothing less than that we should make a definite choice between Russia and Austria, at the same time instructing the German members of the Eastern committees to vote with Russia on doubtful questions." [1]

The Tsar's request to the Berlin Cabinet that Germany should vote in international concerns according to Russia's dictation, coupled with the presence of 400,000 Russian troops on the German frontier, was sufficiently ominous; and it is evident that Gortchakoff believed that he had placed Bismarck between two fires,—France and Russia,—a dilemma from which there was no escape, except in submission to the St. Petersburg autocrat.

When Gortchakoff sent threatening letters to Bismarck he counted on the wrong man for a game of bluff. Alexander had already tried that in regard to the deposition of the King of Hanover, and we have seen what he accomplished by it. The new tariff was on Bismarck's hands at this time, and was not disposed of until the midsummer. He might have pertinently asked the Tsar, "What more do you want?" but he left that to Emperor William, who arranged a meeting with Alexander on the Prussian frontier early in September, and at the same time he went himself to Vienna to consult with Andrassy, a statesman whom he never counted on in vain. It is said that the proposition of an alliance came from Andrassy. Bismarck's face glowed. Gortchakoff was checkmated; for Austria and Germany together could withstand all the rest of Europe. The treaty agreed upon was very simple, and was immediately approved by Francis Joseph. If either empire should be attacked by Russia the other would assist it with two hundred thousand troops. In regard to Turkish affairs it was agreed that the political situation as determined by the Congress of Berlin should be strictly maintained.

---

[1] Memoirs, ii. 261.

Meanwhile the German emperor had returned from an altogether friendly conference with his nephew Alexander at
Alexandrovo, and Bismarck found him in Berlin quite satisfied
that the tone of the Russian papers did not reflect the attitude of the government, and was not in itself a matter of
serious importance. He objected to the Austrian alliance as
a new and revolutionary movement in Prussian diplomacy.
The tradition of the Hohenzollerns had been antagonistic to
Austria, and this had always been encouraged by the Russian
court. The emperor was now over eighty, and such a mental
transposition as this treaty required is hard and difficult at
such an age. Bismarck found that turning the Austrian
empire round on its base was easy compared with turning
the Hohenzollerns. He argued that the policy of Frederick
the Great, while Prussia was an isolated kingdom, could no
longer apply to an united Germany, and that the local independence of the Hungarians had changed quite as radically
the policy of Austria. More than ever now would the Hungarians continue to be the allies of Prussia, since they were
almost surrounded by a cordon of Slavonic states. The Austrians were Germans, and felt the same sympathetic interest in
the welfare of Germany which all Germans must. Finally he
wrote to Von Moltke, who was at Freiburg in the Black
Forest, urging him to meet the emperor on his journey to
Baden, and lay before him a scheme of the advantages of an
alliance with Austria from a military point of view. This
commission Von Moltke was not slow to undertake, but William I. still held out obstinately, trusting always in the good
intentions of Alexander. The crown prince, with his English
proclivities, was, of course, anti-Russian, and the whole ministry sided with Bismarck, but it was of no avail. The emperor's ideas seemed to have become crystallized. Finally
the chancellor played his last trump-card,—resignation.
" Your Majesty, I cannot remain in office and see an opportunity which promises so much for the peace of Germany and
of all Europe sacrificed in this manner." William gave way
before this threat; the necessary preliminaries were soon arranged, and the treaty signed by both emperors by the middle

of November.   Gortchakoff was a neophyte compared to his German rival.

The text of the treaty was not made public until five years later, when the aggressive attitude of Russia in the far East made a little moral pressure serviceable in the interest of political harmony; but the fact that an Austro-German alliance existed was soon proclaimed in Bismarck's favorite journal, the *North German Gazette*.   Alexander at once telegraphed to William his protest against it, but the protest came too late.   Its salutary influence was quickly perceived in the abatement of Russian newspaper attacks on Bismarck's policy, and the withdrawal of Russian regiments from the German frontier.   The Tsarovitch was recruiting at Cannes in France, and was requested by his father to pay conciliatory visits at Berlin and Vienna,—it is said, much against his own will.[1] Bismarck had upset the balance of power only to form a new one, which has continued to the present time, and offers an appearance of greater solidity than has ever been known before.   It was not long before Italy also expressed a desire to enter this partnership, and the combined forces of these three powers, amounting to nearly a million and a half of men, can easily bid defiance to any combination, civilized or barbarous, that could be made up against them.   A more serious check to Russian aggrandizement could not be imagined, and there was equal rejoicing in London and Constantinople at the news of it.   The invasion of Tunis by the French also increased Bismarck's influence with the sultan, and he was thus enabled to become the protector of Greece and Montenegro, besides suggesting some simple reforms in the Turkish administration which have proved much to the advantage of the Ottoman empire.   A coalition between Russia and France was no longer possible, and Panslavism, if not killed outright, had received such a stunning blow that it did not raise its composite head—at least, in a conspicuous manner—for some years to come.   " Beware of the Cossack," said Napoleon at St. Helena.

---

[1] W. Müller, p. 651.

CHAPTER XV

The Austro-German alliance was the last of Bismarck's great diplomatic victories, and the last he could very well have achieved. There was nothing more in that line for him to do. France and Russia were both kept in check by it; the Austrians and Hungarians were contented; the Servians and Bulgarians rejoiced in their liberation from the Turk; Italy, like Germany, was engrossed in its internal development, repairing the waste of centuries; and Spain was trying to discover the kind of liberalism that was best suited to its people. The Poles, of course, were dissatisfied, but, divided as they were among three nationalities, there would seem to be no hope for them even in the near future. Bismarck talked a great deal on this subject, and evidently thought a great deal, but could see no alternative except a continuation of the present order. During the siege of Paris he spoke of the wars of the Great Elector in Poland, which were brought to an unfavorable conclusion by the interference of Holland. If Poland could have been incorporated in Germany, as Hungary was in Austria, it would have been greatly to the advantage of all concerned; but this was a dream of the moment which he was aware could not be realized. However, there had already been a movement in this direction among the Poles, and Bismarck's name had been imprudently connected with it. As Bismarck once said in the Reichstag in regard to Prussian Poland:

"The Polish peasant, from being a despised and mercilessly plundered vassal of some noble, has become a free man and an owner of the soil he cultivates. The usurious Jews are his only plunderers now. German manufactories and machines have promoted an improved method of agriculture. The prosperity of the province has been greatly increased by railways and government roads. Polish children enjoy the advantage of schools for elementary instruction, organized on German principles; and gymnasia teach the higher branches of learning, not by the hollow, mechanical methods of the Jesuit Fathers, but in that solid German manner which enables people to think for themselves. Army service completes whatever is left unachieved by the popular schools. In the army the young Polish peasant learns to understand and speak German. He learns much by association in his company, and through intercourse with the inhabitants of his German garrisoned town he acquires ideas which enrich and emancipate his narrow and fettered intelligence. His notions of right and wrong become clearer; he is obliged to adopt orderly habits of living, which he usually retains after his term of service has expired."[1]

This is perfectly true, and a fair picture of German workingclass culture; but to the average Polish mind only two modes of life would seem to be cognizable,—a luxurious leisure, or serfdom. In the Polish republic there were practically only two classes, and it was the absence of an industrial middle class, and its elective monarchy, which caused the nation to become so weak. They were not satisfied with being a component part of Prussia, but wished to form a separate state within the German empire, like Saxony or Würtemberg, with local autonomy or home rule. They could not be blamed for this; but the decisive objection to it was that such a state as this would be certain to form a nucleus for revolutionary agitation in Russian Poland, and might be the antecedent cause of a life-and-death struggle between Russia and Germany. They continued to agitate this plan, and their deputies in the Reichstag boldly admitted their expectation of restoring the Polish state in one way or another, until in 1886 Bismarck conceived the idea of buying up the large Polish estates in Posen and colonizing them with German farmers.

This was a severe remedy, but a magnificent idea, for it would replace a class of unproductive and unpatriotic citizens with industrious, patriotic husbandmen. The Reichstag did not consider it too severe a measure, and the chancellor re-

---

[1] Our Chancellor, ii. 150.

ceived letters from all parts of Germany and from all classes of Germans commending his plan, which included a system of annual payments for the land on the Von Stein principle. One object which Bismarck had in this colonization was to organize a thickly settled loyal population on the eastern frontier of Germany as a bulwark against Russian invasion; but at the same time the plan gave satisfaction to the Russian government as tending to obviate complications with the Prussian Poles. Whether it was right or not is what every man must decide with his own conscience.

PERSECUTION OF THE JEWS

An anti-Semitic agitation originated in Berlin in 1877,—where or how has not been made apparent,—and extended over a large portion of Prussia and some other German states, lasting a number of years and gradually dying out after the fashion of the Kulturkampf. Jews are much more numerous in Germany than in any other country of Europe, and the explanation would seem to be that they have been treated heretofore in a more friendly manner there than elsewhere. It was not until 1849, however, that they were permitted to hold public offices in Prussia. Bismarck had taken part in this emancipation, but had opposed their appointments to the highest positions in the state; and he found afterwards that in all his legislative measures the Jews, of whom Lasker was the most prominent leader, were a compact body against him. This fact may have aroused the national Prussian spirit, which was so aggressive after the campaign of 1870 for twelve years or more. Petitions were circulated to prevent the appointment of Jews for both civil and military offices. The University of Berlin declared against the appointment of Jewish professors. Hotel proprietors refused to receive Hebrew guests, and even saloon-keepers closed their doors to the unpopular race. In Pomerania there was serious rioting, and many Israelites were driven from smaller places to the large cities, whence the numbers of their brethren could afford them protection. The agitation extended itself into Russian Poland, whence the Jews were forcibly expelled, their property seized, personal injuries inflicted, and even murders committed, without the perpetrators being brought to justice. Exiled Russian Jews were not permitted to find a home in Prussia, and many of them were obliged to cross the ocean in search of a refuge.

Such an order of affairs is by no means pleasant to reflect on, but of course there must have been a reason for it somewhere, though we may not believe the reason to be adequate. The English historian Freeman advanced the theory at this time that a nation has always a right to get rid of any class of people who proved themselves a nuisance, whether it were the Jews in Russia or the Chinese in America. This seems rather brutal, and we hesitate to endorse it; yet the trouble with the Jews is one which cannot be reached by legislation. The majority of them live like parasites on the community. It is true that they take care of their own poor, but otherwise are not public-spirited or helpful. They are not Christians, and do not believe in the golden rule. Those who become Christians seem to change in this respect more or less. It cannot be doubted that they are sharper at bargains than any other races, but at the same time they do not make good financiers for states or empires. Nearly half of the floating wealth of Europe is in the hands of Hebrew bankers, who spend little and give away less. The Semitic persecution had the same characteristics as the Jews themselves. It certainly was not Christian, nor was it remediable in any degree by legislation.

There were attacks upon Bismarck in the Radical papers, and his friends felt it necessary to defend him against them. He was interviewed by a Jew at Varzin, and gave an opinion, which was perhaps somewhat touched up in transition to the press so that it appeared like a stronger statement than he intended. He is reported to have said:

"Nothing can be more incorrect than the notion that I approve of the anti-Semitic agitation. On the contrary, I most positively disapprove of this attack upon the Jews, whether prompted by dislike to their religion or antipathy to their race. It would be just as unfair to fall upon Germans of Polish or French extraction on the pretext that they were not real Germans. That the Jews preferentially devote themselves to business pursuits is a matter of taste; moreover, it may be the national consequence of their former exclusion from other callings; but it is certainly no justification for raising an outcry against their wealth, or reproaching them with being better off than Christians,—a proceeding which I consider reprehensible, because it provokes envy and hatred among the masses. I will never consent to any curtailment of the constitutional rights accorded to the Jews."

This sounds like Bismarck, and, printed at just the right time after the agitation had reached its height, no doubt helped to allay this strange public ebullition. He confessed, however, that he should not like to be governed by a Jew, and wondered that notable Germans should make matches for their daughters with wealthy Israelites. As for Germans marrying Jewesses, he did not think so badly of that, "for then," he said, "their money circulates and does good."

THE DEATH OF ALEXANDER

On March 13, 1881, Alexander II. was assassinated by the Nihilists, and a shudder went across the continent of Europe. He had liberated the serfs, he had emancipated the Christian provinces of Turkey, he had lived a just and pious life, and had done much to mitigate the severity of the military despotism to which he was born and brought up; it has even been affirmed that he had planned to bestow a constitutional government on Russia just before his death; but even more conspicuous virtues would not have saved him from becoming the victim of political bigotry.

There is practically little difference between a Nihilist, a Socialist, a Communist, a Fenian, and an Anarchist. They are differentiated only by the manners and character of the people from whom they originated. There is perhaps more hard ingrained atheism in the Nihilist than in any of the others. Atheism has been popular in the fashionable society of St. Petersburg and Moscow for the past fifty years. It appears on the surface like frivolous talk, but has a deep and dangerous undercurrent which may lead either to ruin or to crime. The realistic literature of the country is one illustration of it,—an art which goes continually round in a circle without coming to any definite result. But Russian literature is only a reflection of French literature, and, though it represents Russian life in externals, is not in itself an exponent of Russian character. The Russian language, as Professor W. D. Whitney says, is the vehicle of civilization to northern and central Asia. This also is the historical justification of the Russian government. In Europe it is a danger to higher forms of civilization, and perhaps a curse to the more enlightened portion of its subjects. It has proved a blessing to the Cossacks, the Finlanders, and the nomad tribes of northern Asia. Any one who has read Vámbéry's travels in central Asia must realize the advantage that has resulted from the Russian conquest of Tartary,—an advantage equal to the British conquest of India. The Russian government has stopped the Tartars from gouging one another's eyes out, and compelled them to give up their nomad way of life.

The death of a man like Alexander II. never happens in vain. It aroused an active sentiment of indignation against the more radical and desperate class of Socialists, impressed the more moderate class with a sense of their responsibility to the moral law, and it helped to disaffect many others from the political doctrines which they had rashly embraced. There were, of course, a few who pretended to consider the event as the natural outcome of Russian institutions, but they might as well have inferred that Nobeling's attempt on the emperor was the result of constitutional government. Bismarck took advantage of its effect on the public mind to introduce his favorite scheme for the establishment of a government insurance fund for the benefit of working-men who might become disabled through accident, ill-health, or old age,—one of his grandest measures, and sufficient in itself to give any man distinction. Certainly it was a gigantic undertaking, for the requisite funds would have to be counted, not by millions but by hundreds of millions. The whole community would have to be taxed for its support, but he considered it only right that the nation should be taxed liberally for the benefit of its humble poor, who really form the foundation on which the whole fabric of society rests.

The outline of his plan was simply this : it provided for the creation of a government department similar to the postal department, which would have agencies in all cities and towns, where money could be loaned and donated to those actually in need, under the direction of a local committee of citizens. Each committee was to consist of ten or twelve members, with a member of the city council for a presiding officer, and always including the city physician of the district in which the agency would be located. In this way it was believed that the whole public would take an interest in the working of the system, which from its nature would be more thorough and efficient than volunteer charities, without at the same time dispensing with the interest and help of private individuals. If the system was to be a machine, it was Bismarck's endeavor to make it a living, human machine. He said in regard to it :

"I am by no means yet convinced that the notion of subsidizing eleemosynary associations by the state is an objectionable one. It seems to me that a possibility of improving the working-man's lot might be found in the establishment of productive associations such as exist and flourish in England. I have talked over the subject with the king, who has the interests of the working classes at heart, and his Majesty paid a sum of money out of his own pocket in aid of an experiment in that direction connected with a deputation of operatives from Silesia, who had lost their employment through differing from their employer in politics. . . . To attempt anything of the sort upon a large scale might entail an expenditure of hundreds of millions ; but the notion does not seem to me intrinsically an absurd or silly one. We make experiments in agriculture and manufactures ; might it not be as well to do so with respect to human occupations and a solution of the social question ?" [1]

Again he said :

"People talk about state Socialism and think they have settled the matter,—as if such things were to be disposed of with a phrase !

---

[1] Our Chancellor, ii. 196.

Socialism or not, it is necessary, the outcome of an urgent requirement. They say, too, the bill would entail enormous expenditure,
an hundred million of marks, at least—perhaps twice as much. As
for me, three hundred millions would not alarm me. We must find
some means of relieving the unindebted poor, on the part of the
state and not in the form of alms. Contentment amongst the
impecunious and disinherited classes would not be dearly purchased by an enormous sum. They must be made to understand
that the state is of some use,—that it does not only take, but gives
to boot. And if the state, which does not look for interest or
dividends, takes the matter in hand, the thing is easy enough." [1]

The laborers' relief bill failed to pass the Reichstag, owing
to the combination of the very parties who, if they had been
consistent, would have given it unqualified support,—that is,
the Liberals, Progressists, and Social Democrats. It is a
peculiarity of the doctrinaires to care more for their theories
than they do for the good which those theories are expected
to accomplish. If the world is to be saved it must be saved
according to their method, and not according to any other;
otherwise they would prefer to have it blown up altogether.[2]
No doctrinaire could ever have succeeded in practical affairs
as Bismarck did. He patiently waited his time, and this
rejected measure has since become the corner-stone of the
present German system of charitable organizations, which
may challenge all other countries to show its equal. A late
writer in the New York *Outlook* says:

"Beyond all question, the care of the poor and distressed in the
cities of Germany is superbly managed. Of course, there is in
every city a general department of poor relief with its specialists
and general advisers, but there is also a system of local committees
which assist in the work. No man in Germany would think of
declining to serve on the committee. But it is the German ideal
at least to abolish poverty. Germans think the present policy of

---

[1] Bismarck's Speeches, Speemann's ed., vol. xvi.
[2] This is especially true of the Progressists and German free-traders. Las-
salle, the most practical of German socialistic writers, is credited with having
said: "If we were to shoot at Bismarck, common justice would compel us to
admit that he is a man ; whereas the Progressists are old women."

the government will ultimately lead to it. For this reason they have inaugurated a system of municipal insurance against sickness, loss of employment, and old age. The German cities also do all they can to encourage small wage-earners and protect those in temporary distress. To this end they have established a system of municipal savings banks and municipal pawn-shops. The Berlin savings-bank system has more than four hundred thousand such depositors. In Aachen (Aix-la-Chapelle) it is said that almost every man, woman, and child has such a bank-book. These banks pay about three per cent. interest on their deposits, and it is paid with the greatest regularity, as the funds are usually invested in government securities of some sort. Experience has shown that the pawn-shops have also been of great practical benefit to the poor."

This system of laborers' insurance has been imitated, or duplicated, by the Pennsylvania, the Burlington and Quincy, and perhaps one or two other American railroads, with excellent success. It had been suggested before, but Bismarck was the first to make the practical application, and should receive credit for it. The supplement of a government pawnbrokerage business was an admirable device, as it cut the ground from under the feet of the Jews, thus helping also to allay the Semitic agitation. In addition to this, the tramps and vagrants in Germany have been collected into villages, and have had cottages built for them, where they work under military supervision. The report of the United States consul-general at Berlin for the year ending 1886 represented a greatly improved and flourishing condition of economical affairs in Germany, and gave a flat contradiction to the statements on the same subject in American newspapers at that time. Simultaneously the London *Times* complained that English commerce in Africa, Asia, and the Pacific was suffering from German enterprise and competition. Bismarck had made personal exertions to secure for his countrymen an immense army contract from the Japanese government, amounting to several millions. "The Germans were improving their foreign trade," said the *Times*, "by their promptness, thoroughness, and exact calculation of means to ends,—those virtues by which English commerce has grown to greatness, but which are not so common in the realm as formerly. German clerks and book-keepers are securing the best places, because they know languages and are more correct. German servants are superseding English servants, because they are more respectful and trustworthy."

Bismarck also made some interesting remarks on the probable effect of a national socialistic experiment. He once said to Dr. Busch:

"It is extremely difficult to discuss the Social-Democratic Realm of the Future, while we are groping about in darkness, like the ordinary audience at a Social-Democratic meeting, who know nothing at all about the matter, but are assured that 'better times are coming,' and that 'there will be more to earn and less to work.' Where the 'more' money is to come from nobody knows; I mean, when every well-to-do person shall have been robbed of his property in order that it shall be divided amongst his despoilers. Then, in all probability, the laborious and thrifty will again wax wealthy, whilst the lazy and extravagant will fall into poverty; or if everybody is to be supplied with the needful by an administration, people will come to lead the life of prisoners, shut up in gaols, none of whom follow occupations of their own choice, but work under the compulsion of the warders. In gaol, too, there is at least an official in charge, who is a trustworthy and respectable person; but who will play the warder in the Universal Socialistic House of Correction? Probably the speechifiers, who gain over the masses by their eloquence."

Doubtless the present organization of society might be improved upon, and it looks as if Bismarck had taken the first step towards this. An association of picked men, like those who made the Brook Farm experiment at West Roxbury, might hold together, under the protection of the government which they pretended to despise, for a single generation, and retain the culture which they had previously acquired; but their descendants would inevitably become farmers, and subject to the limitations of farmer life, and so on forever.

LIFE OF BISMARCK

Even in Germany little is yet known concerning the life and character of Alexander III., but he appears to have been a man of rather frail physique and moderate mental endowments, and yet at the same time possessed of excellent judgment, and, what is quite as important, a good heart; so that, with these two qualifications of true manliness, he struggled through his difficult position until his comparatively early death in 1893 in a highly creditable manner. As Tsarovitch he was much under the influence of the Panslavists, and the assassination of his father aroused grave apprehensions at Berlin and Vienna on this account. Whether the responsibility of power produced a sudden revulsion in his opinions can only be surmised; but certain it is that he had not been six months on the throne before he sought an interview with Bismarck, and from that time was always guided more or less by his influence. A meeting of William I. and the new monarch took place at Dantzic on the Baltic in the autumn of 1881; and though we know nothing of the conference which followed, the Berlin editorials, supposed to be inspired by the chancellor after his return, gave most hopeful indications of the result of this interview for the welfare of Germany and the peace of Europe. Its immediate object appeared soon afterwards in the form of an extradition treaty between Russia and Germany for the benefit of Nihilists and other kinds of dynamiters; and as the French government had declined previously to surrender Hartmann, one of the would-be assassins of Alexander II., it was very natural after this that the relations between the court of William I. and of Alexander III. became more friendly.

European statesmen were fairly astonished the following year when Prince Gortchakoff retired from office and Baron de Giers was appointed in his place. It was supposed that the long ascendancy of Gortchakoff in Russian politics would enable him at least to designate his successor. His term of office had been much beyond Bismarck's, and his extreme age might be taken as a sufficient reason for resigning the cares of state; but De Giers was a German by descent, a man from near the middle of the Russian thirteen classes, who had raised himself by merit and ability to the front rank, and, though he had preserved a diplomatic neutrality during Gortchakoff's *régime*, was understood to be opposed to his predecessor's policy. This soon became evident in the more friendly correspondence between the governments of Russia, Austria, and Germany; and Count Kalnoky, who had succeeded Andrassy in Austria, assured the Hungarian delegation in the following October that the Austro-German alliance had now been supplemented by such pacific assurances from Alexander III. that the prospect of amicable relations with neighboring states had never been more favorable.

Still, Panslavism was an active and fomenting ingredient in the Russian body-politic, and De Giers was obliged to find an outlet for it in some direction; and this soon came to pass in the direction of India. Beaconsfield's Afghanistan blunder had been followed by a grievous political mistake on the part of Gladstone. Why the "Grand Old Man" should have imagined an appalling danger to England and civilization from the Austro-German alliance can only be explained by a lamentable ignorance of continental politics. Gladstone's Midlothian attacks on Bismarck and the alliance were not more injudicious than they were unjust. Writers in Liberal periodicals designated the German chancellor as the demon of Berlin,—with corresponding American echoes,—and the one man in Europe who was most desirous of preserving the peace was represented as continually intriguing for war and conquest. A statement made by Bismarck, as applied to German annexations in Africa, that the existence of a great empire necessitated the idea of its extension, was distorted into a scheme for the conquest of Greece by Austria, and the absorption of Holland and Denmark by Germany. What Russia and France would be doing in such an eventuality did not occur to these ready-witted magazinists. The more improbable these assertions the more readily they would seem to have been believed. It was in vain that Lord Salisbury made a dignified statement to prove that the Austro-German alliance was of great benefit to England, and that the advanced age of William I. and the good will of the crown prince were an adequate guarantee against all suppositions of German conquests; Gladstone and the philistines carried everything before them. The fact was that the English Liberal party had grown old with its distinguished leader, and had outlived its days of usefulness. It had no policy except the ambition for power; no better motive than the love of office; and as a party it was ready to make use of any means that would attain this object.

The net result of this was that Great Britain was left without an ally in Europe, and her enemies were not long in taking advantage of this. After Arabi Pasha had been subdued, the Arabs revolted in the Soudan. The Panslavist party, led by Ignatieff and Skobeleff, pushed forward the Russian boundaries to Afghanistan, and inaugurated a troublesome policy of higgling about the frontier, which might have resulted in open war but for the firmness of Alexander and De Giers. It is certain that there was a strong war party at St. Petersburg, and that for some days the decision of the government was suspended in the balance. When General Skobeleff urged the Tsar to permit an advance of the Russian forces towards Herat, Alexander replied, "The destiny of Russia does not depend on any single movement or political decision. It moves forward continually, and is as irresistible as the rising of the tide."[1] The Governor-General of India made the Ameer of Herat a present of a park of artillery, and the British government chartered transatlantic steamers for the conveyance of troops. The political horizon looked dark and threatening. Late in the summer of 1885 Gladstone was outvoted in the House of Commons; the Liberal ministry resigned, and this political witches' dance, which had been encouraged by his policy, suddenly came to an end. Gladstone was more high-minded than Bismarck in theory, but not in practice. It is well known that there was no parliamentary trick he would not employ to carry his point. In

---

[1] At least, a statement to this effect was telegraphed.

1861 he eulogized Jefferson Davis as the founder of a new republic; and many of his statements on the Irish question were rather dubious, to say the least. He did not lead his party, but was led by it.

During this period Bismarck sat behind his chancellor's table in the Reichstag, steadily transacting business, replying to attacks on the government, and making notes with the long yellow pencils which have become so famous.[1] The Reichstag became more and more divided, and consequently more difficult to deal with. Bismarck had his successes and his defeats in it, but chiefly in regard to matters of inconsiderable importance,—economical questions and the like, such as do not enter into universal history. He accepted both, like an experienced man of business who has become accustomed to the fickleness of fortune. He was virtually emperor of Germany now; for, though William I. was still vigorous in mind and body to a degree which astonished those about him, and caused the Germans to be more proud of him than ever, the long-confirmed habit of deferring to his chancellor's opinion was now fastened irrevocably upon him. The priests no longer caused Bismarck any trouble, and the socialists were little more than a whetstone for his argument. He had spent his whole public life in contention, and needed a strong opposition of some kind for the exercise of his faculties. His later speeches have an air of easy confidence, brightened with occasional touches of humor, which suggests that he was beginning to take more comfort in life. He would have been less than human not to have taken notice occasionally of Gladstone's mistakes and vulnerable performances, for he wished to be on friendly terms with the British government, and it was chiefly Gladstone who prevented this. Lord Granville was the English minister of foreign affairs, and, as his own party afterwards confessed, he conducted them in a very unskilful manner. One day in the spring of 1884, Bismarck amused the Reichstag by stating that their corre-

---

[1] These pencils, so it is said, had to be renewed every day of the session, for some deputy or other was sure to purloin the one that Bismarck had used, as a souvenir for his wife or children.

spondence with the English foreign office during the past six months exceeded in quantity that with all other European governments for several years. When the Reichstag passed a constitutional amendment for the daily compensation of its members, Bismarck did not even permit the bill to go to the House of Peers, but vetoed it at once, saying, "Such a measure in a country which was badly governed, like England, might accomplish mischief, but, thank heaven, I know my place better than to mix up monarchical institutions with republican practices." It does not seem fair or reasonable that a poor man of good ability should be prevented from serving his country as legislator on account of the lack of compensation; but the gratuitous service of parliamentary members in Great Britain and Germany certainly prevents politics from becoming a trade, and is believed to preserve a higher moral tone in the national assembly.

THE SEVENTIETH BIRTHDAY

The Reichstag revenged itself for the salary veto on December 15, 1884, by refusing to grant Bismarck twenty thousand marks a year for a third assistant in the ministry of foreign affairs, although he endeavored to convince the house that his own strength was not what it had been, and that the business of the office was continually increasing with the ever-extending foreign relations of the empire. In fact, quite a number of his associates had given out, from time to time, and been obliged to resign or be transferred to other and less arduous positions.[1] " It is the telegraph," said Bismarck, once, " that produces the strain in the management of foreign affairs. In old times, when everything came by mail-coaches, statesmen had plenty of leisure, and time enough to consider what they were going to do. Now everything is rush and hurry, and it is only a man of exceptional constitution who can stand it."

---

[1] One of Bismarck's secretaries informed an American that he never dared to go to evening parties or even to the theatre, for he might be summoned to the foreign office day or night at any hour.

This action of the Reichstag was severely criticised at home and abroad, and Bismarck's friends were highly indignant at what they called the vindictive parsimony of the legislative body. It was claimed that in refusing to accept the salary bill the chancellor had acted from principle and not from any unwillingness to have the government pay its just dues. As his seventieth birthday was now approaching it was proposed to make him a subscription present, which would defray the expense of additional clerk hire and something more. The plan for a " Bismarck gift" quickly ripened, and the result exceeded the expectation of its originators. Before the 1st of April, 1885, 2,400,000 marks were collected, and with a portion of this the estate at Schönhausen, the greater part of which had been alienated from the Bismarck family in unfavorable times, was redeemed and restored. From the remainder Bismarck donated a fund of 1,200,000 marks, or about $300,000, for the purpose of assisting indigent young Germans for an education as teachers of the higher branches in the public schools. His birthday was celebrated at Schönhausen, and was also made a national celebration. Emperor William attended his reception with many of the royal family, and the most distinguished persons in the realm besides. It was compared with the visit of Henry VIII. to Cardinal Wolsey. If Bismarck's reputation suffered from jealous and unfriendly tongues in foreign countries, he had no lack of appreciation in his own.

AFRICAN ANNEXATIONS

The prosperity of Germany produced its natural effect in a tendency to colonization. In spite of the immense emigration to America, the population of the German empire was increasing more rapidly than that of any other country in Europe. Italy came next on the census list, and for the same causes,—national unity and internal reforms,—while the population of France was almost stationary. Emigration to America could not give employment to German capital, and the enterprising merchants of Hamburg and Bremen were looking about for chances in various parts of the globe. A merchant named Leideritz thought he had discovered rich prospects in southwestern Africa, near the mouth of the Niger, and established factories there at considerable expense. The success of his experiment attracted others to the same neighborhood, and quite a German colony was formed in that vicinity. The development of this settlement into a German territorial acquisition resembled the British conquest of India. As the community grew it required military protection, and Bismarck recognized the necessity of this, though accounts agree that in the beginning he was opposed to colonization, and only consented to this new departure through the mercantile pressure that was brought to bear on him. The imperial flag was accordingly unfurled in the territory of Togo, and the process of annexation proceeded rapidly. On the principle that he might as well be hung for a sheep as a lamb, Bismarck next took possession of the large tract in southwestern Africa known to traders as the Cameroons, and also a large portion of Zanzibar, a tract extending inwards to Lake Victoria Nyanza, from which the Nile rises. The area of these territories is greater than the whole of Germany, but their actual value is less than Alsace and Lorraine. Yet the productive power of nature is so great on the dark continent that it is said a negro can support himself and his family by working only three weeks in the year. Subsequently the northeastern portion of New Guinea was seized by the German government, with the groups of islands to the right of it, which were christened the Bismarck Archipelago. To make these new provinces profitable, lines of steamers to east and west Africa and to the South Sea had to be subsidized, and the means for this were extorted from the Reichstag almost by main force. The subsidies were refused in 1884, and only obtained in 1885 after a desperate parliamentary struggle. People wondered how Bismarck's strength could hold out at his age after so much. It was thought that his indomitable will still kept him in the harness, and but for that he would long since have surrendered his office. That Bavaria and Würtemberg, being inland states, should oppose this new development of the empire was to have been expected.

The sudden entrance of Germany into the commercial arena

raised a general outcry along the banks of the Thames, and the British government, which is really controlled by the commercial interest, made the settlement of these new states as difficult as possible. The new African possessions were all bounded on one side at least by British territory. Special treaties were required, and boundaries had to be definitely adjusted. A voluminous correspondence between the foreign offices at London and Berlin commenced, and continued until the final retirement of Gladstone in July, 1886. If Earl Granville had a genius for anything it was for shifting his ground, and in this way he prevented Bismarck from coming to any definite conclusions with him for nearly two years, while the London papers sustained a vigorous chorus of "unprincipled acquisitions" and the "rights of original proprietors"! Bismarck had also to deal with the Sultan of Zanzibar, who suddenly discovered that he was no longer an independent potentate. But this obstacle was soon removed by the presence of a German fleet off the Zanzibar coast and a liberal "hongo" to his African majesty.

The logic of the matter was that all the powers of Europe were now seizing on whatever they could obtain in Asia and Africa, and there was no good reason why Germany should not have her share. Portugal had annexed the strip of coast between the mouth of the Congo and British South Africa, and was already in troubled water with Great Britain on that account. France was carrying on war in Tonquin, and it was not long before the British government took possession of Burmah and annexed it to India in the same fashion that Bismarck had annexed Togo. There was even danger that France, England, and Portugal would fall out over the possession of the rich interior discovered by Stanley on the Congo River, but this was obviated by the self-appointed arbitration of King Leopold of Belgium, who had taken an enthusiastic interest in African explorations, and succeeded in organizing the Congo Free State on sound international principles,—a rare accomplishment for the ruler of so small a state, and a well-deserved monument to his memory.

Africa was becoming a reflected copy of the map of Europe,

and Bismarck foresaw that, unless some order and method was introduced in the internal relations of this new family of subordinate nations, there was danger that before long the powers of Europe would be involved in a conflict on their account. It was with this end in view that he invited representatives of all parties concerned to meet at Berlin in November, 1884, and hold a conference to determine the proper grounds for annexation of uncivilized territory, and to establish a uniform system of laws and regulations for intercolonial relations. It was likely that Granville would have declined to submit the foreign policy of England to the possible limitations of such a tribunal but for the intervention of Gladstone, who was beginning to feel the strain of complications in so many different countries, and recognized the advantage of a court of appeal for the various provinces of Africa. As for France, Belgium, and Portugal, their foreign ministers were well enough pleased with any arrangement which would tie down the tyrant of the seas to a definite course of procedure, even if England dictated that course herself. The Berlin conference lasted nearly five months, and its proceedings were thoroughly sifted by the ablest jurists of the different countries represented. After the accession of Lord Salisbury in 1886 the friction between Great Britain and Germany was almost entirely removed, and a year later Bismarck was enabled to state in the Reichstag that England no longer " behaved like a raging bull, or a comfortable ox chewing its cud," but could be depended on as a promoter of peace and international justice in the European system.[1] In fact, Great Britain had in an informal manner joined the alliance of Germany, Austria, and Italy, and there was no longer the possibility of any other power making a serious disturbance in the European family.

It is too soon to judge of the success of Germany's colonial policy. The good or bitter fruit of such large enterprises is only gathered after a long season. Some of the companies organized for Africa and the South Sea have paid good divi-

---

[1] Report to the Associated Press.

dends, others little or nothing, and subsidies are still required for some of the steamship lines. On the whole, the prospect thus far is considered a favorable one, and optimists predict better results in the future. Bismarck's attempt to obtain a foothold in the Caroline Islands was the only decided failure. The right of Germany was immediately challenged by the Spanish government, and Bismarck prudently referred the dispute to Pope Leo as arbitrator, who decided in favor of Spain after a thorough legal examination of the question at issue. The loss of a number of war-ships of different nations, German and others, by a terrific hurricane off Samoa while the suit was pending, made a gloomy and unhappy conclusion to this episode.

END OF THE KULTURKAMPF

How was the Kulturkampf to come to an end? The resignation of the inexorable Dr. Falk, in the autumn of 1878, and the appointment of Von Putkammer, a man of mild and conciliatory methods, did not surprise those who were watching the course of events. After this there was neither active resistance on the part of the bishops nor persecution on the part of the government. Von Putkammer evidently intended to interfere as little as possible. An immense number of Catholic parishes were devoid of officiating priests. In some instances these vacancies were filled up by giving proper notification to the authorities of the intended appointments; in others the former incumbents returned quietly to their duties without being molested. There was evidently an understanding between Bismarck and Pope Leo, and what could their agreement be, other than to let the questions at issue gradually subside into the background, and to treat the dogma of infallibility as if it were a dead letter,—a thing of the past?

There was no other course for either party to follow. Neither could very well admit, if they felt inclined to do so, having been in the wrong. The Church of Rome never takes a backward step. Leo could not call another ecumenical council in order to reverse the decision of 1869 without seriously undermining the authority of the Vatican. Bismarck could no more face the Reichstag with a confession that all his anti-infallibility legislation had been a mistake. The dogma of infallibility, however, could be thrown aside for the time and left to an innocuous desuetude. The object for which it was originated—in order to check the encroachments of Victor Emmanuel—had proved a failure. The authority of the pope in the States of the Church was gone, and there was very faint hope that it could ever be regained. Victor Emmanuel was also gone, and the personal antagonism which was felt towards him in the Vatican was not inherited to the same extent by King Humbert. Infallibility had lived its short career, and strutted on its political stage, causing a great sensation for the time being, but its day was done, and nobody cared for it any longer. If the priest who was deposed by the Bishop of Ermland and the Catholic professors at Bonn had not raised their voices against it, perhaps the Kulturkampf would never have taken place; but if a powder-train is laid anywhere it commonly happens that the magazine is fired sooner or later.

It would be neither interesting nor profitable to follow the gradual modification of the May Laws from 1878 to 1887, when they practically came to an end. Almost every session of the Reichstag witnessed some alteration in them, which Bismarck explained in an off-hand manner, as if his hearers understood already what he intended to say, and there was no need of a convincing argument. Every downward step in this change of policy appears to have required a change in the ministry of public worship, and Dr. Falk's successors were as numerous as unimportant in the record of events.

Dr. Windhorst was now one of Bismarck's most faithful supporters (a strong force in his way), and it was not without some reason that the Liberals insinuated that his services were paid for in " money of Canossa." Bismarck had become long accustomed to the taunt of inconsistency, and he could reply with quite as much truth that the May Laws were still on the statute books and could be enforced whenever the government considered it expedient.

The alliance between Germany, Austria, and Italy had been

supplemented by a convenient commercial treaty; the cry of Guelph and Ghibellines was no longer heard in Italy, and a current of similar ideas circulated through the three countries from the North Sea to the Straits of Messina. The word that went forth from Berlin was echoed in Vienna and again in Rome. Never since the Roman empire had the population of so vast a tract been animated by an equally sympathetic spirit. German seriousness and moderation tempered the less stable and more impulsive Italian nature. The Italian government, which for a time seemed to be drifting on a dangerous reef, weathered the promontory, and once more kept its even course. No wonder that Lord Salisbury admitted to a London audience that one man ruled the whole of Europe. "However," he added, "I do not think he is unfriendly to England, but quite the reverse."

The monastic orders were permitted to return to Germany,[1] all except the Jesuits; and when, in April, 1887, the May Laws were finally repealed, with the exception of some simple regulations concerning the appointments of parochial priests, people asked the question whether Bismarck had actually gone to Canossa, after all his defiant protestations. No; he had not gone to Canossa, any more than Canossa had come to him. You may call it a stalemate, if you please; but the object for which the May Laws were enacted had been substantially attained,—the assertion of the supremacy of the civil law. Infallibility was dead as a door-nail. There is no surer way of killing an idea or a dogma than by overdoing it. Everybody was utterly sick of infallibility, and, it may be said, of the Kulturkampf also, and wished to hear no more of it. *Requiescat in pace* was the sentiment in Germany in regard to the whole affair, and Bismarck shared in this. The priests might believe in the dogma so long as they liked, provided only that they did not obtrude it before the public. It had been a tough, obstinate struggle; but the Church of Rome was the only sufferer. If Bismarck had not disconcerted Kullman's aim by raising his hand for the frequent

---

[1] It was called " the migration of the rooks."

salutation, the balance would have been largely on the Catholic side; so narrow a line is there often between success and failure in the most important enterprises. The good understanding between Bismarck and Leo XIII. continued to the end, and the latter expressed himself as feeling highly complimented for having been chosen arbitrator of the dispute over the Caroline Islands. At the close of the same year he presented the German chancellor with the order of Jesus Christ set in diamonds, which had never before been presented to a Protestant prince; and he wrote him at the same time an autograph letter, expressing a respectful recognition of his good services in church and state.

FOREIGN RELATIONS

From 1871 for the next decade Gambetta was the most popular man in France. He upset the septennate of President MacMahon on suspicion of Bonapartist intrigues, whether well grounded or not is uncertain. Von Beust considers that there was really no need of MacMahon's resigning, and that he might have remained in office until his seven years were finished, whether the national assembly liked it or not. Gambetta obtained the passage of a law to place the appointment of general officers under the control of the national assembly, a measure sufficient of itself to shipwreck the French army in a protracted campaign. After the election of President Grévy ministries were formed and resigned so frequently that their average duration was less than six months. Gambetta was the leader who wrought these remarkable changes, which gave the French republic an appearance of political instability. He declined to accept office himself, but finally was obliged to do this in order to escape from the inconsistency of his position. He had no sooner done so than the unpractical character of the man became apparent. His first manœuvre was to seek an interview with Bismarck, and the German chancellor must have been greatly amused at the idea of being outwitted by this inexperienced disciple of Rousseau. If Gambetta was twitted at this meeting for his incendiary philippics against Germany, it is no more than he might have expected. A coalition had already taken root against him before he returned to Paris. The constitution did not satisfy him; he wished to make changes in the suffrage laws, was outvoted in the Chamber of Deputies, and retired from office. Neither did he live long after this. Jules Ferry was the first premier since Thiers's resignation who evinced the capacity to deal with the elements about him. It was during his administration that Tunis was annexed to Algeria, and this was accomplished in a very adroit and skilful manner. He wished to divert his countrymen from home politics by giving them a foreign interest, and it was with him that the annexation of Tonquin in Cochin China originated,—a country almost as rich as India in oriental products. Bismarck congratulated him on his success in governing the French, but spoiled the compliment by adding that no people obey better when they feel the strong hand. This may even have assisted in weakening Ferry's popularity, which was wholly upset by a defeat in the China seas, and he disappeared, like the others before him, never to come to the top again. These continuous changes indicated a decided weakness in the French constitution, for a systematic foreign policy is impossible under such conditions. It was the logical consequence of imitating the English form of government, which is much better suited to a sober, phlegmatic people than to the excitable, capricious French. If the French had modelled their institutions in 1871 more after the pattern of the United States, with an independent president and cabinet, they might have achieved better results in the long run, and founded their republic on a more enduring basis.

Old Manteuffel was made governor of Alsace and Lorraine in 1873, and, though he could not prevent young Prussian officers from swaggering in the streets of Strasburg, he filled the position in an exemplary manner, dealing equal and exact justice to friend and foe. Wherever Manteuffel went order reigned, and confusion fled before him. The anti-German agitation, which had been largely stimulated by the priests, subsided after the election of Leo XIII., and even when Emperor William visited the two provinces in 1877 he was received in a cordial and friendly, if not the most enthusiastic manner. The Alsatians have too much local pride not to feel a certain satisfaction in the military prestige of the new German empire, and this was a partial compensation for their involuntary separation from France. It could not be said that the French had yet become reconciled to the events of 1870; but as time went on they felt continually less inclined to try conclusions again with the German army, and President Grévy is credited with the statement that the man who contemplated another campaign on the Rhine, so long as Moltke and Bismarck were alive, lacked common sense. The acquisition of Tunis was gratifying to the national pride, and, coming as a free gift from the German chancellor, it helped much to ameliorate the feeling towards him.

After the Italian alliance the outlook for peace was particularly good, but Bismarck was not satisfied until he had drawn Russia into the same net. In September, 1884, he effected a meeting of the three emperors, with their respective ministers, at Skierniviece in Poland, intended specially to satisfy the Tsar and De Giers that the Triple Alliance was not in any respect inimical to Russian interests. It was also given out that Bismarck was endeavoring to harmonize the relation between Russia and England in the Balkan states; but it is equally certain that he did not succeed in this, as appeared not long afterward in the Bulgarian imbroglio. This pacific outlook, however, did not last above two years, when it was seriously disturbed by the waywardness of Prince Alexander of Bulgaria in the east, and in the west by one of the most singular phenomena of the past fifty years.

Somewhere about 1885 the populace of Paris fell under the influence of an unprincipled adventurer named Boulanger. He was not a man of exceptional ability or good judgment; audacious rather than brave, and possessed of enormous self-confidence. He had served with credit in the campaign of 1870, and had been promoted rapidly to the rank of major-general. He was thoroughly unprincipled, and subsequent events proved that his pretended patriotism was nothing better than personal ambition. He was ready to sell his soul to any political devil, or political party, for the sake of advancement; but he could deliver a lively off-hand speech, and had that ready good-natured manner which is often mistaken for genuine *bonhomie*. How such an empty character became the idol of Paris it is difficult to imagine, and certainly is not much to the credit of the Parisians; but General Boulanger was so popular in 1886 that he was made minister of war chiefly on that account. He now succeeded to Gambetta's *rôle* as preacher of a crusade of vengeance against Prussia, and he did this so openly and energetically that under different conditions it might easily have caused the outbreak of war. He was secretly supported in this course by the royalists, who hoped to recover lost ground through the confusion which Boulanger created, and openly by the more sensational newspapers and a noisy group of followers in the Chamber of Deputies. The aspect of France was not more belligerent after the Austrian campaign of 1866. People of unregulated imagination already saw in Boulanger a conquering hero, who would recover the laurels and redeem the military honor of the French nation. Slight collisions which occurred on the frontier about this time excited the animosity of certain classes in both countries, and tended to aggravate the situation.

Bismarck knew that diplomacy would avail little with such an undiplomatic cabinet as that in which Boulanger participated, and perhaps he had learned from the Kulturkampf that attempts to muzzle the press of a foreign country were of little avail. He felt strong in the triple alliance, but he thought Germany ought to be able to deal with France single-handed, and he knew that other governments would look at it in that light. Moltke informed him, however, that the present military establishment of France largely exceeded that of Germany. He could not feel confident of success without an increase of forty thousand men in the active service of the German army. Accordingly, in the autumn of 1886, Bismarck went to the Reichstag with a measure to this effect. "In France," he said, "the unexpected may happen at any time, and we ought to be prepared for it beforehand.

An armed peace is, after all, better than war; and if we prepare ourselves for war we shall be less likely to encounter it than if we do not." He asked for an increase of fifty thousand men for seven years to tide over the emergency. The Reichstag, however, looked on this rather as an attempt to obtain an additional support to the imperial authority, and refused to grant it; whereupon Bismarck dissolved the parliament in a rage, and appealed to the constituencies. As happened on previous occasions, the German people supported their chancellor, and the new Reichstag, elected in the autumn of 1887, proved more favorable to his foreign policy. He opened the subject, when the delegates had assembled, in a celebrated speech, from which we cull the following extract:

"That the present bill is not to be looked on in the light of a momentary arrangement—this, I think, will be clearly seen, if I may request you to consider with me the dangers of war to which we have been exposed within the last forty years, without, however, becoming at any time a prey to nervous apprehensions.

"If in my enumeration I should have omitted one single year of all these years, in the terrible experiences of which you have all yourselves participated, one would not have the impression that this state of fear of great wars, of further complications, the results of which as to any possible alliances nobody can judge of in advance, —that this state is a permanent one with us, and that we must prepare ourselves, once and for all, to deal with it; independently of the present conditions, we must be strong, that we, fully conscious of being a great nation, which, if required, is sufficiently powerful to take her destiny in her own hand, even against any and every coalition, with the self-confidence and the trust in God which is born of the consciousness of one's own strength and the justness of one's cause, which will ever be on the side of Germany as far as this is in the power of the government,—that thus, I say, we can look every contingency in the face, and that with tranquillity.

"In short, in these times we will have to strengthen our forces to the utmost; and if it is possible for us to be stronger than any other country of a like number of individuals, it would be a crime not to make use of this possibility. If we do not need our military power, we need not call out the same. The principal point here is the money question, which does not involve a very great expenditure, if one considers that France has spent three thousand millions within the last twenty years for the improvement of her military forces, while we invested scarcely fifteen hundred millions, including the amount for which we now ask you.

"When I say that we must perpetually aim to be always ready for any contingency, I herewith lay claim that on account of our geographical position we must make still greater efforts than other nations do for the same purpose. We lie in the centre of Europe. We offer three sides where we can be attacked. France can only be attacked on its eastern frontier, Russia only at its western. Besides that, we are more than any other nation exposed to the danger of coalitions, according to the development of the history of the world, according to our geographical situation, and also because of the looser organization of the Germans up to the present time as compared with other nations. God has put us in a place where our neighbors prevent us from degenerating through indolence and stagnation."

Bismarck then dwelt on the fact that the war party in Russia had caused an estrangement to take place between the German and Russian empires; and afterwards gave a history of the origin of the Austro-German alliance which is substantially what we have already stated. He then said:

"There is no doubt that if the present bill is passed the alliance with Austria will gain tremendously in power, inasmuch as the power of that side of the alliance represented by Germany will be very largely augmented. As soon as we have the guns for the increase in numbers provided for in the bill, this very same bill will represent a strengthening of the sureties of peace as well as a strengthening of that peace alliance, as powerful as if a fourth great power had joined the league with an army of seven hundred thousand men."

He then went on to say that he did not consider that there was any necessary apprehension of an immediate conflict with either France or Russia. All that was necessary for Germany was that she should be prepared to meet any emergency which might arise. The difficulty of preserving peace was greatly increased by the threatening articles in foreign newspapers. Again he said:

"I would particularly admonish foreign countries to drop these threats. They lead to nothing. The threat which is offered to us—not from the government, but from the press—is, strictly speaking, incredible nonsense, when one imagines that a powerful and proud nation, such as the German empire, could be intimidated by a highly belligerent attitude in printer's ink or by a conglomeration of words. This should be dropped ; then it would be easier for us to take a more conciliatory stand towards our two neighbors. Every country will in the long run be made responsible for the windows which are broken by its press, the bill for which will be presented some time or other by the other nation being seriously offended. We can be easily impressed by friendliness and good-will,—perhaps too easily,—but certainly never by threats. WE GERMANS FEAR GOD, BUT WE FEAR NOTHING ELSE IN THIS WORLD ; and it is the fear of God which induces us to love and cultivate peace." [1]

This was the last of Bismarck's more important speeches, and in the opinion of many the greatest of them all. Its delivery consumed nearly two hours, and during that time Bismarck refreshed himself with more than a dozen glasses of water. It was a mighty effort for a man nearly seventy-three, and these short extracts do it little justice. It must be taken as a whole, and it represented in itself the chancellor's whole public career. It was felt to be a justification of his life-work, and brought to the Reichstag a realizing sense of the man's greatness as never before,—especially that he was at heart a man of peace, and had brought with him a sword so that he might establish peace on an enduring basis. After the oration was finished Count von Moltke came forward and, ascending the steps to the chancellor's table, shook hands with him and congratulated him on his unusual success. The Reichstag then adjourned and escorted the chancellor to the Radziwill Palace in a body, while the audience who had listened in the galleries dispersed and filled Berlin with their enthusiastic accounts of it.

When the army bill came to a final decision all parties

---

[1] Bismarck's Speeches, Speemann ed., xvi. 135. Speech delivered February 6.

united in its support, except the Social Democrats, whose votes were the only ones cast in opposition to it. The London *Times* said, next morning, "The passage of Bismarck's bill for the increase of the German army will give an effectual chill to the belligerent party in France; nor is it likely that we shall hear any more for the present about campaigns for revenge." This proved to be true, and, though twelve or more years have passed since the speech was delivered, there has been no further need of legislation on the subject, nor have the French people required further admonition. Boulanger's downfall followed close upon it (February and March, 1888), so that it almost might seem as if one were the consequence of the other. His turbulent agitation led to his court-martial for insubordination as an army officer, and he was dismissed from the service. He then obtained an election to the Chamber of Deputies, where he distinguished himself by equally violent harangues and by his duel with Floquet, the president of the assembly. A year later he was charged with embezzlement while minister of war, and went into voluntary exile to escape conviction. It was found, however, by a trial election that he had a million supporters among the voters of the French people.

CHAPTER XVI.

DURING the last years of Bismarck's parliamentary service he presented a picture of terrible and almost demoniac energy. Seated behind his chancellor's table, in the white uniform of the Magdeburg Guards, with a stiff yellow collar and gold epaulets, his perfectly bald cranium (much larger than the average man's) rose above his shaggy white brows, which half concealed the nebulous eyes, whose falcon-like gleams flashed through the chamber at every fresh statement or telling argument of his opponents. His stubby nose, obstinate as Martin Luther's, heavy white mustache, and firmly set chin completed a portrait unlike any other in the present century.

More impatient than ever, more determined of his points, and more indifferent to appearances, his oratory was such as might have made a child laugh, or excited a feeling of contempt in a young lady of fashion, but there was neither laughter nor contempt for it in the Reichstag. Towering awkwardly above his table, swaying slightly to the rhythm of his sentences, nervously clutching his coat-buttons, the papers on his desk, or any other object that might be within his reach, he poured forth sentence after sentence of the most telling argument, not like a man who is reading from a book, but rather as if he were writing out his statement, hesitating and revising it as he went along. Sentence crowded on sentence as if one were pushing another out of his mind. Meanwhile, he would continually refresh himself with what appeared to be water, but which was well known to contain a homœopathic quantity of alcoholic stimulant.

When the debate in the Reichstag became tedious Bismarck sometimes retired to an anteroom on the same floor, where he could continue his work to better advantage. On one occasion when he did so the Radicals and Socialists made a desperate attack on some measure he had in hand, and challenged him to come out and reply to it on the floor, and not insult the Reichstag by his absence while it was in session. The chancellor stepped to the door of his room, and informed them that he could hear all that was necessary and essential of their remarks where he was; which did not much improve the temper of his adversaries. Bismarck had long since become a privileged character, even to Emperor William, and, like all such, was often a trial to his friends and an aggravation to others. No man could be more polite or considerate if one happened to catch that side of his nature, but when his thoughts were absorbed in great designs he paid little attention to those about him. His sleeplessness was a national inconvenience, and the most important affairs were sometimes obliged to wait for days until he felt equal to the transaction of business.

That Bismarck was sometimes abusive in the heat of debate is not to be denied. He was in the habit of complaining that his opponents distorted the facts in their statements and misrepresented his own. He sometimes complained of their mendacity, when the truth might be a matter of opinion. At the same time, his friends have always asserted that he never intentionally "struck below the belt," and his arguments in his speeches which have been published are not of the sophistical sort. On one occasion, when he animadverted on the Socialists for their vote upon the army bill, and one of them called "Pfui" (fie) to him, Bismarck rejoined, "Whoever says 'pfui' to me is insulting. As a Christian I may pocket it, but as chancellor of the empire I must resent it, and inform my opponent that I can return insult for insult. We did not make war on France in order to be inoculated by fifteen or twenty Socialists in our own country. The member must understand that this assembly is a meeting of gentlemanly and orderly persons, and if he meets with different treatment here it is because he introduces it himself."

This was called Bismarck's broadsword style, and it is one which he frequently resorted to. Plato, and not Menander

as Goethe says, was the first to preach that it is better to
endure insults than to return them, but it is to be feared that
such an elevated code would hardly appeal to a class of men
like the German Socialists. They would probably have looked
upon it as a confession of weakness, and weakness in Bismarck's position, either real or imaginary, was not to be
thought of. He said himself, in regard to the behavior of the
French troops in killing wounded Germans on the battle-field,
that their wars against barbarians in Algeria, Mexico, and
Cochin China had made them also semi-barbarous. So Bismarck, in his long parliamentary warfare with the Socialists,
had acquired something of the methods and manners of his
antagonists.

THE BATTENBERGER

The organization of the Balkan or Christian-Turkish states,
after the Congress of Berlin, proved a matter of unusual difficulty. There was a conflict of Russian, Turkish, and English interests in most of them which left the native population
small chance to express its own wishes. The only one, however, whose fortunes are directly connected with the life of
Bismarck is Bulgaria, of which Prince Alexander of Battenberg was chosen ruler by the national assembly, with the
advice and consent of the signatory powers, in April, 1879,
and in July he was crowned in the capital of Sofia, and commenced his rule in a vigorous and conservative manner. As
the national assembly proved too radical for his ideas he dissolved it and required fresh elections. As this did not help
the matter much he resorted to a *coup d'état*,—supposed to
have been instigated at St. Petersburg,—dissolved the assembly again and abolished the constitution. Thus we find him
at the outset of his reign acting under Russian influences,
and in direct opposition to the wishes of the Bulgarians, who
are, however, an ignorant and uncultivated people, by no
means well fitted for self-government.

The war followed between Servia and Bulgaria in consequence of the annexation of East Roumelia, and the victorious Bulgarians, having arms in their hands, demanded the

restoration of the constitution, and, though this was opposed by a majority of the officers, especially those of higher grades, Prince Alexander concluded it was best to comply. This placed him, however, between two fires, and his position was certainly a difficult one. A foreigner, and separated from those about him by the gulf of authority, and perhaps also influenced by the Crown Princess of Prussia, it was inevitable that Alexander of Battenberg should seek encouragement against Panslavism in the direction where it was most easily obtained. Unfortunately, this was in a quarter whence he was likely to derive the least material support. It was soon rumored in St. Petersburg that Alexander was acting under English advice, and directing the policy of Bulgaria in the interests of Great Britain. That there was some truth in this is plainly apparent from the course of subsequent events. Alexander travelled about his principality in company with the English envoy in rather an ostentatious manner; and nothing could have been more imprudent, for it not only offended the Russians, but diminished the respect felt for him by his own people. It was considered undignified as well as impolitic. There can be no doubt that he listened to the advice of the English envoy, and received from him expectations of support which were not afterwards fulfilled. There was, in fact, little that the British cabinet could do to sustain him in his position, except through a tedious course of diplomatic manœuvring. The blow which prostrated him was too sudden to be parried by diplomacy. Only Bismarck could have saved him, and he does not appear to have consulted the German chancellor at this juncture. Alexander of Battenberg was nephew to the Tsar Alexander, and that, in the strained relations between England and Russia, he should have permitted himself to be influenced by English interests in opposition to his own kindred exasperated the Tsar and helped to precipitate the events which followed.

On the night of August 21, 1886, his prime minister Karaveloff entered the royal palace, accompanied by a delegation of other officials, and announced to Prince Alexander that Bulgarian opinion was dissatisfied with the policy he was pursuing, and that his deposition was in order. The conspiracy had been kept so perfectly secret that Alexander was astonished, and knew not how to help himself. " I see no friends here," he said ; " I cannot resist you." [1] This reply was dignified but conclusive.

He was escorted by a detachment of Russian cavalry to Widdin, and thence on board ship to Severin in Roumania, where he was set at liberty. Great indignation was expressed at this outrage in Vienna and London, but the indignation in Germany was of an unofficial character. The Roumanian people, and especially the citizens of Sofia, felt that the nation had been insulted by this clandestine removal of their chief magistrate, and expressed themselves accordingly. Under cover of this popular outcry Alexander returned from Austria in a few days, but he found that the conspiracy against him was so wide-spread, and implicated so many of the highest officials, that he decided to resign in a dignified manner and returned to Germany. He is reported to have said that to have punished the guilty would have involved a massacre, and was practically impossible.

Immediately on the return of the Battenberger he was invited to Berlin by the Crown Prince of Prussia and entertained with every mark of distinction.[2] Upon this there were not wanting others to follow so illustrious an example, and newspapers, taking their cue from the heir to the imperial throne, raised a chorus of denunciation against the Bulgarian conspiracy, with slightly disguised insinuations concerning the Russian government. Bismarck, however, said gruffly that Alexander would have done better if he had not fished in troubled waters. The attention of the crown prince and princess plainly indicated the origin of a policy which, if it had been permitted to continue, might have taken a permanent

---

[1] Despatch to the Vienna *Press*, August 23, 1886.

[2] The London *Times* was furious. It said : " The arrogance of Russia and the fall of Alexander were due directly to the cynical attitude of Germany and, in a less degree, of Austria-Hungary. . . . Prince Bismarck has been willing to give Russia a ' free hand' in order to lessen the chances of a Russo-French alliance."

root. Emperor William was now eighty-nine, and though apparently in robust health, so that he surprised his attendants by the slight assistance he required, it was equally certain that the crown prince, with his English wife and British proclivities, might any day be called to the throne. Lord Salisbury had succeeded Gladstone, and wiseacres predicted that the Home-Rule agitation would give him a long lease of power. Then Bismarck would go out of office, and an anti-Russian alliance would be formed between England and Germany. That the crown prince should have been so destitute of political judgment as to lend himself to such an intrigue, which could only result in disasters to Germany, even if it brought advantage to Great Britain, seems almost incredible, but his subsequent course renders the fact incontestable. The old emperor, more and more devoted to his son, appeared to be oblivious of what was going forward right under his eyes, and Bismarck may have considered it the most prudent course not to call his attention to it.

The demonstrations at Berlin in favor of the Battenberger, however, were too conspicuous not to attract attention in St. Petersburg, and they had even become the subject of diplomatic correspondence before the surprising announcement was made that an alliance was in prospect between Prince Alexander and the daughter of the crown prince, Victoria's grand-daughter. Already two years previous the crown princess had attempted to bring this about, but William I. had set his foot down that it should not be done, for reasons of state expediency. Too much depends on alliances between sovereign houses to permit personal inclination to have much of a share in them. Now the courtship was being renewed with better prospect of success. The crown prince did not oppose it, and Victoria encouraged it, but a murmur of dissatisfaction went through Germany from east to west. Bismarck perceived that a storm was coming and prepared himself to meet it. It appears to have been at this time that he promised the Tsar that so long as he remained chancellor the Battenberger should never marry into the Prussian royal family. The excitement suddenly subsided again, and nothing more was heard of the proposed match for nearly a year.

Apart from its moral character the kidnapping of Prince Alexander was a stroke of genius. Bismarck and Count Kalnoky knew the situation perfectly, and would no doubt have interfered in favor of the Battenberger if he had been the right man for Bulgaria.[1] They understood what the editor of the *Times* failed to consider, that the Tsar of Russia, though nominally an autocrat, was no more a free agent than an English schoolmaster is; that there were two parties in Russia, the Panslavists and the party of peace, and that, although the Tsar belonged to the latter and supported it, he was also obliged to conciliate the former or have his way blocked for him in every direction. They realized that it was their duty to assist Alexander III. in this, so far as they could, for the good of Germany and Austria. The Tsar needed all the help he could get, and this fact sufficiently explains Bismarck's attitude towards the Bulgarian abduction. Kalnoky's reticence is also significant. The Austrian government did not fail to interfere from lack of a bold policy, as was proved soon afterwards, but evidently because the emperor and Kalnoky did not consider it expedient.

The following April Prince Ferdinand of Saxe-Coburg was chosen by the signatory powers, and accepted by the Bulgarian assembly, as the Battenberger's successor. He does not appear to have encountered the same difficulties as Alexder, but proved, on the whole, an acceptable ruler to the Slavic population.

In the summer of 1887 Emperor William resorted to Ems as usual, and visitors from foreign countries were astonished to see a sovereign of ninety years so bright in mind, erect in his carriage, and elastic in his step. Optimists predicted that he might yet become a centenarian; but the man who had

---

[1] Minchin says: "He knew, no doubt, that English sympathy was with him, but that material aid was not forthcoming from that quarter. If he had only had Bismarck on his side he might have remained, but the German chancellor had become the colleague of the Russian chancellor."—The Balkan Peninsula, p. 296.

never yet known misfortune was doomed to a severe disappointment in the last hour of his life. The crown prince was already troubled with a slight swelling in his throat, but this was not sufficiently advanced for the doctors to give a decided opinion in regard to it. Early in the autumn it began to be whispered in Berlin that the crown prince's trouble was of a malignant nature, but an English physician, Sir Morrell McKenzie, who had been sent for by the crown princess, made a public denial of this. The popular impression that if the prince was mortally ill he could not, by Prussian usage, succeed to the throne if it became vacant, has been denied by Bismarck in his memoirs. Emperor William was not, apparently, deceived by this stratagem, and recognized the true nature of the malady with fearful clearness. His physical condition changed so much that it seemed as if he preferred not to live, in order that his son might at least leave his name upon the list of German emperors. Bismarck desired to have a regent appointed on account of the age of William and the invalid condition of the crown prince; but William deferred the matter to his son, who either objected to the plan or postponed its consideration. On the approach of cold weather the crown prince was advised by Dr. McKenzie to go to Mentone on the Gulf of Genoa, where he would not only enjoy a more favorable climate, but also his condition could be more easily concealed. It is said that from this time the old emperor did nothing but weep, until he finally died, on the 9th of March, within two weeks of his ninety-first birthday. He was interred in the royal church at Potsdam, where the dust of Frederick the Great rests in a metal casket. Never had Berlin beheld such funeral obsequies, for not only did the position of the man recall the grandeur of the Hohenstaufens, but all Europe respected his character as one that would have distinguished him in a private station, and was the finest jewel in the imperial crown. It is with rather too much effort, however, that his successors attempt to designate him as William the Great. Such a title falls to the lot of few in history, and only by universal acclamation. Compared with Frederick, or Charlemagne, or Alexander he does not appear to such advantage as he does among the sovereigns of his own time.

The crown prince was in a very low condition at Mentone, but he decided at once to return to Berlin and take the reins of government in hand for the short time that remained to him on earth. He signed himself Frederick, without the William, as if to designate that he was the true successor of Frederick II., and to this his military reputation gave him some title. King Humbert of Italy intercepted him *en route*, having made a day's journey for the purpose, and held an interview with him in the railway carriage. Frederick said to him, " I face my malady as I did the bullets of Königgrätz and Wörth." The day after he arrived at Berlin, Frederick III. summoned Bismarck to his couch, received him cordially, and conversed eagerly on public affairs so long as he was able, the empress remaining in the chamber all the while. The following day Bismarck called again, and finding the empress also with him, showed some embarrassment, and finally explained to the emperor that he could not converse with such freedom as he would like in the presence of a third person. The empress accordingly withdrew. It is probable that the Battenberg marriage was brought forward by Frederick during these first days of his authority, and that Bismarck respectfully but firmly refused to consider it, so the matter remained in abeyance.[1]

On March 21 an imperial edict was issued, authorizing the Crown Prince William to act for his father in the consideration or settlement of such state affairs as the emperor should submit to his decision ; and a few days later the project of a marriage between Prince Alexander of Battenberg and the Princess Victoria was again brought forward. Now the storm broke, not only in the royal palace but throughout Prussia. Bismarck declared that he would resign before such a catastrophe should happen in the affairs of Germany. He argued that the marriage was particularly objectionable to the

---

[1] Bismarck alleges that Frederick III. was glad of his support at this critical moment, as against the pressure of his wife and her relatives.

Tsar, and would be certain to disturb the good understanding between the two governments, which for so many years had rested on a most delicate balance, and required the greatest care for its preservation. "I should have been false to my old master and remiss in my duty to the Fatherland," he stated afterwards, "if I had not exercised all my influence against giving to the Battenberger the advantage of this distinction." That he felt any personal animosity to the prince is quite improbable, but he considered the welfare of nations of more importance than the sentiments of individuals.

Not only the ministry supported Bismarck, but most of the Prussian newspapers and members of the Reichstag. When he threatened to resign petitions were drawn up to Emperor Frederick, signed by notable members of the Conservative and National Liberal parties, urging him to retain the chancellor in office. The people who conversed in beer-gardens, the soldiers on duty, even the newsboys in the street, were of one opinion in regard to the proposed marriage. Everybody seemed to understand the question at issue except Frederick himself. The Crown Prince William was inclined at first to support the cause of his sister, for whom he felt a great affection; but Bismarck either satisfied him or talked him over, so that he also joined the opposition, though this brought him in conflict with his own mother. With a dying sovereign and a refractory heir apparent the idea of dispensing with Bismarck's services was not to be thought of. The situation was too critical to permit of such a radical change in state affairs. Queen Victoria started for Berlin to assist the cause of her daughter, but her presence there only served to pour oil on the flames. No people conscious of their own dignity can brook foreign interference in their domestic affairs, and this only served to increase the odium which was now felt towards all the Guelfs. The papers openly declared that the empress was sacrificing Germany to English interests, and that though she had lived so long among them she still remained a foreigner, and could only be considered as a foreigner.

To the emperor this seemed like personal abuse, and he

blamed the ministry for not preventing it and prosecuting the editors, as they had a legal right to do. One of the last acts of his life was to remove Von Putkammer, who was Bismarck's nephew-in-law, from the ministry on this ground. The day before his death, however, he performed an act of magnanimity for which he should always receive due credit: he summoned Bismarck again to his chamber, called for the empress, and, though speechless, joined their hands in his presence. Bismarck was the man to appreciate such an action, and accepted this reconciliation with his former enemy in his most gracious manner.

Frederick III. reigned exactly ninety-nine days, and Germany lost two emperors within four months. After his death his widow retired to her castle at Kromberg, near Frankfort-on-the-Main, where she still continues to reside, with a yearly income of four hundred thousand marks from the German people, who have not yet forgotten the Battenberg intrigue, and pay it very unwillingly. So ended Bismarck's last great struggle.

FREEDOM LIVES HENCE

William II. commenced his reign on June 18, 1888, amid a lively journalistic agitation caused by the Battenberg affair in England and America. It was said that he and his father never could agree; that he virtually imprisoned his mother after ascending the throne; that he was very ambitious, and would certainly lead Germany into endless difficulties; that he hated the English, and intended to make war on France; that he intended to annex Denmark; that he had a withered arm, and that there was an ancient prophecy in regard to this which boded no good.

There was a certain coloring for these assertions in the fact that William had already shown himself a stubborn and self-willed young man, what the Germans call "starrkopf;" but Maria Teresa used to call Joseph II. "starrkopf," and he was the best sovereign that Austria ever had. The true explanation for the condition of his arm is that when he was a baby his mother employed an English nurse, who dropped him on his right shoulder, and so injured the arm-socket that an operation was afterwards required, and his arm was rendered practically useless. Of course, German women of a certain class all believe that if the nurse had been a German this accident would not have happened, and it is thought that the servants about the prince during boyhood instilled this notion into his head. The suffering which it has caused him is apparent in the expression of his face, which otherwise is frank and manly. He has not, however, the intellectual breadth of his father, or the finely proportioned dignity of his grandfather. He looks like a person of more energy than brains.

He was not long in giving proof that he intended to manage his own affairs. No sooner was he crowned than he started on an iron-clad voyage to Cronstadt, for an interview with Alexander III. Immediately on his return to Berlin he went to visit the venerable Francis Joseph in Vienna. What did Francis Joseph think of him? From Vienna he proceeded to Rome for an interview with King Humbert, and to pay his respects to Leo XIII. If he treated the others in the same manner as the pope, there could not have been much satisfaction in these imperial visits. Leo afterwards stated: " I would have liked to have conversed with the Emperor of Germany on politics, but as soon as I entered on the subject he introduced me to his brother, and I did not see much more of him." His characteristics belong to the Guelfs rather than the Hohenzollerns, and in certain traits he resembles his uncle, the Prince of Wales.

It is also true that, having been brought up amongst the most distinguished men of his time, and educated in great events, he has the kind of ambition which naturally arises from this. He wishes to do something to distinguish himself, but does not quite know how. In fact, there is nothing at present of special importance for him to do, except to run the machine which Bismarck and others have constructed; and this, with a corps of assistants who have been trained up at the court of William I., is by no means difficult. He has attempted some slight innovations, but most of them have

failed to pass the Reichstag, and have not been supported by
public opinion. His desire to improve the physical condition
of the German people, who so often suffer from over-study or
from exclusive devotion to one employment, is a commend-
able one. "I want able-bodied men for my army," he said,
"and not invalids with spectacles." At the same time, Germany would not be Germany unless it were the best educated
of nations; and the most important reform in this direction—
that of exchanging their mediæval black-letter, which causes
so much short-sightedness, for Roman type—does not seem
to have occurred to him.

The alarmists forgot—or probably never troubled themselves to learn—that the Emperor of Germany has no constitutional right to declare aggressive war without the consent
of the Kings of Saxony, Bavaria, and Würtemberg; so that
William II., even if he desired to play the *rôle* of a conquering
hero, would find himself shut off in this direction at the very
commencement; and he is, besides, too kindly and good-
humored a man to deliberately sacrifice the lives of his people
for personal glory. Whether he possesses the military genius
which has appeared so frequently in the Hohenzollern family
may never be known; but he is endowed with one talent which
is rare, if not unique, among persons born in his position,—the
gift of speech-making. Under the most favorable circumstances he might not become a great orator; but there is no
man like him to dedicate a statue, or to make an address
to a delegation of citizens. His speeches are not eloquent,
but nicely finished, and delivered with grace and facility. At
first he showed a tendency to make injudicious statements,—
as when he advised the Bavarian army that they should make
up their minds to shoot at their fathers and brothers if he
ordered them to do so,—but as he grows older he has become more prudent in this respect.

Closely allied to this is his talent for dramatic situations—
for grand public effects. Some people are born actors and
actresses from the cradle, and in such cases it rarely happens
that they discover the fact themselves. The newswriter who
spoke of William II. as the Edward Irving of the political

stage was not much out of the way. Neither is it difficult to see through these performances, and they give to the present emperor's actions an air of unreality which detracts from the dignity of his position.

William II. sent fine-sounding telegrams from foreign courts to the government at Berlin, but these had the less value because any information of real importance which he had to communicate would not have been made public. After his return the wheels of state moved smoothly enough; Bismarck and Moltke were treated with distinguished honors; the Battenberg marriage was relegated to the limbo of unsuccessful intrigues, and the shrewdest weather-prophets could not discover a cloud on the political horizon. The only question seemed to be how many years longer could Bismarck's strength suffice for his arduous position. In October, 1889, Alexander III. paid William II. a return visit at Berlin, with mutual assurances of good-will and peaceable intentions. As a matter of fact, the peace of Europe was not in the slightest danger, but there is a continual change in the political panorama to which the minds of statesmen are obliged to adjust themselves. In January, 1890, there was an Industrial Congress held at Berlin to consider the condition of the laboring classes, which was largely attended by delegates from other countries, though not in an official manner. William II. expressed a decided interest in this subject, and there is no reason for doubting his sincerity. Already, in the spring of 1889, when a widely extended strike of mill operatives took place, he summoned a delegation of the disaffected workmen to Berlin, inquired into their grievances, and appointed a board of commissioners to adjust their difficulties; but he also informed them that such independent demonstrations could not be permitted in the future, as they inflicted injury on too large a number of persons who were in no ways responsible for them. If the working-men had good cause for complaint they should apply to him and he would order an investigation.

A council of state was convened at Berlin on February 14, 1890, for a consideration of the labor question, and William II. presided in person. He made an excellent opening address, in which he reviewed the objects of the convention, and said especially:

"The state council should endeavor to frame a scheme for the protection of working-men from the arbitrary systems and operations of employers by which gross advantage is taken of their needs and their inability to help themselves by any other means than the desperate remedy of strikes. It should also attempt to protect women and children against protracted hours of labor. At the same time due regard should be given as to how far German industry will bear the increased burdens thus placed on the cost of production without jeopardy to Germany's position as a competitor in the markets of the world. If that is overlooked the changes I propose, instead of resulting in the improvement I desire, would lead to the deterioration of the working-men's position. To avert this danger a great measure of wise reflection will be needed. The settlement of these questions is essential as bearing upon the agreement as to labor questions, which, it is to be hoped, we shall establish through an international conference."

This is rather better than the average of convention addresses. The young emperor had evidently taken up the subject in earnest and in full confidence that he could improve the relations between the government and the Social Democrats by persuading the laboring classes that he was really their friend. He had yet to learn how impossible this is, and that what the socialists actually desire is not charity but *power*, and the subversion of society in order to obtain this.

This convention was followed by an imperial rescript on the labor question, of which Bismarck disapproved, and, as the subsequent elections resulted unfavorably for the government, Bismarck was convinced that this action of the young emperor had produced an injurious effect on public opinion. Dr. Busch tells us that on the 24th inst. Bismarck's secretary came to him for the purpose of suggesting that he should write a letter to the London *Daily Telegraph* expressing this opinion and explaining the influence of the rescript according to the chancellor's theory. Although the letter was not published, and, if it had been, could hardly be considered

in the light of an intrigue, it was an indirect proceeding
which, if it had come to the emperor's knowledge, would certainly have caused great indignation. Whether Bismarck was
responsible for other proceedings of a like nature at this time,
we do not know, but it is certain that William II. became
suspicious that his chancellor was not dealing fairly with him.

In April the anti-socialist law would come up for consideration in the Reichstag for the fourth time, and a definite
government programme must be decided on previously.
Whether the emperor desired to have it die a natural
death, or wished for some modification of it which Bismarck considered impracticable, still remains uncertain, but
as soon as their disagreement became known in the ministry
it suddenly called into existence an anti-Bismarck clique, the
leader of which was Von Bötticher, minister of the home
department.[1] As already stated, Bismarck had for some
years previously been practically emperor, and his colleagues
often felt this severely. It had long been a saying that Bismarck considered himself infallible; and no wonder if he did.
He had long passed the age when a general in the army
would have been retired from active service. However, a
majority of the ministry and of other high officials of the
government still considered him indispensable, and were willing to endure much for the advantage which they supposed
he might still be to the state. Others were of the opinion
that he was already too old and could as well be dispensed
with.

"Suspicion," says Auerbach, "is a monster with a thousand eyes." About this time it also appears that Von Bötticher insinuated to his imperial highness that Bismarck was
almost living upon morphia,—was obliged to use it all the
time; a base and groundless calumny. Yet no evidence has
come to light that Bismarck was dealing less frankly and
sincerely with William II. than he always had with William I.; nor was there in his directions to Dr. Busch anything more than he had stated openly to the emperor himself.

---

[1] Same as secretary of the interior.

It is significant that when he requested Dr. Busch to have some important documents copied for him, and the latter suggested that there was. danger that the copyist would retain copies of his own, Bismarck replied, "I care little if he does; I have nothing to conceal."

One of Bismarck's first requests of William II. had been to reinstate Von Putkammer in his former position in the ministry, and the emperor agreed to do so after a certain time had elapsed; but when Bismarck mentioned the matter again William II. declined to reinstate Von Putkammer, on the ground that he had become accustomed to his successor, Von Herrfurth, as under-secretary of state, and did not wish to part with him. It was not long after this before Bismarck discovered that Von Herrfurth was holding consultations with the emperor without making any report to the chancellor concerning them. This was contrary to the order of September 8, 1852, which made the minister-president responsible for the policy of the ministry as a whole. It was not until February, 1890, however, that Bismarck considered it advisable to make a decided protest against this, and the immediate consequence was that William II. requested him to draft an order revoking the decree of 1852, by which the relations of the minister-president and his colleagues were regulated. Bismarck declined to do this, and the emperor's next move was to substitute a request that Bismarck should resign his position in the Prussian ministry and retain that of foreign affairs for the German empire. This would have placed Bismarck in an embarrassing position in which he would have been deprived of all direct influence in government affairs. How far Bismarck had encroached upon the prerogatives of his fellow-ministers during his long term of office it is impossible to determine, but there can be no doubt that he had done so to some extent.

For the events that followed only two explanations are possible: either that the emperor was suspicious of Bismarck and feared that he was secretly working to prevent the fulfilment of the agreement between them, or, what is more probable, that he had previously made up his mind to remove the chancellor, and deliberately forced a quarrel with him for that purpose. The motive in one case would be as little to his credit as was his method in the other.

On or about the 15th of March Dr. Windhorst made a call at the Radziwill Palace. This was an exceptional occurrence, but there was no reason why it should attract particular attention, for the two old antagonists had been on cordial terms for the past ten years, and entertained a mutual respect for each other's abilities. Whether William II. was suspicious that Bismarck intended to play false with him in regard to the anti-socialist bill, and wished to make Windhorst his accomplice in the transaction, or whether he was merely seeking a pretext for a quarrel, he pretended to be highly displeased at this interview, and sent a peremptory request (as we may judge by Dr. Busch's statement) to the chancellor not to hold secret consultations with members of the Reichstag.

Such a message was insulting and tyrannical. The emperor would seem to have thought that he was back in the age of Frederick the Great, instead of being the sovereign of constitutional Germany. He had no more right to deliver such an order than Bismarck had to make the same request of him. Would it have been wiser if the chancellor had taken no notice of this affront? If it was suspicion by which William II. was actuated, the thunderstorm might have passed over without taking effect; but if the emperor wished for a rupture with his prime minister the insult would certainly have been repeated. Bismarck acted with his customary frankness. He sent back word that it was impossible to comply with such a request; and this was perfectly true, for if he declined all visits from members of the Reichstag it would certainly cause great offence and produce inextricable confusion among supporters of the government.

William II. then sent a notification to Bismarck that his resignation would be acceptable; and Bismarck replied to this with an inquiry for the reasons for his dismissal. Having received no reply to this request, after a proper interval Bismarck tendered his resignation to the emperor with a statement of his own reasons for doing so. This was followed by an order from the emperor for him to leave Berlin and retire to his estates.

The Countess von Krockrow states that the last interview between the emperor and his first chancellor was a stormy one, and common report in Germany supports this opinion. Bismarck, however, has denied this, and there is no authentic testimony in its favor. The anonymous author of " Bismarck and the Emperor" declares that at no time previous to his writing had Bismarck learned what were the actual reasons for his dismissal. He continues:

" One can say, therefore, that Bismarck asked for the cause of his dismissal from a fourfold reason: first, out of respect for the German nation, which felt such heartfelt sympathy with all the important events in politics, and especially in Bismarck's life; secondly, out of respect for the office itself, the dignity of which had become a part of himself; thirdly, out of regard to his successors; and, fourthly, out of regard for his personal susceptibility,—certainly enough reasons to warrant his demanding for the cause. He never received an answer.

" Considering, therefore, the absolutely mysterious manner of his dismissal (forced resignation), it can easily be conceived that in Bismarck's head, as well as in the heart of the nation, all possible and impossible reasons were discussed in regard to an event of such deep import. Bismarck, at last, came to suspect intrigues and cabals, and probably still keeps to this idea. The people, on the other hand, showed a hankering for more dramatic motives, and thus it happened that not only at that time but even to-day, after five years, those that made the most noise have the greatest chance of being believed."

It would be surprising if some temper had not been displayed on this occasion, for Bismarck must have been raging with indignation. Looked at from any point of view, it was outrageous treatment for a time-honored public servant, whose intentions had never once been mistrusted in an employment of nearly forty years. However, all that we know of the interview with certainty is Bismarck's expression, " The will of his Majesty the Emperor has its boundary at the door of my wife's drawing-room." ' This was a fitting reply, and ought to have brought William II. to his senses. The form of statement would indicate that the interview took place at the Radziwill Palace,—and that a request for the chancellor's resignation followed it. Bismarck in the letter published after his death by Dr. Busch gives his reasons in full for resigning, and claims that the emperor had imposed limits on his official position which did not permit him either to retain a proper share in the transaction of state business and its supervision, or freedom of action in ministerial decisions, or for such communications with members of the Reichstag as his constitutional responsibility required. He also declares that it would be impossible for him to carry out the instructions which the emperor had lately submitted to him with respect to foreign affairs. He finally concluded in this wise : "According to the impressions I have received during the last few weeks, as well as communications from your Majesty's military and civil household, I may assume that my request to resign agrees with your Majesty's wishes, and that I may, therefore, certainly rely upon its gracious acceptance." He was accordingly dismissed from office on March 20 with a request to retire to his own estates. This was really the most politic course which Bismarck could have adopted, for it compelled William II. to place himself on record in a way which would be condemned throughout Prussia, if not all Germany. To counteract this again, and obviate the evil consequences to his popularity, William pretended to feel the deepest regret at the ex-chancellor's departure ; created him Herzog von Lauenburg and a major-general in the army. It was now Bismarck's turn to play his last trump by declining these empty honors and retiring to Friedrichsruhe in sullen indignation. As an old reader of Shakspeare he may have said, like Kent in " King Lear,"—

"Fare thee well, king : since thus thou wilt appear,
Freedom lives hence, and banishment is here."

It was well enough that Bismarck should also pass through this experience, and know something of the evil side of fortune while he still lived on earth. Trouble enough he had met with before,—difficulties almost insuperable,—but here was a difficulty of a new order that he could not overcome. Looked at in its true light it was not a fall but a rise in life to him; but it does not appear that he accepted his dismissal in a philosophical manner.

When Von Beust was relieved by Francis Joseph from the highest position in the Austrian government, the emperor summoned him to his presence and merely said, " I am obliged to you for the assistance you have given me, but I shall no longer require your services." This was simple and dignified. If William II. had treated Bismarck in a similar manner they might always have continued to be friends.

It was now that Bismarck discovered who his best friends actually were. The rumor of his resignation had created surprise in Berlin, but as no one knew the actual facts little indignation was expressed. When, however, it was positively affirmed that he would leave the Radziwill Palace an immense crowd collected in front of the building, and, although this was contrary to law, the police made no attempt to interfere with it. As soon as Bismarck appeared to take his carriage to the railway he was greeted with prolonged and deafening cheers. Never since the news of the battle of Sedan had such enthusiasm been seen in the city. The crowd followed Bismarck's carriage to the station, where another great throng had collected; men wept and ran to his carriage-windows begging leave to kiss his hand. Bismarck was everything, the emperor was nothing; and it is easy to believe that the ex-chancellor made his journey homeward with a lighter heart than any member of the German government felt that day.

Bismarck's personal friends and political supporters received his dismissal in dignified silence. While the *North German Gazette*, which had always been Bismarck's stanch friend, spoke of the event as one which should not be considered in the light of either good or bad fortune, for the great

statesman had fairly accomplished the work of his life, and
at his present age he could not be expected to guide the
policy of the empire many years longer, the *Kreuz Zeitung*,
which was the organ of the court, congratulated the people
on the great things that had been accomplished by William I.
and Bismarck for Germany, but believed that the time had
come for a new departure. In the Reichstag, Count Stirum,
after waiting until Richter and other Socialist jackals had
vented their spite on the dead parliamentary lion, made a
simple and dignified eulogy of the character and achievements of the ex-chancellor in the name of the Conservatives
and National Liberals. Professor Haeckel, of Jena, came
out with an intrepid declaration, enough to show that free
speech is still possible in Germany. He declared that the
removal of Bismarck was a national calamity; that his days
of usefulness had by no means expired; and that Germany
never required his watchful eye and steady hand in its public
affairs more than at that moment.[1] Bismarck had his well-
wishers even in Paris, and a French count said of him at this
time, " He was the capstone of the edifice which he had constructed, and his retirement is a matter of serious concern
to all who take an interest in German national unity." In
America the event was looked upon of not so much importance in itself as indicative of the character and ambition
of William II. The choice of his successor created hardly
less surprise. General Caprivi had held the position, for some
years, of minister of the navy, and was a fairly efficient parliamentary speaker; but he was not considered a man of exceptional ability, nor had he acquired such experience as
might render him capable and fit for his exalted position.
Following after Bismarck, he was almost like a *reductio ad
absurdum*, and it was plain to many that the emperor's chief
motive was to give the impression that he governed Germany
himself, which he certainly could not do so long as Bismarck

---

[1] Haeckel also said, " It is deeply painful for us to find ourselves opposed in
this view to the personal opinion of Emperor William II. But our estimate is
the same as that which the emperor's grandfather had of Bismarck to the end
of his life."

remained at the head of affairs. It would have been better for his own reputation, however, as a man of sagacity, if he had continued Bismarck in office. How cutting to him must have been the silence of the ex-chancellor's friends!

From Berlin Bismarck went first to Potsdam, and entering the royal church of the Hohenzollern family, draped with the battle-flags captured by Frederick the Great, he knelt down before the sarcophagus of William I., and remained there several minutes in prayer or meditation; then to Friedrichsruhe, to pass the remainder of his days with the aged wife who had been his faithful support in all the difficulties and vicissitudes of his turbulent life. She lived to witness the reconciliation between her husband and William II.; and these last four years of peaceful retirement must have been a great satisfaction to her, whatever they may have been to Bismarck himself. " He who has been accustomed," says Goethe, in " Egmont," " to care for the welfare of millions, descends from the throne as into the grave." Bismarck's friends bear testimony that even at seventy-five he was as full of youthful ardor and as deeply interested in public affairs as thirty years before. The long-continued habit of masterful effort was fixed on him, and he could not, like Diocletian, relinquish the cares of an empire for a vegetable garden. The energy within him, swelling like an Alpine flood, must find an outlet, and any accident might determine what direction this would take.

Unluckily, Chancellor Caprivi, in his opening address to the Reichstag, had referred to his predecessor in no complimentary terms. The late chancellor had often neglected to appear in the Reichstag when his presence was desired there; he had been remiss in suitable acts of courtesy to important members of the government; he had not permitted sufficient independence to the heads of departments; he had not treated his opponents with respect, nor his own party with consideration. " All these abuses," says Caprivi, " will be remedied in the new administration of affairs."

Can we suppose that the emperor directed Caprivi to make this statement? Certainly it was most injudicious, and could

not fail to give offence in many quarters; and though there
might be truth in it, Bismarck's venerable age would seem to
require the mantle of palliation for his moss-grown faults.
Immediately afterwards the *Kreuz Zeitung* published a succession of editorial paragraphs in regard to the change in the
ministry, in which various reasons were alleged for its necessity,—that a young emperor and an old chancellor could not
well agree together; that Bismarck was frequently absent at
Friedrichsruhe, attending to a saw-mill which he had erected
there, when public business required his presence in Berlin;
that he had been endeavoring to bring the young sovereign
entirely under his power, and prevent the youthful development of the emperor's personality. If there had been a complicated political problem on Bismarck's tablets at this time,
he might have taken slight notice of these cutting animadversions; but they came at a moment when he was least able to
endure them with patience and had no means of distracting
his mind from them. A warfare with Caprivi sprang up in
this manner, which was continued in a number of newspapers; and this, which had begun in self-defence, extended
itself to the policy of the new administration, which Bismarck
criticised unmercifully whenever it disagreed with the plans
which he had himself laid down, until, finally, the emperor, in
1892, felt himself called upon to interfere, and threatened
Bismarck with prompt and earnest prosecution,[1] unless he
controlled the force of his invective.[2] Perhaps it was only
fair that Bismarck's own weapon against the socialists should
be finally turned against him in this manner. He even
thought of obtaining a seat in the Reichstag, or the electors
of his district may have suggested it to him, so that he could
combat his enemy face to face; but either his friends or his
own better judgment prevailed over this temptation, and he
declined to permit the use of his name. Yet there was an

---

[1] Especially in regard to the publication of the secret treaty between Germany
and Russia, in a Hamburg paper, which was considered a breach of state confidence; though, as Bismarck was no longer in the government service, what he
chose to divulge was a question of good judgment.

[2] Chancellor Caprivi's decree of May 23.

honorable precedent for this course in the proceedings of the
Earl of Chatham after his removal by George III.

To a delegation of manufacturers, who called to obtain his
opinion as to whether the expectation of continued peace on
the part of European governments was sufficiently good to
justify their making extensive improvements, he replied in a
rather ironical vein: "Yes, every government is grasping at
the latest offensive and defensive invention in firearms, and
each feels too weak to attack its neighbor. I think you can
depend on the present condition of political affairs lasting
for a long time to come." He received a great many such
delegations at Friedrichsruhe, and talked to every one of
them as if he were thoroughly versed in their profession or
business affairs. This was a new view of him to the German
people, and naturally served to increase his popularity. An
enthusiastic Teuton said of him in 1895: "If the blows which
the fiery hero has dealt right and left, from above and below,
so that they whistled through the air the last five years, had
hit their mark abroad instead of at home, Germany would
have been infinitely better off than she is now."

Caprivi's administration could not be called a success,
though it was far from being disastrous. He allowed the
anti-socialist law to go out of existence without gaining
thereby any votes for the support of the government. In
fact, the socialists appeared disappointed that their persecution had come to an end, for it gave them the only real importance they had. He found favor in England by slight
modifications of the tariff, and arranged commercial treaties
with Switzerland, Belgium, and Russia, which was supposed
to be a beginning towards a return to anti-Bismarck trade
regulations; but the German people as a whole did not wish
for this, and the newspapers opposed any further reduction.
A reactionary measure in regard to primary education, drafted
by Caprivi according to the emperor's wishes, was laid before
the Reichstag, but created such popular indignation that it
never came to a vote. The hand of William II. was also
visible in a measure to modify the organization of the army.
He wished to reduce the number of years of military service,

but in order to do so he would be obliged to increase the number of men in the standing army. This would have largely augmented the expense of the military budget, and was obstinately resisted on that account by the National Liberals. A majority of the German general staff officers were also opposed to it. Neither were his negotiations concerning the German territories in Africa and the Pacific such as gave satisfaction to the merchants who were interested in those new acquisitions. It was generally felt that the strong man was gone and a weak one had taken his place.

Count Herbert von Bismarck was appointed secretary of legation at London in 1882, and, having resigned two years later, in March, 1885, he was appointed special ambassador to the British government for the purpose of defining the frontiers of the new colonial territories. He was a popular person in London society, which for a German in those times was quite remarkable.[1] We do not hear of him again until June, 1892, when he went to Vienna to marry the Hungarian Countess Margaret Hoyos. There is a certain significance in the union of Bismarck's eldest son to a lady of that race, who indirectly owe their present independence to him. The alliance between Prussia and Hungary was thus repeated again in domestic life. Prince Bismarck and the Fürstin accompanied their boy, and were everywhere received, even in Dresden and Vienna, with the highest enthusiasm by the people; but the doors of government were closed against them. Mayors and deputations of prominent citizens waited on the Bismarck family with complimentary addresses, but there were no invitations from kings and princes. This may not have troubled the ex-chancellor very much, as seems likely when we recollect his remark to Abeken at the battle of Sedan, "For God's sake, let princes be princes." Even old Metternich, always subservient to royalty, could not help relieving his mind in regard to the *ennui* which his court life occasioned him. The wedding passed off happily, with any number of notable Magyars of the highest rank in attend-

---

[1] G. W. Smalley's letter to the *Tribune*.

ance; but the German people were displeased with the slight shown by the Vienna court to their national hero, and arranged a celebration for him on his return, which must have done much to console his spirits, if he required consolation. His daughter, Maria Elizabeth Johanna von Bismarck, had been married to Count Kuno von Rantzau some years previously.

An affecting episode occurred at the celebration of Bismarck's seventy-eighth birthday, when a delegation of friends and admirers called at Friedrichsruhe to congratulate him on the perfect completion of his life's work. In response to this compliment the prince attempted a eulogy of his former master, William I., but became completely unnerved in attempting to do his virtues justice. He wept bitterly when he said, "What could I have accomplished without him, and without our powerful army?" As soon as he could master himself he continued:

"Thanks to our Emperor William I. and his federated sovereigns, more was done than any diplomat could do. If the emperor had not ordered the mobilization of the armies of 1866–70, what would have become of Germany? As long as we can rely upon this true national feeling of our princes I shall not be alarmed for the future of the empire.

"I am not well enough to co-operate with you practically [hurrahs, and cries of 'Yes, you are'], but my ideas are with you, perhaps more than is proper for an old man like myself. You must hold fast to the national idea, and remember that in Prussia, also, we do not follow the Brandenburg or Prussian policy, but the imperial German policy. In this sense I call upon you for three cheers for the Kaiser."

The ex-chancellor retired for luncheon with the presidents of the bodies represented. The deputies departed for their homes on three special trains.[1]

Nothing could better indicate for us how Bismarck felt during this period of retirement.

---

[1] Despatch to the Associated Press.

The most dangerous movement of Gen. Caprivi's term did not come to the surface of parliamentary affairs, but was whispered about in government circles, discussed at court entertainments, and hinted at in the *Kreuz Zeitung* and other official publications. It was to the effect that German unity could not become complete until all governments in the country were abolished but one; that as France and Great Britain had but one capital, so Germany should have but one; that, Prussia having already absorbed Hanover, Cassel, and Nassau, there was nothing to prevent its taking possession of Saxony and the South German states in the same manner, and thus producing a truly homogeneous nation. That there were certain advantages to be derived from this, especially in the reduction of taxes, was not to be denied, and the old Prussian Particularist spirit revived under its influence.

Did this plan also originate with William II.? Was it one of the grand schemes by which he trusted to further civilization? It could only be accomplished by a violent revolution; and when a revolution once begins, who can predict the course it will take? At best it would have required the abrogation of the imperial constitution, and would have been a breach of faith towards the rulers of the smaller German states. It would have divided northern and southern Germany into two hostile camps, and probably have provoked a war with Russia. Bismarck felt no inclination for such a programme. He frowned upon it, and his frown scattered its adherents as a blast from the northwest scatters the clouds of an incipient rain. He spent the summer of 1893, as usual, at Kissingen, and on the third Sunday in August a delegation of seven hundred Thuringians came to pay him their compliments and presented an address to him.

In his reply the prince dwelt especially on the subject of German unity and the necessity of preserving the imperial constitution. He apprehended no further danger from France. The time was now past since the French regarded a campaign in Germany as a sort of pleasure excursion; but there was always some danger in view, and the present one lay in the direction of new experiments and innovations. He said:

LIFE OF BISMARCK

"I refer to the semi-official utterances directed towards the attainment of a 'greater Prussia.' I am sorry to see in the decline of my life the principles of the constitution being undermined by people who are trying to procure the centralization of the imperial power.

"My heart is no murderer's den. I have not learned to lie, even as a diplomat. The people now begin to see what I meant three years ago when I said here that the constitution ought to be the first object of care. The constitution is good. It cost hard work and blood and lives enough. I feel anxious lest it should be meddled with."

The amiability with which Bismarck received these continual deputations is not more remarkable than the manner in which he turned them to account.

THE RECONCILIATION

Bismarck had only three years and a half to wait for his revenge. At a banquet given at Königsberg, in old Prussia, in September, 1893, at which the emperor and many important magnates were present (but Chancellor Caprivi significantly absent), William II. made a stirring speech, in which he attacked the attitude of the Socialists towards the government as ungrateful and unconciliatory, and hinted strongly that it might be necessary to restore the penal code against them. This was a sufficient notification to Caprivi, as well as to the general public, that the emperor had gyrated, and a change of policy might be looked for. Count Eulenberg was requested by William II., at a meeting of the ministry, to draft a new set of anti-socialist laws; and it was not long after that before a personal attack on Eulenberg and his family appeared in the Cologne *Gazette*, and Eulenberg accused Caprivi to the emperor of having instigated it. Caprivi was requested by William II. to deny this if he could; but, having the fate of Von Arnim before his eyes, he concluded it would be preferable to hand in his resignation; and shortly afterwards (October, 1893) Eulenberg also resigned. Germany was electrified.

William II. must have perceived before this that he had

committed a blunder, and no doubt repented of his rashness. The Reichstag had refused to pass his new army bill, and had consequently been dissolved early in the summer. A fresh election had been ordered, but its prospects were not favorable for the government. The ungrateful Socialists paid no regard to the emperor's moderation, or to his interest in the Industrial Congress. What they evidently desired was to obtain possession of the government by force of numbers, and they would be content with nothing less. The National Liberals were disaffected, and would listen to no compromises. The emperor had come up against a blank wall, and found that he would have to take the back track. Bismarck's illness at Kissingen in the autumn of 1893 afforded a favorable opening. The emperor telegraphed to him a sympathetic message, and advised him not to return to the cold, cloudy region of Friedrichsruhe, but to accept his imperial hospitality at some residence in a milder climate. His telegram closed with the words, " I will consult with my court-marshal to designate the most suitable chateau for your Highness." Bismarck, however, was not the fox to be caught in such a trap, and had no intention of endorsing the emperor's policy before he knew what it was going to be. He therefore declined the offer politely, alleging that his trouble was a nervous one, and that the quiet and repose of his own home would be more favorable for him than any new and strange location.

There were many now who expected to see Bismarck recalled to the helm; but this was practically impossible. His present illness precluded it for the time being; he was seventy-nine, and the chances were that if reappointed he would have to be retired again in a year or two more. Old men are apt to forget that they are no longer equal to their former selves; and Prince Kaunitz, of Austria, continued in office until he became so senile that his secretaries were accustomed to trace his signature on public documents;[1] but that would not do for modern Germany. However, a chancellor might be found

---

[1] Annals of the Court of Austria, vol. ii.

who would agree with Bismarck, and could consult with him
on important occasions. Prince Hohenlohe-Schillingsfürst
would seem to be the man. He had been trained for the
diplomatic service under Bismarck's eye, and had held the
two most important positions connected with the German
government during the past twenty years. He had succeeded
Count Henry von Arnim as envoy at Paris, and had assisted
Bismarck in exposing Arnim's misdemeanors. When old
Manteuffel retired from his last post of duty, Hohenlohe succeeded him as military governor of Elsass and Lothringen,
and acquitted himself in that trying position with discretion
and good judgment. There was no one else so well qualified
to succeed to the chancellorship,—a man of rare accomplishments, and with a face beaming with intellectual life. The
German people were delighted, for they knew that public
affairs would now have the advantage of Bismarck's sage
counsel, although his hand might not appear in their management. Hohenlohe has proved the good genius of William II.

As yet there was no reconciliation, but an entering wedge
had been driven in. Bismarck's face looked brighter, and the
tone of his communications was more cheery. He again had
a hand in public affairs, for members of the Reichstag came
to Friedrichsruhe to consult with him on the army bill and
the Socialist laws. He advised them to support the former
with some modifications, and especially advocated a larger
number of non-commissioned officers. "Victory," he said,
"will rest with the side which wins the first battles, and non-
commissioned officers give the best support to the private
soldier." In regard to the laws against Socialists, he believed
that a long term of years would be required to give them a
proper trial. The trouble was a deep-seated one; but if the
laboring classes could finally be made to realize that no other
organization of society was possible, and that those who were
more fortunate than themselves were willing to share with
them, so far as this was feasible, the agitation would finally
die out of its own inertia. He did not regret that Caprivi's
experiment had been tried, for it showed conclusively that no

amount of toleration or magnanimity had much effect on the Socialists.

It was reported all over the world that at his Christmas dinner Prince Bismarck proposed and drank the health of the German emperor. Following this, on the 26th of January, 1894, William II. sent his aide-de-camp, Colonel von Moltke, to Friedrichsruhe with a bottle of Johannisberg,—called by a witty editor *Lachrymæ Caprivi*,[1]—and with an invitation to attend the emperor's birthday celebration on the following day at Berlin. There could be no more friendly testimonial than this, and Colonel von Moltke reported that Bismarck had accepted the olive-branch which was thus proffered to him. On the 27th the emperor met Bismarck unceremoniously at the railway station, shook hands with him, kissed him on both cheeks,—not the most pleasant subject for that purpose,—and accompanied him to the imperial palace, where he was made honorary colonel of the Seventh Cuirassiers, a famous regiment in Prussian history. The Cuirassiers escorted Bismarck back to the railway, amid the acclamation of thousands. The Berliners were delighted.

This ovation was succeeded by a visit of the emperor to Friedrichsruhe in the following month, and birthday presents on the first of April. The reconciliation might now be called complete, but it is questionable whether Bismarck and William II. were ever on wholly cordial terms again. The political capital which William II. made out of his visits to the ex-chancellor must have interfered with this, and Bismarck was finally obliged to call public attention to the fact that Prince Hohenlohe had introduced a certain measure in the Reichstag immediately after one of them, as if to give the impression that it resulted from a consultation with him, whereas it was a proposition for which he felt no inclination.

---

[1] After the wine made from the grapes on Vesuvius, called *Lachrymæ Christi*.

CHAPTER XVII

FÜRSTIN VON BISMARCK lived to see the good understanding renewed between her husband and the emperor, to her very great joy, but her death followed soon after this. As Jules Simon says, "Bismarck always wore his heart upon his sleeve,"—in private life one of the simplest and most unaffected men,—and he made no attempt to play the Spartan and disguise the irrevocable loss which he felt in the death of his life's companion. He hated publicity on such occasions, and the funeral ceremonies were only attended by the family and their nearest relatives. The emperor and empress sent messages of condolence, which we can believe in this instance were devoid of political purpose or any interested motive.

Bismarck, unlike Burleigh and many other statesmen, never attempted to advance his sons to positions beyond their true deserving. In 1895 his second boy, William, was appointed governor of East Prussia, and holds that position at the present date. The expectation that Herbert Bismarck would be employed in state affairs after his father's retirement has not been fulfilled,—and this, considering his training and experience, would seem to be a loss to the diplomatic service.

Bismarck's birthdays had now come to be affairs of European importance, and his eightieth, following so soon after the reconciliation, naturally became an exceptional occasion. There was even felt to be danger that his now fragile life would be crushed out of him by the accumulated attentions of injudicious admirers, and faithful Dr. Schweninger—the only man, it is said, whom Bismarck was ever afraid of—was on guard to protect him against the effects of over-exertion. The number of presents sent to him, not only from Germany but from all parts of the world (including a Chickering piano from the United States), filled three additional baggage-vans, and

412

were considered sufficient to refurnish Friedrichsruhe from gable to foundation. The railway station at Friedrichsruhe was decorated with banners of all the German states, and with the flags of the allies of Germany, besides being ornamented with boughs of evergreen. A company of infantry, a company of pioneers, a squadron of hussars, and a battery of artillery were ordered by the emperor to assemble at Ahmcule, the next station to Friedrichsruhe, where William II. himself alighted from a special train, and placing himself at the head of his small army marched with flying colors to Bismarck's residence.

On March 24 previous a complimentary resolution to Prince Bismarck had been defeated in the Reichstag by a narrow majority, but the emperor telegraphed the resolutions to Friedrichsruhe on his own responsibility. The London *Times* remarked at this: " There can be no question that the emperor's telegram to Bismarck expressed the true sentiments of the German people. The vote injured none but the Reichstag." It is difficult to see how it could in any manner injure an old man of eighty, who had retired from public life, and whose bitterest enemies could accuse him of nothing worse than they were guilty of themselves.

There is a noble kind of pathos in the gradual extinction of the powers of genius by the course of time, and we feel this especially in the old age of men like Michael Angelo and Bismarck. The hand moves on the dial, and the man changes with it irresistibly. As Emerson said at a much earlier period,—

> " I feel the hastening of the stream,
> I hear the roaring of the fall."

Not only Bismarck himself felt this, and his family felt it, but all Germany was conscious of the same thing, and dreaded the sudden shock which would take their world-hero from them. All that a man lives after eighty is a free gift of nature, and, though Bismarck's constitution evidently intended him for a centenarian, Dr. Schweninger forgot his sleepless nights, his late hours of concentrated work, his severe journeys, and mighty efforts in the Reichstag, when he opined that Bismarck might yet see his ninetieth year. Happy is the man on this advanced stage of life whose faith in God and immortality remains unshaken. We know that Bismarck had this faith. He did not believe, like the German physicists and the English Darwinians, in an impersonal, scientific deity, but in the God of Moses, Isaiah, and Luther—the God of heroes and sages and poets, whom all truly great and noble men have reverenced·in all centuries and countries. He believed also that he was accountable for his sins, but he must have been conscious that the main effort of his life (and such an effort as it was) had been for the good of his country, and through Germany for the good of mankind. Whatever he might be called to account for hereafter, he knew that the deadliest sin of the nineteenth century, the sin of cant, pretension, and hypocrisy, had left no stain upon his mantle. In fact, his whole public life had been a continual warfare against it. The constellation of great men of which he had formed the centre in middle life had all gone before him. William I., who had greeted him at court as " the young advocate of justice," and to whom he owed all his chances in life, was gone; Von Moltke, Manteuffel, the Crown Prince Frederick, Prince Frederick Charles, and Von Roon were all gone. So were Louis Napoleon and Victor Emmanuel. Francis Joseph alone was left, after a long reign of nearly fifty years. Bismarck had outlived his best friends and fellow-workers, and all the delegations to Friedrichsruhe, all the plaudits of the Berlin streets could not make him forget this.

In the autumn of 1897 complications between the Russian and the English governments in the China Seas assumed a threatening aspect, and Hohenlohe considered it necessary to send a German squadron to the scene of action for the protection of German interests. Before the fleet sailed its commander went to Friedrichsruhe and held a lengthy consultation with Bismarck in regard to the course he should pursue in the various contingencies which might arise through the uncertain proceedings of two such hostile governments. Subsequent events justified the wisdom of the ex-chancellor's advice, and the best proof of this is that the presence of the German iron-clads produced no irritation either to the English, Russian, or Chinese.

This was the last of Bismarck's services to Germany. On January 9 a report was telegraphed that he was dangerously ill: facial neuralgia and swelling of the veins, which caused him intense pain. Dr. Schweninger, however, succeeded in relieving the disorder in the course of some weeks, and on April 1 Bismarck was able to entertain his friends at dinner. As pleasant weather came on and he was able to obtain more air and exercise, he felt still better, but his family were aware that the sand in the hour-glass was running low. Dr. Schweninger spent the greater part of his time on the railway between Berlin and Friedrichsruhe. It was thought that Bismarck would live through the summer, but another sudden attack of neuralgia seized him on July 20 and confined him to his bed, from which he never rose again. His sufferings during the last ten days were like those of a man consumed in a fire, but he endured them with unwavering determination. The final scene is said to have been distressing and very affecting, for not only his family but all his domestics were devotedly attached to him. He died July 30, at eleven P.M. He was eighty-three years and four months old, almost exactly the same age as Goethe.

Bismarck's body was embalmed to await the erection of a mausoleum in Berlin, of which William II. had already notified his family. This is an honor that has never before been conferred upon a German, or any modern except Napoleon. One of his last requests was that his remains should be spared what he called "the monkey show" of a state funeral. This was dignified and worthy of him. There was not a drop of vain blood in his body, and though the emperor made a request for it, as Bismarck may have expected, Prince Herbert Bismarck positively declined it as contrary to his father's expressed wishes.

The funeral services took place late in the afternoon of August 2. Only the emperor, the empress, and a few of the

LIFE OF BISMARCK

chancellor's most intimate friends were permitted to attend it, but an immense crowd, chiefly of Hamburgers, collected about the grounds and at the railway station, while the peasants of the neighborhood stood respectfully with uncovered heads in a group by themselves. Bismarck's two sons met the emperor at the station and were greeted by him with royal cordiality. Prince Herbert conducted the empress into the death-chamber, and the emperor followed with the Princess von Bismarck, after whom came a few members of the emperor's suite and the rest of the Bismarck family, together with Dr. Schweninger. All knelt down while Dr. Westphal, Bismarck's country pastor, offered a prayer; after which a hymn was sung and Dr. Westphal delivered a short discourse. Then a second hymn was sung, and the service was closed with a benediction. The emperor deposited a beautiful cross of flowers on the casket, and the empress a wreath of white roses. On their return at the railway station the emperor kissed Prince Herbert Bismarck and shook hands with Count William, speaking to them both in a very sympathetic manner.

The text of Dr. Westphal's discourse had been chosen by Bismarck himself in the last days of his illness. It was from Paul's First Epistle to the Corinthians, xv. 53–57, and expresses the most confident belief in a future life: "For this corruptible must put on incorruption, and this mortal must put on immortality. . . . O death, where is thy sting? O grave, where is thy victory? . . . But thanks be to God, who giveth us the victory through our Lord Jesus Christ." Such was the end of Otto Edward Leopold von Bismarck, who ruled the continent of Europe for twenty years, moulded sovereigns to his will, and filled the earth with his fame. I think we may say of him, in the words of Schiller's apostrophe to Ajax,

"*Rest in peace, proud name thou leavest.*"

CONCLUSION

The tendency of the present age, especially in England and America, is to judge of men rather by good intentions and the absence of faults than by positive virtues and actual accomplishment. Such a measure can hardly be applied to Bismarck in fairness and equity. Rather he reminds us of the Greek sculptor, who, when his guild were invited to compete for a colossal statue to be placed on the roof of the senate house, easily obtained the prize by requesting the commissioners to set up his strange-looking model in the position for which it was destined, and to consider how it would appear from that distance. At the base of the mountain its summit is obscured by foothills, and only those who ascend above these, or who retire to a distance from them, can see it in its beauty and in its grandeur. Thus it happens that only those whose lives have raised them to a more or less elevated position are now able to recognize Bismarck for what he was; but as time goes on he will loom up more and more grandly in the records of the past as the mountain rises behind us while we are being hurried away from it. In the course of another century mankind will have changed its opinions, the echoes of party passion and the feeling of party antagonism will have died away. No one will care whether Bismarck made war on Austria, persecuted the Catholics, or domineered over the Reichstag; but the question will be asked, was he a useful man in his time, and helpful to the human race? To answer this now we have only to consider what he accomplished for Germany, and what Germany is to Europe,—the most sober, well-educated, and spiritual-minded of nations. It is only in Germany that an American chemist—to take a single instance —is able to publish the fruit of his labors and receive due credit for them.

On hearing of Bismarck's death the secretary of the navy said, " He had a marvellous career, and reached a ripe old age." The secretary of war said, " In my estimation, he was the greatest man of his day."[1] Persons in their position know, much better than the average journalist, the difficulties which a great statesman has to contend with and the allowances which ought to be made for him; as we have to allow also for the difficulties and temptations of journalism. The

---

[1] Mr. Long and Mr. Alger.

most creditable witness to Bismarck's character is the French
statesman, Jules Favre, one of the greatest of his political
antagonists, and certainly the most high-minded. Among
his German opponents in and out of the Reichstag—Windhorst, Lasker, Eugene Richter, Von Beust, and others—there
is not one who can be compared with Favre in the general
estimation of Europe. In his report on the Government of
the National Defence in 1870 he says:

" Although fifty five years of age, Count Bismarck appeared in
full vigor. His tall figure, his powerful head, his strongly-marked
features gave him an aspect both imposing and severe, tempered,
however, by a natural simplicity amounting to good-nature. His
manners were courteous and grave, quite free from stiffness or affec-
tation. As soon as the conversation commenced he displayed
a communicativeness and good will which he preserved while it
lasted. He certainly regarded me as a negotiator quite unworthy
of him, but he had the politeness not to let this be seen, and appeared interested by my sincerity. For myself, I was immediately
struck with the clearness of his ideas, his vigorous good-sense, and
originality of mind. His freedom from all pretension was no less
remarkable. I consider him to be an extraordinary political business man, taking account only of what is, occupied with positive
and practical solutions, indifferent to everything which does not
lead directly to a useful end. Since then I have seen much of
him ; we have treated numerous questions of detail together, and I
have always found him the same. The great power he has causes
him no illusion, neither is he haughty ; but he is tenacious of it
and does not attempt to hide the sacrifices he makes to preserve it.
Convinced of the worth of his talents, he continues to apply them
to the work in which he has succeeded so well ; and if to accomplish it he has to go further than he desires, he resigns himself to
do so. For the rest, impressionable and nervous, he is not always
master of his impetuosity. I have found in him repulsions and
indulgencies to me inexplicable. I had heard much of his great
ability ; he has never disappointed me ; he has often wounded me,
even revolted me, by his severity and exactions ; in everything I
have always found him upright and correct." [1]

---

[1] Government of National Defence, p. 119.

This is the typical Prussian character, and something more, and it corroborates Von der Pfordten's statement in 1866 that Bismarck was simply the incarnation of Prussia. John Lothrop Motley combines the friend, the statesman, and the historian when he says of Bismarck:

"Such enormous results were never before reached with so little bloodshed in comparison. They are national, popular, natural achievements, accomplished almost as if by magic, by the tremendous concentrated will of one political giant. . . . Intellect, science, nationality, popular enthusiasm are embodied in the German movement. They must unquestionably lead to liberty and a higher civilization. Yet many are able to see nothing in it but the triumph of military despotism." [1]

Count von Beust also finally concluded that Bismarck was not such a bad sort of man. He says in relation to their last official interview with the two emperors at Gastein:

"To those whom he likes Prince Bismarck is the most agreeable of companions. The originality of his ideas is only surpassed by his expression of them. He has a spontaneous and therefore pleasing *bonhomie* which mitigates the asperity of his judgment. One of his favorite sayings was, 'Er ist ein recht dummer Kerl' (he is a right stupid fellow), without meaning any offence to the person to whom he referred. 'What do you do when you are angry?' he once asked me ; 'I suppose you do get angry as often as I do.' 'I get angry,' was my answer, 'with the stupidity of mankind, but not with its malignity.' 'Do you find it a great relief,' he asked, 'to smash things when you are in a passion?' 'You may be thankful,' said I, 'that you are not in my place, or you would have smashed everything in the house.' " [2]

Great reformers, who stir human nature to its depths, are certain to receive a large share of the world's obloquy in return for it, even if they are still permitted to live. "Cromwell," said Bismarck, "was the first English ruler who made Great Britain a factor in European politics." He was the

---

[1] Curtis's Correspondence of Motley.
[2] Memoirs of Count Beust, ii. 257–258.

greatest of English statesmen, and perhaps the greatest of
English soldiers, and yet he was obliged to wait two centuries
for his country to do him justice. Bismarck has already received justice in his own country, but it may be long before
he obtains it in others. Yet he is fortunate in escaping the
rather vulgar accusation, which is brought against Cæsar,
Cromwell, and Napoleon, of " having aspired to the sovereignty." The most superficial examination of his life shows
that whatever may have been his methods of dealing with
others, he did not advance his own interests at the expense
of his rivals, but by the royal appreciation of his ability and
deserts. What are called ideal characters are never the ablest
kind of men, for to reach the limit of one's capability requires
a freedom of action which conscientious scruples too often
interfere with. " To gain something," said Grant, " a general
must risk something ;" and it is the same in morals as in war.

John Adams was a great man without being a genius ;
Hawthorne was a genius without being a great man. Bismarck was both, and yet his genius was so inscrutable that it
defies all analysis. How he accomplished what he did no one
has told. We can study a chart of the battle of Austerlitz,
and the manner in which the victory was won is made clear
to us ; but how Bismarck gained his diplomatic victories may
always remain a mystery. It would seem to have been an
innate quality in the man which he did not even understand
himself. We recognize the faculties of mind and character
which might lead to such results, but they are the same traits
which we perceive in other people, only in his case magnified
to an exceptional degree. If his peculiar ability were to be
described in one word it would be *comprehensiveness*,—the
faculty of mentally grasping the largest number of facts at any
one time.[1] The extent of his knowledge was enormous, and
it always seemed to be available at the moment when he required it. Add to this the faculty of recognizing any situation or complicated series of events better than others could ;

---

[1] In his memoirs Bismarck often embraces so many facts in a sentence that it
is difficult to follow his reasoning.

to decide more quickly than others, and to act always according to his thought. "The foolish think as they will; the wise will as they think."[1] It cannot be doubted that Bismarck acquired a Shakespearian knowledge of human nature. Even speculators like Jay Gould depend on that for their success. Given his man, Bismarck could always reckon how he would act under certain conditions. He knew just how far human nature could be trusted. The statesman who imagines people are better than they are becomes popular very readily, but is certain in the end either to miscalculate or be deceived. Even Bismarck was occasionally deceived in his man,—as happened in Von Arnim's case,—but the few errors he made he repaired in a masterly manner. Neither was he suspicious or sceptical of those with whom he dealt. Like Napoleon, he saw into a man at a glance, and watched the eye of his interlocutor.

Bismarck's reasoning was of the topographical order,—a kind which is not yet taught in the universities. He placed his subject before him as if it were a chart, and studied the relations of its different facts to one another as he would countries on a map. The map of Europe was to him something more than an outline, a drawing of cities, mountains, rivers, and seas; it was filled with human life, and every nation on it was a special and a continuous study of which he had volumes already in his head. From 1862 to 1865, when William I. could see nothing before him but darkness and chaos, Bismarck never forgot that Hungary and Venetia were two swords pointed at the throat of Austrian absolutism, and that Napoleon III. could never afford to surrender Rome to the Italians.

One evident cause of his success, which he noticed himself, was his entire freedom from political theories. He objected to theories as tending to dogmatism and the illusion of preconceived notions. Government was to him a growth, or rather a structure, to which every generation of men made additions or changes, and his study was to discover what were the most necessary and suitable additions he could make to it. He never troubled himself with Plato's *Republic*, Machiavelli's *Prince*, or Mill on *Liberty*, but went to the Muse of History for his instruction, and studied statesmanship in the lives of statesmen. A keen French journalist, who visited him in June, 1866, when all Germany was practically in a state of revolution, told Bismarck plainly that he treated the Prussian Landtag as Louis XIV. treated the French Parliament, and yet at the same time he was declaring that the popular wish of Germany for political unity was the only foundation for a national government, and that the German Reichstag was the only cure for their present evils. Was this consistent, or was it even sincere? Bismarck was pleased with the frankness of his visitor, and explained the whole subject to him in an equally candid manner,[1] finally adding, " I am obliged to use such materials as I find ready at hand: I did not make Germany or Prussia as they are." The history of the subsequent five years showed that Bismarck was consistent, and intended what he said. A theoretical monarchist or republican would not have succeeded in dealing with the situation. It was a transition period, and required exceptional methods.

Bismarck's death produced a flood of anecdotes in regard to him, many of which should be taken with due allowance, while others are no doubt apocryphal. The change of a single word in a sentence will often pervert its original meaning, and it should be remembered that these incidents were mostly written down some days, or perhaps years, after their narration. When history or biography gets into its anecdotage it deteriorates rapidly. Many statements, like Bismarck's saying that " God made man in his own image, but Italy in the image of Judas," have a relative and temporary significance. He was probably thinking of La Marmora's unprincipled calumnies against him, which might be described as the very essence of ingratitude. Likewise many of his French criticisms, reported by Dr. Busch, were made under

---

[1] Hesekiel's Biography, chap. iv.

the influence of strong belligerent feeling. The most unique story that we have of him is that of the death of his mastiff Tyras, called the Reichshund, whom Bismarck refused to leave so long as there was life in him. His son Herbert attempted to draw him from the room, but one look from his faithful old companion decided the chancellor that he ought to remain, and so he did. He had a strong liking for mastiffs, and kept a succession of them. In fact, he was himself the mastiff of Germany.

Professor Francis J. Child was fond of relating how the Iron Chancellor, once passing through Göttingen, noticed the old janitor of the University walking on the street, and immediately leaped from his carriage, ran after him, embraced him, and detained his escort some twenty minutes while he talked with this old friend of his youth on the sidewalk.

Nothing better ever came from his pen than his tribute to the character of William I.,—" my old master,"—as expressed to General Grant at the time of Hödel's attempted assassination. He said:

" The man never lived who had a more simple, magnanimous, and humane character than the Kaiser. He is different in many respects from those who are usually born to so high a position. Princes of the royal blood, as you may know, are accustomed to look upon themselves as made of different material from ordinary men, and they commonly pay little regard to the wishes and interests of others. The Kaiser, on the contrary, is in all respects a man. I do not believe he has ever wronged another, or consciously injured any one, or treated any man with unnecessary severity. He is one of those persons whose kindness of nature attracts all other hearts, and the constant aim and occupation of his life is the welfare of his subjects and of those who surround him. I cannot imagine a more high-minded, pure-hearted, more amiable or beneficent type of a sovereign, or a man, than he is." [1]

We hear a good deal of Bismarck's humor, but the specimens recorded of it are not very brilliant. Like many of his critical sayings, it may have had a local and charac-

---

[1] Bismarck after the War.

teristic value, which has now evaporated. It would seem to have been rather a kind of playfulness which pervaded his actions than penetrating wit. His enemies likened it to the playfulness of a cat who has caught a mouse; but all who knew him admit that it added much to the pleasantness of the man. It indicated that Bismark was in his element and enjoyed his work. Louis Napoleon said of him: "What danger can there be in a person who thinks aloud?" Dangerous enough to the French emperor, for it showed that Bismark was intellectually his master. No man was ever more capable of concealing the truth when necessary, even if he appeared to be thinking aloud. Such is the measure of the diplomat.

The government of the future is evidently republican. The worldly extravagance and excessive magnificence of royal life, which kept nations in awe during the middle ages, is not in harmony with the modern idea of government. We wish to revert to Roman and Athenian simplicity during the best days of the classic epoch, but there are obstacles in the way. What was possible formerly in a single city is not so easily accomplished in many cities and over large tracts of country. Those who can appreciate the value of plain living and high thinking are still a minority in the most favored nations. The greater proportion either live plainly from necessity, or, having obtained riches, surround themselves with luxuries, and assert an aristocratic superiority over their fellow-men. Not until this order of affairs becomes the exception shall we have a *genuine republic*, in which men and women are respected for what they are worth morally and intellectually, not for the money they can spend or for the titles they inherit. In such a state the franchise will not become the right of every ignorant loafer, simply because he is a man and walks on two legs, but rather the privilege of a good citizen, who has proved his capacity to decide in regard to public affairs by an efficient management of his own and a proper respect for the rights of his neighbors.

The government of the future, therefore, will have to be exempt from socialism, or even from anything that appertains to the idea that the will of the people echoes the voice of God. Only *right* and *justice* have a divine emanation, and the question for the law-giver is how can we approximate to these as closely as possible? The masses of mankind must learn that politics is not like a game of cards, which people play for their amusement, but an intensely serious matter, on which the fortunes of their posterity depend, and that it is not each man's individual interests that he is to consider and vote for, but the interest of the community as a whole. Until this becomes properly realized monarchical institutions will still have a kind of justification, and a large portion of the sensible and thinking classes of Europe will continue to give them support. France has finally become a republic, after eighty years of revolution and reaction and the loss of a million human lives. No wonder if Austria, Germany, and Italy dread such a change; nor is it certain that the French have yet escaped the worst consequences of it, although the signs are more favorable now than they were twenty years ago.

It will be noticed that geographical position has much to do with the form of government in Europe. Russia and Turkey are military despotisms. Germany, Austria, Italy, Spain, and the smaller central states are constitutional monarchies. France is a republic, and so is England, practically, at all events, when the Liberal party is in power. There is good reason for this in the fact that a liberal form of government would be hardly possible in close contact with Asia. So, likewise, the form of government in Germany and Austria is affected by the contact of those empires with Russia. If the revolution of 1848 had succeeded in transforming Germany to a republic, it would have been crushed while in the process of formation, as the Hungarian revolution was crushed by Russian bayonets. *It is only through German national unity that Germany can ever become a republic.* So long as the nation was divided into a number of independent states, each with a sovereign of its own, an attempt at revolution might succeed in some of them, but would be quite as likely to fail in others; and even if it succeeded in all, there would be no central organization by means of which the different states and provinces could act in concert. One part of the country would soon place itself in antagonism to another, and such confusion would prevail that orderly and sensible people would soon be glad to return to the previous condition of affairs. *The national government which Bismarck has created and the military system which Moltke has perfected are the sure foundation on which the future republicanism of Germany will rest.* A revolution that gains possession of the central government of Berlin would control the whole of Germany and be well prepared to resist foreign interference. *A nation of soldiers is a nation of freemen:* witness Rome in the time of Scipio, and Athens in the time of Pericles. When the German army shall decide that a republic is preferable to a monarchy they can obtain it without a blow; but the great middle class of Germans will never come to that conclusion so long as the Social Democrats set themselves in opposition to all constituted authority and oppose the right of holding and inheriting private property.

INDEX

427

INDEX

INDEX

INDEX

INDEX

THE END.

www.ingramcontent.com/pod-product-compliance
Lightning Source LLC
Chambersburg PA
CBHW021321110726
47900CB00005B/1307